D0378994

The Medium

THE MEDIUM

NOËLLE SICKELS

FIVE STAR

A part of Gale, Cengage Learning

GALE
CENGAGE Learning

Detroit • New York • San Francisco • New Haven, Conn • Waterville, Maine • London

GALE
CENGAGE Learning

LIBRARY OF CONGRESS CATALOGING-IN-PUBLICATION DATA

Sickels, Noëlle, 1945–
   The medium / Noëlle Sickels. — 1st ed.
     p. cm.
   ISBN-13: 978-1-59414-618-3 (alk. paper)
   ISBN-10: 1-59414-618-7 (alk. paper)
    1. Mediums—Fiction. 2. Guides (Spiritualism)—Fiction. 3. World War, 1939–1945—Fiction. I. Title.
   PS3569.I269M43 2007
   813'.54—dc22   2007031872

Published in 2007 in conjunction with Tekno Books.

Printed in the United States of America
4 5 6 7 12 11 10 09 08

To Jude, my wind of happiness

ACKNOWLEDGMENTS

I am very grateful for the efforts, advice, and encouragement of my enthusiastic agent, Jeffery McGraw, of The August Agency.

The author is grateful for the access granted to the archives of the National Spiritualist Association of Churches in Lily Dale, New York.

CHAPTER 1
AUGUST 1937

Rich man, poor man
Beggar man, thief,
Doctor, lawyer
Indian chief
Rich man, poor man
Beggar man—

"Thief!" a voice shouted.

Helen lost her rhythm and stepped on her jump rope. Billy Mackey's grinning face appeared at the top of the fence between their yards.

"You're gonna marry a thief!" he cackled.

"Am not!"

Helen wished she could be more clever in her retort, but there was something about Billy Mackey recently that could leave her feeling flustered and unsure of herself. Sure, he was two and a half years older and two grades ahead and had taken to acting like that suddenly made him smarter and wiser than she, but she'd turned thirteen last week, and his annoying teases shouldn't be able to get to her so. There'd been a time—most of their friendship, actually—when he hadn't been such a tease, when they'd run across lawns and roller skated down sidewalks and tumbled in leaves and snowbanks together like twins. His brother Lloyd, who was her age and in her class at school, always had taunts and practical jokes at the ready, but Billy had been different.

Billy had lots of pals, but he had never minded spending time with Helen. When they were littler, he had unashamedly hunkered down and made mud pies with her, and even nowadays when he spied her sitting in the shade reading, he'd still sometimes come plop down beside her and spread out model airplane plans to study.

He had once confided to Helen that he liked it that she wasn't too "girly," by which she supposed he meant she wasn't above putting worms in her pocket or getting dirty. So, why, lately, had he been treating her as if she *were* too girly? She hadn't been behaving differently, at least not around him. She had a new habit of evaluating herself in mirrors, but he didn't know about that.

The golden curls of Helen's younger years had mutated into waves the color of clover honey, a regrettable change, she'd decided. She had her father's serious brown eyes and thick eyebrows, her mother's straight nose and wide mouth. Her grandmother said she had a strong face and that she would grow into it and be a beautiful woman, but Helen couldn't see it. What did Billy see? Was wondering that too girly?

"It doesn't count if someone makes you miss," she protested.

"Okay, do it again. I'll keep quiet."

Billy had put on a sober expression, but his hazel green eyes twinkled with warning. Helen wound up her rope.

"I don't feel like it," she said.

"Don't you want to know what kind of man you're gonna marry?"

"It's just a game."

Jumping rope was beginning to feel like a mortifying thing to have been caught at.

"Say, maybe one of your grandma's spooks will jerk the rope

and make you miss when you get to the right answer," he said, laughing.

Righteous anger welled up in Helen. Now he had truly trespassed. No one was allowed to make fun of Nanny and her séances. She gave him a scorching stare. Pride made him hold his smile, but his eyes, by which she always knew his true feelings, spoke remorse. She held his gaze until she saw his brave grin waver, then she spun on her heel and marched away.

"Hey, Helen," he called, "I didn't mean it. C'mon back. I've got some nougats."

She looked over her shoulder. He was holding up a small white paper sack.

"Whad'ya do, steal 'em?" she said fiercely. "Or did your bum father send them to you?"

She ran to the house. He wouldn't call after her again. Because now she had trespassed, too. As soon as she'd hurled the barb, she was sorry. She knew how worried the whole Mackey family was about Mr. Mackey, who had been riding the rails for nearly four years, having left the family when the youngest, Linda, was still a baby, so that it would be easier for them to collect relief. She knew Billy feared his father would never come back. Now she'd taken that fear and twisted it into a weapon. She didn't understand how such meanness could have sprung up in her, even considering his provocation.

Hearing the voices of her mother and grandmother in the kitchen, Helen wheeled upstairs to her room. She was too dangerously close to tears to meet anyone. She honestly could not have told them why she was upset, anyway. The bare facts might seem sufficient, but she had a gnawing sense that they really weren't and that trying to explain would only prove another kind of trespass.

Her room was stuffy, but she didn't open the window. She lay on her bed and stared out into the thick foliage of the large sugar maple in the backyard. She wondered if Billy were still standing by the fence, as surprised by her outburst as she was. Most likely he was furious. He'd be blind to her presence next time they met. If she apologized, he'd act as if what she'd said hadn't touched him. He didn't often get mad at her, but when he did that was how he handled it. Coolness, then a turning aside of her efforts to talk, then after a pause of a few days, an unblinking resumption of easy commerce. Those first reconciled exchanges always left her feeling a little sick to her stomach, as if she were telling a lie.

A squirrel ran down one branch of the maple and leapt to another, shaking the leaves along his path. Helen was sure she heard the leaves rustle, though with the windows shut, it had to be her imagination. Her mother said she had a good imagination.

Perhaps, Helen thought, she'd imagine herself apologizing to Mr. Mackey. She'd insulted him as much as she'd injured Billy. Helen knew full well that Mr. Mackey was not a bum, but a hobo. Her father had carefully explained the difference once when they saw a man on the street wearing a sign saying "I will work for food." While both bums and hobos hitchhiked or hopped trains, hobos were looking for work, while bums lived by begging.

If Mr. Mackey were here, it would be an awful trial to apologize to him, not because he was intimidating but because she'd have to admit her cruelty. But once it was done, she could face Billy more freely. Yes, apologizing to Mr. Mackey would definitely make her feel better. And if she couldn't do it in person, she'd do it in her mind. Nanny had said the mind was like a box of magic tricks, and that if you believed hard enough in something, it was like it was real.

Helen shut her eyes and pictured Mr. Mackey, his red hair and freckled forearms, his pants that were always a little too short and showed a flash of white socks. In her mind's eye, Mr. Mackey appeared in a plaid woolen shirt, but the last time she'd seen him, he was wearing a brown jacket and a brown hat and carrying a small cardboard suitcase. It was that image she was trying to bring up, Mr. Mackey standing in front of his house looking it up and down, right before he turned and walked away. Yet there he was in her imagination wearing a plaid shirt. Actually, it was draped over his shoulders, wrapped around him as if he were cold. She could see he had another plain shirt underneath, with dirt smudges on it. Helen decided to go ahead no matter how he was dressed.

"Mr. Mackey," she said aloud, her eyes still closed, "I said something terrible about you today, and I'm sorry."

She wondered if she ought to be specific. Should she say she'd accused him of being a thief? That wasn't precisely accurate. Should she explain she only called him a bum because his Billy had made fun of her grandmother? Or would that detract from the purity of her repentance?

As she was pondering this impasse, Helen heard again the distinct rustle of leaves. She opened her eyes and looked out the window. No squirrel in sight, but the leaves were moving. Wind, she guessed.

Then she smelled smoke. It wasn't a cooking smell. And it wasn't smoke from someone's trash fire, either. It was stronger than that, blacker and denser, she somehow knew, though she didn't see even one wisp in the air outside.

Suddenly, Helen sat up, her heart pounding. It was Mr. Mackey. Mr. Mackey was in a fire. She was as sure as if the flames were roaring up right before her. She was gripped by terror, both because of Mr. Mackey's peril and because her knowledge was so absolute. She rushed to the door of her room. She had to find Mama or Nanny. Her hand on the knob, she stopped and tried to calm herself. If she went to them hysterical, they'd just think it had been a bad dream. As she stood there, a new certainty came over her. Mr. Mackey was not in the fire anymore. He was safe. Someone was taking care of him. He was going to be all right.

She went to the window and pushed up the sash. A soft breeze entered, bringing no smell of smoke. Despite the warm air, Helen shivered. Seeing Mr. Mackey was not a completely new experience. There'd been other times when a phrase or a picture had appeared unexpectedly in her mind like a stray puppy nosing insistently at a screen door. These words or sights were invariably meaningless to her and fleeting. They'd slip out of her awareness as cleanly as they'd entered. She'd never given them much notice. But this time was different.

"It never came so strong before," she murmured. "Never so strong before."

CHAPTER 2

"They got the wire from the Red Cross this afternoon," Helen's mother was telling her father at dinner the next evening. "It seems Will and some other men were sleeping in the warehouse. It's a miracle they were saved. The firemen weren't looking for anyone to be in there."

"Will Mackey has no business being away from his family," Helen's father said.

"I guess he thinks it's best."

"He is coming home now, Emilie?" Helen's grandmother, Ursula, asked.

"I don't know."

That her vision had proved true excited Helen, but her stomach churned with worried guilt, as if she had broken some rule and was bound to be found out. Even so, she was curious about the details of Mr. Mackey's ordeal.

"Was Mr. Mackey burnt?" she asked.

Her mother was slicing another piece of meat loaf. She placed it on her husband's plate.

"Gravy, Walter?" she asked. He nodded and she passed him the gravy boat.

"I don't think so, Helen. They only kept him overnight in the hospital because he had breathed in a lot of smoke."

"Was it black smoke?"

"I don't know. Any kind of smoke from a big fire like that is bad for you."

"Was he wearing a plaid shirt?"

"What kind of question is that?" Helen's father interrupted. He preferred quiet dinners or ones in which he led the conversation.

"Why do you wonder such a thing, Helen?" Ursula said with genuine interest.

"No reason."

Helen shoveled a large piece of meat loaf into her mouth. She wouldn't be expected to say more with her mouth full.

"Helen, don't take such big bites," her mother scolded. "Really, you're too old for me to have to tell you that."

Helen tried to keep her cheeks from sticking out as she chewed the soft wad. She stared at the row of steins on the sideboard in order to avoid her grandmother's quizzical gaze.

Helen's parents had already forgotten her odd question and poor manners. They were on to the familiar topic of "hard times." Though the Schneiders had lost their savings when the bank failed a few years ago, and Walter's job as a bookkeeper had been cut back to three days a week, at least he still had a job. Household economies like buying day-old bread, coupled with Emilie selling vegetables from her garden and Ursula contributing the fees she got for séances had enabled the family to weather the worst years of the Depression without being subjected to hardships suffered by so many others.

Shocked at first, Helen had gotten used to seeing people living in their cars, businessmen in suits digging sewer pipe ditches, schoolgirls wearing dresses made from feed sacks, and idle men loitering in parks and libraries to postpone the shame of going home empty-handed. Now, thanks to federal assistance, people could get rent money and shoes and food from their local townships. Just last winter, Helen had helped Billy and Lloyd pull home sleds loaded with free turnips, potatoes, and cornmeal for the Mackey family. The Schneiders hadn't needed food

16

hand-outs, but Helen was aware that the adults often ate less so that she was sure to get enough.

Helen expected her grandmother to press her about the plaid shirt when they were alone together in the kitchen getting dessert ready, but Ursula was all business, scooping noodle pudding into glass dishes, skimming cream from the top of the milk bottle to pour on Walter's serving, steeping the tea. Helen scraped the dinner plates and stacked them in the sink. They exchanged only a few utilitarian comments. Helen was so relieved that she didn't even mind not knowing if she'd been right about the shirt.

But her relief was short-lived. After dessert, Walter and Emilie went to the living room to listen to the radio, while Helen and Ursula, as usual, cleaned up in the kitchen. Helen was drying the last platter when Ursula finished sweeping the floor and came to stand beside her. Helen felt an eruption of nervousness.

"Mr. Mackey," Ursula said. "He was lucky, no?"

Helen nodded yes to the rhetorical question.

"Did you see him, Helen?"

"See him?"

"Did you see him in that fire?"

"No. No, I didn't. How could I?"

"*Ach,* there's no answer for that."

Ursula shook her head slowly.

"When I was a girl, near your age," she said, "I had a dream about an avalanche. A man from our village was in it. Our baker. I saw his skis go over and over down the mountain. My Papa said I only dreamed so because I knew the baker was away visiting in Austria. But a few days later, we learned there *was* an avalanche, and he was killed in it."

Helen waited for her grandmother to go on, but she didn't. A lump burned in her throat.

17

"I was thinking about Mr. Mackey," she finally whispered. "And I kind of saw him."

"It was my first time," Ursula said, as if Helen had not spoken. "Dreams is how the spirits start you sometimes. To get you used to it."

She patted Helen's shoulder.

"But, Nanny, I didn't see him in a dream. It was daytime. I was awake. And I just knew."

Ursula raised her eyebrows.

"Then, *Liebling,* I can not help you so much. You are already past me."

CHAPTER 3

Helen came home from the park one Wednesday afternoon two weeks later to find her grandmother in the kitchen ironing one of her Sunday dresses. Usually, this was done on Saturday. Not curious enough to ask about it, Helen merely said hello and headed for the cookie jar.

"Go take a bath, Helen," Ursula said, sprinkling water on the dress's pique collar. "And wash your hair."

Helen took two fruit shortbread cookies out of the jar and went to the Kelvinator for milk.

"Is someone coming for dinner?"

"No one for dinner. We go out afterwards, you and me."

"Out?"

"I have some people at Mrs. Durkin's."

A séance, then. When Helen was younger, she often had to accompany her mother and grandmother to séances. At Mrs. Durkin's, she got to wait outside under a huge weeping willow. At other homes, she was required to sit quietly in a boring kitchen while the grown-ups met in another room. But Helen had not been to a séance in almost a year. Her mother felt she was old enough to stay at home alone during the day, and in the evenings her father was always there, except when the *Sängerbund* met. As one of only three baritones in the singing society, Walter didn't like to miss meetings. But Wednesday was not their night.

"It could be you can help a little tonight," Ursula said, not looking up from the ironing board.

"Help?"

Ursula slipped Helen's dress onto a hanger.

"You'll wear this," she said. "And we make your hair into nice, shiny braids. So you look like the sweet girl."

"But what am I going to do, Nanny?"

Ursula shrugged. "We will see."

Helen was glad to encounter in Mrs. Durkin's living room several familiar faces. Mrs. Durkin herself, pillow-bosomed and round-faced, gave Helen a hearty welcoming hug, as if it had been years since she'd seen her, though she'd passed Helen's yard only last week while walking her collie. Old Mr. Grauer made a courtly bow in Helen's direction. Miss Simmons from the dentist's office smiled at her. It was strange to see her without her white uniform. Instead she wore a red blouse with a pleated plaid skirt and red ankle socks and loafers. Her hairy calves seemed mildly indecent absent the accustomed white stockings.

Mrs. Durkin, Mr. Grauer, and Miss Simmons were all "regulars." Tonight, Miss Simmons had brought her young man, Mr. Howard from the Esso station. He put out his hand for Helen to shake. It was thick and hard, black grease outlining his cuticles. When her hand touched his, Helen caught a momentary image of a violin.

There were two other people, a man with thick bifocals that made his eyes look as round as those of the fish on ice at Dohrmann's market, and a stylish woman wearing two red fox pelts over her tailored suit, each fox grasping the tail of the other in its pointy mouth. It was an unusual costume for August, even though the evening was cool, the air freshened by a promise of rain. These strangers stood apart from the others, at opposite sides of the small room. It was, overall, a rather large group.

Perhaps, Helen thought, that's why her grandmother had wanted her along, though she still didn't know how she could help.

Mrs. Durkin led the way to the adjoining room, lit only by four candles in a silver candelabra in the center of her circular dining table. A squat vase of dark red roses sat beside the candelabra, and there was a row of potted geraniums and violets on the windowsill.

The man with the thick eyeglasses sat across from Helen. Candle reflections danced on his lenses. Ursula sat on Helen's right, Mr. Grauer on her left. The old man smelled of Old Spice and shoe polish.

Although the ages of the people around the table entitled every one of them to wield authority over her, Helen somehow did not feel subject to them. In a quick series of glances, she detected in each person some degree of wishing or wanting. It was in the eyes, or in the nervous, foraging movements of hands and fingers. In some, it had grown into need. And she saw that it was their wishes and their neediness that had diminished their power. It was a novel feeling, a bit disconcerting, but interesting, too.

At a nod from Ursula, the group placed their hands flat on the table, the pinky fingers of neighboring sitters touching.

"May the Divine Spirit and the Spirits of the Universe guide us this evening," she said.

Staring at the candles, Ursula asked if anyone had a particular spirit they wished to contact. The regulars didn't answer. They were content to accept whomever came.

Mr. Stewart pushed his thick glasses up higher on his nose. "My daughter Dorothy," he said hoarsely. "She was just a little girl when . . . Is that all right?"

Ursula made no sign of having heard his question, but Mr. Grauer sent him a reassuring nod.

"My late husband," said the lady with the fox pelts. Her voice was crisp and challenging.

Mrs. Durkin handed Ursula a Bible.

"This belonged to Mrs. Vole's husband," she explained.

Ursula placed the book next to the flower vase and rested her hands in her lap. Helen was just wondering if she ought to stretch her right arm toward Miss Simmons to bridge the gap in the circle when her grandmother tapped her elbow, indicating Helen was to place her hands in her own lap. Copying her grandmother, she crossed her wrists left over right. At a nudge from Ursula's foot, Helen also crossed her ankles. When her grandmother shut her eyes, again Helen copied her. She heard Ursula breathing loudly and deeply beside her.

The noise of the breaths slowly grew softer, as if her grandmother were walking away from her, until Helen couldn't hear them at all anymore. The perfume of the roses filled her nostrils, the flowers warmed by their nearness to the candle flames.

When she heard a child crying, Helen tried to open her eyes, but her lids felt immovable. Then she saw the child, though her eyes were still closed. It was a young boy in short pants, crying in a corner. Over his crying, she began to discern another sound. Music. The boy raised his face and stopped weeping. The music grew louder. It was a violin, plaintive and lonesome, but at the same time sweet and soothing. Helen felt the desire of the little boy that the playing go on and on. He desired it the way small children do desire things, with absolute totality.

"He wants you to keep playing," Helen said aloud, not knowing or caring whom she was addressing. The boy's desire was so strong, she just had to communicate it.

"You have a message, Helen?" came her grandmother's voice, distinct but far away.

"Play the fiddle some more, Buddy. Never stop playing,"

Helen said. It was her voice, but the child's words.

"Oh, my lord," a man exclaimed, also from a distance.

The image of the boy began to fade. The sound of the violin wavered and also faded. Helen was aware, all at once, of the hard seat of her chair and of the presence of other people. Her limbs felt heavy and tired.

"Buddy—that's what my family calls me," Mr. Howard was saying excitedly. "It was my little brother started it, 'cause he couldn't say Bertie. My little brother that died of the scarlet fever. He was only five. I never thought . . . I came tonight just 'cause Molly hounded me to. I never thought I'd—"

"But you don't play the violin, Bertie," Miss Simmons said.

"I used to, Molly. I used to. And he did think it was swell, too. Only one that did, in fact."

Helen opened her eyes. Everyone was staring at her with frank curiosity. Mrs. Durkin brought a tall glass of water, and Helen drank half of it down.

"Did you get a little boy?" her grandmother said carefully, as if Helen might not understand her.

Helen nodded.

"Children come more easily to their own," Ursula explained to the sitters.

"Then my daughter might—?" Mr. Stewart ventured.

Ursula raised her hand to cut him off. Then she closed her eyes and bent her head back.

"Yes, now I see the boy. His cheeks are red."

"From the scarlet fever," Mr. Howard interjected.

"He wants to thank you for playing for him," Ursula said. "He remembers it still."

A small moan escaped Mr. Howard. Miss Simmons laid her hand comfortingly on his arm.

"He has someone beside him," Ursula continued. "Another child. He's pulling her forward. She has something in her arms.

A doll, perhaps. A rag doll, worn out with use. Does that sound like Dorothy, Mr. Stewart?"

"Dorothy never had a rag doll. But she had a teddy bear she carried most everywhere."

"Yes, now I see it more clearly. It *is* a teddy bear. With long arms and legs, like a rag doll."

"That's it. That's my little girl's bear. What does she say?"

"She's holding the bear close to her face," Ursula said. "She's too shy to speak in front of all these people. She's stepping back."

Ursula rubbed her forehead.

"There's someone else trying to come through. A man. He's feeling . . . pleased. . . . Pleased to see . . ."

Ursula reached for the Bible. She smoothed her hand over its cover.

"He's pleased that his book is here. He watches you, Mrs. Vole, when you take it out and hold it."

Mrs. Vole leaned forward and scrutinized Ursula, whose eyes were still shut. The tip of a fox tail swung forward and brushed the tabletop.

"Why did he do it?" Mrs. Vole asked, each word hard and singular.

"He says . . . He says he had his reasons."

"Oh, Al, why did you do it?"

"He says he didn't ever mean to hurt you."

Ursula opened her eyes and regarded Mrs. Vole, who remained canted forward. Helen looked at her grandmother. No one seeing that face could imagine its owner able to be prevailed upon a moment longer.

"Let us each quietly thank the spirits who visited tonight," Mrs. Durkin said, lowering her head as if in prayer.

All the regulars, plus Helen and Ursula, immediately followed suit. The three agitated newcomers felt constrained to lower their heads as well. When Mrs. Durkin rose, everyone except Helen and her grandmother also rose. Mrs. Durkin ushered the sitters out of the dining room and into the process of retrieving their hats and handbags. Helen heard Mrs. Vole inquiring about future meetings. Mr. Stewart was asking about a private sitting.

"Was there anything else?" Ursula asked Helen when they were alone. "Any *one* else?"

Helen shook her head.

"I should maybe have let you hold that Bible," Ursula mused. She smiled, patting Helen on the knee. "No matter," she said. "There's ways to call the spirits. You will learn."

"Do they always come?"

"*Nein.* They got their own business, just like us. But there's ways, too, to make it look like they come. That you can learn, also."

It sounded to Helen as if her grandmother's suggestion was very close to, if not the same thing as, outright lying. Her concern must have showed on her face because her grandmother gave her an encouraging wink.

"We keep open the doors, *Liebling.* The doors to the spirit world, and the doors to Mrs. Durkin's house. Because what is the good when the spirits do come, if no one is here to listen?"

Chapter 4

"First, how to sit," Ursula was saying. She crossed her wrists and her ankles.

"I know that already," Helen said, recklessly unwilling to edit resentment from her voice.

She longed to be outdoors in the final hours of the afternoon. Instead, she was sitting at a card table in her grandmother's overfurnished bedroom. She wished she'd gone with her mother to do the marketing. That would have been dull, too, but at least she would've been out. In only a week's time, school would begin again, cooping her up on a regular basis.

To Helen's surprise, her grandmother did not reproach her, but only nodded.

"But do you know why we sit so?"

Helen allowed herself a loud exhale.

"To be comfortable?"

Ursula shook her head. "It is not comfortable, sometimes, to meet spirits. *Nein,* we cross our hands and feet to shut off from the other people and to save our energy."

"Okay. Then what?"

Ursula stood up, folding her arms over her chest. She was a short woman, but her erect, stout figure was imposing in the small room where the only sound was the pointed ticking of an antique Bavarian clock.

"Maybe we are not ready for 'then what.' Maybe you are not so special as I think, but just a girl with a too big imagination.

26

Or maybe you want to stay only skipping rope and singing songs, and make believe you are not different."

Helen had regretted her recalcitrance the moment her grandmother pushed back her chair to stand, but now she regretted it more deeply because Ursula's words had delivered a sting. She was, in fact, different and had always been so.

"I'm sorry, Nanny. It's just that I wanted to go outside a while. All morning I was helping Mama make jelly."

Ursula sat down.

"I would not keep you in, but our lessons must stay a little secret for now. So, when your mother went to the shops, we could not miss the chance."

"Why do we have to be secret?"

"It is like how Emilie starts her seedlings in the kitchen window in spring. She does not put them out in the dirt until they are strong enough for some cold night or some day of sleet."

"I don't understand."

"There are people who will be afraid, Helen, when they know what you can see and hear. Or they will think you make it up, or that you are a little crazy. They will say things to make you feel bad, maybe bad enough to stop. That is why, first, you must become a strong seedling."

Helen sensed truth in this. She'd noticed the whispers at their backs when she and Ursula passed certain neighbors on the sidewalk. When her parents had told her it was not proper to discuss family matters with outsiders, she knew they meant the séances. Hadn't even Billy Mackey succumbed to teasing her about it? What might someone who was not her friend be capable of?

"Could I make it stop, Nanny?"

Ursula stared out the window with a faraway look in her eyes. She turned her diamond wedding ring with her thumb, a habit when she was mulling something over.

"If you are in a room," Ursula began, still staring out the window, "and there is an opening to another room, you can turn your back and pretend you are alone. But you can not make the other room disappear."

The old woman faced Helen.

"I have only a keyhole to look, but for you, Helen, there is maybe a wide doorway. Better to learn how to live in two rooms than how to move always carefully to keep away from the other room."

In reply, Helen crossed her wrists and ankles.

"So," her grandmother approved. "That is for a mental circle. The medium alone will hear and see the spirits. In his mind. For a physical circle, the medium leaves uncrossed the hands and feet."

"A physical circle?"

"When there are things everyone can see and hear. When the table moves or there are raps, or when a spirit takes form and shows itself. Uncrossed lets you draw up energy."

Ursula reached across the square table and tapped Helen's wrists, indicating she could relax them.

"But not so much anymore do spirits materialize. Not like you read about one hundred or even fifty years ago."

"Did you ever see one, Nanny?"

"*Nein.* But Mrs. Durkin, she is hoping all the time. So she keeps her plants near our circle. Such a romantic. Waltzes she likes, too."

Helen knew that her grandmother insisted on cut flowers on the séance table. She said flowers, especially dark flowers, increased the vibrations of spirit voices and made them easier for her to hear. But Helen had never considered that the rows of potted geraniums and violets on Mrs. Durkin's windowsills played any part.

"How do the plants help?"

"To take physical form, a spirit must pull energy from people in the circle and from magnetic currents in the earth and pass it through the medium's body. A growing plant has energy strength the same as several people."

"Jeepers, I don't know if I'd want a spirit to . . . to . . ."

"Materialize."

"Isn't it scary?"

Ursula shrugged.

"You see them in your mind, you see them in the house—not so different, I think. And everyone else gets to see them, too. It could be good for sitters coming back and telling friends."

Helen wasn't so sure about that. Mightn't Mr. Howard have been badly shaken if he'd actually seen his little dead brother crying in the corner? What about when the spirit left? Wouldn't its loved ones get upset then?

"Don't worry, Helen. This won't happen. There are special ways the room must be, and still, the spirits may not show themselves, even with a medium practicing for years. But we don't say this to Mrs. Durkin, because hope is not a thing to push down."

There it was again, Helen thought, another slippery version of honesty. She looked hard at her grandmother's face, as if it might provide some clue to explain this unsuspected side of her. There was nothing, of course, but the same face she had known all her life, although Helen did see in sharper relief than ever before the signs of old age on her grandmother's features— the deep wrinkles around her eyes and the lavender shadows below them, the soft folds of skin at her neck, the brown spots on her cheeks.

"You can go outside now. We are done for today," Ursula was saying. "Next time we will try the automatic writing."

Helen hesitated, consumed by a tender affection for her

grandmother. She felt the urge to embrace her, but no one ever embraced Ursula except at her instigation.

"Go, go, child, or you will be a fidget at supper, and I am too tired to hear your father complain."

Reluctantly, Helen left the room. At the doorway, she glanced back and saw Ursula still seated in her chair, again playing with her ring and staring out the window into the golden glow of the summer dusk.

CHAPTER 5
SEPTEMBER 1937

The automatic writing was not going well.

Helen followed her grandmother's instructions scrupulously. She would get comfortable in her chair and listen to her breathing until she felt sleepy. Then she'd pick up a pencil, hold it loosely in her fingers over a sheet of paper, and wait. Once, her hand had trembled and she'd felt it being pulled to the paper, but she produced only a few unrelated letters, which her grandmother said were the spirits getting used to the feel of Helen's muscles. The start of school had limited Helen's free time, but Ursula had admonished her to keep practicing.

"Just ten minutes," she'd said. "Every day."

"Every day?"

"So the spirits know you are serious, and maybe a guide will come."

"Do you have a spirit guide, Nanny?"

Ursula considered a moment, and then she nodded.

"What does it do?"

"Sometimes he calls other spirits to come, ones that the sitters want. Sometimes he speaks for them. But . . ."

Ursula clasped her hands in her lap and looked down at them.

"My guide comes not so much."

"Why not?"

Ursula looked at Helen.

"It is no matter," she said. "Every sitter brings spirit companions. In the séance, other spirits visit. Always I find one

31

who will talk. Or I can guess good at what they would say."

"Well, when he did used to come," Helen persisted, "what did he look like?" She didn't fancy the idea of encountering a spirit alone in her room.

"His name is Gerard. He is dressed in hunting clothes, like my *grosspapa*," Ursula replied. "But I cannot see the face. Only light there."

"What should I do if someone comes to me?" Helen asked nervously.

"Like with anybody. Tell your name. Ask his name. Ask how to make the contact again. If it is a person, not an animal, maybe ask who he was in this life. If you have the curiosity."

Helen didn't think curiosity would be her foremost reaction. Her grandmother clucked her tongue.

"A spirit guide is a helper, Helen. He is like a part of you, the part that can see the unseen and know the unknown. You have a pure heart. Your guide will be a good spirit. And remember, if ever any spirit frightens you, order it to leave and it will go. It is your own fear that gives such a spirit power."

Helen nodded, only somewhat reassured.

"It can happen slower," Ursula continued, "if you ask that the guide comes first to your dreams. One night, maybe after many times of asking, you will feel him behind you. Turn around just when you are ready. Look at the feet, then slowly up. Speak, too, only when you are ready. You can use many nights. The spirits are patient."

Helen had been attempting automatic writing daily for ten days now, and last thing before sleep every night she'd asked for a guide to come into her dreams. So far, neither exercise had borne fruit. Still scribbles. Still dreams populated only by schoolmates and neighbors, or blank nights of no dreams at all. Helen wondered how long her grandmother would expect her to keep trying without any sign of success.

Today's practice was extra onerous because she didn't feel well. Since mid-morning her stomach had been aching in a strange tugging way, as if some small animal were methodically pawing her insides. She'd gone to the school nurse, but since she showed no fever, the nurse had only let her recline on the couch in her office for twenty minutes and then had sent her back to her classroom without even a note to excuse her from making up the math quiz she'd missed.

Helen hadn't bothered to tell her mother or grandmother when she got home. They, too, would simply have taken her temperature, then passed over her complaint as indigestion or growing pains, maybe offering her a cup of heavily sweetened chamomile tea. Helen went to her bedroom, closing the door to shut out the sounds of *Mary Noble, Backstage Wife* from the radio in the living room.

Resignedly clearing a space on her desk, she set out pencil and paper and sat down. As she slid into the familiar float on her breaths, the dull pain in her abdomen gradually muted until it was just one other vaguely registered physical fact, like the sweep of hair into her barrette, or the ribs of the braided rug under her stocking feet. As she continued to ride her breaths, she felt suffused with warmth. The sensation was such a pleasant relief she put off picking up the pencil.

Then, between one breath and the next, she knew someone else was in the room. Her heart heaved with apprehension. There was the same prickly feeling in her armpits as when she had to walk at night past the overgrown yard of the spooky old house two blocks over, and the same lurch of dread. She sat rigidly still, and resolutely shut her eyes.

For almost intolerable long minutes, nothing changed. Helen realized that playing possum was not going to work, and doing nothing was itself becoming distressing. Remembering her grandmother's advice, she decided to find out who was there.

She wasn't brave enough to move or open her eyes, but she shifted her mind toward the presence as pointedly as if she had actually turned around and looked.

She saw a tall woman wrapped in the graceful folds of an emerald green hooded cloak. Her feet were clad in thin sandals. One pale hand held a single iris so rich a purple it was almost black. Helen made out a soft, close-lipped smile and widely spaced dark eyes within the shadows of the hood. A deep calm close to joy fell upon Helen.

"Who are you?" Helen said.

The figure did not stir or speak.

"Are you my guide?"

The woman bent her head over the flower as if she were smelling it. Could she be nodding yes?

"I'm Helen Schneider," Helen said.

"I know," the woman said. Except that she didn't really *say* it. Her voice came into Helen's head as smoothly as one of her own thoughts.

"Why are you here? Is it for the writing? Will I see you again?"

A slight inclination of the head. The hood slid forward, further obscuring the face, which Helen now imagined must be beautiful.

"When? How?" Helen asked urgently.

A flood of words cascaded into her mind, tumbling over one another, yet she was able to comprehend perfectly. The woman told her she'd come whenever Helen wanted to contact someone in the spirit world, that Helen only need open herself and wait. Helen understood that she could dispense with the automatic writing practice, that it was not to be her way until later in her life.

Surprisingly, after the first rush, no further questions bubbled up in Helen. She was content simply to behold her visitor, who shimmered like a reflection on quiet water. Again, words came to Helen from the woman, this time in a dreamy flow even more like the winding circuits of her own mind. The woman let her know there would be times when she'd come to Helen unbidden and that at those rare times Helen might experience her only as a strong desire or a strong distaste, or a nudge to unaccustomed action. Helen wondered how she'd be able to tell when such feelings were her own and when they'd been sent from the woman, but at the moment it seemed an unimportant quandary.

Helen felt a cool breeze. The woman withdrew the flower into her cloak and was gone. So was the warm, floating feeling. The pain in her abdomen reasserted itself.

She stood up and stretched and looked around her room, half expecting it to be different, but, of course, it wasn't. Or was it? The colors in the worn patchwork quilt didn't seem as faded, the starched linen dresser scarf looked crisper, the windowpanes more clear, the jumble of books, games, and old toys on the open shelves tidier. Something had definitely happened here.

Helen knew she ought to feel special, and in a way she did. But special had two sides. When the woman was smiling and speaking, Helen had felt large and strong. Now what she mostly felt was empty, and that let a little of the fear creep back. She worried that something about her might show that she was a girl whom spirits visited, and that kids at school would notice. Surely it wouldn't be as obvious a badge of difference as that fifth-grader Charlene Thatcher's big bosom or Harvey Winkel's stutter. But what if it were?

The woman had promised to return. Helen wondered if it would feel as good every time and whether she could stop her from coming again if it didn't. She wished she knew her name. She thought that would make it feel safer somehow, friendlier, more ordinary.

She decided to call her Iris. She also decided that she

wouldn't tell her grandmother just yet. Iris hadn't wanted to answer too many questions right away, and neither did Helen.

Helen was silent at dinner, which was not unusual enough to provoke comment. She couldn't stop thinking about her encounter with Iris, but not in a dissecting way. The enormous fact of it was simply claiming all the space in her mind. Eventually, however, the adult conversation snagged her attention. Her grandmother was recounting a letter she'd gotten from a nephew in Berlin.

"Otto says things are better. Everyone has jobs."

"The radio says there are still shortages of meat and butter and fruit," Walter said. "And long lines at food shops."

"Better are lines for food than no food at all," Ursula retorted.

"But at a price," Walter said. "The Reichstag a powerless sham. Nazis in charge of everything. They arrest anyone who speaks against them, even priests. Why, they don't hesitate to kill members of their own party who aren't loyal enough."

"What do we know?" Ursula argued. "Only that Germany was on its knees and now it is not. That people were in despair and now they are not."

"We can be glad for that, I suppose," Emilie put in.

Walter nodded grudging agreement.

"Remember in 'thirty-three when Herr Hitler first took charge?" Ursula said. "Otto wrote then that people lit bonfires on every hilltop to show the nation had awakened."

"But awakened to what?" Walter said. "I'd like to see Germany on its feet again, and I know the state has to be strong for that to happen, there must be order, the people must make sacrifices, but I still think placing all law in the hands of one man is dangerous."

"Otto does not complain," Ursula sniffed.

"Maybe Otto doesn't dare."

Ursula had grown up in Germany, coming to America when she was twenty, while Walter and Emilie had both been born right here in New Jersey, but of late, news from Germany, whether from the radio or family letters, seemed to interest them all equally. Helen had never met this cousin Otto, nor had her parents. Yet her father acted as if Otto's plight were a part of their lives they must not ignore, like cobwebs in the corners of an otherwise well swept room.

Helen only half-listened to the news reports on CBS, but she was aware of Adolf Hitler and his rise to prominence. Her father's concern that Hitler now constituted the whole of the German government intrigued her. In their home, her father was the holder of all the rules. The fact that her mother and grandmother might find ways around him from time to time didn't dispute that. And wasn't a country a more difficult thing to manage than a family? How much more necessary for someone to be clearly in charge. Like FDR was here. In his second inauguration at the beginning of the year, he'd said he saw one-third of the nation still ill-housed, ill-clad, and ill-nourished. How would he fix that if not with a strong hand on the reins of government, even now when things were so much better than they had been when he was first elected? But maybe strength wasn't the only way to judge a leader. Maybe, as Walter implied, Hitler wasn't a safe man to give the reins.

Helen went to bed early, curling up in a ball around the lingering ache in her belly. She was disappointed to awaken some time later and find she hadn't yet made it to morning.

She fumbled out of a tangle of blankets and went to the bathroom. When she stood up from the toilet and turned to flush, she saw by the glow of the night light something dark in the bowl. She flicked on the overhead light. A bloody cloud was seeping through the water. Then she felt small splashes of warm liquid on the insides of her thighs. She thrust her hand into her pajama pants and with a gulp of terror brought it back, the fingertips wet with bright red blood.

"Oh, oh," she said aloud.

She wanted her mother, but she shrank from the thought of what would come next. The rousing of the rest of the household in alarm, the summoning of Dr. Nichols. It would be mortifying to have the doctor and her father learn the nature of her illness, but with such dire symptoms how could they be left out?

She pictured them all standing funereally around her bed. They would speak softly and smooth her covers. Her mother would wear a brave smile. Dr. Nichols would tell them to get some rest. He wouldn't even give her a shot or any foul-tasting syrup because what remedy could there be for someone whose insides were leaking out?

Was this Iris's doing? Helen couldn't believe Iris would wish her harm, but there was no denying the succession of events. Maybe it was Iris's mark on her. Like when Lloyd Mackey and Owen O'Brien sliced their fingers to pledge themselves blood brothers. If it were just a mark, then it would be okay. If it were just a mark, it would stop, and she wouldn't have to tell anybody. With shaking hands, she pulled off her pajama pants and was shocked to discover a huge scarlet stain spread across the seat. This was no brotherhood mark. What a stupid idea. This could mean only one thing. She was dying. That's why Iris had come.

She threw the pajama pants into the sink and turned on the faucets. Taking her bathrobe from a hook on the back of the bathroom door, she hastily put it on and hurried to her parents' room.

She knew her mother slept on the side of the bed nearest the door. Clutching her robe tightly, Helen inched forward through the darkness until her knees bumped the edge of the bed. She gently shook her mother's shoulder.

"Mama," she whispered. "Mama."

Emilie raised herself up on one elbow and glanced at the Big Ben alarm clock, whose luminous hands indicated two-thirty. She waved Helen back and got up, pushing her feet into terry-cloth slippers. They went out onto the landing. Emilie shut the door behind her and turned on a small table lamp at the head of the stairs.

"What's wrong?" she said, laying an assessing hand on her daughter's brow.

"I don't know."

"Bad dream?"

Helen shook her head.

"I think I'm sick. Really bad."

"What do you mean? You were fine at bedtime."

Helen led her mother to the bathroom and pointed to the sink. Her pajama bottoms lay in a pool of pink water. Helen began to cry.

"And it's still happening. I'm still bleeding. Down there. My stomach hurt all day, but the nurse at school said I was okay, so I was just waiting for it to go away. But it didn't, and now—"

"Sh, sh," her mother said, pulling out the sink plug. "You're all right."

She unfurled a long strip of toilet paper, folded it into a square, and handed it to Helen. "Wait here."

Sniffling, Helen pressed the square of paper between her legs and sat down on the edge of the tub. She was astounded at her mother's calm. All right? How could she be all right?

Emilie returned with a cardboard box and an elastic strap. She drew a thick, rectangular white pad out of the box.

"This is a sanitary napkin," she said. "It works like this."

She showed Helen how to fasten the tails of the napkin into two little metal S-hooks on the elastic strap, then she helped

Helen step into the strap and pull it up around her waist so that the pad was positioned firmly between her legs. Although it was soft, its bulk was uncomfortable.

"Tomorrow we'll go out and get you your own belt," Emilie said, adding cheerily, "You won't mind missing a half day of school, I guess?"

"Whose is this one?"

"Why, mine, of course."

"This happened to you once, Mama?" Helen felt hopeful. Maybe she was going to be all right after all.

"Yes, yes. It happens every month. It will to you, too."

"Every month?"

Emilie took both of Helen's hands in hers and looked deeply into her eyes.

"You know, Helen, that babies grow inside their mothers, right?"

Helen nodded.

"Well, a woman's body makes a sort of nest every month just in case a baby wants to grow. When one doesn't, the body throws the nest away, so it can start fresh the next month."

"A nest of blood?"

"It doesn't sound very nice when you put it like that, but yes, a nest of blood. It's what babies need when they're inside their mothers."

"But I'm not a woman."

Emilie bit her lip, as if it might be her turn to cry.

"Actually, my dear, now that this has happened, you *are* a woman. In one way, anyway." She leaned forward and hugged Helen tightly. "But you'll always be my little girl, too."

Emilie straightened up and smoothed her nightgown over her hips. "Maybe you can get a book from the library that will explain it better."

"Then I'm not going to die?"

"Heavens, no! Everything is as it should be. Just sneaked up on us is all. Now, let's get back to sleep, shall we?"

CHAPTER 6

Helen was excruciatingly aware of her body below her waist. She worried constantly that the outline of the ungainly sanitary napkin might be visible through her skirt. Afraid to turn her back on anyone, she didn't volunteer to write on the blackboard, and she sketched with a dull nub of lead rather than go to the pencil sharpener. At recess, she kept on her long tweed coat even though an Indian summer sun had sidetracked autumn's chill. The coat would have hampered her at tag or jump rope, but the pamphlet in the Kotex box had advised avoiding strenuous exercise, so she'd declined all invitations to play.

Watching the other girls play, she wondered if any of them had been struck yet. She looked at the teachers and at women on the street and even her own mother as if she'd suddenly acquired x-ray vision, like Superman, and had just discovered that beneath their dresses and slips, these women had bodies that did amazing things quite apart from their wills or wishes.

On Helen's third day of sitting out recess, Rosie O'Brien came over and put her foot up on Helen's bench in order to re-tie the shoelaces of her scuffed brown and white saddle shoe.

"We're gonna play Giant Step," Rosie said. "Wanna come?"

Helen looked up from the book on her lap, smiled, and shook her head no. Rosie sat down beside her. Helen read a few more sentences of *Lad, A Dog,* then closed the book.

"You don't have to sit here with me, Rosie."

"Oh, I don't mind. Not enough time left for a good game, anyway."

Together they gazed at the schoolyard of children noisily engaged in various pursuits, most involving running and tagging, as either part of an official game or as a tease.

"Is it a good story?" Rosie pointed to Helen's book.

"Pretty good."

"Good enough to keep you on this bench an awful lot."

Helen felt herself blushing. She knew Rosie was looking at her, but she kept her eyes focussed on the playing children.

"You got the curse, don't you?"

"The curse?" Helen gave her a startled look. She hadn't heard the term before, but she was sure she was guessing its meaning correctly.

"How can you tell?"

"You don't usually mope around."

"I'm not moping."

"You're not playing Giant Step, either."

Rosie's tone was conclusive. As one of the younger children in a large family, she had learned early to put forth opinions with a confident air, and she could rarely be shaken from them, even by indisputable evidence to the contrary. Rosie believed there was always room for dispute.

"I just don't feel like it," Helen asserted.

"Could if you wanted to."

"You don't understand."

"Do so, too."

Helen searched Rosie's defiant, freckled face for any trace of bluff. She was not above it. But this was too tender a topic for Helen to let Rosie get away with a fib.

"Makes you feel kinda sick," Rosie described, "and like you don't want anyone looking at you. And me, I even get worried sometimes . . . well, can maybe anybody . . . *smell* me."

43

Though she stressed the word smell, her voice was almost inaudible when she said it.

"But you get used to it," she continued more robustly. "And it doesn't always hurt. My mom said it ain't nothin' next to having babies."

"I didn't ever know you had it," Helen said, impressed. Rosie was thirteen, too, but a few months younger than she.

Rosie nodded. "A few times. Five now, I think. Or maybe four."

An electric bell on the side of the brick building rang loudly and long. Children began swarming into lines. A pack of boys some distance from the building were jostling one another against the chain-link fence. There were usually five or six who waited until the last possible moment to line up. Lloyd Mackey was always among them. Helen remembered Billy often being part of such a pack, too, but now he was in his second year at high school. They didn't have recess in high school.

Rosie and Helen stood up from the bench, but neither girl took a step. For Helen's part, she didn't want to leave because for the first time since that alarming night in her bathroom, she did not feel alone. The pamphlet from the library had said menstruation happened to every girl, but she still felt her experience to be overwhelmingly solitary and unique. Rosie's bluntness had broken through that.

"When my sisters got it," Rosie said seriously, "they stopped being much fun. They used to throw balls with me and jump off swings and all, and after, they only wanted to lay around looking at movie magazines and trying new ways to comb their hair."

"Why?"

"Dunno." Rosie looked at Helen appraisingly. "You won't change, will you, Helen? I'm sure I won't. I don't care what anybody says."

Helen wondered how Rosie could believe herself capable of standing firm against the forces of nature. The library pamphlet, which the librarian had taken from a drawer behind the check-out counter, had revealed that the messy business of periods was only the start. More changes were coming. Some would be upon them soon, others down the road, after they were married. The pamphlet was hazy about men's part in making babies, but it was clear they were essential.

"Rosie, do you know about the nest?"

"The what?"

"You know, the blood. How it's for a baby."

"Oh, yeah, that. Kinda nutty, huh?"

A few teachers had come out onto the yard, their Miss Thompson among them. The girls started walking toward the lines of children.

"But how do the babies get in there?" Helen dared to ask. She figured in the O'Brien family of eight children such information might be more available than in her household of close-mouthed adults.

"My mom said it's like a garden. The dad plants a seed and a baby grows from it."

Helen frowned. The pamphlet, though it used medical terms and diagrams, had presented a similarly inadequate metaphor.

Grinning, Rosie linked her arm in Helen's and inclined her head confidentially. "But I heard my brother Jimmy telling his friend Tom a joke about a tootsie roll and a lifesaver, and I think that's the real scoop."

An ungenerous person would have deemed Rosie's face plain, but even an ungenerous person would have to admit it had a certain elfin charm, especially when Rosie was smiling, as she was now, her upturned eyes sparkling with merriment at her own boldness.

They had arrived close enough to the lines to hear Miss

Thompson clapping her hands to signal for silence. The eighth-graders always led the school in. Rosie ran ahead. Helen reached the end of the line just as it began to move forward. Lloyd and fat Ron Greenberg thundered up from behind and cut in front of her. Ron, his wrinkled shirttail hanging out of the back of his pants, didn't look at her, but Lloyd approximated an apology by turning around and winking at her. Another day she would have said something, and Lloyd would probably have let her go ahead of him, but today it seemed unimportant, a child's matter.

She walked up the two flights of stairs to the classroom in a daze. The joke about the candy was still not the bald information she craved, but it was more vivid and felt more genuine than any of the facts she'd had laid carefully before her over the past few days. She didn't have to puzzle it out. It made sense to her so quickly, she realized she must have possessed the answer somehow all along. She felt embarrassed at knowing and embarrassed on behalf of all the mothers and fathers of her acquaintance. She wished she could un-know it. She resented Rosie for telling her.

Miss Thompson was writing page numbers on the blackboard, and Helen's classmates were taking out geography books. She did, too, opening to a chapter titled "The Dark Continent." She shook off her disgruntlement with Rosie. After all, she had asked. She had wanted the secret, for a secret it clearly was. It was just that she'd never before considered that asking and finding out could result in a burden of knowledge impossible to ignore, an actual weight on the mind and heart. She wondered if further revelations lay in store. And she wondered what other hidden things she already knew.

CHAPTER 7
OCTOBER 1937

Helen heard honking and paused in her raking to look up at a V-formation of Canada geese flying by. They were the first flock she'd spotted this year. They seemed bulky in the sky, their wings pumping valiantly, necks strained anxiously forward.

After they'd passed, Helen became aware of another sound, the metallic *swish, swish* of a grass rake. She went to the plank fence and stepped onto the wooden soda crate kept there as a stool. Next door, working intently at the far side of his yard, Billy Mackey was also raking. His task was harder than hers, because the Mackeys had more trees, including three old apple trees. He was wearing baggy wool trousers and a snug sweater vest, and he had rolled his shirtsleeves up. Yellow jackets were circling him, disturbed from feasting on the rotten windfall fruit he was raking up along with the leaves.

Helen delayed calling to him. There was something enjoyable about watching him when he didn't know she was there. She admired how the muscles of his arms moved with each pull on the rake and how his torso twisted rhythmically like a little piece of a Fred Astaire dance. His sandy hair, usually tamed with brilliantine, had shaken loose with his exertions, and a couple of locks hung down over his forehead, the ends curled like commas. She wondered that it didn't bother him, and if she'd been close enough, she didn't think she could resist reaching out and pushing it back for him.

"Hey!" he said in greeting, noticing her at last. She'd been

47

standing there only a minute, but it had seemed much longer.

"Hey," she answered.

He leaned his rake against a tree trunk and walked toward her. He was smiling, and to see that smile warmed her ridiculously.

"What's cookin'?" he said when he reached the fence. He had to tilt his head to look up at her, and when he did, the errant locks of hair fell back off his forehead. Her desire to brush at them with her fingers remained, however.

"I've got to rake our yard, too," she said.

"Yeah?"

"How come your brother's not helping you?"

"Basketball practice."

"Oh, right," Helen remembered. Lloyd Mackey was the star of the eighth-grade team.

"But I'm gonna leave some for him," Billy said. "Maybe in the corner where there's the most apples. Darn yellow jackets bit me twice already."

He held up one arm to show her a red swelling near his elbow, then turned his head and pointed to another, meaner swelling on the side of his neck. Helen felt a quick, dropping sensation in her gut, like when her father drove too fast over a dip in the road.

"Want some baking soda?"

"Naw. Can't even feel the one on my arm anymore."

He backed away, turning after a few steps and trotting to where he'd left the rake. Helen climbed down and resumed her own raking. Soon she'd accumulated three satisfying piles.

"Helen, hey, Helen!" she heard from the Mackey yard.

She went to the crate. Billy was right at the fence, his hand over one ear, a grimace of pain on his face.

"Got me again," he said. "I'll take that baking soda this time."

She hopped down and ran into her kitchen, where she mixed

baking soda and cold water into a paste in a small Willoware bowl.

To get around the fence, Helen had to go to the front of her house and up the Mackeys' driveway. She found Billy on a bench next to the garage, his head leaning back against the garage wall.

Businesslike, she set the bowl on the bench, scooped up a gob of paste, and applied it gently to the angry lump on his ear. He winced, but he didn't complain. He made no objection when she smeared some paste on the bite on his arm, and when he saw her swabbing up more from the bowl, he obligingly turned his head so that she could reach the bite on his neck. Her fingers trembled a little as she put the paste on his neck with a careful, stroking motion. He glanced sideways at her with a questioning look.

"It's getting dried out," she explained. "Doesn't want to stick."

As if to prove her right, two powdery clots, one from his neck and one from his ear, broke off and fell inside his collar. Laugh ing, he stood up and pulled his shirt out of his pants, shaking his shirttails to let the clots of dried paste fall free. Helen laughed, too, and sat down, leaning her back against the garage wall and wiping her pasty hand on her pleated wool skirt. Billy perched on the forward edge of the bench, his body angled towards her as if he were about to relate something important. Though he was still grinning, his expression had turned serious, and Helen wasn't sure which part to address, his easy smile or his vehement eyes.

"Did you see the geese went by before?" she said.

He shook his head no. She looked up into the sky, searching for geese, listening for their noise.

"Hey," he said softly, "Florence Nightingale."

He must have been moving as he spoke because when she

turned her face to him, she was surprised at how near he was. There was only a small space left to close before his mouth was on hers, a feathery swipe of lips, then a brief withdrawal, then a firmer press, less tentative, long enough for her to feel his breath against her cheek, long enough for his hands to cradle her hips as if he wanted to steer her. She clenched her fingers around the splintery edge of the bench and twined her ankles together beneath it.

When he pulled away, she regretted his leaving. She knew she was supposed to be outraged, that she should slap his face like they did in the movies, but instead she wished fervently that he'd kiss her again right away.

Billy abruptly stood.

"Gee, Helen, I hope you don't think I'm a heel."

Helen looked down from his worried face and began scuffing the dirt with the toe of one shoe. She couldn't think of a single thing to say. Instead she gave a shrug of her shoulders so slight it could have been taken as reproof or release or a little bit of both. He waited, but she continued to watch her foot kick up dust.

"Well, it's not like it was a *real* kiss," he finally said in a different, louder tone. His voice had lost all trace of plaintiveness.

She looked sharply at him and found that he didn't appear as decisive as he'd sounded. But she saw, too, that he would not back down.

"Didn't seem like you minded much, anyhow," he said, and he dared a smirk.

Now she did feel like slapping him. Not for the kiss, but for the amusement in his face, however much put on. Maybe, even, because it *was* put on. She grabbed the bowl and ran down the driveway.

In her own yard, she crouched behind a bush that hid her from the sight of anyone looking out a window and from Billy, should he decide to peer over the fence.

In a few minutes, she heard the sound of Billy's rake again. And he was whistling. She put her hands over her ears and started counting aloud. When she reached a hundred, she decided, she'd go into the house. Her father could scold all he liked, she'd do no more yard work today.

Walter was in a temper that evening, but it wasn't about Helen's shirking. He was stony throughout dinner. Emilie kept casting assessing glances at him, but she didn't question him, which told Helen that her mother already knew the source of his irritation. Her grandmother chose to ignore his mood, and it was taken for granted that Helen wouldn't be inquisitive. The three females maintained intermittent conversation on easily exhausted topics—Helen's homework, the butcher's new kittens, the possibility of frost overnight.

Helen was surprised when her father made a rare after-dinner appearance in the kitchen, where she was scraping the plates and her grandmother was filling the sink with hot soapy water.

"Nanny," he said, "if you would join us in the living room?"

The request, though polite enough, was not really an invitation.

"We'll soon be done here," Ursula said.

"Helen can manage on her own," Walter countered. "Let her finish one job today."

"Very well," Ursula said. "Helen, don't forget to wipe down the stove."

Helen washed and rinsed the dishes and flatware and pots. When she couldn't dislodge some bits of crisped pork from the roasting pan, she put it to soak. She went into the dining room to brush crumbs off the tablecloth. The sliding doors to the living room stood slightly ajar. When she heard her father mention her name in a loud voice, she tiptoed quickly to the partially closed door to eavesdrop.

"To have a neighbor tell me what my own daughter is up to!" her father was saying.

"I thought it was Emilie Mrs. Durkin told it to," her grandmother replied calmly.

"The point is that you planned to have Helen perform at a séance next week without so much as a by-your-leave from either of us. I won't have it, Nanny. I just won't have it."

Helen was startled. Her grandmother hadn't consulted her, either, about another séance.

Emilie spoke then, but her voice was so low, Helen couldn't make out what she'd said.

"It's unseemly for a girl of her age to exhibit herself like that," Walter asserted.

"I was not much more when I began."

"You weren't my daughter."

"*Nein.* And still I am not. You cannot forbid me."

"Walter doesn't mean—"

"Don't presume to explain me, Emilie. What I can forbid, Nanny, and what I do forbid is for Helen to assist you in any way with your séances."

"The girl has a gift," Ursula said, as if she were noting something as obvious as the furniture around them.

"A gift for what? Charlatanism?"

"Walter! My mother is not a charlatan!"

"No? And will you swear you have never tilted her table with your foot, or moistened an envelope with alcohol so that she might see through to the secret question sealed inside, or some other such shenanigans?"

A lengthy silence ensued after this outburst. Fearing that one of the adults might be about to slide the door open, Helen reluctantly turned away. Then she heard her grandmother's voice, hard and strong.

"You are right, Walter," she was saying, though somehow she made it sound like she was telling him he was wrong. "Sometimes my Emilie must help. Even if she doesn't like to. Sometimes it is the kindest thing, instead of sending a sitter home still with fears and questions. But do you really doubt the dead can reach the living?"

Now Helen could not even consider leaving her listening post.

"Ursula," Walter said. It was the first time Helen had ever heard her father use her grandmother's name. "I am a man of business. I have a practical mind. I believe that God could not mean so marvelous a creation as man to end at death, but I don't know if spirits can return to our world, or if they would want to. You say they can and do. I won't dispute that. I know you to be an honest woman at heart, in spite of the séance mischief. But I will not have my daughter become a target for people sunk in grief, nor for nonbelievers ready to ridicule."

"She truly has a gift," Ursula repeated.

"She's a child," Walter countered.

"She is not so much a child anymore. Emilie told you? At such a change, the ability to meet spirits, it grows."

Helen blushed fiercely.

"That's neither here nor there. She is still child enough to be under my direction."

"Nanny," Emilie said, "how are you so sure Helen has a gift?"

"I have seen it at work."

"Well, I've seen nothing," Walter declared. "Nothing at all. Have you, Emilie?"

"Well, no, but—"

"No buts. There is evidence, or there isn't."

"And must you be witness, Walter, to trust that something is true?" Ursula challenged.

"Not always. But certainly if it's something that could well be an exaggeration or someone's imagination."

"Then there can be only one answer."

A quiet followed. Helen pictured her father and her grandmother staring each other down, like in the game she and Rosie played to see who'd blink first. It was Ursula who broke the silence, though Helen did not suppose from that that she'd been the one to lose the contest.

"Helen must come to the séance, and you, Walter, must come, too. Then perhaps, as you wish, you will see for yourself."

Helen heard her father clear his throat loudly, which meant he was about to agree to something he had originally opposed.

"There can be no tricks," he said suspiciously.

"No tricks. Of course."

"Absolutely not," Emilie added.

"And only this once."

"So we are settled," Nanny said. "It was a good idea, Walter. *Danke.*"

Heart skipping, Helen hurried back to the kitchen to wipe down the stove.

CHAPTER 8

They walked to Mrs. Durkin's house, Walter and Helen in the lead, Emilie and Ursula behind. Walter was holding Helen's hand. At another time, she might have objected, but this evening she welcomed the firm clasp of her father's large, warm hand. Watching their paired shadows lengthening and shortening on the slate sidewalk as they passed below street lamps, she was able to push down the nervousness in her chest.

Still, she'd been glad when they'd got past the Mackeys' front walk. She'd have hated Billy to spot her in tow with her father like a little girl. She hadn't spoken to Billy since their encounter in the yard a week ago and had only seen him at a distance twice. She checked every time before leaving the house to be sure he wasn't around. She knew it couldn't go on like this, but she had no idea how it would change, much less how she might make it change.

"Mr. Schneider, so nice you could come," Mrs. Durkin said.

She stepped back and opened her door as wide as it would go, as if Walter were entering on horseback. After she'd taken all their coats, Mrs. Durkin turned to Helen and cupped her face in both hands. Her fingers smelled of onions.

"Helen, Helen," Mrs. Durkin said, beaming. Helen wondered for one panicky moment if her face were about to be plunged into the broad, hilly expanse of Mrs. Durkin's flowered dress front. But the woman only repeated Helen's name once more and let her go.

Mr. Grauer led Helen to a milk glass bowl of hard candies in the living room, his advanced age permitting him the liberty of acting as host in a home not his own. Helen untwisted the crinkly cellophane from around a butterscotch and popped the candy into her mouth.

"Ursula," Mrs. Durkin said in a confidential tone although she was standing in plain hearing of all of them, "I've had to let in one new sitter tonight. She was so anxious. Her son, you see. Only twenty-one years old. Some murky business, I gathered."

"No matter," Ursula said.

The doorbell rang, and Mrs. Durkin floated over to answer it. The other sitters had arrived all at once—Miss Simmons from the dentist's office, this time without her beau; chirrupy Miss Portia Macy, an occasional client; and the first-timer, Mrs. Samuels, her gray hair pulled back into a tight bun, her black shirtwaist dress too loose for her slight form. She reminded Helen of a scrawny, wild kitten. She had that same air of wanting to be fed but also not wanting to be picked up.

While Mrs. Durkin was introducing Mrs. Samuels to the rest of the group, Helen's grandmother drew her out of the living room into the hallway leading to Mrs. Durkin's sewing room.

"You remember what I told?" she said quietly.

"That I don't have to work to make something happen? That I should just wait?"

Ursula nodded. "You cannot tell a tree it must grow faster, or the sun it must come up earlier. So also here. The spirits will decide. And we will accept."

"But what if nothing happens?"

"You are like the phone, *Liebling*. It only carries the voice that wants to use it. And we do not blame the phone if no one calls, do we?"

In the dining room, there was some shuffling about before everyone got seated. Ursula specifically did not want Walter beside any member of the family, which meant Mr. Grauer had to give up his accustomed chair. This disgruntled the old man, even though he knew that the proper positioning of sitters was essential to making the spirits feel welcome, and that unsuitable arrangements could not only block visitations, but also might open the door to disruptive spirits.

"Never before have they required *me* to move," Mr. Grauer grumbled under his breath. No one inquired whether "they" referred to people on this side of the grave or the other.

He was mollified when Ursula seated him next to her. The places on either side of the medium were the most important ones. Ursula had told Helen these places should be filled by people with gentle, open hearts. Helen was assigned the other seat next to her grandmother.

There was only one slender candle in the center of the table, and all the electric lights in the house were turned off. Ursula explained to everyone that the darkness would encourage communication from Mrs. Samuels's son, who was recently departed. Apparently, new spirits could be self-conscious.

"Let us put away doubts," Ursula said, "for this little while. The spirits do not mind the skeptic. They like to come and teach the skeptic. But in the circle we must have harmony of purpose. If you cannot believe, you must at least suppose it may be possible."

Emilie intoned a brief invocation, and hands were laid flat on the table. Within seconds, Ursula removed her hands to her lap and closed her eyes. Helen did the same.

The regulars began to sing softly, a German lullaby. Helen heard her father's strong baritone join in after a few bars. Soon, however, no voice was distinct from any other. The tempo of the song corresponded to the tempo of a subtle buzzing in her ears that seemed to be coming from inside her own body. It wasn't unpleasant, like a mosquito's buzz. In fact, the sensation was euphoric. Her mouth, seeming to act on its own, slowly formed a smile. The singing stopped. Helen felt as if the top of her head were opening up. Lazily, she opened her eyes. The people around the table looked like silhouettes cut from black paper.

"Are there any spirits present?" Ursula said to the air.

Suddenly, Helen felt a constriction around her neck. The peace and pleasure of a moment ago vanished. She put her hands to her throat and gasped for breath.

Walter pushed his chair back from the table. Mr. Grauer rebuked him with a gesture one might make to a boy squirming in church.

Ursula gently grasped the back of her granddaughter's neck. "What is it, Helen?"

The constriction began to lessen.

"Something . . . something around my neck . . ."

"Hands?"

"Not hands. Like a scarf . . . but tighter."

"Are there any spirits present?" Ursula repeated loudly, addressing the ceiling.

The constriction was completely gone now. Helen let her hands fall to her lap.

"Yes," she said.

It seemed to her that her voice was coming from the back of her head or, impossibly, from behind her head.

"What is your name?"

Mrs. Samuels made a small whimpering sound.

"Mrs. Samuels," Ursula asked, "does the neck or pain of the neck mean anything to you?"

The woman nodded. A large tear was making its way down one cheek.

"My boy . . . my boy hanged himself," she whispered.

Helen coughed.

"Won't you tell us your name?" Ursula looked at Helen as she rephrased her question.

Helen swayed a little, then nodded.

"Iris," she said.

"Iris," Ursula said, engaging the spirit directly while still looking at Helen, "do you have someone with you?"

"Yes," Helen answered.

"Is it possible to speak to them?"

"I will speak for him."

"Is it my boy?" Mrs. Samuels interrupted. Emilie put a restraining hand on the distraught woman's arm.

"Who is with you, Iris?" Ursula said.

Helen leaned back in her chair. She could feel sweat on her brow and on her upper lip.

"Sammy," she said almost inaudibly.

"That's him! That's my Moshe. His friends called him Sammy. I never liked it. But boys—what can you do with boys today?" She gave a nervous laugh.

"Do you want to ask him anything?" Ursula said to her.

"Are you all right, Moshe?"

Helen saw Iris hovering serenely beside Mrs. Durkin's sideboard. One sleeve of Iris's robe was rippling as if she were standing in a breeze. Helen couldn't see Moshe, but she sensed an agitated presence next to Iris and knew that he was the cause of the sleeve moving. Then Iris's voice was in her mind, at once strange and intimate.

"Iris says Sammy is on the road to perfection," Helen said.

"I didn't get to tell him . . . to tell him good-bye."

"Iris says Sammy knows you love him. There is no time for regrets. The past is not here."

Iris was fading. Helen looked away from her to the sputtering candle. "They're going," she said.

"No!" cried Mrs. Samuels.

Mrs. Durkin got up and turned on a floor lamp. Now they were only seven people around a table in an ordinary dining room. Mrs. Samuels was weeping into a large white handkerchief.

"He hasn't really left you, Mrs. Samuels," Emilie consoled her.

"Nothing is lost but it changes," Ursula added. "We are none of us ever alone."

CHAPTER 9

The next morning, it was raining. The air was the color of pussy willows. Helen was reminded it was Saturday by the fact that no one had knocked at her door to hustle her out of bed.

Just as she reached to push open the swinging door to the kitchen, she heard her name mentioned in conversation. This was getting to be an uncomfortable habit, catching news of herself while hidden behind a door.

"How can you be so sure, Nanny, that Helen wouldn't have been hurt?" Walter was saying.

"You heard how Emilie begins by calling on good spirits," Ursula answered.

"But bad spirits can show up anyway," Emilie reminded her.

"Bad," Ursula mused. "We must be careful to judge when we do not understand all."

"I judge someone who would choke a young girl as bad," Walter insisted.

"He was perhaps only inexperienced in making contact. Suicides do not like to be called."

"I'm not convinced spirits were involved at all," Walter replied. "Maybe Helen's gift, as you call it, is in reading thoughts. Maybe somehow the agonies of that wretched woman emptied into Helen's innocent mind."

"Maybe," Ursula admitted. "But what about Iris?"

The conversation seemed stalled, so Helen entered the kitchen. Everyone was at the table, though they'd obviously

61

finished breakfasting. As usual, her father and grandmother had newspapers spread in front of them. Walter gave Helen a nod in response to her "good morning," then turned his attention to the front page, and Ursula answered *"guten Morgen"* quite normally before taking up her morning ritual of memorizing obituaries. Emilie smiled at Helen, put down her coffee mug and got up to fix some Wheatena.

"Feeling better?" she said from the stove.

Helen stared at her mother's back, unsure how to respond. She did feel differently this morning from how she'd felt last night. Quieter. Cleaner. Was that better? Should she call last night bad? She'd been dizzy on the way home, had leant her head against her mother's shoulder as they walked, but that hadn't been bad exactly, only odd, as if she'd just gotten off a fast merry-go-round. At home, her mother had helped her out of her clothes and into bed. Her freshly laundered sheets had smelled lovely.

And before, at Mrs. Durkin's—to say that she'd felt badly then was not a big enough description. The sensation of choking was frightening, but it hadn't lasted long. And she'd gotten to see Iris again, which was nice, though now that she considered, she didn't like that Iris had come unasked. Was the mere act of sitting at a séance table invitation enough?

Helen rubbed her forehead. No, she wasn't feeling better. She was muddled and embarrassed and uneasy in her own skin.

"Yes, I am better, thank you," she answered anyway.

Emilie set a steaming bowl in front of her. Helen watched a pat of butter melt into the brown sugar, which in its turn was melting into the hot cereal. One by one, the three adults exited the kitchen to attend to separate errands, and she was left with only the thrum and drip of the rain to listen to.

The adults' careful casualness annoyed her, especially after what she'd just overheard. Suppose she had suddenly sprouted wings? Would her family fail to mention them as long as she kept them neatly folded on her back whenever she was in the house? Would it be deemed her problem to figure out how to deal with them in the bathtub? Would her mother simply remake her blouses and quietly set a bottle of preening oil on her dresser?

Helen began to eat. The first few swallows were tight. She wondered what she really wanted. To be sized up face-to-face and fussed over, or to be granted privacy? Probably a bit of both. She sighed. She'd had no preconceived notion of what this business of contacting spirits would be like, but she'd never thought it would leave her lonely.

The rain and muted light continued all day, which suited Helen's slack frame of mind. When Rosie called with a plan to go to a matinee, Helen declined. The idea of a crowd and bright noise and commotion was as unappealing to her today as it would have been irresistibly enticing on any other rainy Saturday.

By late afternoon, she was contentedly ensconced in the living-room window seat, reading the latest Nancy Drew mystery. Her mother was in the armchair by the fireplace knitting. Her father had gone out for tobacco, and Nanny was napping.

Coming to the end of a chapter, Helen lifted her head and looked out the window. The movement of someone in a yellow slicker on the Mackeys' back porch caught her eye. It was Lloyd, stuffing rolled newspapers into a canvas sack in preparation for going out on his route. Helen watched him hoist the sack over one shoulder and trudge down the wooden steps to his bicycle. She watched him pedal down the driveway. He made a crooked path, hitting every puddle. She imagined him laughing, not caring whether his corduroy pants got wet and muddy, not worrying about losing his balance or dropping his bag. Lloyd was a joker and a daredevil. Mrs. Mackey said every gray hair she had was because of him, but everyone inside the family and out knew he was her favorite. When Lloyd turned out of sight, Helen opened her book again.

Nancy Drew was just jumping into her roadster in order to pursue a mysterious stranger she'd spotted lurking near the railroad station, when the print on the page swirled. Trying to focus, Helen saw a flash of yellow. Feeling nauseated, she shut her eyes. Immediately, an image of Lloyd on his bicycle was before her. Lloyd just a block away, making a quick veer as a large black car rounded the corner. Car and bike skidding on the slick street. Lloyd flying over the handlebars. Then motionless and twisted on the wet macadam.

Helen leapt up and ran out of the house. She took the Mackeys' front steps two at a time and pounded on their door with both fists. Billy opened the door with a bewildered look. His mother was right behind him. She was balancing her youngest, Linda, on her hip, and in her other hand she held a mixing spoon coated with chocolate batter. Helen pulled Billy's wrist.

"Come on!" she shouted and ran down the steps.

Billy followed without hesitation. At the end of the block, a small crowd was gathering around a black Hudson. When Billy spotted his brother's bicycle sprawled at the curb, he picked up his pace and passed Helen. Her speed was hampered by being in her stocking feet. She looked back at Mrs. Mackey standing in front of her house peering up the street.

"It's Lloyd," Helen yelled to her.

Mrs. Mackey screamed. Frightened, Linda began to cry. Helen saw her mother coming out of their house with an umbrella. She took the little girl from Mrs. Mackey, who rushed up the street. As she dashed by, Helen noticed she was still holding the chocolate spoon.

"Helen?" her mother was calling. "Helen!"

But Helen ignored her. A siren sounded in the distance, getting nearer. Helen walked to the accident scene. There was Lloyd, just as he'd appeared in her mind's eye, one leg turned at a sickening angle, a smear of blood at his temple, his newspapers spilled around him. The only addition was Mrs. Mackey, kneeling beside him sobbing, with Billy next to her, gripping her shoulders. And the babble of people telling and retelling versions of what had happened.

Helen forced herself to look at Lloyd in order to check the accuracy of her vision. As she stared at him, she discerned a band of pale light around his body. She glanced at the sky, thinking the clouds had opened and let through a beam of sunlight. But the gray cover was uniformly dense. Looking at Lloyd again, she noticed that around his bent leg and his head the light had a greenish cast. No one else nearby was touched by the soft glow surrounding Lloyd. Was he dying? As soon as she thought it, Helen sensed that wasn't the correct interpretation. To the contrary, it came to Helen that the strange halo meant just the opposite.

When the police arrived, the onlookers were pushed back, and most moved on. Disregarding the wetness, Helen sat down on a low wall one house down from the accident corner. Mrs. Mackey climbed into the back of the ambulance. Billy watched it pull away, then he began walking slowly home. When he reached Helen's spot, she joined him. Neither of them spoke. They stopped at his front walk.

"He looked bad, didn't he?" Billy said.

His voice broke on "bad." He looked up at the roof of his house as if he were inspecting it for loose shingles. Helen knew he was trying to hold back his emotions. He swallowed, and she saw his Adam's apple slide up and down under the stretched skin of his throat. She'd never noticed before that Billy had an Adam's apple. She looked away quickly, as if she'd seen something she shouldn't have. Billy lowered his head and swiped his sleeve under his nose.

"Where's Linda?" he said.

"My mother's got her."

"Do you think she can keep her a while? I want to go inside and . . . I want to find my Mom's rosary and . . ."

"Don't worry. I'll help with Linda. You can come get her later."

"Thanks. You're a pal."

He turned toward his house, then turned back. His eyes were filling up with tears.

"He looked . . . broken. Why does he always have to be so . . . ? Oh, geez, Helen, I don't know what my Mom's gonna do if anything happens to Lloyd."

Helen took both his hands in hers.

"Listen to me, Billy. Lloyd will be all right. You'll see. He's gonna be fine. I'm sure of it."

He looked at her questioningly for a moment, then nodded and managed a half-baked smile. She let go of his hands, and he stuffed them in his pockets.

"Okay," he said. "Okay."

After he'd gone inside, Helen stood on the sidewalk a while pondering. A pal. That'd been good enough before, and it would have to be good enough again. It was clearly better than their recent estrangement. She wouldn't let herself think any more about the kiss or his Adam's apple or the way his hair sometimes fell over his forehead. Pals didn't think about such things, and they certainly never mentioned them if they did think about them.

"Okay," she said aloud, encouraging herself. But even at that moment of resolve, she was aware of a cranny in her heart where a tiny part of her sat waiting for the time to come when such things could be thought of and mentioned.

CHAPTER 10

Lloyd was out of the hospital in a week, walking without crutches or cane after six weeks. He still got headaches sometimes, but less and less often. Mrs. Mackey said he'd probably be dead if he didn't have such a hard head, but that it was his hard head that got him in trouble in the first place. Hadn't she warned him over and over about that intersection, and wouldn't he always tell her not to be a worrywart?

In the excitement that day, no one except Emilie had wondered how Helen knew about the accident so soon. Helen explained that she'd heard the squeal of tires, and having just spotted Lloyd leaving on his bike, she'd feared the worst and run out to see. It was the first large lie Helen had ever told.

Helen watched Lloyd's homecoming from her bedroom window. Billy went down the walk to meet the Checker cab, while his older sister held back Linda, who was trying desperately to get to her mother inside the big, exciting yellow car at the curb. Lloyd emerged slowly, hotly refusing the cabbie's offer to carry him. Billy stayed beside his brother as he struggled with his crutches, but made no attempt to assist him. Mrs. Mackey circled her sons like a collie herding sheep.

Lloyd had the air of a wounded soldier. It was the effect, mainly, of the bandage around his head, but also of his gallant insistence on making it under his own steam. At least, that was how soldiers were presented in the history books at school, as men who did not act hurt when they really were, men who did not ask for special consideration just because they'd had bad luck.

Helen thought repeatedly of Lloyd as a soldier in the weeks that followed—when she saw him in a chair in the backyard with a blanket on his lap, or shuffling up and down the driveway trying out his cane, or running his hand gingerly over the long red scar that curved across his shaved scalp. If she let her eyes go a bit out of focus, Helen could see again the shimmering light she'd noticed around him the day of the accident. There was always a narrow, milky band close to his body, and one or two layers of color around this. The colors changed from time to time. Orange occurred most often. It was the right color for Lloyd, Helen decided, a confident, proud color.

Sometimes at school, Helen would look up from writing out spelling words or plotting graph points, to scout the lights around one of her classmates. It worked best if she didn't stare directly at her subject, but off to one side.

Each individual had a characteristic color that was almost always present and others that came and went. In trying to understand the colors, it helped to know a person's basic nature, plus his or her immediate circumstances. Brown all the time apparently denoted a liar, yet someone who was outlined in brown during a history test was probably just confused. Rosie's main color was a happy, lively pink, but when fat Ron tripped her, the pink was shot through with angry red. Red could also mean someone was afraid, just as bright yellow seemed to say someone was having fun making something, like during art period, while dull yellow said someone was being selfish, like when Mary Steltman wouldn't let Ginny Taylor try her new jacks, even though everyone knew Ginny was the best player in school.

Helen's father had said he wouldn't allow her to go to any more séances, and she didn't regret it. She didn't like the hungry way people looked at her, even people she'd known all her life, like Mrs. Durkin and Mr. Grauer. She supposed seeing the lights was linked to what Nanny called her "gift," but it felt more like a knack, like how Rosie could wiggle her ears. Helen considered reading the colors simply a game. It didn't get anyone excited because it was a secret. The one time she had put it to use, that first time with Lloyd, it had enabled her to help Billy not feel so scared.

Once Helen had worked out a system of meanings for the colors, she sought out the lights less frequently. For one thing, her interest was flagging, and for another, Miss Thompson kept reprimanding her for not paying attention. She'd even had to stay in at recess one day to write "I must not daydream" a hundred times on the blackboard. Occasionally, she'd still perceive a glow around someone when she wasn't trying, most often the red spikes of anger or fear, or the green shimmer of beginning illness, but after the blackboard humiliation, she resolved not to get distracted again.

November 1937

During the week before Thanksgiving, Miss Thompson foreshortened afternoon lessons so that the eighth-graders could collect decorations from all the classes and put them up around the school. Hallway bulletin boards and the auditorium windows were decked with construction paper Pilgrim's hats, leaf rubbings, hand-print turkeys, and cornhusk dolls. A huge papier-mâché cornucopia graced the counter in the principal's office. The whole of Wednesday morning was given over to weaving baskets out of strips of shirt cardboard and attaching tissue paper carnations to the handles. The Women's Club would fill the baskets with walnuts and tangerines and peppermint candies for the County Home for Orphans.

Wednesday night, Rosie and Helen were playing Scrabble on Helen's dining-room table. Spicy aromas of pumpkin and apple pies curled in from the kitchen.

"Nanny made these for you girls," Emilie said, putting down a plate of baked pie crust trimmings that had been folded into triangles filled with cinnamon, sugar, and melted butter.

"And when you're done with your game, I want you to take a pie across the street to the Steltmans."

"Is Mrs. Steltman still sick?" Rosie asked.

"I'm afraid so. I saw her yesterday, and she's as thin as a stick. Her sister's coming to make their dinner tomorrow, or they wouldn't have any, likely."

Emilie turned to go back to the kitchen, then paused in the doorway.

"Why don't you ask Mary over to play?"

Rosie, whose back was to Emilie, rolled her eyes at Helen. They didn't much care for the company of Mary Steltman, who had strong tendencies to whining and telling tales.

"Mary doesn't like Scrabble," Helen said quickly.

"Well, you might think of something else to do," Emilie replied, but her tone of voice said she wasn't going to push it.

It was dark when they crossed the street to the Steltmans'. Helen carried the warm, heavy pie wrapped in a clean dish towel, and Rosie held a jug of whipping cream carefully upright.

When Mary opened the door, she didn't look especially pleased to see them. But when her mother called in a husky voice to ask who it was, she had to step back and let them in. They followed her into the living room.

It was a small room, crammed with overstuffed furniture covered in floral chintz. A fire blazed in the fireplace, and to Helen, fresh from the crisp November night, the room felt overheated, the air stale and vaguely sour. Mrs. Steltman sat in an easy chair with afghans around her shoulders and across her legs. The thinness Emilie had described was evident in her caved-in face and in one bony hand fidgeting with an edge of the lap rug.

"So thoughtful," she said, when Helen explained their errand. She was smiling, but she looked sad and terribly tired.

Mary received the bundled plate from Helen, and after letting her mother lift a corner of the towel to admire the pie, she took it to the kitchen at the back of the house. Rosie accompanied her, valiantly chattering about whether the pond might freeze this weekend and if Mary had gotten her skate blades sharpened yet and how she would have to use her brother's old hockey skates again this season but was hoping for figure skates for Christmas.

At Mrs. Steltman's insistence, Helen sat on the end of the couch near her chair. There was the usual exchange about how she was liking school and how her family was, and then they fell quiet, both of them directing their gazes to the fire, whose occasional crackles kept the silence from feeling awkward. When Mrs. Steltman sighed audibly, Helen turned to look at her.

The woman was still staring into the flames, either unaware of Helen's attention or ignoring it, and around her glowed the lights. They were different from any Helen had encountered before, sky blue with silver sparks, and there was a hole in them near her stomach. As Helen was puzzling over this, she sensed the presence of someone else in the room. Twisting around, she expected to find Mary and Rosie, but instead an old man was standing at the hall door. He was looking at Mrs. Steltman, and his eyes shone with kindness and concern. He took two steps forward and stopped. Helen checked on the sick woman, but she continued to watch the fire, obviously sunk deep in her own thoughts.

Suddenly, Helen knew who the old man was, as certainly as if he'd spoken. He was Mrs. Steltman's father, and he'd come to help her die. His being was so gentle and loving, Helen felt no fear at this knowledge. To the contrary, she saw that Mrs. Steltman had been suffering for a long time, and that death would be a release for her. Helen knew that Mary and Mary's father and Mrs. Steltman's sister would be very sad when she left them, but surely they would come to see that it was better for her than living on in pain and discouragement.

At the sound of Rosie's laughter from the hallway, the old man disappeared and Mrs. Steltman looked away from the fire.

"Sorry, dear, I guess I dozed off for a moment," she said, though Helen hadn't seen her eyes close.

"Did you dream?"

"Dream? I don't know. I suppose maybe I did."

"Did you dream about . . . about a person?"

Mrs. Steltman appeared briefly startled, then she shook her head slowly.

"What a queer child you are, Helen."

Mary and Rosie burst into the room, both giggling. It was hard to get Mary to laugh at the best of times, and since her mother fell ill six months earlier, she'd been even more somber. Helen guessed that after seeing Mrs. Steltman's condition, the soft-hearted Rosie had made a real effort.

"Go on, you silly girls," Mrs. Steltman scolded jokingly. "Let a person have some peace."

"Want to go out back and watch for shooting stars?" Mary offered.

"Sure," Rosie agreed.

Helen was the last one out of the room, and when she glanced back, she saw that Mrs. Steltman's father had returned and was standing closer to her.

There was no moon, so the sky was populous with stars. The Milky Way was clearly visible through the leafless tree branches. Mary had brought out a couple of old, moth-eaten blankets. She spread one on the ground, and when they had all lain down, Rosie in the middle, they arranged the other blanket over themselves, with much tugging and good-natured squabbling.

Once settled, they lay scanning the sky and listening to the wind brush through the tall pines at the end of the yard. The top blanket was scratchy under Helen's chin, but she rather liked the cozy setup. She was almost able to forget the tough times ahead for poor Mary. If only there were some way to reassure her in advance.

"My mother says a shooting star is an angel bringing someone an important message," Rosie said.

"That's daffy," Mary scoffed. "Everyone knows shooting stars are *meteors*."

"It's not daffy," Rosie bridled. "It's a pretty story, like the pot of gold at the end of the rainbow, or the tooth fairy."

"Baby stuff," Mary insisted.

"Stories aren't just for babies," Rosie countered. "Stories are fun. Or sometimes they're exciting."

"Or sometimes sad," Helen put in. "But sad in a good way."

"Sad in a good way?" Mary said scornfully.

"Well, sometimes when you feel sad, you can feel glad at the same time. About some other part of something. Oh, I'm not explaining it very well."

"You can bet on that," Mary said.

Rosie twitched her legs, and Mary complained she'd pulled the blanket off her feet. All three had to shift around to make it right. Helen sensed Rosie's forbearance waning. After a few immobile minutes, Rosie sat up abruptly, bringing the blanket up with her.

"Hey!" Mary complained.

"Bah, I don't think we're going to see any *meteors* anyway," Rosie said.

Mary rose to the bait. "Yeah, I guess the *angels* don't have any messages tonight."

Rosie stood up and marched off, heading back to Helen's. While Mary folded up the blanket that had covered them, Helen shook out the bottom one to get off bits of dried grass.

"You know, Mary, maybe it's not from angels, but there *are* messages that can come from the other side."

Mary hugged the folded blanket to her chest.

"My mother told me, Helen, never to talk to you about stuff like that. You know, about your grandmother and those nutty people who believe in . . . in all that."

Helen's temper flared momentarily, but she quelled it. Mary was only obeying her mother, after all. A mother she'd shortly have to mourn.

"Well, your mother might think differently after she's on the other side herself."

"What do you mean?" There was panic in Mary's voice.

"She's going there soon, Mary."

"What are you saying? Are you saying my mother's going to die?"

"Don't worry. Your grandfather is there waiting for her. And she'll feel so much better. You want her to feel better, don't you?"

To Helen's shock, Mary started screaming. All the agony of her heart was in that scream. It filled the night. Helen expected neighbors to rush out of their houses any minute. And there she'd be, an obvious culprit, standing suspiciously close to the hysterical girl.

Helen stuffed the grassy blanket over Mary's face to muffle her scream. Instead of fighting back, Mary burrowed into the balled up blanket and started, quietly, to cry. Helen looked around at the lighted windows of the surrounding houses. No one was peering out. No doors were slamming open.

Mary lifted her head and sniffled, stifling her tears. She pulled the blanket roughly out of Helen's grasp.

"You've never liked me, Helen Schneider, so I guess you think it's okay to be so mean," she said. "But what you said is much more than mean. It's plain and truly crazy. Lucky for you I don't want to upset my parents by telling them what you did. But when we get to school Monday, I'm going to tell everyone there how crazy you are. All the gang and Miss Thompson and everyone."

She spun around and beat a self-righteous retreat to her back door, leaving Helen, stunned and frightened, shivering in the cold.

Chapter 11
November 1937

All Thanksgiving morning, Helen was kept hopping. Dust the living room, polish the silver coffee urn, cut the last chrysanthemums from the garden and trim their dead leaves, iron the linen napkins. Emilie and Ursula were busy in the kitchen, where every surface was cluttered with bowls and spoons and chopping boards and food. The two women were not so much cooking as dancing the feast into being.

During her chores, Helen struggled to hold at bay the alarm that had been thudding inside her since Mary's terrible pronouncement. She'd been afraid to tell Rosie about it. Mightn't even Rosie's loyalty falter at the prospect of befriending an outcast? For that's what Helen would be if Mary made good on her threat, and there was no reason to think she wouldn't. Maybe it wouldn't even come to a question of loyalty. Maybe Rosie, like any sensible person, would be staggered by Helen's claims and would recoil from her in fear and abhorrence. It would be the natural reaction. It was she, Helen, who was unnatural.

Helen dawdled over sweeping the porch, stopping periodically to stare across the street at Mary's house. Would Mary really refrain from telling her parents what Helen had said, or would the urge to inform be too delicious to pass up?

"Helen," her father called from the driveway, where he was washing the Ford. "If you want to ride with me to the bus stop, you'd better stop wool-gathering and finish that sweeping."

His warning was without teeth. Helen always went with him to pick up her uncle and aunt and cousins from the bus stop on Thanksgiving, and she always rode along when he drove them back into Brooklyn that night. She loved the lights of the bridges, the looming up of the city as they went in, the dark silhouette of the Jersey palisades on the way home. Helen's going on these rides was a tradition as firm as Nanny's chestnut stuffing or Walter's German blessing over the turkey. It couldn't be jeopardized by lackadaisical sweeping. Nevertheless, Helen briskly resumed her work, pacing herself to her father's whistling, and she didn't look over to the Steltmans' again.

The meal was sumptuous, the diners festive. After dinner, the children were sent outside so that the grown-ups could enjoy a tranquil dessert. Helen and her cousins, Teresa and Terence, twins one year younger than she, were glad to escape their chairs after the long meal. They'd get dessert in the kitchen later and not have to keep their voices down while they ate it.

There were always extra kids in the neighborhood on Thanksgiving, and unless it was raining, they all made it outside some time in the late afternoon. This year, when Helen and the twins went out, the Mackeys, minus seventeen-year-old Barbara, were already in front tossing a football with their three cousins. Within fifteen minutes, eight other kids assembled from both ends of the block. Helen was glad not to find Mary Steltman among them.

A game of ring-a-levio was quickly organized. Helen and Teresa were on Billy's team, Terence on Lloyd's team. As a rule, the twins liked to stick together, but Lloyd had insisted they split up.

"If we call Terry, see, we won't know which one if you're on the same team," he explained, brushing aside their objection that neither of them used the nickname Terry.

They didn't protest very strongly. Lloyd's head was covered

with longish stubble by now, but his formidable scar was still visible, and coupled with his charisma, it rendered him an irreproachable leader. It was he who chose the center of Dohrmann's corn patch at the street's dead end as base. With the tall, dried stalks surrounding prisoners, it would be more difficult, and more thrilling, for their teammates to secure their release by running in, tagging the central plant, and yelling "ring-a-levio, caw, caw, caw." Lloyd talked little Linda out of one of her red hair ribbons and tied it to the corn stalk that had to be tagged.

The game was wild, requiring almost constant running. Soon sweaters were unbuttoned and caps cast aside. If someone tripped, they scrambled to their feet without a whimper and ran on. Helen gloried in it. At last, the tightness in her chest from last night's interaction with Mary was gone, unlocked by the force of her pounding heart and swelling lungs.

As the afternoon crawled into twilight, some children had to leave, but the game continued. With fewer players, it was harder to catch people, and it took longer to be freed once you were caught. At one point, with the light nearly too dim to make out the racing, dodging figures, Helen and Billy found themselves prisoners together at the corn plant with the red ribbon. A breeze rasped through the stalks. The shouts of their companions reached them from different directions. Billy kept turning his head from side to side, watching for a teammate to crash through the stalks to free them.

"Be ready to go," he said to Helen. "It's gonna be hard to see anyone coming."

Helen nodded, pulling up her anklets, which had slid down into her shoes at the heels.

"Lloyd's running pretty good," she said. "Guess his leg's all better."

"Yeah, it's jake." Billy stopped scanning the rows to bestow a teasing smile. " 'Course, it don't take much to catch a girl."

"You think so, Billy Mackey?" she answered, playfully shoving his shoulder so that he stumbled a bit over a broken corn stalk on the ground behind him.

In response, he shoved her gently, but she had braced her feet apart and didn't budge a step. Seemingly satisfied with the uneven exchange, Billy hunched down like a sprinter and resumed watching for a rescuer.

"You do sorta run okay," he admitted, peering through the stalks.

"Well, thanks," she said sarcastically.

He straightened up and looked at her. She smiled to show there weren't really any hard feelings. He kept looking at her, and she began to feel embarrassed.

"Good thing we're on the same team," he said. " 'Cause I could catch you easy any time. Any time at all."

Helen felt the need to swallow, but her mouth was too dry.

"Maybe you could, and maybe you couldn't," she answered. "Leastways, not *every* time."

"What if you decided to slow down?"

Helen couldn't hold his gaze any longer. She bent to tighten her shoelaces.

"What if I did?"

She stood up. Maybe it was a trick of the twilight, but his familiar face looked slightly different to her. She noticed for the first time a strong resemblance to his absent father, in the line of his jaw and the spacing of his eyes.

"What if I did?" she dared to repeat.

"Well, then, I guess I would—"

"Ring-a-levio, caw, caw, caw!" screamed Teresa as she burst through the corn stalks and tagged the one with the red ribbon.

Billy bolted at once. When Helen hesitated, Teresa pulled on her arm, and the two of them took off. When they emerged from the stalks and paused on tiptoes to locate the other runners, they spotted Walter standing out on the sidewalk in conversation with a neighbor, Ted Robertson. Terence stood waiting beside them. He beckoned to the girls, and they ambled over, calling out general good-byes.

Helen spotted Billy on the other side of the lot, where Linda was leaning against a tree sucking her thumb. He waved before squatting to pick up his sister, and Helen waved back. The Mackey crew was going home, too, but Helen didn't expect them to walk with her group. Billy would hold them back, within sight perhaps, but out of speaking range. It's what she'd do in his place. It was the only way to keep that confusing private moment private. It was the only way to protect its possibilities.

"So that young Robertson was in a Lincoln Brigade, was he?" Helen's uncle Franz asked her father.

They were in the car on the way to Brooklyn, the two men up front, Helen, her aunt and cousins in back. The twins were asleep, Terence leaning on Teresa and snoring softly, Teresa slumped heavily against Helen.

"That's right," Walter answered. "Just back from Spain this week because of a bad chest wound. Been gone close to a year."

"What's he got to say for himself?"

"Seems just as fired up against General Franco as when he left, but I got the impression he won't be going back."

"Had his bellyful of fighting, eh?" Franz said.

"The boy's not a coward, if that's what you mean. More like discouraged. He said Hitler and Mussolini are giving Franco so much help, the Loyalists don't stand a chance. Stalin gave them some support early on, but it hasn't amounted to much."

They were crossing the George Washington Bridge. Helen pressed her forehead against the cold window glass to watch the black gleam of the Hudson River far below.

"Is this Ted Robertson a Communist?" Helen's aunt asked in a horrified whisper.

"No, Marie," replied Walter. "No, I don't think so."

"Then why'd he volunteer to fight in Spain? It's a civil war. It's nothing to do with him."

"He's young, idealistic. He sees fascism gaining footholds everywhere in Europe. He wants to stop it. That's how he explains it, anyway."

"And he has no worry about Communists?" Marie said incredulously.

"Young men," Franz said, shaking his head. "They're always drawn to the glory of the fight."

"Pooh," exclaimed Marie. "He should know better than to go against someone who has got the German air force on his side."

Terence moaned and twisted about in his sleep. His mother stroked his hair. It was quiet in the car for some minutes. When the adults began speaking again, it was of family matters.

After the Thanksgiving guests had been let out in Brooklyn, and thank-you's, good-bye kisses, and handshakes had been exchanged, Helen stretched out in the backseat and dozed. Her father roused her when they were on the bridge again because he knew how much she enjoyed crossing it.

She propped herself up for a good look all around, then flopped down when they reached the Jersey side and were cruising down Route 4. As she lay curled up with her hands tucked under her cheek, she began to wonder about Billy's odd question and about what else he might have said if Teresa hadn't interrupted. Worry over Mary was snaking in once more, too, with the added anxiety that her defamation might reach Billy's ears.

It wasn't fair. She'd only been trying to help that bonehead Mary. Helen slid slightly as the car, off the highway now, met a sharp curve in the road. They'd be home in minutes, but home didn't feel like a refuge tonight. Home was a place in which to wait for the sky to fall. Helen felt trapped and helpless, like a captive no one would risk rescuing.

CHAPTER 12

Mary was not on the playground Monday morning. She wasn't there when they formed up lines to go inside. Was she going to be absent, or was she just tardy?

Helen's heart jumped each time the classroom door opened, once for a girl delivering mimeograph stencils, once for the safety patrols coming in from their posts, once for a hall monitor with a note from the office. After Miss Thompson read the note, she stood up and turned to the blackboard. Helen was amazed to see her teacher's neat handwriting spell out Mary Steltman's name and address.

"Class," Miss Thompson said. "I've just learned that your friend Mary's mother passed away yesterday. Take out your grammar books and look up the guidelines for a condolence letter. I expect proper form and proper punctuation. The salutation may be to Mary or to Mary and her family."

She sat down, nodding to Susan Edelman, whose job it was to pass out the good white paper. Susan went to the storage cabinet and began counting out sheets. Three students got up to sharpen their pencils. There was a low buzz among the rows of children.

"If you're not sure what to say," Miss Thompson instructed, "do a rough draft first. I don't want any erasures on the final letters."

Helen's fingers felt numb as she paged through her grammar book. She didn't notice Susan go by, but she must have, because when Helen looked down at her desktop, a smooth sheet of lined white paper was lying on it. Uncapping her fountain pen, she carefully wrote the date in the top right corner, just as the sample in the grammar book showed.

The book said a condolence letter should be brief and should focus on memories of the deceased, sympathy for the survivors, and an offer of help to the survivors. Helen decided she would omit that last one, but with a sinking heart, she realized that her mother would be sure to make offers of help to Mr. Steltman and that she might even make promises that Helen would spend time with Mary. Helen would tackle that problem later. Now she had to concentrate on the tricky task of the letter. She would tell Mary, first, she was sorry her mother had passed away. That was true, however Mary might doubt it. And she could also honestly say that Mrs. Steltman had always been nice to her. Helen was trying to recall some specific instance of Mrs. Steltman's niceness to mention when Miss Thompson called her to her desk.

"Helen," Miss Thompson said, "you and Mary are neighbors, aren't you?"

"She lives across the street."

"Good. Then we can put all the letters in one big envelope, and you can hand deliver them."

"Me?" Helen said, panicked.

"It would be much more personal than mailing them. And I'm sure Mary would appreciate your stopping by."

"Are you going to visit her, Miss Thompson?"

"I expect so, in a few days."

"Then can't you take the letters?"

Miss Thompson's expression showed exasperation competing with self-control.

"Helen, there's no need to feel nervous about this. Such sad events are part of life, and you are old enough to respond in a polite, grown-up manner. Now, take your seat."

Before Helen had reached her seat, Miss Thompson called her back.

"Helen," she said in a low tone that even the first row of students would not be able to make out, "are you frightened by the illness that Mrs. Steltman had?"

"No, ma'am," Helen said, not adding that she didn't know what Mrs. Steltman had had, except that the lights had shown there was something very wrong in the area of her stomach.

"Because it's only ignorance and superstition that make people shun people who have cancer."

"Yes, ma'am."

Miss Thompson seemed to be searching Helen's face for signs of fear or false beliefs.

"Why don't you choose someone to go with you? Two students would make a fuller representation of the class, and you can be company for each other. I know it's not an easy job I've set you."

"Thank you, Miss Thompson."

"But why'd you pick *me?*" Rosie asked again on their way to the Steltman house. "If you remember, last time I saw Mary, we were kind of mad at each other, so I don't think she's gonna be too happy to find me at her door now."

"Look, Rosie, I picked you for *me,* not for Mary. Because you're my best friend, and I didn't want to go alone, and I thought you'd want to help me out. But if it's so hard, then just forget it."

"Forget it? What about the letters?"

"I'll pick somebody else and take them tomorrow."

"Miss Thompson won't like it."

"I won't like it, either."

"Oh, all right. Anyway, I don't *really* care what Mary Steltman thinks about me."

They walked on in silence. The sky was thick with gray clouds threatening the first snow. The resulting light washed the color out of everything. Dark objects, like tree trunks and brick walls, looked darker, while brighter objects, like shop signs, appeared faded and tired. There was an indifferent flatness to everything.

A black-ribboned floral wreath was hanging over the knocker on the Steltmans' front door. It hadn't been there when Helen left for school that morning. She remembered how much Mrs. Steltman had liked flowers. Her roses had won prizes.

Rosie pushed the bell. A woman looking like a plump version of Mrs. Steltman in better days answered the door. Helen guessed she must be Mrs. Steltman's sister.

"We're from Mary's class," Helen said. "We brought her some letters."

"I'm afraid Mary's not up to receiving visitors yet," the woman said, taking the proffered envelope, "but I'm sure she'll see you for a moment."

Before the girls could protest, the woman had gone inside, leaving the door ajar. In a few minutes, Mary appeared, looking as if she'd just woken up, though it was four o'clock in the afternoon. Her eyes were puffy and red. She held around her the same afghan that had been draped over Mrs. Steltman's shoulders the night before Thanksgiving.

"Hey, Mary," Rosie said gently, reaching out to pat the girl's arm. Helen envied her poise. "We're awful sorry about your mom."

"Miss Thompson told us this morning," Helen added. "We all wrote letters. That lady has them." She pointed to the interior of the house.

"She's my aunt," Mary replied.

"When will you be back to school, do you think?" Rosie asked.

87

"Next week, I guess."

"Well, we'll see you then."

Rosie turned to go, and Helen, grateful for the lead, also turned. But feeling she hadn't really said the right things, she glanced back at Mary, unmoving in the doorway, and said, "I really am very sorry, Mary."

Mary made no answer, not even a nod. Helen and Rosie had reached the street when Mary called out.

"Helen! Wait up!"

Rosie continued on, telling Helen she'd see her tomorrow. Helen took a deep breath and faced Mary, who was coming down the walkway. The unkind light of the gloomy day made her look even more miserable.

"I decided not to tell," she said, as bitterly as if she were uttering a curse.

Helen supposed she ought to thank her, but somehow it didn't seem appropriate.

"I don't want people thinking about you whenever they remember my mother. I don't want any more whispering about her. She was good, and you're . . . well, you're like a kind of witch."

"Mary, I only—"

Mary put up her hand to stop Helen. The afghan slipped from one shoulder.

"I don't want to hear anything from you. It's like it didn't happen, got it?"

"Got it."

"Except . . ."

"Except what?"

"If you ever do anything like that again, not just to me, but to anybody, I *will* tell. I'll tell and tell. I'll put it in the newspapers if I can. And I won't stop until you haven't got a friend left, until even the milkman is afraid to come to your house."

88

★ ★ ★ ★ ★

That night, Helen waited an hour after the rest of the household had gone to bed, and then she summoned Iris.

She pulled her desk chair into the center of her bedroom and sat doing the deep breathing her grandmother had taught her as séance preparation. She tried to keep herself "open," as Iris had advised, driving out thoughts that strayed into her mind by listening to the ins and outs of her breaths. Finally, just as she was beginning to think she should give up and try again the next night, she felt an elating lightness infuse her body. Opening her eyes, she found Iris standing before her, the signature flower held loosely between long, slender fingers.

Helen didn't know how to begin. Iris gave Helen to understand she'd wait patiently for as long as it took Helen to collect her thoughts.

"I didn't get to say, but thanks for helping me out with the man with the pain around his neck," Helen said at last.

"Sammy is grateful, too," Iris said, in her usual nonspeaking way. The smiling lips did not move. Instead, her voice slipped into Helen's mind like mercury. "You helped him comfort his mother. He couldn't have done it without you."

Helen was surprised. She had known that mediums could be helpful to living people, but she'd never considered that they could be of service to the dead as well. Or that the dead might have desires as piercing as those of the living.

"Well, I couldn't have done it without you, Iris."

"One day you will do such things and more without me. Somewhere these things are already coming to pass."

Helen squirmed in her seat. Could Iris read her mind? She had come painfully close to the reason Helen had summoned her.

"I won't be . . . calling you anymore."

Iris gave no reaction.

"I don't want to hear things or see things other people can't. I want to be a regular person."

"Deaf and blind?"

The question was soft, hushed, and Iris seemed quite disinterested in what choice Helen made, but the words angered the girl. Iris was supposed to help her, not mock her or get her mixed up. Iris was supposed to understand.

Helen rarely felt anger towards adults. Even more rarely did she show it. Where did it ever get you but in a worse spot? But Iris was in a different category. Could a spirit really be adult or child? In any case, in some strange but definite way, Iris was *hers*, and that freed Helen to feel and express anything in her presence.

"Yes, all right, deaf and blind, if that's how you want to look at it!"

Helen thought she saw the tiniest lift of Iris's shoulders.

"I continue, but I will keep away, if that is what you wish," Iris told her. "There are many ways to make the same journey."

"You'll fix it so I won't see or hear things anymore?"

"I continue, and it is always happening. Beside you, behind you, before you. You will have to post a guard. Not against me. Against yourself."

"How do I do that?"

"When they come, look away. When they speak, hide your ears. Don't carry their messages. Don't be ruled by tenderness. Don't dream."

Helen wondered how all that would work in reality, if it would work at all, but before she could form another question, Iris was gone. As a first step toward becoming "regular," Helen did not call her back.

CHAPTER 13
JULY 1938

Helen and Rosie lay on their backs in the shade in Helen's backyard. Racketing cicadas made the heavy afternoon seem even more sweltering. Rosie was plucking blades of grass and pressing them between her index fingers to use as whistles.

"Wanna go to the river?" she said, crooking her elbow and propping her head on her hand.

"What for?"

"Dunno." Rosie picked the flower head from a stalk of clover and ate it. "My brother and his buddies went over to Peck Park for a ball game," she said hopefully.

"They won't all be at Peck Park."

"Yeah, I guess."

Hunter's River marked the town's north border. Afternoons spent floating on inner tubes in its slow-moving waters or sorting through stones on pebbly Oratam Beach were as definitive of summer as ice cream cones and lightning bugs. Other years, the girls had spent part of nearly every sunny day there, as small children in tow with Rosie's big sisters, and after the age of ten, on their own.

Oratam Beach used to be merely a swath of tough grass and gravel between the woods and the river, with a few splintery picnic tables. But early in the Depression, the township had repossessed adjoining land parcels from people who had defaulted on their taxes, and WPA workers had filled in boggy spots, trimmed away underbrush, made paths, and built more tables, a shaded pavilion, and a bandstand. The new park had been grandly renamed Brinker's Green, after the mayor who pushed the project through, but people still called the swimming area Oratam Beach.

This summer, Helen and Rosie had avoided the park as assiduously as they did the strictly forbidden railroad tracks. There had been no discussion, no overt decision. It was simply something they'd always known—that the river beach was for younger children and high school kids only. Helen and Rosie felt like they were neither. They'd graduated from eighth grade, but they hadn't yet spent one day in the high school's large, intimidating brick building. They had left a school where their age and size made them royalty, and they were facing an institution where they'd be like first-graders again.

They might have surmounted this unsure status enough to be able still to enjoy the river if it were not for the problem of bathing suits. Helen and Rosie and most of their friends had begun to develop figures, and bathing suits had become occasions of anguish. Bodies filled them out either too little or too much. Some styles allowed pubic hair or cleavage to show. A suit might look all right dry, but when wet, might cling too closely to nipples or to the curving cleft of a rear end. Rosie's suit, after having been stretched over the varying charms of three owners, was incapable of rendering even a Hollywood glamour girl presentable. For economy's sake, Helen was expected to make do with a suit bought two years ago. Its little pleated skirt and its straps trimmed with eyelet ruffles clearly and embarrassingly marked it as a child's bathing costume.

All the shortcomings, of both bathing suits and figures, would be, at the river, put on parade for boys. There were always boys at the river. Older boys who took an interest in ogling and didn't hide it, and boys the same age as Helen and Rosie who took an interest in acting like the older boys.

Older girls didn't seem to mind the scrutiny. If anything, at times, it was the boys who seemed nervous and tentative, especially if the girls arrived in a big group, as they often did. But the presence of those girls was no comfort to Helen and Rosie and their friends. They only made them feel like interlopers. Not by anything they did or said directly, but by how they slipped their shirts off bare shoulders, how they rolled over on their blankets, how they waded, shuddering, into the river up to their knees and scooped water over their rounded arms. There was some kind of power in all that, and the way to it was still a mystery to the new ninth-grade girls.

"I've got an idea," Rosie said. "What if we go swimming somewhere else?"

"Somewhere else?"

"In the river, but not at Oratam Beach."

Intrigued, Helen sat up. Why hadn't they thought of that before? In the woods lining the river, there were a few narrow footpaths that wound through the tangle of briars and ferns, then widened at the river's edge to muddy banks with room enough cleared for two or three people to sit. These were fishing spots. They didn't attract swimmers. Except at Oratam Beach, the river close to shore was reedy and its bottom slimy. If Rosie and Helen went to one of these places, it wouldn't be as pleasant as Oratam Beach, but it would be private. And if they brought inner tubes, they could push out away from the reeds and the dreaded touch of green ooze and imagined eels.

"We could take the trail behind Dohrmann's field right down the block," Helen said, standing up.

"Now we're cookin' with gas," Rosie said. "I'll go home for my suit."

"I'll get the tubes out of the garage."

Rosie started out of the yard, then stopped.

"How's about I take the trail off Cedar Street that joins up with your trail? It'll be quicker than coming back here."

"Okay. See you at the river."

Helen held up her bathing suit and regarded it with disdain. She was still slender enough to fit into it, but she would've liked cups or bones to give her chest some shape and lift, even if Nanny said she didn't need that much support yet. She put the suit on, pulling Bermuda shorts up over it. She braided her hair and pinned the braids on top of her head. Sliding her bare feet into a pair of beat-up moccasins, she felt something hard under the ball of her left foot. Perching on the edge of the bed, she shook out the offending object. A small stone dropped to the floor. It had probably been in the moccasin since last August, when she'd last been at Oratam Beach.

Helen picked up the stone. Out of the blue, she felt dizzy. She closed her fist around the stone and shut her eyes. Billy's face appeared in her mind. He was dappled with shadows, and there was something odd about his smile. "C'mon, let's go," she heard him say. He was looking at her, yet he didn't seem to be speaking to her. Then the vision was gone.

As these things went, it hadn't been too bad an episode. Puzzling, but brief and bland. Ever since her run-in with Mary Steltman at Thanksgiving, Helen had been struggling to sidestep or ignore seeing and hearing things outside the normal range of experience. She no longer played with looking for the lights around people, and she rarely saw them spontaneously anymore. No spirits had appeared to her. Iris had kept her word to stay away.

Helen had come to recognize a kind of hum emanating from a person that meant she was about to find out something about them, and she had learned to obfuscate whatever images or thought-messages came, however compelling, by reciting the multiplication tables under her breath. Sometimes, simply getting away from the person prevented anything coming through. Today had been a little different.

Helen had never been in a physical fight with anyone, but she imagined it might feel something like what her bouts against her abilities felt like—moments of mastery alternating with thumping setbacks, constant effort and alertness and enforced bravery. Until the fight was over. Helen believed there must exist a switch to turn off her abilities permanently, not merely disregard them, and she meant to keep groping in the dark until she hit it.

What meaning did today have in her struggle? Was the mildness of the event a sign she'd gained more control, or did the novelty of it indicate the spirits had found a new path into her mind? She didn't want to dwell on it. That was part of her plan, too. She walked to the open window and tossed out the little stone.

Helen was walking at a good clip through the woods, despite the awkwardness of the fat inner tubes, one slung over each shoulder. From time to time, a tube would strike a tree and bounce her slightly to one side or the other, but she didn't slow her pace. She wanted to reach the river before Rosie, to ease herself in and be already floating when her friend arrived. Rosie might be as queasy as Helen about the sucking mud and nipping crayfish of the murky shallows, but she'd never show it. She was sure to plunge in without hesitation, stirring up muck and marsh gas and creating an unappealing stew for Helen to enter.

At the point where the Cedar Street trail joined hers, Helen paused to look for Rosie, but there was no sign of her. Helen hurried on. Soon the glint of the river was visible through the trees. Near the trail's end, where it turned to meet the small stretch of cleared bank, Helen spotted a white shirt hanging on a bush.

"Drat!" she said, stopping short.

But maybe Rosie was waiting for the inner tubes. Helen could still have a chance of getting into the river first. If she could overcome her reluctance about cold water and the icky shoreline, she could run by Rosie and jump in before Rosie even knew she was there. Helen's plotting was interrupted by the sound of laughter from the riverbank, a girl's voice.

A young woman came from the other side of the bush and retrieved the white shirt. She was wearing a plaid halter and a dirndl skirt, with a yellow scarf as a belt. Here was someone who would have no trouble with any kind of bathing suit. She was lifting her long, dark hair over the collar of the shirt when a young man stepped around the bush behind her and put his arms around her waist. She leaned back against him, and he kissed the side of her neck. She laughed again.

Helen coughed loudly to let the couple know she was there. When they saw her, they parted with a little jump that would have been comical had not Helen suddenly recognized the boy.

Billy's face was dappled with leaf shadows. He moved in front of his companion as if he were shielding her and smiled crookedly at Helen.

"Hey, hi," he said with artificial cheer. "What are you doing here?"

"Going swimming," she said, her heart hammering.

She saw the girl examining her over Billy's shoulder. Her appraisal was bound not to be as flattering as the one Helen had given her.

"This is Helen, my next-door neighbor," Billy said, turning to the girl.

"Cute," the girl said. Then to Helen, "I'm Beth."

"Oh, yeah, sorry," Billy added. "This is Beth."

Helen had heard the expression about wanting the ground to open up and swallow you, and now she fervently wished for just that. Anything but to have to stand there one more second with her stupid pinned-up braids and her stupid patched inner tubes. At least the tubes were hiding the awful, babyish ruffles on her bathing suit straps.

"C'mon, let's go," Billy said.

Beth slid her fingers down Billy's arm, and he reached back and let her take his hand. They had to sidle carefully past Helen single file to fit on the narrow path. Thickets of poison ivy on both sides prevented any of them from stepping off the trail. The protruding inner tubes grazed first Billy's chest, then Beth's breasts.

Helen ran to the river. Kicking off her moccasins and dropping one tube to the ground, she stumbled into the water with the other tube. She hadn't stopped to take off her shorts. Holding the tube out in front of her, she beat her legs in the water to propel herself out into the river. Twice, to keep down sobs threatening to erupt, she ducked her head underwater and held her breath as long as she could. She worked her legs until they ached, and worked them some more, then climbed into the tube and used her arms to row herself downstream. In a few minutes, she was around a shoal and out of sight of the mud flat where she was to have met Rosie. Let her friend think what she liked, she couldn't face her or anyone just now.

The exertion of kicking and paddling was both an outlet and a container for her churned emotions. She would keep going until she felt calmer, until the sky and the woods and the bridge upstream no longer looked like scenery flats but became three-dimensional and regular again. In this suspended piece of time, only her feelings seemed real, and in this suspended piece of time, being real was thorns and gouges and stinging nettles. She didn't think about where she was going. She wasn't thinking at all, only moving. Pushing through the water. Getting away. Off the too-solid ground, out of the enshrouding woodlands, beyond people and clumsy talk.

Finally, she was too exhausted to go on. She laid her head back on the tube and drifted with the current. Her skin dried quickly in the hot sun, and her face and shoulders and knees soon achieved an agreeable sensation of baking. When they began to smart, she splashed water over herself, and the lovely process of drying and baking resumed. She knew she was getting a sunburn that would cause her misery tonight, but she didn't care. It was blessedly quiet on the river. She was far enough out that sounds from shore were muffled, and there were few of them, in any case.

"Billy," she whispered, trying out the name to see how it would feel, waiting for the tailspin.

No tailspin happened. Only a terrible tug at her heart and a tiny flash of anger.

"Billy," she repeated more loudly. "Billy!" she shouted, safe from all hearing.

A motor boat sped by the far shore, and a minute later, the inner tube was rocked gently by its wake. Helen picked one ripple and tried to track its progress all the way to shore.

What should she do when she saw Billy again? She was sure he would be as reluctant as she to mention the meeting in the woods. But it would be there between them all the same.

Unless. Unless she could convince him that it needn't be and wasn't. She would behave toward him exactly as if there were no secret, no embarrassment, no rotten Beth. And he would see that she could be counted on, that she wasn't silly or small-minded. After a while, maybe it would feel that things were the same. Maybe even better.

She noticed she was opposite a familiar sandy spit and started paddling toward it with long, smooth sweeps of her cupped hands. She wanted to go home. She wanted to rinse the river out of her hair and put lotion on her shoulders. And she wanted to throw away her contemptible bathing suit.

CHAPTER 14
OCTOBER 1938

It was the end of October, and high school had come to seem to Helen not only a congenial environment, but a mildly intoxicating one. She liked having different teachers for different subjects, and she liked sharing complaints about them with her friends. She liked hugging a pile of heavy books to her chest, and writing with her grandfather's thick fountain pen, which Walter had ceremoniously given her on the first day of school. She liked the loud, bustling halls, the noise of metal lockers banging shut, the babble in the crowded girls' rooms, the way students poured out the doors at the end of the day in clamorous throngs, the way the throngs gradually diverted into side streets like cooling lava. There was excitement in all of it, and a sense of being part of something large and dynamic.

Of course, she still had uncertainties. She was already beginning to worry about mid-term exams and how she'd ever manage to hold in her head all the information needed to get through them. The marvelous confidence of the juniors and seniors as they moved splendidly in small groups through the halls could make her feel gangly and dull. The gang showers in the gym were a challenge to composure. And both the logic and the allure of football remained inscrutable. She went dutifully to every home game, joined in the chants the cheerleaders led, stood up and shouted when everyone else did, but she was only aping form, as she would have done at services in a strange church.

Once, she had spied Beth standing with three other girls near a water fountain. Helen ducked round a corner to avoid passing her, but not before taking in the girl's attractive stance, weight shifted to one foot, hip nudged outward. Helen and Billy had never spoken directly of Beth, but Helen would not let herself presume his interest in the girl had waned.

Billy had stopped by the very next day after Helen encountered him and Beth in the woods. He was going away for the rest of the summer to work on a road gang in the Ramapo Mountains and had come to say farewell to the Schneiders.

"That's good work for a young fellow," Walter said. "Out in the open air, being useful. You're fortunate to get it."

"Yes, sir, I know. I wanted to go to the CCC—those fellas make thirty dollars a month, and the CCC sends all but five dollars straight to your family. They're digging drainage ditches and building dykes in the Hackensack Meadows and in Secaucus to control mosquitoes, but I'd have to sign up for at least six months, and my mom doesn't want me skipping school."

"Your mother will miss you," Emilie said.

"It's only 'til September," Billy said. "Barbara's got some hours down at Woolworth's now, and Lloyd can look out for the family. My Mom would rather have him home than me, anyway."

"Well, you take care of yourself," Emilie said. "Will you have an address? We'll send you cookies."

"Oh, Em, don't fuss at the boy," Walter grumbled.

"There's a post office box," Billy answered. "I have the number at home." Looking straight at Helen for the first time since entering the house, he added, "If Helen can come to the fence, I'll pass it over."

Helen didn't have to wait long at the fence, but every second was agonizing. Would she be able to keep her pledge to herself to behave as if the meeting in the woods had never happened? When Billy arrived, he didn't immediately give her the address.

Instead, he rested his arm on the top of the fence, the folded square of paper tucked between two fingers like a cigarette.

"Helen, you know . . . I . . ."

Helen concentrated on keeping her face blank.

Billy shook his head ruefully and laughed a short laugh.

"So, did you have a good swim yesterday?" he said.

"Yes, I did."

"Kinda muddy there, though."

"I went way out onto the river."

"Well, then, that's okay."

A dog barked somewhere, and Billy peered toward the street, as if trying to locate the dog exactly. He looked at Helen again and held out the paper.

"Tell your mother she doesn't really have to send me anything," he said.

"All right."

"Except if she does, maybe you could put in a note, huh? You know, just about what's going on around here, if my Mom's okay, stuff like that."

"If you want me to."

"Yeah, sure. I'll even try to write back."

He smiled, and she was sure she blushed. She stepped down from the box on which she'd been standing and began walking to her house.

"Hey, Helen!"

She turned. He was still on the box on his side of the tall fence, only his head and shoulders in view.

"Thanks," he said, and waved.

She managed a smile. He jumped off his box and was gone.

It was eight o'clock Sunday night, time for the *Chase and Sanborn Hour* with Edgar Bergen and his dummy Charlie McCarthy. Tomorrow would be Halloween. Helen had decided she was too old to go trick-or-treating this year, but she'd carved a large jack-o'-lantern to set in the bay window in the living room. From her seat on the sofa beside her mother, she could catch the pleasant scent of raw pumpkin warmed by candle flame.

Walter lit his pipe and leaned forward in his easy chair to turn on the radio. Ursula took her customary seat. She turned on the floor lamp beside her chair and pulled a ball of yarn, a pair of needles, and a partially finished sweater out of a basket at her feet and began knitting. The theme music from the *Chase and Sanborn Hour* swelled into the room. It was a favorite program with all of them. In the opening ten minutes, they shared several laughs over Charlie McCarthy's brash joking.

When Nelson Eddy came on to sing *Neopolitan Love Song*, Walter turned the dial. It was a habit of his, switching to another station during commercials or unappreciated musical interludes. He stopped at the sound of a man's excited voice. The man identified himself as Carl Phillips, a CBS news correspondent, reporting from a farm in Grover's Mill, New Jersey. It sounded like one of those flash bulletins that sometimes interrupted programming, like when Japan had seized Chinese cities last year, or this spring, when Hitler annexed Austria, and only a few weeks ago, when German troops, with the acquiescence of the British and French, had occupied parts of Czecho-Slovakia.

What I can see of the object itself doesn't look very much like a meteor, at least not the meteors I've seen, Carl Phillips was saying. *It looks more like a huge cylinder.*

"What is he talking about?" Ursula said, pausing with her knitting needles raised.

"Grover's Mill," said Emilie. "That's in south Jersey, isn't it?"

"Near Trenton, I think," said Walter.

The reporter was interviewing the farmer on whose land the object had fallen. In the background, you could hear a crowd and the gruff commands of policemen trying to keep them back.

The reporter held his microphone out to pick up a scraping sound coming from the object.

"Now what's that supposed to be?" Ursula said. The ball of yarn had dropped to the floor, but she didn't retrieve it.

Carl Phillips asked the same thing of Dr. Pierson, a Princeton professor who was on the scene. The professor was unsure about the strange sound, but he did express doubt that the object was a meteor.

The metal casing is definitely extraterrestrial—not found on this earth, Dr. Pierson said authoritatively.

"Not found on Earth?" Emilie echoed nervously. "What does he mean, not found on Earth? Walter, what does he mean?"

Walter made a shushing motion with his hand. In rapid succession, Carl Phillips narrated the incredible facts that the scraping sound was the cylinder opening up and that a huge, tentacled monster had emerged, dripping saliva from quivering, rimless lips. People in the crowd were gasping and shouting. He described a small band of men waving a white flag as they carefully approached the creature.

Walter stood up and tensely faced the radio. They were all concentrating on it, straining to sort out Carl Phillips's words from the confused voices and noises around him. Helen's heartbeat thumped so loudly in her ears, it almost seemed another element of the broadcast. Whimpering, Emilie put her arm around Helen's shoulder.

Then from the radio, screams and shrieks. A jet of flame from the cylinder had incinerated the little group of approaching men and set the whole field on fire. Automobiles were exploding. More flames were shooting out of the cylinder, aimed at the fleeing crowd. Carl Phillips cried out that it was coming his way. Then, dead silence.

"Walter?" Emilie said weakly.

"There's something wrong with the radio?" Ursula asked.

104

Helen heard a distinct quaver in her indomitable grandmother's voice.

An announcer stated that due to circumstances beyond their control, they were unable to continue the broadcast from Grover's Mill, but that they'd return to it at the earliest opportunity. In the meantime, they'd continue with the musical program the news bulletin had interrupted. A piano began playing.

"I'm going to try another station," Walter said. "Somebody's got to know more."

But before he could turn the dial, the piano was abruptly cut off, and another announcer relayed a phone message from Grover's Mill that forty people had been burned to death there. The governor had declared martial law in Mercer and Middlesex counties. Militia were heading to the area.

Helen was trying hard not to cry, fearing once she began, she wouldn't be able to stop. She tried to picture the map of New Jersey on the wall of her history classroom. How near was Grover's Mill?

A sober announcer reported that of the 7,000 militiamen, only 120 survived; the rest had been burned or trampled to death. Communications were down in central Jersey from Pennsylvania to the ocean. Highways were jammed with terrified civilians trying to escape.

"My God," Walter intoned.

Ladies and gentlemen, I have a grave announcement to make. Incredible as it may seem, both the observations of science and the evidence of our eyes lead to the inescapable assumption that those strange beings who landed in the Jersey farmlands tonight are the vanguard of an invading army from the planet Mars.

The Secretary of the Interior came on to caution the public to remain calm, reminding them that the Martians were contained in one area. But on his heels, various bulletins

contradicted him. More cylinders had landed. Martians in fighting machines were advancing northward, tearing up railroad
tracks, bridges, power lines. The Schneiders listened, horrified,
to Army officers in bombers as they were engulfed by a black
cloud of poison gas. The same gas was blanketing Newark. They
heard a newsman choking to death. The Martians were headed
for New York City.

"We must call Franz and Marie," Emilie cried, jumping up
and running to the phone.

Helen wondered how soon the Martians would reach Brooklyn. Would her relatives have time to get out? But they had no
car. Where could they go anyway? Where could anyone go?

"I can't get through," Emilie wailed. "The lines must be
down. I can't get through."

She covered her face with her hands and began sobbing. Walter seemed not to notice. He was circulating the room in
agitated strides, stopping momentarily when he neared the radio
to stare expectantly at it. Helen knew she should go to her
mother, but she couldn't move.

Ursula went to the sofa and took Helen's hand.

"*Aufstehen!*" she said, pulling her to her feet. "We must leave."

"Leave?"

"We must go to the north, or west. Away from towns. To
hide, so we can see what may happen later."

As she spoke, they could hear voices in the street, the slamming of house doors and car doors, a small child crying loudly
and bitterly. Though muffled by the closed windows, they were
unmistakably the sounds of panic, and they further inflamed
the family's already tossed emotions.

"Let's call the police first," Walter said. "They've probably
closed some roads."

"Go, Helen, get our coats. And your father's flashlight,"
instructed Ursula. Her voice was still shaky, but Helen was glad

to hear her giving orders. "Emilie, some oranges there are in the kitchen. Bring what else you see quick to take."

Emilie wiped her eyes and looked around with a bewildered expression, then hurried out of the room. Helen ran to the hall closet.

"Can't get through there, either," Walter said, putting down the phone. "We're on our own."

When Helen returned laden with coats and hats, an announcer was reporting from the roof of a building in New York. The faint drone of people singing hymns was floating up to him from the streets below.

Enemy now in sight above the Palisades. Five—five great machines. First one is crossing the river.

Helen imagined the Martian machines tall as the George Washington Bridge, similar in structure, but gruesomely animated. She thought of Terence and Teresa. Could they see the black smoke advancing over the skyscrapers as the announcer was describing? Everything was happening so fast. Only a short time ago, Carl Phillips was contemplating a strange object in a farmer's field, and now Carl Phillips was a charred corpse in a Trenton morgue. And what of Trenton's population? Were they all either dead or running? Helen wondered wildly which would be worse, to die by fire or by gas.

Walter took his and Emilie's coats and hats and the flashlight from Helen. He, Helen, and her grandmother put on their things, then went to the kitchen to get Emilie, and out the back door. While Walter ran to the garage to get the car, the others went to the front.

In the middle of the street, two cars had collided. Both drivers had come out of their drives at high speed, one going forward, one backing up, neither bothering to watch for traffic. Now the two men, standing beside their interlocked bumpers, were shouting at each other and seemed close to blows. One man's wife, a woman who played cards sometimes with Emilie and Ursula, was trying to pull him away. Tears were coursing down her face. Her little boy, also crying, had the hem of her skirt bunched up in his hand so tightly her garters were showing.

"How do you expect us to get away now?" her husband was shouting at the other driver. "We need a tow truck to pull these cars apart."

"You're the damn fool drove right through your own garage door," countered his opponent.

"Well, we won't be needing the garage door anymore, but we damn well need a working car."

Mr. Steltman rushed across his yard and put himself between the angry men.

"Gus, Sam, it's too late to leave now, anyway," he said. "Go back inside. Stuff wet towels around your doors and windows to keep out the gas. Take your families into the basement. In the morning, if the coast is clear, we can get together as a neighborhood and make a plan."

The men scowled at him, but they backed away from each other.

"Got no time to argue," one said. "Me and mine'll just walk out. Keep to the woods by the river. Radio says the roads are jammed, anyway." He pulled a shotgun out of the trunk of his disabled car and strode off down the street, his wife and three children scooting after him.

Walter pulled the car to the curb and got out, his motor idling. Mr. Steltman had moved on to other neighbors who were loading cars or standing in their doorways looking up fearfully at the sky. He advised them all to the same course of action he'd urged on the disputing motorists. Most shook their heads and turned away. Elderly Mrs. McMahon nodded at him and went back into her house. Living alone, without an automobile, she had little choice.

Mr. Steltman was making his speech to Walter when a neighbor from the end of the block arrived. Helen knew his name, Mr. Collins, but his children were older than she, and the two families had only a nodding acquaintance.

"Steltman," Mr. Collins said, "you're wasting your time."

Mr. Steltman was gathering himself up to respond when Mr. Collins continued.

"Ain't no Martians."

He looked around at his neighbors, some still scurrying around, some pausing to think over Mr. Steltman's ideas. Now the Mackeys were out in the street, too. Mrs. Mackey and her sons each carried pillowcases stuffed with objects. Barbara held Linda by one hand and their dog on a leash by the other. Billy spotted Helen and came up to her.

"I'm going to ask your father to take my mother and baby sister," he said.

"What will the rest of you do?"

"We'll get Barbara in a car somehow. Me and Lloyd, too, if we can. If not, he and I'll lay low, like Mr. Steltman says."

Billy moved closer to where Walter was standing, near Mr. Steltman and Mr. Collins.

"Hey, all of you," Mr. Collins said, raising his voice. "Ain't no Martians."

"Have you heard something new on the radio?" a woman asked.

"Nope. Same as you."

"When I was closing our door," Billy said, "there was a short wave guy on the radio trying to call New York, but nobody was answering. Nobody."

"Sonny," Mr. Collins said, "they can't raise up anybody in New York 'cause the Krauts have cut the lines. It's not Martians done all this. It's Nazis. That goddamn Hitler's invaded, see, and just fooling us about Martians so's we'll give up without a fight. That meteor thing was a zeppelin in disguise, I figure, and the gas, well, the Germans used gas in the Great War, didn't they?"

Helen saw the Dohrmanns, on the edge of the small crowd, turn and walk away.

"Could be Japanese," someone suggested. "They're crafty devils, you know."

"Get in the car," Walter said, and Helen and her mother and grandmother complied without comment.

"Mr. Collins," Walter was saying, "the radio said Martians. The Secretary of the Interior was on, and Army people, and reporters. We heard some of those people die, for God's sake."

"You expect us to put stock in what *you* have to say?" Collins said ominously.

"Hell, no," someone said. Concurring mumbles came from some of the men.

In the backseat of the Ford, Ursula leaned over to whisper in Helen's ear.

"Are you picking up anything?"

Helen just stared at her.

"Take a moment. Listen," Ursula said. "All those deaths. Everything else. Do you feel anyone? A message?"

Helen didn't want to do it, but she closed her eyes, and for the first time in nearly a year, she deliberately let her mind fall open to whatever might come. She didn't go so far as to call on Iris, but she drew her attention inward, found a placid hollow in the midst of the fear and stayed there patiently waiting.

Nothing came. No visions, no words, no physical sensations. Only a hazy impression of being clogged, as if she had a bad head cold. She was sorry she could be no help to the terror-stricken people around her, but at the same time, she was elated. If she couldn't pick up anything in as dire a situation as this, she must finally have conquered her tendencies. If this really were the end of the world, her victory was of little import, but it pleased her nonetheless.

"Nothing," she said to her grandmother.

"Not me, either," the old lady replied, and for the first time since Walter had tuned the radio dial to the alarming story of invaders from Mars, her voice was ordinary.

Walter opened the car door and slid into the driver's seat.

"That's right," a man at the back of the crowd called out. "You go. They probably told you where to hide out to be safe."

Collins turned to the milling neighbors. "If any of you still want to run away, maybe you oughta follow the Krauts," he said. " 'Course, then, you just might end up prisoners."

"Hey, hey, everybody!" Mr. Goldberg from four houses over was running down the middle of the street shouting. His doughy wife, in a wrapper and bedroom slippers, ran behind him, puffing hard in her attempt to keep up.

"It was a play!" he shouted. "A play! Mercury Theater of the Air. We just heard. *The War of the Worlds.* For Halloween, get it?" He stopped beside the Schneiders' car because the most folks were collected there. Mr. Goldberg was smiling sheepishly. "Scared the pants off me, I'll tell you."

Slowly, the neighbors headed back to their houses. Some loitered to review the broadcast, which details had convinced them of its truth, which details, in retrospect, pointed to fiction. Walter waited for the space around the car to clear of people, then he drove it into the garage.

Ursula made cocoa. No one told Helen it was past her bedtime. No one said anything at all. While they drank their cocoa seated around the kitchen table, Helen looked from one adult face to the other. In each one, anxiety lingered, plain to see.

CHAPTER 15
JULY 1939

"Teresa, show Helen our official guidebook," Marie said as the family was waiting at Penn Station for the train to the World's Fair. "It says the Fair is the most stupendous, gigantic, super-magnificent show on earth, and they're right! We should go straight to the Trylon and Perisphere first."

"That is customary," Franz pontificated, "but the view of the Trylon and Perisphere from the Lagoon of Nations is much finer, in my opinion."

"Oh, he's right," Marie told Emilie. "I do wish that had been *our* first sight of them. That's what's so nice about going to the Fair more than once. You get to do everything, and you get to do it right."

Normally, Helen would have resented the lording air her aunt and uncle were assuming, but today their attitude didn't bother her. Let them guide. Let them crow. By tonight, she, too, would be a Fair veteran, with her own memories and favorites. This would be her only visit, an early fifteenth birthday gift from her father, and she wasn't going to let anything mar it.

Helen's cousins were pulling the guidebook back and forth between them in their eagerness to display different pages. The twins were sharing their knowledge of the Fair not as tutors but as comrades.

"They've got a whole Swiss village," Teresa said, "with real snow and yodeling."

"We gotta do the Parachute Jump," Terence declared.

"It scared me too much," Teresa said, shaking her head. "Let's go to the Aquacade instead."

"Futurama's the best," Terence told Helen excitedly. "You go to 1960, when there's gonna be fourteen-lane superhighways across the country, and cars will only cost two hundred dollars, and fruit trees'll grow under glass jars, and a bunch of other stuff. At the end of the ride, they give you a button that says *I have seen the future.*"

Helen had to admit that her aunt and uncle had been right about the view from the lagoon. It was spectacular. Gazing from a bridge down a long avenue of trees and statuary, they were able to see, through the mist of fountains, the Fair's symbols, a huge obelisk and sphere that glowed blindingly white in the July sun.

Leaving the adults to take the Fair bus, the young people set off jubilantly down Constitution Mall towards the Trylon and Perisphere. How could anyone bear to sit on a bus and simply pass by the myriad surprises and marvels on every side—acres of national and commercial pavilions, lawns studded with thousands of tulips, murals, statues, bands, shows and exhibits?

"The Trylon's six hundred ten feet high," Terence said when they reached it. "Taller than the Washington Monument."

Terence's visits to the Fair had sparked the idea he might become an architect some day, so he was interested in dimensions and measurements, especially impressive ones. Helen smiled, remembering that only two years ago his future plans had centered on becoming the next Green Lantern.

The three companions boarded an escalator that ascended as steeply as a roller coaster into the sphere. They stepped onto a slowly rotating balcony that passed through a tunnel and carried them out into a great space. Helen gasped. All around them, awestruck people were exclaiming, "Look, look!" A colossal, blue-lit dome arced high above them, while below sprawled a model American city in the year 2039. "Democracity" and its suburbs fanned out in concentric half circles from one central skyscraper. None of the city's streets intersected.

"No auto accidents," Terence pointed out.

As the balcony revolved, the dome darkened and stars emerged. Lights went on all over Democracity. The majestic sound of a choir welled up. Projected images of workers appeared on the dome, marching closer and closer—teachers with books, miners with headlamps, engineers with blueprints, farmers with hoes and pails, factory men with wrenches.

The cousins exited down a spiral ramp to a plaza graced by a sculpture called *The Astronomer,* a male nude staring upwards. Helen thought he looked worried. It was a strange expression for a statue, especially one standing beside the splendid promise of Democracity.

As arranged, the adults were waiting for them near *The Astronomer,* Emilie waved as they approached, but no one else acknowledged their arrival.

"No, Walter, I don't agree," Franz was saying. "Herr Hitler is willing to let the Jews go, but no one is willing to take them in. The Poles sent thousands back. Boatloads have been turned away from Argentina, Paraguay, Costa Rica, Mexico, Egypt, Turkey. The British have quotas in Palestine to keep the Arabs calm. There are quotas here, too. It's easy to criticize Germany, but what the critics actually *do* doesn't add up."

Walter sighed in frustration. Helen could see he didn't like conceding a point to her uncle.

The family began strolling, and the conversation resumed.

"It's still not right, Franz, for the Nazis to put them in camps," Walter persisted. "Or to use the threat of camps to force them to leave. The nations that turn their backs are wrong, yes, but it's Germany who's causing the problem."

"German civilization is one of the highest in history," Marie objected. "Didn't the Führer give Richard Strauss a lavish birthday luncheon in Vienna just last month? He is a man of culture, and he can be relied on to behave as one in state matters, too, I think."

"I don't know about that, Marie," Emilie said. "The little bit of news out of Germany is often troubling."

"Which news?"

"Did you see the newspaper photos of the Italian Minister of Culture inspecting Jews at Sachsenhausen concentration camp? They looked so grim, so sad."

"Pooh," Marie said. "So would anyone with a shaved head and wearing those baggy striped uniforms. They're prisoners, after all. I expect the food is not good. They're probably at hard labor."

"I've read much worse than that happens in those camps. Terrible cruelties. Every month, hundreds of people commit suicide by throwing themselves into the Danube rather than be taken."

"Who knows what to believe and what's propaganda? We don't hear the whole story, I'm sure."

"You're probably right there," Emilie admitted.

"What about the *St. Louis?*" Ursula said.

The adults all turned to look at her, as if they'd forgotten she was there.

Helen remembered well the story of the Hamburg-Amerika liner. Her grandmother had told her about it in May. It had made a deep impression on Ursula.

"More than nine hundred Jews on it," Ursula said now. "Whole families. All approved for the United States, going to Cuba to wait. That was all. Only to wait until the entry numbers came up. Round-trip tickets they had to buy, though no one planned to return."

"The *St. Louis*," Walter jumped in. "There's a case in point. While they were at sea, the President of Cuba decreed that they'd need more money to enter, plus additional documents. It was only a trick to keep them out. The ship circled the Caribbean for weeks before finally heading back to Germany."

"I remember," Emilie said. "The Coast Guard followed them when they were near Florida so no one would try to swim ashore."

"Cuba already has nine thousand refugee Jews," Franz said. "Why should they take more if they don't want to?"

"But Franz, while the *St. Louis* was at sea, tens of thousands of Jews in Germany were given notice to leave the country within weeks or sometimes hours, or face internment. How could anyone send them back into that?"

"The Jews have made their bed, now let them get out of it on their own," Marie said. "And they're not on their own, anyway. All those countries you fault for turning some away, Walter, they've taken thousands of them in, too."

"Most of the *St. Louis* Jews ended up in England and France, and in Belgium and Holland," Franz added.

"Because the League of Nations twisted some arms," Walter said.

"The newspapers helped," Franz said, seeming to complain. " 'Cargo of despair,' the *New York Times* called them. I don't know why those Jews got singled out for special attention."

"Lucky for them they did," said Walter.

"They say sometimes," Emilie put in, "if a captain can't land anywhere, he just dumps them on an island in the Mediterranean or at some remote spot along the Palestine coast. I guess they have to fend for themselves then."

"As I said earlier," Marie sniffed. "But come now," she added in a cheerier tone. "What dark talk on such a lovely day. And with the children probably hungry, no?"

She looked appealingly to Helen and the twins. Terence nodded.

"It's like being on a mountain here," she went on, "looking at what this great country has achieved and the even better life it will bring us all."

She linked arms with her husband. He smiled affectionately at her.

"This is a good spot," he said, pointing to a restaurant at the Court of Railways. Helen could see that her father was reluctant to drop the debate, but that he was going to do so anyway. Her mother, too, was rearranging her expression to one of conviviality.

"When the ship was in Havana harbor," Ursula said, "a man cut his wrists. A man with a wife and children."

"Nanny, please," Marie began, but the old woman scowled at her, so she didn't go on.

"They took him to a hospital. But they would not let his family on shore. The ship left, and they were parted."

These were the kinds of details Helen could understand. She didn't know what happened in the concentration camps in Germany. She couldn't comprehend how the Jews could be so dangerous that all of them, all ages and occupations, had to be regulated and watched. But she could imagine the pain of leaving home and losing loved ones. That's what her grandmother had wanted the odyssey of the *St. Louis* to explain to her.

"And when the ship left Havana," Ursula continued, "out into the harbor came many little boats, with the aunts and uncles and grandparents and cousins and brothers on them. The little boats went alongside the big one and kept company until the sea was too wide and rough. There was sobbing on the big ship and sobbing on the small boats. And they all were calling *auf Wiedersehen,* back and forth, again and again."

They entered the restaurant and ordered. Marie leafed

through the guidebook, making suggestions for the afternoon, asking Franz's advice, Emilie's preferences. She succeeded in drawing Walter out by blathering on about the RCA exhibit and then letting him correct her on how television broadcasting actually worked. Ursula was quiet. They had all had their say. No one was going to change anyone's mind.

The world was at peace at present, and everyone had their fingers crossed that it would hold. In March, the Civil War in Spain had ended, and Hitler had annexed the areas of Czecho-Slovakia that hadn't been already given to him by France and England the previous September. It was hoped he'd be satisfied with that.

The whole Fair was keyed to the world of tomorrow, and to the conviction that in the decades to come, technology and hard work and democracy were going to make a better life for everyone. But in many homes in Europe, Helen considered as she listened to the careful cordiality of the adults and thought again about the plight of the *St. Louis,* tomorrow didn't mean 2039 or 1960 or even, perhaps, 1940. Tomorrow there meant the very next day and queasy speculations on what it might bring.

CHAPTER 16
AUGUST 1940

It was Helen's sixteenth birthday, and Billy had given her his yearbook photo, signed "fondly," and a nosegay of violets. He'd passed them over the fence, as they'd been passing items back and forth for years. But things were deliciously different now.

In May, they'd started walking to school together, a day here and there, when they chanced to leave their houses at the same time. By the middle of June, Billy was waiting on his porch for her every morning, and they often met to walk home together, too, dropping the pretense of happenstance.

After his graduation, Billy went to work at Benson's Hardware, but he and Helen spent every Saturday and some Sunday afternoons together, bicycling, swimming, fishing. They'd been out at night three times, to a movie, a band concert, and the roller rink. The summer jaunts had reinforced and broadened the mutual attachment nurtured by their school-day walks, and the gift of the photograph cinched it.

Helen had tucked the photo in a corner of her dresser mirror and was arranging the violets in a vase when her grandmother paused outside her open bedroom door.

"So, you have Billy Mackey's picture. Does such a thing mean what it did when I was young?"

"I don't know," Helen said shyly.

"No?"

"Sorry, Nanny. I don't know what it used to mean to you, but I do know what it means to me."

She gently pushed the photo more tightly into the mirror frame. "To us," she added.

"To us?" Ursula repeated archly.

Helen didn't wince under her grandmother's inspecting gaze. The bravery of saying "us" had released her from shyness.

"It means I'm his girl," she went on. "That I won't go out with anyone else. And he won't, either."

"Ah, your first sweetheart."

"First and last."

September 1940

The band concerts at Brinker's Green were a pleasant way to pass a summer evening, but Helen preferred the latter concerts of the season, played on the first three Saturdays of September. The weather was crisper, the crowd smaller, the music somehow brighter and more bracing. This year's final concert was scheduled for tonight. Helen would wear Billy's varsity letter sweater. It was too big for her, but that was part of its charm.

"Mama," Helen said, walking into the kitchen, "I need snacks for tonight."

"Look around," Emilie replied, "There are chicken wings in the fridge, some squares of *Pfefferkuchen* in the cookie jar." She was sitting at the table leafing through *Life* magazine.

Chicken wings are too greasy, Helen thought, rummaging in the meat drawer for cold cuts. But she'd definitely take some gingerbread. It was one of Nanny's specialties, and she knew Billy liked it.

"Dear, dear, look at this," Emilie said.

Helen came to peer over her mother's shoulder. She was pointing to a photograph of a group of children crowded together in a deep, narrow ditch. They were all looking up, not at the photographer, but higher, beyond him. What you noticed first were their intent faces. Then the hands. One boy's hands were clenched together, another was using his hands to shade his eyes, another had his fingers in his mouth. Two girls had their arms around younger kids, their hands curled tenderly around little shoulders. The headline over the picture read "Hitler Tries To Destroy London."

"It's a trench shelter in Kent," Emilie explained. "They're watching Spitfires intercept bombers."

The Germans had been dropping bombs on London for the past sixteen days, with no signs of stopping. Thousands had been killed. In *Movietone News*, Helen had seen people digging in rubble piles, sometimes with their bare hands, and rescue workers carrying stretchers, but this magazine photo gripped her more than any of the moving pictures had. The children were so average-looking, so clean and well-fed, their upturned faces trusting in spite of their obvious anxiety.

The children's faces seemed to acquire throbbing color. Helen knew suddenly, without reading the text, that they'd all survived that day in the trench, but she also knew that the little boy in the foreground would die later, when a bomb hit his church, and that the girl with her hair pulled back from her brow with a barrette would also die, during an air raid that would take out a whole block of houses.

Helen turned away. Everything had been so quiet for so long, two whole years. She'd been sure she was really done with such things. Why should it come back now, in her own kitchen, on a happy Saturday afternoon, just because of a photograph? She'd been seeing newsreels and hearing radio broadcasts about the war in Europe for a year with no such effect.

Though the United States remained neutral, Helen's American history teacher had colored a world map to show occupied countries and inserted little flags to mark embattled areas. In the spring, German armies had overrun Denmark, Norway, the Low Countries, and France. With Japan and Italy as allies and Russia signed to a nonaggression pact, Hitler seemed unstoppable. Helen knew that people were suffering and dying every day and night overseas, yet neither the classroom map nor the teacher's daily review of current events had sparked any visions or intuitions. Helen hadn't even had to resist them. They just weren't there.

"Honey, are you all right?"

Helen turned to find her mother standing beside her. Only then did she realize she'd been leaning against the edge of the counter and softly moaning.

"It's that picture," she said. "I saw . . . Well, I didn't actually *see* anything, but two of those kids—I know they're going to die."

"Oh, Helen." Emilie put her arm around the girl's shoulders.

"I don't like finding out things like that, Mama. I don't know what to do with them."

"Shall we ask Nanny about it?"

"No. I want to forget it."

Helen could see her mother struggling to think of what to say. Abruptly, Emilie opened the breadbox.

"All right then," she said. "I was saving these rolls for supper, but why don't you use them for sandwiches?"

She peered into the refrigerator. "I know I've got some sweet pickles . . . Here they are. And, Helen, I believe there's a bit of lettuce still in the garden. Go pick it. It'll only be wasted if the weather turns."

Helen stood staring at her mother's industry as if she were watching a circus act.

"Well, go on," Emilie said.

Still Helen hesitated. Emilie moved close to her and spoke quietly.

"It's just these times," she said. "All the terrible news, the wondering where it's leading. Anyone could have premonitions or dreams. I'm sure people do who have never had such things before. Don't worry about what to do about it."

Helen knew it was not as simple as that, and she knew Emilie knew it, too. But she decided she would take the route her mother was laying out. She would pretend she hadn't received any communication about the children in the photograph, at least not anything almost anyone might imagine, as her mother said, in times like these. She would make her bologna sandwiches and go to the band concert and hold Billy's hand while they listened to the music, and she'd stop with him in the shadows on the way home and kiss him and let him touch her breasts if he wanted to, which he had taken to wanting often lately. She could forget anything while that was happening. She could forget anything just by thinking about that happening.

February 1941

In the months that followed, Helen was repeatedly reminded of the children in the trench. The *Life* photo had been made into a poster supporting America's providing armaments to the Allies. The enlarged photo, with the slogan "Help England—and it won't happen here," was posted in store windows, in the lobby of the movie house, and at the bus terminal. Helen kept her eyes averted whenever she passed one of the posters, but she couldn't stop herself wondering if the two doomed children had died yet.

Billy had taken a job at Wright Aeronautical in Paterson, but he still worked Saturdays at Benson's. Mr. Mackey had come back from his trampings and gotten a job at the Wright plant, too. President Roosevelt said America should be "the arsenal for democracy," and Helen supposed he was right, but she regretted that Billy's work schedule meant he had less time to spend with her. Sundays were often taken up by his family. Mr. Mackey had embarked on a number of overdue repairs on the house, and he expected Billy and Lloyd to pitch in.

"Do you think he's changed?" Helen asked Billy some weeks after Mr. Mackey's return. She'd noticed a wrung out quality to the man that she didn't remember him having before. Even standing in the midst of his family or busily engaged in some task of carpentry or yard work, he had an air of solitariness and motionlessness.

It was a clear Saturday night in February, and Helen and Billy were trudging home from sledding on steep Maitland Avenue. Rosie and her brothers had been there with their ten-person toboggan, and the snow on the backs of Helen's and Billy's coats attested to numerous hilarious spills.

"I'm not sure," Billy answered after some thought. "It's different with him now, but I don't know if it's him or me."

"What do you mean?"

"Well, he gives me my head most of the time. Lloyd, too. Which I think is 'cause we're not kids like we were when he left. But he kind of stands off from all of us, doesn't even shush Linda when she's making a racket. He hasn't looked at the model planes I made while he was gone, and when I told him about a great new fishing spot we could go next summer, he didn't say anything."

"You sound disappointed."

Billy stopped walking and kicked at a snowbank, gradually boring a dent in the packed snow.

"It's funny, Helen, but I still miss him. He's back home, and I still miss him."

"I guess you can get an idea in your head of somebody when the person isn't around, and then, later, if they don't match that idea, it can be sort of sad."

Billy left off kicking the snowbank and playfully pulled Helen to him.

"And what about my idea of you, huh?" he said, hugging her,

his voice teasing, but his regard serious.

"What about it?" She laughed.

"If I wasn't around, would you change?"

"Where would you be?"

"Oh, I don't know. My uncle—you know, the one who's a pilot—he joined the RAF. Could be he's dog-fighting some Stuka or Messerschmitt right this minute."

"But he's an American."

"Eagle Squadron. It's all American pilots."

Helen stared into Billy's eyes.

"What are you going to do?" she said fearfully.

"Oh, nothing," he said, giving her a little shake. "Guess the Brits don't need any hardware store jockeys. I'm better use to them here making fighter plane engines."

Helen rested her cheek against the scratchy wool of his coat shoulder.

"Better use to me, too."

He put his fingers under her chin and lifted her face. Slowly, eyes open, they kissed, then kissed again. Arms about each other's waists, they resumed walking.

"I wouldn't change," she said softly after half a block.

"I'm not asking for a promise, Helen."

"And I'm not making one," she said earnestly. "It's just the truth. I wouldn't change. No matter where you go."

June 1941

By June, the March of Time newsreels proclaimed, there were 10,000 American volunteers in the RAF. The war news continued to go up and down, hope and discouragement trading places almost daily. The Allies, originally successful against the Italians in North Africa and Greece, were later bested in both places by the Germans. England was still under brutal bombardment—in Edward R. Murrow's broadcasts from

London you often heard the noise of bombs and the shouts of fire wardens in the background—but the English remained unbowed, and the RAF was regularly downing German aircraft and bombing the German homeland. The powerful and dangerous *Bismarck* had been sunk. On the other hand, the Nazis were marching into Russia with half a million horses, as well as thousands of planes and tanks and heavy guns. Sometimes, during newsreels, people in the audience cried, and sometimes they shouted angrily at the screen, especially when Hitler or Mussolini appeared.

Amid the welter of bulletins and commentary, Helen found it difficult to weigh the ultimate import of events, or to discern in what direction the war was heading. Added to her confusion were the laments of her grandmother for all the German deaths, especially of civilians, and the careful positioning of her parents and other German-Americans in the neighborhood. Her father's singing society had cancelled its annual concert and indefinitely suspended meetings. The front garden of the Dohrmanns sported little American flags beside their hydrangea bushes. The Smiths, whose great-grandfather had been Schmidt, had dropped out of Ursula's séances, which they'd been used to attending every few months. The frequency of séances had been cut in any case, Ursula saying the spirit world was too much in turmoil to make visits from there as calming as in peacetime.

"Some do not even know yet they are dead," she confided to Emilie in Helen's hearing one evening as the three sat in the living room, the older women mending and Helen reading. "They come to our circle confused, like drifting boats."

"How can that be?" Helen asked in spite of herself.

Ursula considered her before answering, as if pondering whether someone who had disdained learning about spirit deserved explanation now.

"When death comes sudden or violent," she finally replied,

"the person can be as if dreaming. He stands in a spinning fog, afraid to go forward, even though he may see light ahead."

"What happens to them?" Helen said.

"Some awaken slowly to understand this life is done. Sometimes a higher spirit leads them. In our home circle, we have called such spirits to help the lost ones. It is good work, but it is tiring, and I cannot ask Mrs. Durkin and Mr. Grauer and Miss Simmons to do it too often."

Ursula paused, again seeming to consider whether to proceed.

"You, Helen, younger and with your natural gift, could help. Just in this, not more. I do not let customers in the home circle."

Helen swallowed. She wanted to say that she couldn't do what her grandmother was asking because she believed it would open a dam already straining. And she feared that what would come through would be not a measured flow, but a wild torrent that would wash away the normal life she'd been carefully building. What justification would not sound small and selfish? What equality was there between her wishing to count on flat-footed, ordinary days, and ghosts needing to be taught that they were dead? How could she say she was in her own struggle to find a place? How could she admit out loud that she didn't want to risk losing the affection in Billy's eyes, the touch of his hands?

"Nanny," Emilie said, stepping into the taut silence, "remember when you and the others helped my babies leave?"

Ursula shifted her gaze to her daughter. She seemed annoyed by Emilie's interruption, but the change of topic was too sensitive a one to dismiss.

"*Ja*," she said.

"You were too little to remember," Emilie said to Helen, "but when my pregnancies failed, your brothers' spirits were confused and unhappy, like Nanny just described. The circle talked to them and told them not to be afraid. We imagined them floating up into the sky like beautiful soap bubbles. It was a great comfort to me to know they had found their way."

It was only the second time Helen had ever heard her mother talk about her miscarriages. Helen recalled them happening largely because she'd been sent both times to stay a few nights at Mrs. Durkin's house so her mother could rest. Mrs. Durkin had told her that Emilie's babies had gone back to heaven because they weren't ready yet to come live on earth. Helen had wondered in what way tiny babies could be unready. She'd considered all that had to be done before she was ready to go anywhere—the finding of shoes, the brushing of teeth and hair, the matching of outerwear to the weather. None of that applied to the case of her puzzlingly fickle brothers, but when she returned home, the subdued manner of the three grown-ups informed her that questions would not be welcomed.

Helen had waited, a usually trustworthy course, and soon enough they took up their normal ways of speaking and moving about the house, but she had never felt the time ripe to ask for more information on why the babies hadn't been ready, and eventually, she forgot about it. It was only last year, when a neighbor lost a baby, that Emilie had talked briefly with Helen about her own miscarriages and how slow the sadness had been to lift.

"Nanny helped me see that my babies were still part of my life and your father's, and life in general, no matter how briefly they'd existed here," Emilie had said then. "You see, she'd lost babies, too."

Though her grandmother had resumed her mending, Helen knew she was still waiting for her to respond to the suggestion that she join the séance circle. Ursula would let Emilie unwind her digression, but she wouldn't be thrown off by it.

"*Ja*," Ursula said, "babies need help. Sometimes, too, there are spirits who know they should let go, but who cannot because they love too much this world or someone in it, or something they feel is left to do."

"Are you finding more of those since the war?" Emilie asked.
Ursula sighed.

"They worry, some of them, that their people here need them, or that if they go forward, ties to those people will break. Such spirits we must push a little, so they may see that we do not really lose each other."

"Nanny," Helen began carefully, "I know all this is important, but I'm just not sure that I could . . . I don't want any more . . ."

"It's not fair to put Helen on the spot," Emilie said to her mother.

Ursula looked from one to the other.

"*Zwei gegen einen.* I am outnumbered."

"Maybe *I* could help at the séances," Emilie offered. "I haven't the gift, but I did take part for my babies, so I know how it's done."

Ursula nodded concession, though it was clear she begrudged it.

"Your mama told me about the picture in *Life,*" she said to Helen. "Has it happened again since that?"

"No."

"This I am surprised to hear." She raised her eyebrows. "You have more strength than I supposed."

"Well, I'm going to have a bath," Emilie said, standing up and putting her sewing things into a lidded basket.

Emilie obviously believed everything was safely settled, but Helen didn't want to stay in the room alone with her grandmother, who suddenly felt like an adversary. Helen hadn't asked her mother to keep her experience with the photograph a secret. But Nanny hadn't said anything, so Helen had assumed she didn't know. It was distressing to realize the old woman had stayed deliberately silent all these months, as if she'd been waiting for the best time to bring it up, a time at which it might serve her own aims.

"I have a report to finish," Helen said as soon as her mother had exited. She closed her book and rose from her chair.

"So near the end of school?" Ursula said suspiciously.

"The last one of the year!" the girl answered with calculated gaiety.

She had just reached the doorway when Ursula muttered to herself. Her voice was low, but Helen caught the words distinctly.

"*Ja*, I am outnumbered," she said. "If you do not count the dead."

CHAPTER 17
DECEMBER 1941

On tiptoes near the top rung of a tall ladder, Helen reached above her head to fasten a strand of silver garland looping from the corners of the high school gymnasium to the center of its ceiling. The ladder wobbled.

"Hey!" she called to the girl below who was supposed to be steadying it.

"Huh?" Madeline Darby turned her gaze dreamily up at Helen. She'd been absorbed in watching a group of boys assemble a bandstand. A Victrola was playing the hit *Take the A Train*, and one of the boys had stopped working to dance extravagantly across the unfinished stage, evoking raucous complaints from his comrades.

"Never mind them," Helen scolded. "Hold the ladder still."

"*Jawohl*," Madeline said sarcastically. "But don't take all day about it, would you?"

A number of retorts sprang to Helen's mind, but she didn't utter any of them. It had been like this most of the school year, veiled and not-so-veiled rudeness. From Madeline and a few others. Not from everyone, not even from a majority of the students, but you never knew who might throw out a biting comment or when. In Civics, Jeff Keller had declared that Germans as a race were bloodthirsty and heartless, citing as examples not only the armies of the Kaiser and the Third Reich but also Bruno Hauptmann, who'd been convicted of murdering the Lindbergh baby several years ago. Not even a gangster would be so cruel, Jeff had said, and the teacher hadn't contradicted him.

Helen tried not to provide any cause for criticism. That meant holding her tongue when she would have liked to speak, pretending not to hear certain remarks. It meant she felt constrained from doing anything as public as running for Student Council or trying out for Color Guard.

Helen knew from her grandmother's stories that the situation wasn't anywhere near as bad as it had been during the Great War, when it was illegal to teach German, or to speak it on the street or on the phone. Books about German history and literature were taken out of schools and libraries. In some places, German churches were burned down, German men forced to kneel and kiss the American flag. There'd been lynchings in Illinois, floggings in Texas, imprisonments in Georgia. It was having lived through all that that had made Ursula so disturbed by the passage of the Alien Registration Act last month, which meant she'd have to go to the post office to be photographed and fingerprinted

"Like the common criminal," she'd said indignantly.

"The government files fingerprints on upright people, too," Emilie had said, trying to soothe her. "Policemen, civil servants . . . Even J. Edgar Hoover has been fingerprinted."

"I will obey the law," Ursula said, unappeased, "but I will not believe it is fair or harmless."

She'd made Helen accompany her to the post office. Pretending not to know English, she wouldn't deign to speak to the officials.

The occasional barbs and snubs at school were blemishing Helen's senior year, but no one could truly feel carefree this year. The start of school in September had coincided with the beginning of the German siege of Leningrad, now in its fourth month. News was scant and all bad—people freezing and starving, dying of simple illnesses in the cold and dark. The use of convoys had diminished the success of U-boats in the Atlantic, but the stealthy submarines were still making lethal strikes, including sinking two American destroyers that were escorting British supply ships. The Japanese, too, had launched a fleet of subs. The Americas seemed a huge island surrounded by bloodshed and misery.

Madeline walked away when Helen was only halfway down the ladder, leaving her to drag the heavy thing to the custodian's closet on her own.

As Helen walked home, the bright afternoon lifted her spirits. It was warm enough to leave her coat unbuttoned. The snow of last week was melting. Drips glistened from tree branches, black against the azure sky.

The shops on West Main Street were decked out for Christmas. Helen walked by leisurely, thinking about what gifts she might get her parents and grandmother.

She stopped in front of McCutcheon's Gift Shop to consider an arrangement of cut-glass bowls and goblets. Sunlight was slanting into the window, and the glassware refracted it against the shelves lined with shiny blue and green foil paper. Helen squinted against the glare. It seemed, then, that she was looking down on a glimmering sea from a great height.

The street sounds around her ebbed, replaced by a dull drone that became louder and louder, burgeoning into a roar. Helen turned around, expecting to find other pedestrians stunned by the awful noise and searching apprehensively for the arrival of whatever massive machine could be making it. But as soon as she looked away from the shop window, the sound stopped. She met only the familiar Saturday street busy with unfazed citizens and ordinary automobiles.

Oh, Lord, Helen thought, it's happened again. Though this was a new variation, a set of sensations inserted into normal surroundings like a joker slipped into a deck of cards. Her heart was glutted with foreboding. What could the innocuous vision of the sea and the deafening noise mean? Unlike the specific knowledge that had come from the *Life* photo, this experience resisted quick interpretation.

Just because she couldn't decipher the sea scene didn't mean it had no significance. Was someone going to drown? It was December, for heaven's sake. Who went swimming in New Jersey in December? Billy had talked about taking a life-saving course at the Y in February. Should she stop him? Would he listen? And what about the noise? That had been the frightening part. She'd had a quick sense of expectancy when she'd seen the sea, but the noise had felt like a dire threat. Maybe Billy or his father was going to have an accident with some machinery at the engine factory.

Absorbed in her ruminations, Helen didn't hear running feet behind her and was startled when someone whizzed by and snatched her crocheted hat from her head.

Billy skidded to a stop on the slushy sidewalk five yards ahead of her, laughing and waving her hat in his hand.

"A penny for your thoughts," he called. "They must be deep ones."

"How much for my hat?" she answered, as she came up to him.

"I'll give it back only if you promise not to put it on."

"You dislike it that much?"

He handed her the hat.

"It's all right, I guess, if you don't mind looking like an acorn. It's warm enough, anyway, don't you think?"

Helen stuffed the hat into a pocket. They walked side by side, turning off the commercial street onto a residential one.

"I told old man Benson he ought to put out some beach umbrellas next to the snow shovels, but he didn't go for it,"

Billy went on. "Where you coming from?"

"We were getting the gym ready for the winter dance tonight."

"You going?"

"I have to. I'm on the decorations committee. I already told you."

"Right. Guess I forgot."

A chilly breeze had kicked up. Helen took her hat out of her pocket and pulled it down over her ears, buttoned up her coat. They turned onto their block. The breeze had brought in wispy clouds. The houses, white clapboard on brick foundations fronted by flat yards patched with muddy snow, had an air of desertion about them. It was an effect of the paling of the sun, and the emptiness of the sidewalks. The quiet neighborhood, like the featureless sea in Helen's vision, seemed poised for some momentous change.

"Billy," she said meditatively, "what could change the sea?"

"Change it?"

"What could happen to make it different?"

"The sea's too big to change. Unless you mean a typhoon or something. You could say that changes the sea for a while. Bigger waves, high winds, lightning—things like that."

"And thunder?"

"Yeah, sure, thunder. But thunder doesn't do anything. It's just noise."

She nodded, unsatisfied. Billy started up the walk of his house, and Helen went on to her own.

"Say," he called, "I'll come over tomorrow, and you can tell me how the dance was, okay?"

The next day, Helen stood at the sink washing luncheon dishes while Billy and her father listened in the living room to a Giants football game being broadcast from the Polo Grounds in New York. Her mother and grandmother were at the church sewing

135

circle knitting scarves and socks for "Bundles for Britain." Helen was daydreaming at her task, once more turning over the ordeal she'd been through in front of McCutcheon's window display. She still could make no sense of it. But a feeling of dread lingered.

When shouts came from the living room, her skittish heart leapt.

"Good grief," she chided herself, "it's only a touchdown."

In the next instant, the swinging door slammed open. She turned to admonish Billy, but the look on his face checked her.

"Helen, come quick," he said excitedly.

She rushed across the room, fearing her father had been stricken in some way. Billy followed close on her heels.

"We've been attacked," he was saying behind her. "We've been attacked by Japan."

At the threshold of the living room, she spied her father standing safe and sound by the radio. Belatedly, Billy's incredible announcement hit her.

"What?" she said.

"At Pearl Harbor."

"Where's that?"

"Be quiet!" Walter commanded.

Helen and Billy went to stand beside him. There were easy chairs on either side of the big Philips, but none of them made a move to sit down. As they listened in horror to garbled reports of bomb strikes on American bases in Hawaii and Guam that morning, Billy put his arm around Helen's shoulders. She leaned against him. Never before had they been so demonstrative in front of her father. Walter said nothing, not noticing or not caring. He kept staring at the radio, shaking his head. His rigid jawline showed how tightly he was clenching his pipe.

The newscaster was describing a scene of devastation and chaos. Fires raging. Dead and wounded sailors floating in the harbor. Hawaiian boys swimming through flaming oil slicks to pull them out. Civilian casualties in Honolulu, from both enemy strafing and Navy shells gone astray. Helen's stomach churned.

"Dirty Jap rats," Billy said, his voice breaking.

The reporter repeated again and again how the Japanese warplanes had swarmed in, some so low people on the ground were able to see the faces of the pilots and rear gunners. They had attacked in waves, first torpedo bombers, then dive bombers and high-level bombers. In two blistering hours, they had sunk or badly damaged eighteen ships, destroyed hundreds of planes, and killed thousands of Americans. Marines were being sent to look for Jap paratroopers in the island valleys. It was feared that California cities would be hit tonight. Parents in San Francisco were being advised to give their children identification tags in case of separation.

Helen began to cry quietly, tears sliding down her cheeks.

A local reporter came on to say that although President Roosevelt would not address Congress until tomorrow at noon, New York City and the nearby New Jersey cities of Bayonne, Jersey City, Newark, and Paterson were already on a war footing. Mayor LaGuardia had confined Japanese nationals to their homes and closed their social clubs and other meeting places.

"We're in it now," Walter said, reaching over and turning the volume down. "God help us, we're in it now."

"I'd better get home," Billy said.

"I'm going to the church for my wife and mother-in-law. I'd appreciate it, Billy, if you'd keep Helen with you until I get back."

"Of course, sir."

Even as the two men conspired to watch over her, Helen felt oddly shunted aside, as if she were watching them through a closed window. They had somehow formed an indivisible unit, indivisible, at least, by her. She was glad not to be left at home alone, but she sensed that if she had wanted to be, they wouldn't have allowed it.

But advice was what she needed more than protection. She was filled with fear, shock, and a strange kind of guilt, and no amount of comforting could make a dent in those feelings. Wait, she wanted to say to them. I have things to tell you. I heard the Jap planes coming yesterday. *Yesterday.* Thousands of miles from Hawaii. I saw the Pacific, though I didn't know that's what it was, and the reflections of sunshine on the sea. And I think I could have found out more. If I'd tried. Ought I to try now? But she could discover in their mobilization and unity no chink through which to insert her revelations and questions.

Next door, Mr. Mackey and Lloyd were sitting in the living room, leaning forward in tense conversation. They stopped talking when Billy and Helen came in. Nevertheless, their agitation was obvious, and Helen thought she detected something close to exhilaration as well. The radio was on, redelivering the same terrible news.

"I was just tellin' Pop," Lloyd said, jumping up, "he's gotta sign for me so's I can join up first thing tomorrow. Don't want to miss the show. 'Course, there won't be any problem for you, ya lucky slug."

Helen's whole body flushed hotly, and she looked quickly at Billy. There was nothing in his profile to reveal whether or not he agreed with Lloyd. She was possessed by an urge to grab hold of Billy, to force him to face her. She wanted to wrest his attention away from Lloyd's wild talk. But his posture and his silence forbade such dramatics. Helen swallowed hard. As dazed as she'd been by the news of Pearl Harbor, she had not, until now, thought how it might reach into her life to touch her directly.

"We'll talk more later," Mr. Mackey told Lloyd. To Helen he said, "Mrs. Mackey and the girls are in back."

Helen left the room. Her legs felt like they were made of wood.

She found Mrs. Mackey sitting blankly at the kitchen table, a damp handkerchief clutched between her fingers. Barbara was at the stove making a pot of coffee. She greeted Helen with a warm hug. Perched on a stool near the table, Linda was licking a large, round sucker, her nose and chin sticky red. The women exchanged a few comments on what they'd heard and how awful it was and how awful it was going to be.

"Are the Japs gonna bomb us, Mommy?" Linda piped up.

"Be quiet, Linda," her mother said.

"But are they gonna come here? Are they?"

Mrs. Mackey twisted around in her chair and gave the seven-year-old a resounding slap on her bare arm. The child dropped her lollipop on the floor and started to cry.

"I told you to be quiet, missy," Mrs. Mackey shouted.

With great effort, Linda stifled her sobs. Her sister picked up the lollipop, rinsed it in the sink, and gave it back to her. The child judiciously slid her stool beyond her mother's reach.

Helen was surprised at the outburst. She'd never known Mrs. Mackey to strike her children. It was a measure of her upset, Helen supposed. She felt sorry for Linda, but she was glad for the ensuing quiet. She couldn't have said more or listened well. She kept imagining the bright, innocent Hawaiian morning with maybe people playing tennis or eating breakfast in a flowering garden or on the deck of a ship, maybe walking dogs and pushing baby carriages, setting out for church or sleeping in, when the noise of the bombers first boiled up. Like herself on Main Street, people must have been confused and curious, then unnerved. But unlike her, they had turned around to find death and destruction pouring down on them.

CHAPTER 18

That night Helen dreamed she was treading water in the inlet of Pearl Harbor, surrounded by men sinking beneath the churned surface, planes roaring overhead. Some of the men stretched out burned, blackened hands towards her, some only threw her anguished stares, but she knew that for all of them, she was the last of life they had beheld.

The strongest feeling that lingered as she lay staring at dawn light on her bedroom ceiling was a sense that she had let the dream-men down, not by being unable to save them, but in some other worse way. But what could be worse than not being able to rescue someone from death?

She walked through the morning at school in a fog. She had to keep pushing the desperate faces from her dream out of her thoughts. Some teachers were carrying on lessons as usual, but most gave the students a study period and didn't scold if they talked among themselves. Helen spent those periods gazing out the window and humming to herself, locking her mind onto the nonsense lyrics of *Hut Sut Ralston*. At noon, everyone filed into the auditorium to listen to President Roosevelt demand that Congress declare war on Japan, which it readily did. Afterwards, the principal brought a Navy recruiting officer on stage. When the officer said it was not only the senior boys, but the sophomores and juniors who'd win this war, clapping erupted in several parts of the auditorium. Lloyd, seated at the end of Helen's row, put his fingers in his mouth and whistled loudly.

Walking home, Helen tried to recall every detail of her experience from Saturday, the flash of the blank sea and the surge of engines. Her head ached with trying to figure out how she could have read a message there.

When she found her grandmother in the living room listening to the soap opera *Life Can Be Beautiful,* Helen sat down on the floor near her chair, waited for a commercial, then rapidly explained her dilemma. Ursula turned off the radio.

"So, this is a big question you are putting."

"Questions, Nanny. Questions, plural. Not only what was it that happened to me, and what could I have done with it, but why me? Why leave something so important with me?"

"Such signs were probably not given only to you."

"You think other people saw and heard the same things?"

"Or something like."

"Good."

"Good?"

"Because then it's not all my fault. I mean, it's not my fault that I didn't tell anyone, that I didn't give the warning."

"But you did not understand."

"Right," Helen said eagerly. "So how *could* I give a warning?"

"Not understanding: that, maybe, is the fault."

Helen drooped. Her own train of thought had already taken her to her grandmother's position. There was no getting around the possibility that if she had continued to study with Ursula, if she hadn't banished Iris, she might have been better equipped to understand the vague portent that had come to her.

"It's a long time you have kept the world of spirit from your doorstep. *Nicht Willkommen,*" Ursula said, tapping her chest over her heart.

"I thought it would go away," Helen muttered.

"*Nein.* There is too much *Liebe.*"

"Love?"

"How else do you imagine spirits can return but through love?"

Helen leaned back against the couch, tucking her legs under her skirt. She remembered the well-being she'd felt in Iris's presence and supposed it could be called love. She remembered the gentle approach of Mrs. Steltman's father, and the clear sense of attachment to the living that she'd gotten from both the crying little boy and the young suicide. And would she have received her visions of Mr. Mackey, or Lloyd, or Billy in the woods if she hadn't had affectionate ties with the family?

"But what about the children in the *Life* photo? Or the sea and the noise the other day?"

"The spirits send messages like . . . like radio waves," Ursula said, pointing to the Philips. "Where there is someone who can receive it, he does. If the radio is on, we get sounds, whether we want them or not. If we turn the dial, we clean the static, we have a better chance to understand."

"You mean I'm a kind of radio, only I didn't know I was on?"

Ursula nodded.

"Well, how do I work the dial?"

"You must begin again the séances. When the student is ready, a teacher always comes. For you, I think, are spirits already waiting."

Helen didn't like that answer, though it was what she'd expected.

"If I go to séances, will I know what it means when I see things? Will I be able to explain it to other people?"

"It is not like reading the newspaper. More like telling stories about pictures. And spirits can make mistakes. Just to be dead does not mean you know all things. But many spirits are very wise. We always hope for such ones to come."

"If it's so ticklish, why should I bother?"

himself so that he was perched on the edge of his chair, with his elbows resting on his knees and his hands clasped together. They all looked concerned, and the men also looked angry. But Helen detected something more in them than worry and anger. As she waited for one of them to speak, it struck her that they were afraid. Not for Erich and Freida, but for themselves. This made Helen, too, suddenly afraid.

"Mama?" she said feebly.

Emilie came out of her reverie and turned to Helen, but she didn't answer her.

"That's why I didn't call," Franz said softly. "They could be spying on me, too."

"Oh, surely not," Emilie said nervously.

"They picked up a Jap at the train station in Newark just because he was holding a map of Brooklyn!"

"You have something to hide, *Junge?*" Ursula queried Franz.

It was in all their minds, Helen thought, though only Nanny could have asked so bluntly and so soon. Even she had tempered the near-accusation by calling him "lad."

"I don't want Marie to know," he said, looking pointedly at Walter. "Not that I've done anything wrong, anything to be ashamed of. I just don't want her worrying."

Walter nodded. "I won't tell her unless I have to. But as her brother, I reserve the right to do what's in her best interest."

Franz looked at Helen then. She expected to be dismissed from the room.

"If there is nothing wrong or shameful," Ursula interjected, "our Helen may hear."

Franz cleared his throat.

"A while ago," he said, "I went to some meetings of the German-American Bund."

"What?" Walter said. "You're a member of the Bund?"

147

"No, I'm not a member. I just went to some meetings. Years ago."

"The Bund! Hooligans and crackpots who like to dress up in uniforms and march around giving the *heil* salute. Did you know that last summer they burned a cross down at their Camp Nordland in Sussex County? They give us all a bad name, Franz. People start presuming every German is a Nazi. Whatever were you thinking?"

"It's a perfectly legal organization, Walter."

"You call that an excuse?" Walter said loudly. He tried to reinsert the fireplace poker into its stand, and when he couldn't get it in easily, he threw it down on the hearth.

"Walter," Emilie said, "Franz didn't come here to be yelled at. The Bund is finished now, anyway."

Helen knew all about the Bund's recent demise. The organization had been in the news a lot this year because seven of its leaders had been tried for breaking New Jersey's 1935 law prohibiting the promotion of hatred based on race or religion. Her history teacher had used the case as a study in the American legal system. Just last week, two days before Pearl Harbor, the New Jersey Supreme Court had overturned the convictions on the grounds that the 1935 law violated the state constitution. Helen's teacher said the Bund Nazis might gloat that the reversal demonstrated the weakness of democracy, but, in fact, it showed just the opposite. Besides which, the teacher added, Bund Führer Fritz Kuhn was doing his gloating in Sing Sing, where he'd been sent in 1939 for grand larceny after he'd been caught stealing Bund funds for himself.

"Yes, the Bund is bankrupt," Franz said, "but there may be lists somewhere. Not just of members but of . . . I don't know . . . of sympathizers or something."

"Why *did* you come, Franz?" Walter said coldly. "Trying to pull us all down, are you?"

Franz stood up.

"I don't want to put you or anyone in jeopardy," he said with, Helen thought, a surprising degree of dignity. "I just wanted to make you aware of what might happen to me so that, I hope, you're prepared to take care of my family."

"Nothing's going to happen, Franz," Emilie said, crossing to him and putting her hand on his sleeve. "You're an American citizen."

"Even so," Ursula said, "he is right to make ready."

Walter took a deep breath. He picked up the poker and set it in its place.

"I'm sorry, Franz," he said. "Of course I'd take care of Marie and the kids. But I doubt that I'll have to. If all you did was go listen to a few speeches, I think you're safe."

"That's all, Walter. I swear."

"And if all Erich did was read trash and make beer hall boasts, he and Freida will probably be released soon. But you'd better drum it into his thick head he's got to watch his step from now on."

"Right," Franz said and extended his hand to Walter.

Walter hesitated only a moment before shaking his brother-in-law's hand, but Helen noticed it, and she was sure Franz and everyone else had, too. She wondered if it signaled a lingering annoyance that would pass, or if it went deeper than that. Did her father distrust her uncle? Was he trying to draw a boundary between them?

Helen thought she herself would never look at her uncle in the same way. She had never considered before what kind of a man he might be. He was a presence at the dinner table a few times a year. When she was younger, he'd been a dispenser of peppermints and pennies. Now the picture was messier, sadder. He had used poor judgment; perhaps he had even coddled ugly beliefs. She felt sorry for him, even as she realized she didn't understand him. During the past couple of days, in the lap of war, everyone around her—at school, in the neighborhood, on the radio—had been talking as if the world were a clear, black-and-white pattern of good and evil, right and wrong, with or against. But maybe it wasn't as simple as that. Maybe it never could be.

CHAPTER 19

Four days after Pearl Harbor, Germany and Italy declared war on the United States. So did Hungary, Romania, and Bulgaria. That whole week was dense with news. Helen began reading the *Bergen Evening Record* more thoroughly than she ever had before.

Every day the paper carried stories about war-related activities throughout the state. In Newark, the Red Cross set up a blood drive. Students at the New Jersey College for Women started knitting for the Army. Guards and roadblocks were posted at key facilities like the R.C.A. plant in Camden and the Standard Oil refinery in Bayonne. Mines were laid in the ocean off Sandy Hook. Communities everywhere devised strategies for air raids, including siren signals and evacuation plans. Housewives were buying black fabric for their windows, fire buckets to douse incendiary bombs, and crowbars and hatchets to dig out of a caved-in house. In Paterson, the Italian National Circle, a civic club, changed its name to the Panthers of Paterson. Two Jehovah's Witnesses were fired from a factory in Hillside because they refused to recite the Pledge of Allegiance. An "America First" anti-war rally in Jersey City was cancelled. And every day, as the telegrams arrived, obituaries of local men killed at Pearl Harbor appeared.

Many of River Bend's young men enlisted. Recruiting stations all over New Jersey were open twenty-four hours a day to handle the crush. Lloyd, tall for his age and brimming with self-confidence, managed to convince the Army to take him without proof of age. Billy told Helen that when Lloyd came home with his triumphant announcement, Mrs. Mackey had begged her husband to take Lloyd's birth certificate to the recruiting station, but he had said the deed was done and not worth undoing since Lloyd would be eighteen in six months. Rosie's brother, Owen, had also lied in order to sign up, and he was only sixteen. His mother had provided him a letter attesting that he was of age. The high school band took to playing at the bus station when groups of boys went off for their physicals, just as it used to do when the football team left for an away game.

Billy confided to Helen that he thought it was foolish for Lloyd to drop out of school, but when she was too vehement in her agreement, Billy had snapped that at least Lloyd was a brave fool. Lloyd had worked on his brother to join up, too, but Mr. Mackey convinced Billy he would be more valuable to the war effort working at Wright Aeronautical than in uniform. Besides, Mrs. Mackey wasn't in any shape to see another son become a dogface soldier.

Helen was glad Billy's job made him eligible for draft deferments, but if the war lasted any time at all, he was bound to get restless. She'd already noted embarrassment in his manner whenever they met friends about to go off to boot camp. Shaking their hands to wish them luck, he often held on a moment too long, as if he wished they'd pull him along with them. She'd thought, watching him on these occasions, that a part of him *was* pulled along with every boy who departed, and that eventually there wouldn't be enough gravity to anchor him at home.

January 1942

Helen continued to dream about the sailors at Pearl Harbor, and some nights, she also encountered planes crashing in a desert, or contorted bodies strewn in jungles and snowbanks.

She never saw unique facial features or identifiable uniforms. She awoke from these dreams gasping for air, as if she herself were trapped inside the plummeting, smoke-filled plane, or lying facedown in rotting foliage or icy puddles. Her appetite declined, and circles showed under her eyes.

As the war news worsened, so did Helen's dreams. By mid-January, German submarines were sinking American cargo ships off the Atlantic coast at the rate of ten a week. Bodies and wreckage washed up on the beaches of New Jersey and other eastern seaboard states. In one dream, Helen found herself at familiar Point Pleasant, watching a man's body roll up and back with the surf.

Ursula insisted Helen was having visions, while Walter claimed she was only fashioning images out of news reports. He stopped talking about the news at dinner and discouraged Helen from reading the paper. But she caught fragments of radio bulletins, overheard conversations on the bus, got information from classmates and teachers. The war was on everyone's lips, especially since it was not going well. The Japanese were sweeping through the Pacific, driving the British out of Singapore and Burma, battering American and Philippine forces in Bataan and Corregidor. The British Eighth Army had kept the Suez Canal out of the hands of General Rommel, but the crafty "Desert Fox" had not been beaten, and his German and Italian tank divisions were mounting a fearsome counteroffensive. And although at Moscow, for the first time in the war, the Nazis had been forced to retreat, it was due, in part, to "General Winter," which froze into inactivity guns and radios and engines, as well as the sick and dying. Come spring, Moscow might yet be taken.

After one spate of four straight nights of repeated nightmares, Walter sat with Ursula and Helen at the breakfast table. Emilie was sleeping in. She'd had even less rest than Helen, getting up each time the girl called out and at other numerous times to look in on her.

"This can't go on," Walter said.

"You are still against the séances, *ja?*" Ursula asked.

He nodded glumly.

"I don't mind, Papa," Helen said, "if it'll make the dreams stop. Besides, I think it's something I *should* be doing anyway."

"I don't want you to," Walter said firmly.

"All right, Papa."

Walter reached across the table and patted Helen's hand, but he looked so worn out and worried, she thought it should be she patting him.

"Here is another idea," Ursula said. "Helen will sleep in my room, and when the dreams come, she will quick tell me their story."

"What good will that do?" Helen asked.

"Together we will find a path so that you can come and go as you want inside the dreams."

"You can do that?" Walter said dubiously.

"I can make the good try."

Walter rubbed his forehead, considering, then stood up. "I'll get the camp cot from the garage. Emilie will want to scrub it down."

Ursula reached out and wrapped her fingers gently around Walter's wrist. It was unusual for her to make such an intimate gesture towards him.

"Walter, if this ends the dreams or not, still you must let Helen work in spirit."

"I'm sorry, Nanny, my mind's made up."

The old woman let go of his wrist. "It is not the right decision."

"We've been through all this," Walter said in an aggrieved tone. "You admit yourself that your séances aren't completely aboveboard. You and Emilie say there is always some kind of truth behind the fabrications. All right, I'll accept that. I'm sure many people leave your séances comforted. Maybe they don't care whether they've been duped. But I don't want Helen entering that world of half-truths. I don't want her thinking it's all right to deceive people if it will make them feel better. I don't want her learning to lie so well she begins to believe her own lies."

Ursula glared at her son-in-law.

"I could make many answers to you, Walter," she said, "but I give only one: Helen will not need to lie because Helen is real."

As tired as she was, Helen felt a thrill, part pride, part fear.

Silence congealed around Ursula's last word. Outside, it had begun to snow. Walter crossed to the door and opened it. Cold air coiled into the room.

"After the séance with the hanged boy," Ursula said to him, "you said she might try again some day. Her day is here, Walter. She wants to serve."

Walter looked wearily at Helen.

"Are you sure?" he asked her.

"I think so."

"As I recall, Nanny," Walter said, turning to Ursula, "we agreed on possibly *one* other séance."

"One is enough. If you can keep open your mind."

"With your home circle only. No paying customers looking for advice."

"Not so much now do clients want advice," Ursula replied. "Just one more contact with their soldier. To have a more easy picture than the storm of blood and pain they keep imagining."

"Nevertheless, no clients."

"We will do as you say."

Walter took a wool shirt from a hook beside the door.

"I'll get the cot."

"*Gut.* To tame the dreams must come first."

February 1942

Ursula began by suggesting Helen try to wake herself up when a dream became too frightening. There was a point in every dream when Helen realized she was dreaming, but until her grandmother advanced the idea that she could secure her own release, she had remained ensnared in the dream until some unendurable image or slamming terror jolted her awake.

Eventually, Helen became adept at escaping a dream when she wished, but it was always a struggle, an amazingly physical struggle in which she had to will her heavy, supine body slowly up through an invisible, viscous substance, as if she were hauling a full bucket out of a well. The required effort was greatest at the start, the drag and weight of the thick matter holding her down the strongest then. Once awake, Helen would rouse her grandmother, and the old woman would sit up and calmly ask questions to help her revisit the dream and pick out details.

Ursula told Helen to call on Iris at bedtime to accompany her into the dreams. Helen did, and once in a while in the midst of a dream, she would catch a glimpse of something purple, in the shadow of a shattered doorway, at the edge of a battlefield. Helen came to feel that Iris was with her even when she couldn't find the purple, and so she felt less frightened and almost curious about what she was seeing. She waited longer and longer before waking herself up, and sometimes she let the dream run its course. Oddly enough, as the dreams came to disturb her less, they diminished in both intensity and frequency. By the beginning of February, she was able to move back into her own room.

But she had found no communications in the dreams, beyond the human tragedy of war, which any magazine or newsreel could tell as well. Her grandmother assured her that clearer meanings would emerge during séances. Though Walter had agreed to only one sitting with the home circle, Ursula was confident that if all went well, he could be convinced to allow Helen to do more. If not, she intimated, Helen would have to decide for herself which dictates were more important, her father's or spirit's.

The séance was set for late March. Ursula wanted to be sure the dreams had been corralled, and she wanted to prepare Helen with exercises like billet reading and self-inducing light trances. She had her try automatic writing again, too, which came a bit easier than it had in the past. No definite messages came through, but she did get a few evocative phrases like "we're going down," and "sweet rest beyond the river," and many variations on the word "mother."

One preparatory task Helen set on her own was to explain to Billy her intention of becoming an active medium. He had always known of Ursula's doings, though he'd never asked Helen about specifics, except to inquire once, years ago, if her grandmother had a crystal ball. The Schneiders and the Mackeys were cordial neighbors, and the Schneiders had helped Mrs. Mackey whenever they could during the hard years Mr. Mackey had been away—sending over cabbage soup or macaroni and cheese, saving Helen's outgrown clothes for Linda, once even giving them coal when they had no fuel and were burning old tires for warmth. Helen was counting on all this history to ease the way for Billy to accept her mediumship.

She chose Valentine's Day. They'd decided to spend the day in New York. Billy had quit Benson's when they lengthened the shifts at Wright Aeronautical, so his Saturday afternoons were free. They went ice-skating at Rockefeller Center, window-shopped on Fifth Avenue, and ate at the Broadway Automat. They'd seen lots of young men in uniform on the streets, prompting Billy to drop into St. Patrick's Cathedral and light a candle for Lloyd, who was in basic training at Fort Bragg in North Carolina.

Twice, Helen noticed auras around soldiers who passed them, but she looked quickly away. Her grandmother had instructed her to close down attention to any psychic information that tried to break through when she hadn't sought it. She'd be more powerful in séances then, as well as more relaxed in her day-to-day life.

It was not until they were on the evening ferry home, leaning tired and dreamy on the outside railing despite the cold, that Helen summoned enough nerve to have her talk with Billy.

"I have something to tell you," she began.

He was peering over the side of the boat at the dark water. "Hmm?"

"About some dreams I've been having."

"Dreams?"

"Things like this have happened to me before, but not as much as now."

"What do you mean?" He turned his head toward her.

"I've been dreaming about sailors. From Pearl Harbor. And sometimes soldiers. Dead sailors and soldiers."

"I guess a lot of people have been doing that."

"Well, maybe. But I'm going to do something about it."

"You're not making much sense, Helen."

"I'm sorry. I'm a little afraid to say it out plain. Afraid of what you might think."

He gave her a quizzical look.

"I guess you better try," he said. "But give me the real dope, okay?"

Helen nodded, more to bolster her courage than to answer Billy.

"I'm going to try to get messages from spirits. I'm going to be a medium."

"A medium?" he said sharply. "You don't really believe in that stuff, do you?"

His tone was scornful. Helen felt a spike of fear in the pit of her stomach.

"I kind of have to believe in it."

"Have to?" Still a breath of scorn, blunted, with some effort it seemed, to mere doubt.

"My dreams aren't like regular dreams, Billy, not even like regular nightmares. And there've been times . . . times that I've seen things . . . when I was awake."

"Holy cow," Billy said, shaking his head. He turned his gaze away from her, lifting it to the sky, which was full of stars. Helen recalled the perturbed *Astronomer* statue from the World's Fair. Maybe he'd been oriented skyward because there was something on earth he didn't want to face.

"I always figured your grandmother was only pretending," Billy said after a few moments. "I thought the people who came to see her must just be lonely, or out for some fun, or maybe a little . . ."

"Crazy?"

He looked at her as if he'd just noticed that she had a big, ugly birthmark on her face.

"You said it, not me."

He kept on staring, and she couldn't think what to say next. She wanted him to hold her, or blow warmth from his mouth onto her gloved fingertips, or tell her that her hat made her head look like an acorn. Anything but this pensive study.

"Could we wait and see, Billy? Could we just wait and see?"

He let out a long sigh.

"You really think you're gonna talk to ghosts," he said, shaking his head.

It was almost a question, but Helen decided to act as if it weren't. She also decided not to press him for reassurance. It was enough that he'd softened his voice, that he'd propped his forearms on the railing again and resumed watching the ferry's wake. When he shifted his observation to the silhouette of blacked-out Manhattan, she slid closer to him so that the padded shoulders of their thick coats were touching. He didn't put his arm around her, but he didn't pull away, either, so she told herself to be satisfied and not go looking for trouble. Trouble was completely capable of finding its own way to her, if it was interested.

CHAPTER 20
MARCH 1942

Rosie and Helen were walking home in a light rain, having stayed late at school to take first aid classes with the Junior Red Cross. The early evening air was minus the bite of winter. Though it was only March, the day's mildness promised an early spring. Rosie was telling Helen about a visit to relatives in south Jersey.

"There's an INS camp in Gloucester City," Rosie was saying, "and my cousin Harry took me and my brother Joe to watch them bring in some Germans from Philadelphia."

"Why'd you do that?"

"The boys aren't old enough to go fight, and they said it was their only chance to see the enemy."

They stopped at a corner, standing back from the curb to avoid getting splashed by passing cars. When traffic cleared, they crossed to the other side of the street.

"Harry and Joe had counted on seeing a bunch of tough guys marching around," Rosie continued, "but there were only a few people, and some of them were ladies. They were pretty ordinary, too, all loaded down with suitcases and packages. It looked like they'd slept in their clothes. Most of them kept their eyes down, like they were ashamed."

Listening to her friend, Helen, too, felt something like shame. She wanted to defend the internees, but she was tongue-tied. For one thing, she didn't know if they were guilty of anything or not. More than that, she felt a desire to distance herself from them, to avoid any stain of similarity.

Helen had told Rosie about her upcoming séance. Rosie's re-action had been more moderate than Billy's. She liked to consider herself unflappable. She'd asked a few questions, then let the subject drop. But to know that members of Helen's fam-ily were internees might strain even Rosie's tolerance.

She hadn't told Rosie about Erich and Freida and their children, who were still in custody, now on Ellis Island. Hear-ings had finally been scheduled for them, though Erich was considering voluntary repatriation to Germany.

Franz claimed that the only reason the United States was rounding up so many Germans was so that they could exchange them for thousands of Americans trapped in Germany. The Swedish ship *Drottningholm* had already taken six hundred Ger-man diplomats and their families to Portugal, where they traded places with six hundred American students, tourists, and businessmen arrived from Germany on another humanitarian ship.

Walter had advised Franz to keep his theories to himself. But when FDR signed Order 9066 in February, Franz once again began spouting suspicions and worries, though only to other German-Americans.

Order 9066 allowed the War Department to create restricted zones anywhere in the United States and to exclude anyone they wished from living in or entering those areas. General De Witt, commander of all the Army units west of the Mississippi, had already evacuated thousands of Japanese and Japanese-Americans from the West Coast to "planned communities" inland.

"A Jap's a Jap," General De Witt told the newspapers.

He said even Japanese born on American soil could never be Americanized enough to dilute their race loyalties. News of Japanese ferocity against American prisoners of war forestalled

162

public sympathy for Japanese-Americans being forced to leave their homes.

The general also wanted to relocate German and Italian aliens from coastal areas. But, as Walter took pains to point out to Franz, a congressional committee had opposed that mass roundup. The Japanese had to be evacuated as a group, the reasoning went, because their habits and biology were so different from other Americans, it was impossible to distinguish saboteurs from harmless people, while Germans and Italians could be evaluated case by case.

"You know, Rosie," Helen finally managed to say, "just because they're Germans doesn't make them the enemy."

"Maybe," Rosie said.

"My uncle knows a man who was arrested because somebody said they heard him say he hoped Germany wins the war. One of those civilian hearing boards interviewed him for two hours, and he had to fill out eighteen pages of questions."

"Did he get sent to a camp?"

"No, they let him go. He told my uncle he never said anything to anybody about wanting Germany to win."

"What about the person who heard him say it?"

"They wouldn't tell him who it was. He thinks it's a neighbor he had an argument with about her noisy dogs."

"I don't know," Rosie said dubiously. "If they ask somebody that many questions, he's probably fishy somehow."

Helen and Rosie had come to the street where their paths diverged. They hesitated, neither wanting to part on an awkward note.

"We got a letter from my brother at boot camp," Rosie said.

"What's he say?"

Though Helen didn't feel she'd successfully made her point about arrests and detentions, she was happy to move on to a new topic.

"He's got bags of complaints. The sergeants are crabby, the uniforms are too big, they have to get up at five in the morning. Mostly, though, he's homesick."

"Is your mom sorry she let him go?"

"Yeah, I think so. It made her cry when he told about seeing some fellows from Pearl Harbor who were missing arms and legs. But he had really pestered her to let him sign up."

"What about Jimmy?"

Rosie's older brother Jimmy had been in the Army since 1940 and had trained for jungle combat in the swamps of Louisiana. He was fighting in the Philippines, where things were going so badly, the President had ordered General MacArthur to escape to Australia, leaving the troops to fight on under General Wainwright. MacArthur had said he would return to help them, but no one knew when that might be, since the Navy remained crippled from the Pearl Harbor attack, and much of the rest of the armed forces consisted of raw recruits still in training.

"All we know is he's somewhere in Bataan," Rosie said. "In his last letter, he said we might not hear from him for a while 'cause things were heating up."

"When was that?"

"Beginning of February."

"Oh, well, that's not so long ago."

"Yeah," Rosie said. "I keep writing him every week anyway. I guess he's not too busy to read a letter."

"Give me his address, and I'll send him a note, too."

"Okay."

The rain started to come down harder, making little drumming sounds on their umbrellas.

"Better get home," Helen said.

Rosie nodded and turned away, then quickly back again.

"Say, Helen," she said shyly, "you know you're aces with me, right?"

164

Helen smiled. She felt both relieved and guilty about being relieved.

"Right," she said.

Gathered around the Schneiders' dining-room table were Helen, her parents and grandmother, Mrs. Durkin, Mr. Grauer, and Miss Simmons. Walter had insisted the séance take place at home as a guard against artifice. He trusted Ursula, but he knew the members of her home circle were eager for Helen to join them on a permanent basis and so might be tempted to enhance her performance somehow. He himself had provided the pencil and blank papers for automatic writing, should Helen be moved to that. The long, draping tablecloth had been removed so that the area underneath the table was clearly visible. At Walter's request, all the women were wearing short-sleeved dresses, and Mr. Grauer had removed his jacket and rolled up his sleeves.

The usual candles stood in the center of the table, but Walter had carried a floor lamp in from the living room. It gently illuminated the entire room. Ursula hadn't liked this addition. Darkness, she'd declared, was required for many everyday happenings, and no one found it sinister then. Babies grew within their mothers in darkness, seeds sprouted deep in the soil, photographs were printed in darkrooms.

"How would you see stars if the sky never was dark?" she'd complained.

Helen sat between her grandmother and her father. Neither of them was touching her except at the tips of her pinkies, yet she itched to stand up and stretch, to throw them off as she would a heavy coat on a warm afternoon. She knew they each had her welfare at heart despite the fact that they had opposing hopes for the evening. She was bound to disappoint or confound at least one of them. She gave her head a little shake to clear away these thoughts. Her grandmother had told her that being anxious or doubtful could make it difficult for spirits to approach.

"We expect, tonight, to meet with war dead," Ursula said to the circle, "as have often come to us when we do not call for anyone by name."

She gave Walter a sidelong glance.

"But, as always," she continued, "we receive whatever happens with patient, unlocked minds. And because Helen is new in her mediumship, we will not expect to understand everything we hear."

Ursula nodded across the table at Emilie.

"I chose tonight's invocation from Proverbs," Emilie said. "It says: the hearing ear and the seeing eye, the Lord has made them both."

"Let us sing," said Mrs. Durkin, and Miss Simmons began *I Dream of Jeannie,* her voice as clean as a bell. Mr. Grauer's gravelly atonal voice joined in, the two forming a surprisingly pretty harmony.

By the time the others also began to sing, Helen had already started to enter her trance. She was picturing herself in front of a door, her hand on the knob. The knob was smooth and warm, and as she imagined her fingers wrapping around it, the bones in her neck and spine seemed to loosen, and she felt as if she were pleasantly floating. In her practices with her grandmother, this was as far as Helen usually went. Ursula had had her call up Iris a couple of times, but no other spirits.

Now, Helen silently summoned Iris. The darkness behind Helen's closed eyelids slowly thinned to a dawn-like softness, and she was able to discern her green-robed guide standing there waiting.

"She's here," Helen informed her grandmother.

Helen could not have said where her grandmother was, nor

where she herself was, though somewhere at the far back of her mind, she was aware that she was in her dining room and that her grandmother was right beside her.

"Ask Iris if she has any spirits to bring through," Ursula instructed, her words reaching Helen as if through a thick curtain.

Helen put the question wordlessly to Iris, who responded by stepping back a few paces. A shadowy form was emerging to her right. Because of all the dreams, Helen quickly recognized it as the form of a young soldier.

"A soldier," she said, "in light-colored clothing." She was performing as trained, giving a description without interpretation, attending to the spirit without making any demands on it.

"He's next to a tank with a big hole in its side," she added as the vehicle shimmered into view. "In the desert. He's not alone." Other soldiers had appeared behind the young man.

Helen felt as if there were cobwebs on her hands. She divined that she was meant to write, that the first soldier was yearning to tell her something long and intricate. She groped for the pencil and papers. Someone shoved them within her reach.

As soon as Helen had grasped the pencil, the young soldier began talking, and she raced to get down his every word. It was exhilarating. A current of radiant energy swept up and down her spine, with occasional bursts travelling across her hips and down her legs in fluttering waves. Her body felt large, soft, joy-ridden. Nothing else mattered. There was no family, no home circle, no Iris. Only herself and the soldier and the labor of her writing.

Finally, the soldier was finished. He thanked her and turned away, his companions shuffling after him. Iris stood alone beside the damaged tank.

"There are others," Iris communicated.

Helen was exhausted. Her fingers ached.

"The attending can be yours," Iris offered. "They rest outside time."

Iris and the tank faded from sight. Helen opened her eyes to find twenty or so pieces of paper spread in front of her, all covered edge to edge with her hasty handwriting. A small, neat number had been put at the top of each page, presumably by her grandmother. Helen carefully stacked the pages in order, handling them tenderly.

"Helen?" her father said. "Are you all right?" He had spoken gently, but the sound of his voice made her wince.

She nodded and dredged up a smile to reassure him. She felt averse to speaking, and she sincerely hoped no one else would speak, either. Everything felt like too much. The light hurt her eyes, her belt and her collar and her shoes were too tight, and Mr. Grauer's raspy breathing was scouring her eardrums.

Ursula made a sign with her hand that everyone seemed to understand to mean they should quietly leave the room, which they did. Helen heard her mother making good-byes at the front door.

"Now, Helen," her grandmother said very softly, "you take your pages to your room to look at when you are ready. We will see them later."

Helen stood up.

"I'm really fine," she said to allay the worried expression on her father's face. "Just tired." The words scratched her throat.

"I'll bring you up some soup," her mother said, returning from the hallway.

That sounded perfect. Helen billowed with gratitude.

CHAPTER 21
APRIL 1942

Helen practically had his story memorized. For a week after the séance, she'd taken out the bundle of pages daily and carefully reread them. Every time, she felt a muted version of the excitement she'd experienced while taking down the young tank driver's recitation. I did this, she thought. I brought this to light.

Growing up, Helen had accepted the idea of spirits and spirit communication as uncritically as another child might have accepted a sister who tap-danced or a house with warped floorboards. It was part of her personal atlas, part of who her grandmother was, only one of many defining characteristics of her family and her home life, and by childish extension, of the wider world. Though she'd resisted her own psychic abilities, and known by adolescence that they were not common, she hadn't been surprised by them. But the tank driver had accomplished what years with her grandmother had not, what even her own visions had not. He had convinced her that death did not exist. Other soldiers came with similar stories and cemented her conviction, but she didn't really need them. He was the first, and he was enough.

The thing I hated most was the noise. Guns, explosions. Shell splinters banging on the sides of the tank. It gave me awful headaches. All that's over now, and I'm plenty thankful.

We were in the thick of it, see, and my captain was shouting at me to alter our course, but it was too late. We were hit, and I remember the captain cursing and saying,

"Christ, we've got it this time." Then we were all standing outside the tank, wondering how we got there and feeling pretty lucky. The tank was in bad shape, though. I thought how it was my fault for not dodging quick enough and how now we'd have to walk back to base, which wasn't gonna be easy with all the Germans and Italians between us and there. Me and a buddy went with the captain to give the tank a look-see in case maybe she was still able to move. We'd just got the door wrenched open when a shell came and knocked it clear off. But our luck was holding, 'cause we weren't even scratched. Another strange thing—I noticed my headache was gone, even though that shell hit so close and the battle was still going on around us.

Then we looked inside the tank, and we saw bodies in it. Our bodies. The whole crew. And my buddy starts laughing and says, "Didn't I tell you we'd wake up dead one day?" I laughed, too. Somehow I didn't care, except that at the same time, I cared terribly. Then the captain says we'd better be going, but he doesn't know where. He set out anyway, and since he's the officer, we all followed, right through the battlefield. I could see the fighting like I was looking in the wrong end of a telescope.

As we went along, other guys joined in one by one. Didn't say anything, just came up from somewhere and started walking with us. You didn't see them coming. You'd just look around, and there would be another joe walking next to you or behind you. Even some of the enemy. That didn't bother me. It didn't seem important.

Then we got to a forest. It shouldn't have been there, in the desert. It was beautiful, cool and green, and we all sat down under the trees and went to sleep. When we woke up, we felt different. We looked the same, but where our bodies oughta been tired and achy, they weren't. I felt like I was standing on air. There was someone with us, a Messenger, he calls himself, and he went around to each of us and touched our heads. Let me tell you, when he touched me, it was like he was pouring something into me, I felt so happy and alive.

He says more's going to happen to us. We'll get stronger and have work to do. We won't have bodies, not even these other, refreshed bodies, and it will be a great release, he says. Some of us might take longer than others to get used to everything and to stop missing home, but we'll all come through eventually. There's helpers here for us. It's easier for me 'cause I was raised that there's an eternal soul and that God's in His heaven waiting for us.

The Messenger let me come tell you all this because love and prayers from earth can help us go on to the next part sooner. And another thing: lots of fellows have tried real hard to appear to their folks or their sweethearts, and they didn't notice them. If you're too sad, we can't get through. It hurts to see you like that. It holds some of us back. We want you to know we're okay. There's thousands of us here, more arriving every day, and we are all okay.

Helen's father wasn't as affected by the results of the séance as she was, but he'd been impressed enough to allow her to continue sitting with the home circle twice a week, once at Mrs. Durkin's and once at the Schneiders'. If there really were brave soldiers wanting to impart messages from beyond, he'd said, it would be unpatriotic to block their way. He still drew the line at including outsiders seeking to contact specific spirits or address private concerns. That smacked too much of a sideshow.

The séances at Mrs. Durkin's house focussed on contacting what Ursula called *Reisende,* or wanderers. Unlike the tank driver and his comrades, *Reisende* hadn't yet embarked on their new lives in the hereafter. Most of them were neither happy nor unhappy, though some felt lonely. They existed in a gray mist that emanated from themselves and prevented them from seeing the spirits around them waiting to help. Some of them were still too tied to earth, either longing for the pursuits and people of their earthly lives, or required to stay near earth in order to learn the lessons they had refused while alive. Chief among these lessons was the foolhardiness of living in isolation, with thoughts only of oneself.

Though Helen attended both séances every week, Ursula acted as medium in the *Reisende* sessions because of the danger of contacting "dwellers on the threshold." Dwellers had passed away without having cultivated their spiritual natures. They were not necessarily evil, but they could be. There was always the chance that a dweller might try to control a medium in order to recite his past misdeeds or gratify his sensual desires. He might enter the medium's eyes to see the physical world again as a living person does. He might amuse himself with the thoughts in the medium's mind. Young, inexperienced mediums like Helen were especially at risk because they were more likely to be swayed by a dweller's flattery or importuning. The home circle always called on strong teaching spirits whenever a dweller appeared, both for the benefit of the dweller and to protect Ursula.

Helen's mediumship was confined to the circles in her own dining room. As on the first occasion, the group made no requests. Helen called Iris, Iris brought spirits, and Helen recorded their stories. Details varied, but the message was always the same: I didn't know I was dead, someone came to guide me, I rested and awoke revived and joyful, I am all right, I am moving ahead in a land of light and love.

I blacked out. This was in Libya. When I came to, I hailed some passing trucks, but they ignored me. TARFU, we call it. "Things are really fouled up." Then here's this Arab in those long robes that they wear coming toward me, and I'm thinkin', what's he doin' out here? When he gets to me, I see he's really tall, maybe seven feet, and his face is real friendly and calm, so calm. It made me realize how much I was used to seeing men with strained faces all the time. He put his hand on my shoulder, and a feeling of intense life and joy went through me. It was everywhere in me. I could see colors—colors in the desert, where everything always looks the same—and I could smell roses. I heard music. I didn't want him to ever take his hand away, but he did, and I still felt happy and well.

The Arab went to help some poor mug who was lying on the ground nearby, looking pretty beat up. I went over to watch. He touched the guy's head and a kind of shadow grew up out of the guy's body, slowly taking on the same features as the body. I could see he was feeling the same strength from the Arab's hand that I had, and I was thinkin' this Arab was one swell doc. Then I noticed the Arab was standing so that the guy who'd gotten up couldn't see the body that was still on the ground, and it hit me that we must be dead. I coulda cried. "Are we dead, sir?" I said, and the Arab just looked at me. There was pity in his eyes, and I felt that he knew everything about me, that he understood me, and I didn't feel like crying anymore.

Not all the spirits were from the desert. A seaman told of his ship sinking. He dove down to free his canary and discovered two birds, a dead canary in its cage and a live one singing. Underwater. He left the ship, passing easily through walls, which made him realize that he was dead. When he reached the surface, he heard bells, and he felt radiantly alive.

A pilot stood bewildered beside a crashed plane in France. Spotting a body hunched over the controls, he rushed to free the man, only to discover it was himself. Horrified at the awful condition of being apart from his body, and feeling too weak to extricate it from the wreck, he lay down to rest, whereupon he left his second body. "It was like shelling peas," he'd said, "and I seemed to go on and be just as much myself outside both bodies." A stranger arrived and took him to a place called the Garden of Awakening. The pilot lay down on the grass and immediately experienced amazing refreshment, as if the grass were electrified. He'd always felt, the times his plane was under attack, as if he were on the end of an elastic that would snap him back to safety, but now the elastic had been cut, and he felt at peace.

CHAPTER 22
MAY 1942

"These stories," Billy said, tapping the pile of handwritten pages he'd just finished reading, "you made them up, right?"

"No! Why would I do that?"

Helen had known Billy might well express disbelief in the automatic writings, but when he actually did, she was not only disappointed but also annoyed and even a bit startled. As the stories had accumulated over the past few weeks, they'd shored one another up, each one rendering its predecessors both more credible and less extraordinary. By now, Helen regarded them almost as routine—amazing and wonderful, but routine.

"I don't know why," Billy said, irritated. "Maybe because you didn't want your grandmother and her friends to think you were the bunk."

"Are you calling me a liar?"

"No, no. Pipe down."

"Well, I'm not lying. Or play-acting. I swear."

They were sitting in Billy's backyard, on a circular bench Mr. Mackey had built around the biggest apple tree. The tree was just starting to break out in clusters of white flowers. Helen was reminded of the song *I'll Be with You in Apple Blossom Time*. It was a pretty tune, both words and melody brimming with longing and faith in the future. The old song had been on the radio a lot this spring.

"I don't think you're a liar," Billy said. "But maybe you heard a story somewhere sort of like these and then forgot about it, and now your imagination is bringing it back and fiddling with it to come up with new stories. They are all a lot alike."

"They're alike because they're true."

Billy leafed through the pages and held one up to her.

"What about this one? This poor sap watches his pals carry his body to a hospital tent. Next, his brother—his *dead* brother— shows up and takes him to the Rest Hall. C'mon, Helen, do you really believe there's a place called the Rest Hall? Made of crystals? Where the fountains make music, and everyone feels happy?"

"I remember him," Helen said, taking the page from Billy. "Later a Messenger came and took him to the Hall of Silence to rest some more. And the Messenger told him not to describe to me too much of what he'd seen, because a lot of it was illusion."

"See? Even the spooks know it's in your imagination!"

"No, Billy! These spirits are all very new, and what they see at first comes partly from their own ideas." Iris had taught her that. "And they're not poor saps."

Billy stood up and shoved his hands into his pockets.

"I don't like it, Helen," he said quietly.

"What do you mean, you don't like it? You can refuse to believe it—though I don't see how—but what's to like or not like about it?"

"It's . . . I don't know . . . it's too . . ."

"Too what?"

"Too different." He looked at her and frowned. "It makes you different."

"But I *am* different. You already knew that."

"Yeah, but you were always still a regular person, and we were together just like anybody else, and now you're kind of . . . apart."

"Apart?" Helen felt a tremor of anxiety.

"It's almost like you've been going around with another guy."

Helen reached out and tugged at his rolled-up shirt cuff. "That's silly," she said.

"Is it? You should see your face when you talk about them. It's like they're alive."

"They *are* alive, in a way. But they're gone. And it's their stories I think about, not the boys themselves."

As Helen said this she realized guiltily that it was not quite true. The boys Iris brought to the séances were all individual personalities to her, even though their stories repeated the same themes. Helen could bring up in her mind's eye the look of each one, the color of his hair, the condition of his uniform, the peculiarities of his face and posture, the relative degrees of puzzlement and peace in his eyes. For the time of the séance, and to a lesser degree whenever she reread their accounts, she experienced them as dear and particular, not simply as anonymous bearers of engrossing tales. "My boys," she'd thought more than once.

"It's hard to explain," she told Billy, "especially since you've never been to a séance."

"So tell me how it works. Exactly."

He positioned himself expectantly in front of her. Because he was looking down at her, the usual errant lock of hair fell across his brow, and it had the usual effect of making her want to touch him, but she resisted, straightening up as if she were a teacher about to begin a lesson.

"Well, I close my eyes and relax, and I slip into a sort of dream, except I'm awake. And then I see them."

Helen judged this was not the right moment to introduce Iris.

"Then what?"

"Then I get this pins and needles feeling in my hands, or sometimes like they're covered with spider webs, and I know it's time to write. The spirits talk—one by one—and I take down what they say. I don't look at the paper while I write, or even know what I'm writing until later."

Billy was staring at her in a peculiar way. Perhaps he was simply trying to absorb what she was saying, but she couldn't help feeling it was she herself he was appraising.

"You enjoy it, don't you?" he said in an accusing tone.

Helen felt caught out in a misdeed. He was right. She did enjoy it. There was an intimacy to the séances that was uniquely and almost physically satisfying. Those boys made her feel special and important, chosen, even loved. She knew she'd never make Billy understand. With sudden clarity, she realized it would be dangerous to try. She stood up and drew his hands out of his pockets, entwining her fingers with his.

"It's just a kind of job," she cajoled. "If I were in a steno pool, you wouldn't be jealous of the men who dictated letters to me, would you?"

Billy pulled his hands away.

"I'm not jealous," he scoffed. "How could I be jealous of dead guys? *Imaginary* dead guys."

They stood in silence a few moments, each one looking at a different part of the yard. Finally, she tentatively laid a hand on his waist. When he didn't reject her, she slid both arms around him and pressed her body against his.

"Trying to change the subject?" he said with put-on gruffness.

"Do you mind?"

He drew her behind the large tree to shield them from view and began kissing her. His hands rested at the small of her back and gently urged her to move against him. They swayed together, their hips travelling a small, exquisite ellipse again and again. Then, abruptly, Billy put his hands on her shoulders and firmly held her away. He took a deep breath, and grinning, raised his eyebrows at her. His face was flushed.

"Wanna take a walk?" he said.

He didn't need to name where. He could only mean the tree house he and Lloyd had built years ago in the woods behind Dohrmann's field. Helen thought of it as their place now, hers and Billy's, even though the single-minded Lloyd occasionally brought girls there, including, two or three times, the detestable Beth of the yellow sash, who had become less detestable to Helen after Lloyd's conquest of her. Helen and Billy used the tree house for rainy day picnics and star-gazing. They also regularly achieved dizzying heights of pleasure in that crude structure of scrap lumber and branches, but so far, by mutual agreement, they'd stopped just short of crossing the line Lloyd had erased.

"It'll be getting dark soon," she said.

"Even better."

She rolled up the pages of automatic writing, stuck the scroll between her belt and the waistband of her skirt, and turned to leave the yard, relishing the few seconds he stayed behind, imagining his appreciation of her gait. When he fell in step beside her, there was no more talk of spirit stories or differences.

Helen was careful not to bring up the soldier spirits again with Billy. She stopped attending her grandmother's séances, and she cut back her own work with the home circle to one séance every other week, hoping to lessen the hold of "her boys" on her thoughts. But she was still enthralled by their messages, and she still derived a visceral pleasure from the process of automatic writing. To pretend that this wasn't happening or that it didn't mean enough to her to talk about it made her, at times, feel hollow and almost fearful in Billy's company. His outlandish likening of her mediumship to her having another beau had come to fit, in that she grew nervous at lapses in conversation and felt false when she rushed to fill them with inconsequential chatter, as if she really did have an amorous transgression to hide.

It used to be that something inside of her lit up when Billy arrived at her door or called over the fence, or even when she caught sight of him from her window painting one of his models at the workbench in his yard. This had not gone, but now she was likely to experience foreboding, too.

Fortunately, their physical relationship remained untainted. Their bodies possessed superlative knowledge of each other. Every kiss, every touch beguiled and entreated. They pounced on any opportunity to be alone. Billy so regularly loosened Helen's clothing, she took to wearing shirtwaist dresses that buttoned all the way down the front to make the task easier.

One day, she went to Bamberger's and bought a lacy, powder blue silk slip. It was the most expensive item of clothing she'd ever owned. The supply of silk from Asia had been cut off by the Japanese, and what silk there was had to go into parachutes. Bamberger's had a huge barrel near the front door for women to deposit old silk blouses, scarves, and stockings. There was a barrel for nylon stockings, too. Nylons could be refashioned into tow ropes for military gliders and powder bags for naval guns.

The collection barrels made Helen feel a little guilty at her indulgence. Posters, billboards, and radio spots repeatedly admonished everyone to conserve resources. "Use it up, wear it out, make it do, or do without." Yet, she reminded herself, other ad campaigns insisted women should continue to wear make-up and look pretty to keep up morale. On the bus ride home, the slip stuffed into a zipper compartment of her handbag, Helen fluttered in anticipation of Billy's reaction.

Billy had groaned in delight when he saw her in the slip. Later, when they lay happy and expended in each other's arms in the tree house, he told her about a letter from Lloyd, who was training in England. He'd written that to mark the United States' entry into the war, girls there were wearing slips with little American flags embroidered on the hems and on the cloth between their breasts. Despite the popular British song, *You Can't Say No to a Soldier,* Lloyd insisted that he'd seen these slips only in shop windows, but Billy was sure that was to keep from unnerving their mother.

"Lloyd doesn't like Ma fussing and brooding over him," Billy said. "He's said so right out to her, sometimes not too kindly, but I guess from thousands of miles away, he can afford to be more tenderhearted with her."

"I wonder if your mother fusses because Lloyd is so wild, or if it makes Lloyd wild because she fusses."

"Both, I think. But they're each mostly being their natural selves. Ma's always favored Lloyd, and Lloyd has always gone his way and fought anybody keeping him down. Even when Pop was gone, we couldn't rely on Lloyd."

"But he helped, didn't he? He had that paper route. He worked around the house?"

"Only when he decided. Never if Ma wanted it, or if he thought I was asking for her sake."

Billy sat up, the signal it was time to prepare to go home.

"You know the maddest I ever saw Lloyd?" Billy said as he was buttoning his shirt. "Once we were wrestling, and I threw a blanket over his head and held him tight in it." Billy shook his head at the memory. "He fought like a trapped tiger."

"What'd you do?"

"I had to let him go. He actually scared me, he was so angry. He's not one to stand against when he has a mind to go ahead."

They finished straightening their clothing and climbed down the ladder of the tree house. A clump of lily-of-the-valley was growing at the base of the tree. Helen picked a sprig and put it in her top buttonhole. She wanted to remember this afternoon because it had been the debut of the slip, and because it was getting to be a rare thing to have more than an hour to spend with Billy. The federal government had built a huge new plant for Curtiss-Wright Aeronautical in Wood-Ridge, and Billy had been transferred there. He was working most of the time, and collapsed in sleep when he wasn't.

Air Marshal Goering had said American industry was good at making refrigerators and razor blades, but they couldn't make airplanes. But all over the country, old plants were refitting and new plants were being built, hurrying to produce planes, locomotives, jeeps, munitions, trucks, tanks, ships, and all their related parts. Billy's plant made engines for B-17s and B-29s. Elevator manufacturers were now making landing gear and gun turrets, optical plants were producing bombsights. Prisoners at San Quentin were making antisubmarine nets and nightsticks. No civilian automobiles had been made since early February, nor any new bicycles, and none were planned. Only six months after Pearl Harbor, what had been pastureland outside Detroit was now a Ford factory a half mile long. Raw materials went in one end and came out the other end as a long-range bomber ready to fly.

Given Helen's new sense of unbalance, Billy's shortage of free time was actually a boon. She was easier when their time together was measured. They were more likely to spend it necking, which banished any hesitations either of them had about the other. If they didn't talk, they couldn't disagree.

CHAPTER 23
JUNE 1942

Helen's graduation was a low-key affair. Lloyd was not the only boy who had left school to join the Armed Services, and their classmates decided to leave empty chairs on the stage in the alphabetical places where they should have been seated. There was one such chair next to Helen, with a rectangle of oak tag taped to it lettered with the name Michael Scully. Mike was training in Colorado with the Tenth Mountain Division, learning to fight on skis.

The principal read a list of past graduates who'd lost their lives, most in the Pacific, including two in the recent Battle of Midway, the first big victory against Japan, and it was impossible not to wonder how many of the boys on stage would also leave and never come home. Helen had spotted a few gold-starred flags in people's front windows, indicating a family member had died in the service. You didn't need to be psychic to know the number of those flags would be increasing, as would the number of flags with blue stars. There was even one such banner in a window of the White House. It had four blue stars, one for each Roosevelt son in the military.

As the valedictorian droned on about the grave responsibility of this graduating class to save the world from fear and evil, Helen surreptitiously laid her hand on Mike's empty chair. She received no intimations of what lay ahead for him. Such premonitions were rare for her, but they did come, especially now when men in uniform were encountered daily in every public place. She'd gone a few times with Rosie and other girls and women to take baked goods to the troop trains stopped at the water tank at the south end of town, and it took only a brush against a uniform sleeve as some boy reached out the train window to take a donut from her tray, for Helen to get a flash image of that arm blown off and lying beside him on a muddy battlefield. She met twenty or thirty soldiers for every one that presented her with a vision, and the visions were not always gruesome, such as the time she saw a shy farmer from Iowa lifting the skirt of his first woman in a dark, cobblestoned alley. But the possibility of a disturbing mental ambush was always there.

She never told anyone of these seeings, not even her grandmother, who would have scolded her for not keeping her abilities in closer check. Helen believed it wasn't right to try to prevent the premonitions. It seemed her own particular brand of sacrifice for the war effort. Those boys, so jocular and flirtatious as they crowded at the train windows, were actually going to have to face what she foresaw, and more. How could she presume to protect herself from merely seeing it for a moment? Still, she didn't dare join the bus trips to the USO canteens at Camp Kilmer and Fort Dix, where she'd have to dance with soldiers. What more thorough visions might such contact provoke?

Emilie had offered to host out-of-state soldiers for Sunday dinner, so once in a while there'd be two or three green privates at the table, politely conversing with Walter about war news or their hometowns, praising Emilie and Ursula's cooking, smiling at Helen as she leaned to clear their plates. Luckily, only one young man so far had provided her with dire foreknowledge. She saw him lying in the arms of another soldier, his chest covered with blood, his eyes glazed with pain and bewilderment. She found some comfort in the discovery that just before he died, the grime and noise around him would disappear from his awareness and he'd believe he was reclining on the grass in his West Virginia backyard watching his little son toddle after a butterfly, the scent of freshly baked cherry pie wafting from an open window in the tidy white house behind them.

Strangely, Helen's certitude that after his dying agonies he'd attain peace and a new kind of existence was less consoling than that he'd have that final glimpse of earthly contentment. The stories of "her boys" had not lost power for her, but they couldn't assuage the tragedy of too many people dying too young.

Being at the latter end of the alphabet, Helen was one of the last to receive her diploma. Soon after she'd resumed her seat, the class stood to sing the alma mater, followed by *God Bless America* and *The White Cliffs of Dover*, which the graduates had chosen because it recognized the current plight of the world yet managed to be hopeful. The song had been recorded by five different big bands and their singers, and all had been Top-Twenty hits, Kay Kyser's making it to number one.

> There'll be bluebirds over the White Cliffs of
> Dover
> Tomorrow, just you wait and see
> There'll be love and laughter and peace ever after
> Tomorrow when the world is free.

Ursula had badgered her, Walter and Emilie had granted their consent, and Billy had stopped short of forbidding her, but it was Rosie who finally convinced Helen to begin taking clients at séances.

A week after graduation, Rosie and Helen were pulling wagons door-to-door, collecting scrap metal to bring to a depot at the Elks Lodge. The Elks had affixed placards to each wagon.

Rosie's placard urged "Slap the Jap with the Scrap," while Helen's cheerily asserted "Praise the Lord, I'll Soon Be Ammunition."

Housewives pulled odds and ends out of garages and cellars to give to the girls. One woman proudly presented them with a stack of washed, flattened tin cans she'd gathered from her neighbors. After only two blocks, one wagon was nearly full.

Turning up the next sidewalk, they spotted a woman only a few years older than they hanging laundry in her side yard. Most of it was diapers. A fat baby sat on the grass gnawing a piece of zwieback, his chin smeared with wet crumbs. The woman turned towards the girls. She removed a wooden clothespin from her mouth and put it into her apron pocket. Her face evinced only mild curiosity.

Helen made an admiring comment about the baby, which failed to produce the customary maternal smile, and then Rosie launched into a brief spiel about the salvage drive, winding up with the impressive announcement that the town of Englewood was even tearing up its trolley tracks to donate.

"Sorry," the woman said, bending to lift another diaper from her basket. "We got nothin' here."

"Not even newspapers?" Rosie said. "We're not collecting those, but you can leave them on the curb first Sunday of every month, and someone will come by for them."

"Don't read newspapers," the woman said, continuing her chore. "Don't need newspapers to know the world's in a jam."

Rosie threw Helen an exasperated glance.

"You don't have to give anything big," Helen said. "Most people are surprised what they've got laying around."

"Like razor blades," Rosie suggested. "Did you know twelve thousand razor blades can make a two-thousand-pound bomb?"

"Don't have twelve thousand razor blades."

"Well, of course not," Rosie said, an edge coming into her voice.

Helen pulled her wagon closer to the woman.

"Just look at what we've gotten so far," she said. "Maybe you have something of the same kind? Like this old iron shovel. This shovel can be converted into four hand grenades."

The woman glanced briefly at the contents of the wagon, then shook her head. From an upstairs window came the sound of a young child crying. The woman looked up, squinting against the sun.

"My other boy's awake," she said. "And I got dinner to start." She picked up the baby and started to walk away. She hadn't finished hanging the laundry. As irritating as the woman had been, Helen had the urge to do the job for her.

"Don't forget to save your used cooking fat," Rosie called after her. "The butcher will buy it when you've got a pound."

The woman didn't acknowledge that she'd heard Rosie, though the baby graced them with a gummy grin from over his mother's shoulder. The screen door slammed behind them.

"Let it lay, Rosie," Helen said, seeing her friend was tempted to follow.

"I was just gonna tell her how the glycerine in one pound of fat can make a pound of powder for bullets."

"She doesn't want to know."

"If those boys were bigger, she'd want to know all right."

"Let's hope so."

"I'm gonna leave her a booklet anyway," Rosie said. She put a copy of *A Kitchen Goes to War* on the worn welcome mat at the front door.

They'd been giving everyone the free booklet of recipes for meatless dishes and sugarless desserts. There were no serious shortages of food in the United States, as there were in Britain and Europe, but the federal government had set ceilings for food prices and distributed ration books to everyone, even children. So far only sugar was being rationed. Meat was still unrestricted, but people were being asked to cut back to guarantee that the troops would be well-fed.

"Do you plan to stop by Tuesday to see if you can smell a pot roast cooking?" Helen teased. Observing "meatless Tuesdays" was considered a patriotic act.

"I just might," Rosie replied, smiling.

After the girls had delivered their loads and received the list of the next day's addresses, they went to the library square and sat on a bench watching the fountain splash in the sunshine. A nearby kiosk, in the past posted with minutes of civic meetings, announcements of church social events and bake sales, and offers of free kittens, was now plastered with war-related posters. A handsome pilot grinned on a recruiting poster declaring "Fly to Tokyo, All Expenses Paid." A man in a suit stood admiring a woman dressed for factory work in a kerchief and overalls as she announced "I'm Proud: My Husband *Wants* Me to Do My Part." And emblazoned across a drawing of two tall red gasoline pumps was the reprimand "When You Drive Alone, You Drive with Hitler."

"My mother told me Mary Steltman's gotten a job at Bendix making instrument panels for planes," Helen said pointing to the poster of the woman worker.

"Old whining Mary? I wouldn't think she had it in her."

"Even Mary must've figured out nobody wants to hear whining these days."

Rosie walked over to the kiosk and studied the poster with the pilot.

"You heard about that new Women's Army Auxiliary Corps?" she said.

"Yeah."

"I'm gonna join."

"Really?"

Rosie turned to her friend. "Really."

"Gosh, what'll you do, do you think?"

"Whatever they tell me. The idea is to do things like office work and driving trucks and making maps so the guys can go fight. But I hope I get an overseas assignment."

"What about your folks? With your brothers already in it, will they let you go, too?"

"They can't stop me, Helen."

One look at Rosie's face would convince anyone she was immovable. But Helen knew her well enough to spy a tiny flicker of uncertainty in her defiant eyes. Some part of her wanted approval, even though not getting it wouldn't prevent her following through.

"Have you told them?"

Rosie nodded.

"What'd they say?"

"My mother never says much about anything. She took it pretty good, said I was grown now, and she supposed I could make up my own mind. And my father . . . he . . . well, he kind of laughed, but not in a way like when something's funny. He just laughed, and then he stopped short, like he was gonna cough or spit, and then he said . . . he said he already had enough sons."

Rosie sat down again.

"I keep thinking about Jimmy," she said, "stuck in a Jap prisoner-of-war camp, maybe sick or hurting, and Owen in England with bombs dropping, waiting to ship out somewhere and get shot at, and then I think about them coming home some day and asking what it was I did to help the war. I want to be able to look them straight in the eye and say I did all I could."

Helen took Rosie's hands in her own.

"You're grand, Rosie," she said. "Absolutely grand. And you'll be the best soldier any girl could be. I just know it!"

Beaming, Rosie threw her arms around Helen, and the two hugged enthusiastically.

"Helen," Rosie burst out when they'd disengaged, "why don't you join, too? We'd make a super team!"

Helen shook her head slowly.

"I don't think so, Rose. It's not for me."

"Don't say that. You haven't even thought about it. Say, what if I go in first and send you a scouting report, and then you decide?"

"You sure better write to me! But not as a scout."

As she spoke, Helen had stood up to go, but Rosie remained seated.

"What are you so worried about?"

Helen took a deep breath and let it out.

"I can't be around too many soldiers, Rosie. I don't want to be finding out who's going to die and who's going to make it back."

Rosie stared soberly at her.

"You can do that?"

"Sometimes."

"Could you tell about my brothers?"

Helen sighed. "No. I have to be with the person. To get a really strong picture, I have to touch him."

"I thought you only knew about people who were already dead."

"That, too."

Rosie frowned, thinking.

"Remember when I won the school relays in sixth grade?" she said. "And then the all-town race? But I still couldn't go to the regionals because only boys went to the regionals?"

"I remember," Helen said.

"If they'd have let me go, I would've brought back a trophy

for the school showcase. I know I would have. I was that fast."

"And?"

"Nobody should be kept back if there's something they can do, especially something that does some good not just for that one person. And for sure, nobody should keep themselves back."

"I'm sorry, Rosie, I just don't think my being in the Army would be a good idea."

"Never mind that. I'll take your word on that. But, Helen, there's got to be some way you can use what you have. There's got to be people who need it."

CHAPTER 24
AUGUST 1942

So many women in New York wanted to sign up for the new Corps, Rosie had had to stand in line eight hours to register. It was the same story all across the country, bowling over officials who hadn't expected such a turn-out. In July, Rosie was sent to Fort Des Moines for basic training. Helen received one letter in smudged pencil and lacking margins. As she read, she could almost hear her friend's characteristic speaking pace.

Dear Helen,

Owen's complaints about basic were all true, and I could come up with some of my own, but tired and sore as I am, I feel happy as a pig in a puddle, which is lucky because we hike and do calisthenics every day, rain or shine, and I've been eye-to-eye with mud more than once. So, let's see, what have I learned? To dig a slit trench, to take a bath in a helmet, to pick up a pencil with my toes (for stronger arches), to forget about there being no shades on the windows and no walls in the latrine. There's thirty of us on each floor of the barracks, and I'm with one tiptop bunch of gals. Our cots are set head to foot so we won't spread colds (have to pass that tip to my mom), but we still manage a little palaver before we conk out. I've got to choose a specialty. Word is it's typists and telephone operators that'll ship out to Europe first. I guess you've seen news pictures of our uniforms—not exactly smart, are they? The skirts are cut so that even the skinniest girl looks like she's got a pot belly. They say they're still working on it. But there's not going to be any slacks. Director Hobby said she wants us to look neat and military but still feminine so John Q. Public keeps his shirt on about ladies in the Army. In the motor pool, at least, they've got the sense to give you coveralls. But we run obstacle courses and do drills and just about everything else in a skirt, and you'd better keep those stocking seams straight, too, sister! Basic is going to be four weeks instead of three months. General Marshall says casualties have left them so short of ground forces, they're going to need five times the number of WAACs they thought, even though the draft's started to take eighteen-year-olds and fathers, plus defense and farm workers, too. So they're working us hard, but that's okay by me. Maybe I'll get home a few days before specialty school, and you can see for yourself what this man's Army has made so far of . . . your friend, Rosie

In her reply, Helen was less voluble about her own designs for contributing to the war effort, except to tell Rosie that she'd taken her advice to heart to put "what I can do" to use for others, namely by holding séances for new widows and grieving parents. What she didn't tell Rosie was what the séances did for *her*. When Helen successfully contacted the dead, she felt exalted and powerful. Her grandmother often used the phrase "serving spirit," and Helen knew she was, indeed, a kind of servant and that her abilities were a privilege, but she couldn't suppress a hearty dose of personal pride in her mediumship.

Emilie was present at every one of Helen's séances. She was determined her daughter not fall into the fast shuffles Ursula employed. The old woman researched the histories of her clients, picking up personal facts from school directories, church newsletters, gossip, newspaper archives, *Who's Who*. She had an excellent memory and could readily bring up researched facts. Simple things like the utterance of a family nickname could work wonders on a client whose belief was wavering.

Emilie had gone along with her mother's little cheats because they derived from a wish to maintain the flow of exchanges between this world and the next. Ursula didn't tell outrageous or dangerous lies, and the businesswoman in her never completely trumped the sympathetic advisor who wanted to send clients home more at peace than they'd been when they arrived. Nevertheless, Emilie wasn't proud of the subterfuges she'd been party to over the years. Especially now, they seemed dishonorable.

Especially now, Ursula had insisted, they were important.

"Just let me teach her cold reading," she said before Helen's first sitting with a client, a woman who, in one week, had been notified of the deaths of both her brother and her husband.

"No," Emilie said. "Helen picks something up or she doesn't. If that's not good enough for people, they can go elsewhere."

Ursula sometimes had to do cold reading when she knew nothing at all about a client. It entailed asking lots of questions and seeing which ones hit a mark.

"I'm getting an S name," she'd say. "Who is that?"

"The spirit is showing me something orange. What is that?"

"I'm seeing a photograph on a bedside table or a mantel. Do you have a photograph of your loved one displayed at home? Yes? He's so pleased."

"You have a piece of jewelry that belonged to your loved one, don't you? Do you have it with you? She's glad to know you wear it."

But Helen hadn't needed cold reading techniques for the séance with the bereaved young widow. Iris had delivered both spirits, a Marine who'd died landing on Guadalcanal and a paratrooper who'd perished during a training exercise in Ireland.

The Marine assured his wife he'd gotten her letter telling him she was pregnant and that he hoped she'd name the baby Maurice or Maura after someone in his family.

"Or maybe he's saying Mort and Maureen," Helen said. "It's not clear."

"Maurice," the tearful widow confirmed. "Maurice was his father's name. He passed away while Bob was in basic training. It broke Bob's heart he couldn't get home in time to see him."

The paratrooper said nothing, but Helen saw him holding a pole, causing the client to exclaim that it must be her brother because he used to love to hike in the mountains and sometimes used a walking stick.

After this reading, performed in a conversational manner, Helen surprised everyone by emitting a soft groan, closing her eyes, and bending her head back. When she began feeling about on the table for her writing materials, Emilie had to rush to the desk in the living room to retrieve them. Unasked, Iris had brought another unknown soldier eager to relate the story of his death. Almost every subsequent reading ended this way. Emilie made sure paper and pencil were always at hand. These testaments became part of Helen's renown. Even clients who received scant information on their departed relatives left Helen's séances feeling consoled by the evidence of life and peace after death given by her boys.

I was struck by a shell splinter and I fell down, but I didn't black out. When I got up, I was outside my body. I stayed nearby 'cause I figured I'd be going back into it again some time somehow. I felt hot and out-of-breath, like I'd been running hard, but otherwise I was okay. I sat by my body all night and finally I slept. When I woke up my body was gone. I guess the medics took it. Then I got it that I had to be dead. It was a shock. Not actually being dead, but finding it out. Then I got the feeling that everything that wasn't really "me" was dropping into a bottomless pit. I didn't feel like I was losing anything, more like I was being set free.

Next my cousin arrived—my cousin who passed a couple of years ago—and with him a Light Angel. They were on their way to hell, they said, to try and get some guy out. The Angel didn't want to take me along, but my cousin convinced him. It turns out hell ain't a place but a thought. The guy they were after wouldn't come even though he said it was awful there. He was afraid if he went somewhere else it'd be worse. The Angel said no one could unchain the guy but himself. I felt sorry for the bum, but the Angel told me some day the guy will see his fear is only an illusion and he'll be released.

The Angel and my cousin kept close to me in hell 'cause even though it's dark and gloomy, it kinda gave me a thrill and was pulling at me to stay. After, they took me to a garden to rest. You folks on earth can get that same kind of rest, if you just shut out the thunder of war and look inside yourself to where it's silent. And if, the Angel says, you give love, if you pour yourself away.

Chapter 25
November 1942

Franz and his family arrived early for Thanksgiving dinner to allow time for a family visit. There were to be extra guests at the table this year—two Midwestern soldiers from Camp Kilmer—and their presence would stifle talk of personal matters. Ursula and Helen hustled the pumpernickel dough into bread pans for its second rising, then joined everyone in the living room, where Franz was just pulling out Erich's letters.

In early spring, an Alien Enemy Hearing Board had released Freida unconditionally and put Erich on parole, judging him a German nationalist, but not a Nazi. But in June, Erich had been taken into custody again, after the FBI had "dropped by" their home and ransacked it, coming up with a short wave radio and some letters from Germany.

Because the contraband radio, forgotten at the back of a closet, was found not to be in working order, and the letters from Germany were family notes from 1938, the hearing board might have continued Erich's parole except for an unfortunate coincidence. That same month, eight saboteurs had been apprehended landing from a U-boat on the East Coast, and two German-born naturalized U.S. citizens had been arrested in Detroit for helping an escaped German prisoner-of-war. Though the cases were unconnected, the men were tried together in a military court, four of them turning state's witnesses. The other six were executed, one right after the other in the electric chair. Justice had been swift and severe, but the public was nervous, and the hearing boards knew it. Erich was assigned to Camp Fort Bliss in Texas for the duration of the war.

When Freida requested to join her husband, they were all sent to Crystal City, also in Texas. Fort Bliss was for Italian and German men only. Crystal City was for families—around 2,000 Japanese, about half as many Germans, and a handful of Italians.

"When they were on Ellis Island," Marie was saying as Helen and Ursula entered, "Franz was able to visit and bring Erich cigarettes. Erich had a job sweeping up for ten cents an hour, but cigarettes are hard to get now that Lucky Strikes and Camels are saved only for servicemen." She frowned significantly, as if the cigarette allotments were a personal affront. "I used to send magazines, too, though Freida said the German Red Cross and the YMCA had stocked a good library there."

"They don't have this at Crystal City? A library and jobs?" Ursula asked, settling into her customary chair.

"Yes," Marie said, "but Erich says all the best jobs go to the Bundists and pro-Nazis. They're the ones get elected to be spokesmen to the camp commander. Natural leaders, I guess."

There followed an awkward silence during which Walter made a great show of refilling his pipe. Helen knew it took effort for him not to remark that Erich had been a Bundist, or close enough to one to get himself incarcerated. Franz was shuffling through Erich's letters, looking for some particular passage. Helen glanced over at the handwritten sheets. The censor had blacked out a sentence here and there, but the lengthy correspondence stood largely intact.

"At least he's not complaining about the heat anymore," Franz said.

"It was awful in the summer, they said," Marie explained. "Over a hundred degrees most days. It's complete desert. Used to be a camp for migrant laborers. For the spinach crop. Maybe

Mexicans are accustomed to heat and scorpions and mosquitoes, but Erich and Freida suffered. Each cottage was given a block of ice a day. It was the only relief."

"The children did get to swim," Franz put in.

"Pooh, children," Marie said. "Children don't feel things the way adults do. Do you know, Walter, that Erich's girls go to school with Japanese children and play with them and never think there's anything wrong? Erich makes sure they attend German classes, too, of course."

"So the groups do mix?" Emilie asked.

"Only the children," Franz answered. "The adults keep apart from one another, unless they happen to work in the hospital or the bakery."

"Does Erich have a job?"

"He teaches metalworking in the machine shop. Ten cents an hour. All the jobs in all the camps pay the same."

"They offered Erich a job at the camp farm," Marie said, "but he refused. Germans don't stoop, he said. Japs are better suited for such work, anyway. Erich says lots of them used to have truck farms in California."

"All in all, it doesn't sound too bad," Helen said.

"That's what I was thinking," agreed Teresa.

"Not so bad?" Marie burst out. "Are you forgetting that they're prisoners? And for no good reason?"

"The government may be trying to provide decent conditions," Walter calmly told the embarrassed girls, "and the Swiss inspectors will hold them to it, but Erich and Freida and their children—their children, who are American citizens—are, indeed, prisoners. The cottages, the school, the swimming pool, the social hall, and all the rest of it are surrounded by barbed wire and armed guards."

"Here, listen to this," Franz said, holding up one of Erich's pages. "Three times every day we are counted to be sure no one has escaped. A whistle blows, and no matter where you are, you must return to your cottage and stand in front of it. It makes you feel like a criminal. There are ruffians here, drunks who get into fistfights at the Vaterland Café, thieves who steal lumber and coffee, bullies who bar families from the mess hall and the food shops if they don't obey them. We live among bad company. But it is the counting that makes me feel *verdorben*."

"*Verdorben?*" Helen said.

"Corrupted," Ursula translated.

Walter slowly shook his head. "I fear that if Erich and people like him didn't go into the camps as Nazis, it's how they may well come out."

Marie puffed herself up to deliver another comment.

"Do not blame the girls," Ursula said. "They have no way to know. They mean no disrespect."

"No, we didn't," Helen said. Teresa nodded agreement.

"Now, come, Marie," Ursula said. "We go check *Herr* turkey, and you lend me your magic hand with the gravy, *ja?*"

Marie's gravy drew high praise all around, one of the soldiers going so far as to say it rivaled his mother's. In deference to the soldiers, Emilie had added sweet potatoes to the menu. Usually, the side dishes were the same ones Ursula's mother had served: stuffing from the bird, potato salad, green beans, and carrots. An immigrant, she'd been unfamiliar with sweet potatoes and pumpkins, and had merely shifted the October harvest meal of *Ertendanktag* to her American Thanksgiving table. The Schneiders had been saving up sugar for weeks for the crumb-top apple pies. Marie had brought plum cake. With coffee now being rationed, she'd also brought some of that.

Inevitably, by dessert, the conversation had worked around to war news. New American troops were finally seeing action, three large task forces having landed in early November in

North Africa. Lloyd Mackey was there with the First Infantry. Marines, pounded by torrential rains, were still fighting bitterly on Guadalcanal. They hadn't been able to go on the offensive yet, but they'd held Bloody Ridge. Both sides knew that the victor at Guadalcanal would likely be the victor in the Pacific overall. In the waters surrounding Guadalcanal, American and Japanese warships had clashed again and again, with many sinkings. The cruiser *Juneau* had gone down only two weeks ago, taking with it 690 of its 700 men, including the five Sullivan brothers from Iowa, whom everyone knew from news stories about their patriotism in signing up together. But at the Schneiders' Thanksgiving table, talk centered on Europe.

"I'm no general," Private Horn asserted in his Minnesota accent, "but attacking across the English Channel still seems like a better idea than heading to Germany through Greece or Italy, like Churchill wants."

"There are generals who agree with you," Walter said. "But we won't have men and supplies enough for a Channel crossing for at least a year, and the British don't want to wait."

"We're going to have to cross the Channel some time," Private Horn repeated. "And with troops in North Africa now, it'll take even longer to build up for it."

"I have a friend in the Women's Auxiliary Corps," Helen said. "She said they're rushing WAAC training so more men can go to combat units and the invasion won't have to be delayed too long."

"That'll help," Private Horn said. "The Army's expanding so fast right now, some of us had to train with wooden rifles, and we still haven't been issued winter uniforms."

"I say we ought to beat the Japs first, put all our muscle in the Pacific," Private Ryder said. "Before they can get even stronger." Ryder was from Chicago, with the hard instincts of a city boy. "After we whip Tojo, we can concentrate on licking Hitler."

"Well, the Navy's certainly working on that," Emilie said.

Helen thought of the boys mentioned at her graduation who'd been lost in the Pacific. Unlike the Sullivans, they'd gone unheralded to war. Of course, someone knew them. The name of every person killed was being cherished by someone somewhere. At least, she hoped that was so.

"But why pick North Africa for our first fight against the Nazis?" Terence asked.

"The English, as usual, are worried about their colonies," Franz said. "They're afraid Rommel will capture Suez."

"There's Stalin, too," Emilie added. "Wasn't there some worry that he might pull out of the alliance if the British and Americans didn't move against German forces soon? To draw some of them away from Russia?"

"All those things are true," Walter said, "but I think that Roosevelt simply wanted to get into the thick of things quickly. He's trying to keep up morale. For the troops and for the folks at home."

"Keep up morale?" Marie scoffed. "How does men dying keep up morale?"

"Marie!" Walter said sternly, casting apologetic looks at the two soldiers. Camp Kilmer was a staging area. Men stationed there were on their way overseas.

"Fighting keeps up morale, ma'am," Private Ryder said. "Waiting and doing nothing doesn't."

"I'm sorry," Marie stammered, blushing furiously. "I didn't mean that either of you might . . ." She nervously picked up and put down her teaspoon, making a loud clink on the saucer. "And on top of everything, we can't even find out what's happening to our friends in . . . in Europe . . . or whether any of them are . . ."

"No offense taken, ma'am," Private Horn said. "We know the risks. I believe we're ready for 'em."

"I think you're both very brave," Teresa said admiringly.

Private Ryder laughed. "I was drafted," he said.

"I still think you're brave," Teresa insisted.

"Isn't it kinda exciting, too?" Terence asked. "Risks and all?"

The soldiers exchanged glances.

"Sure," Private Horn said.

"Don't get me wrong," Private Ryder said. "Just because I was drafted doesn't mean I'm not gonna give it everything I've got. And I plan on coming home, too. Promised my little brother I'd bring him a Luger."

At the word "home," it hit Helen that the two soldiers would, indeed, survive. She turned to the pimply young Chicagoan sitting beside her.

"I'm sure you'll do just that," she said. Glancing across the table at Private Horn, she added, "I know you're both coming home."

Walter cast a quick glance at Emilie, who pushed her chair back from the table.

"Helen," she said brightly, "why don't you and your cousins show our guests the river? Cold air is good for the digestion."

"But we were gonna go see that new picture, *Casablanca*. It's opening at the Oritani," Terence said.

"There is time for that, too," Ursula told him.

"Care to walk with the young folks, Franz?" Walter suggested. "When we get back, we may even find room for another piece of pie."

Franz assented, and everyone was set in motion, either getting coats or clearing the table. Ursula drew Helen into the empty living room.

"You saw, didn't you, Helen?"

"No. I just knew. But it came too fast, Nanny, to block it out."

"I don't complain about that. I only worry for you to have pain from this."

Helen didn't reply. Pain was unavoidable, wasn't it?

"It is lonesome," Ursula went on. "I cannot do all that you can, and still people stand back from me, afraid I will read their minds, find their secrets." She gave a little laugh. "Even though they tell me themselves sometimes the confessions."

It was the closest Helen had ever heard her grandmother come to asking for sympathy.

"Now, I make a confession," Ursula said. "I had, once, envy of your gift. Not anymore. But it made me, perhaps, not always the best guide for you."

"Oh, Nanny, don't say that."

Terence, dressed for outdoors, appeared in the doorway to the hall.

"Aren't you coming, Helen?" he demanded.

Helen was reluctant to leave her grandmother.

"Go," Ursula said. "I am done."

CHAPTER 26
JANUARY 1943

Helen's séances were getting crowded. She didn't like doing more than two a week, because the whole next day, she'd be listless, as if she'd just come off a fever. The effect was the same with two sitters or twelve, so to meet demand, she convinced Emilie to schedule up to a dozen clients at a time. With a larger group, more spirits came. Sometimes Iris had to act as referee, directing spirits to step forward or back, to speak or to wait.

The larger numbers of sitters and spirits seemed to create a magnetic force that drew in spirits whom no one at the table had sought. Helen's boys remained chief among these uninvited visitors, but other spirits were appearing as well, soldiers and non-soldiers, newly dead and long-dead. There was always a connection to someone in the circle. So far, no dwellers had shown up, and Helen was relying on Iris to block any that might try. But though they weren't dwellers, nor any other kind of troublesome spirit, the interlopers invariably caused a commotion, simply because they were interlopers.

The first had been the worst. After that, Emilie expanded her warnings to clients. She'd always prepared them for disappointment by saying that there was no way to command spirit communication. Now she also told them they might hear from people they hadn't expected, and that Helen couldn't control that, either.

The first one had come just before Christmas. Helen had found the spirits of four young men for their relatives, when another figure moved forward from behind Iris and silently stood, wearing overalls and twisting a soft, black cloth item in his hands. He didn't speak, but stray words came to Helen that were definitely from him.

"I'm getting the name Tim," she said, keeping her eyes closed to better study the spirit.

No one had asked to contact a Tim.

"He's got something black in his hands. A wool beret."

"Does this have meaning for anyone?" Emilie asked.

There was no reply, though Emilie told Helen later that Mrs. Knudsen, who'd come about her husband, killed on Bataan, hadn't looked around quizzically like the other sitters, but had remained fixed on Helen. The difference in the young widow was so slight that Emilie didn't realize she'd seen it until later, after Mrs. Knudsen started screaming.

"He's looking for a little girl, a little girl with a big pink bow in her hair and a white dress with a pink sash. He wants her to know it wasn't her fault."

Mrs. Knudsen began to whimper. Helen opened her eyes and looked directly at her.

"I was wrong," she said. "It's not Tim. It's Tom. Thomas. I was wrong."

That was when Mrs. Knudsen had screamed.

"Daddy! Daddy!" she cried, leaping up and reaching across the table in an attempt to grab Helen. Luckily, it was too far. Emilie moved quickly to the woman, taking hold of her arm. A man on her other side did the same.

"What are you doing?" she yelled at Helen. "I didn't ask for him. Not him. Of course it wasn't my fault. Everyone said so. Everyone."

She began to cry then, which made her more docile. Emilie and the man easily led her out of the room. Ursula took Helen, shaking, into the kitchen.

The next day, Mrs. Knudsen had come to apologize and to tell her story. Thomas was her father, who'd fallen off a roof to his death just at the moment she, a little girl, had rounded the corner of the house and called up to him so that he could admire her new white dress. He hadn't spoken to her for three days prior to this, as punishment for some childish infraction, a punishment she felt much more keenly than she would have a spanking, for she was his favorite child and she adored him.

His last words, spoken to his wife, were "I was wrong." The wife thought he meant he should never have gone onto the roof, because of his clubfoot. She'd wanted to hire someone to make the roof repairs. They'd quarreled about it. Mrs. Knudsen had hoped her father's dying words meant he was sorry that during their last three days together he'd been silent. But she could never be certain, just as she could never be certain that if she hadn't called to him, he wouldn't have turned so quickly, he wouldn't have slipped.

"Until now," she said gratefully to Helen.

Word got around about the incident with Mrs. Knudsen's father. Other similar incidents occurred, though thanks to Emilie's precautions, with less spectacular reactions, and word got around about them, too. There was pressure on Helen to add a third séance to her weekly schedule. But word had also gotten to certain parties who wanted Helen's activities to diminish rather than increase. This pressure was substantial and official, and it was delivered to Helen through Captain John Fitzpatrick.

They had just finished supper one icy January evening when the doorbell rang. When Walter opened it, he was surprised to find an Army officer standing there.

"Captain John Fitzpatrick," the man said before Walter had recovered enough from his surprise to speak.

"Yes?"

"Is this the residence of Miss Helen Schneider and Mrs.

Oskar Hauser?"

"Yes, it is."

"May I come in?"

"Certainly. Forgive me." Walter stepped back to let the captain enter.

Emilie had come into the hall by then. She took the man's overcoat and hat and gloves. He kept hold of a flat leather case. Walter sent her to fetch Helen and Ursula while he ushered the captain into the living room. Behind their visitor's back, Emilie threw Walter a questioning look. He responded with a mystified shrug.

"I'll come right to the point," Captain Fitzpatrick said after everyone was assembled. "And let you get on with your evening." He flashed a charming smile.

"We've had reports of certain activities that concern us. Meetings, shall we say, at which you, Mrs. Hauser, and you, Miss Schneider, have provided citizens with information that is best left to our government to supply when and how it sees fit."

"Information?" Walter said.

"Information, sir, about servicemen missing in action."

"You mean the séances?" Emilie asked. "But those people already know what's happened to their sons and husbands. They come to us to contact them."

The captain pursed his lips.

"A discussion of fraud is beyond the scope of my orders," he said curtly, all trappings of charm gone. "I am here to ask you to refrain from giving people details not already in their possession. Where a death occurred, how, when. Even if you're just guessing. Such details could compromise the safety of men still in the field. It's everyone's duty to avoid any action or conversation that might do that."

"Fraud?" Ursula said testily.

"Contacting the dead, Mrs. Hauser?" Captain Fitzpatrick said.

"Just so," Ursula replied.

"Believe what you like, ma'am. But when you trade on the desperate hopes of the bereaved, when you take money under false pretenses, there's a good case for fraud. And if you refuse to cooperate, we will see that the civil authorities pursue one."

"It is only contributions we take," Ursula said, taken aback. "And my granddaughter spends hers for the war bonds."

"I might add, Mrs. Hauser, that as a citizen of an enemy nation, you would place yourself in a highly questionable position were you to continue your activities after the Army of the United States has specifically requested you to desist."

Helen's heart leapt. Did he mean Nanny could be sent to a camp? She reached over and took her grandmother's hand. The old woman, uncharacteristically, didn't brush her away.

"I don't think threats are called for, Captain," Walter said. "My mother-in-law's been in this country forty years. It's her home. This is where her loyalty lies."

"I'm here to present facts, sir, that's all. And to appeal to the good sense and patriotism of these ladies. Of all of you."

The captain unzipped his leather case and took out some papers.

"In truth, Mr. Schneider, it's your daughter we've heard more about."

Helen's heart skipped.

"Heard about?" Emilie said.

"On three occasions," the captain said, skimming over his papers, "relatives of servicemen have come to us requesting confirmation of information they obtained from Miss Schneider. Two had questions about details of locale. And one . . ." He looked up and stared directly at Helen. "One mother wanted to know if it was true her son's ship had gone down with all hands.

The Navy hadn't notified her. There'd been nothing in the newspapers. Seaman Joseph Fellini."

Helen remembered him. He'd been one of the interlopers. Mrs. Fellini had been attending the séance as companion to a friend. She had sobbed at the unexpected news of her son, though she said she'd already felt in her heart he was gone.

"How did you know about Seaman Fellini, Miss Schneider? Who told you about his ship?"

"He was all wet," Helen said. "He was standing there all wet. A ship's name was stitched on his shirt. His lips were blue, and—"

"That's enough, Helen," Walter interrupted. "What, exactly, is it you require, Captain?"

"As I said, we want no supplementary or augmenting information provided to anyone on the condition, location, or demise of any serviceman." He looked pointedly at Ursula. "No matter what the source."

He turned his gaze to Walter. "My personal advice would be for all such meetings to stop for the duration."

The captain put away his papers and stood up to go. Walter and Emilie also rose, Emilie exiting to retrieve the captain's outerwear.

"Out of curiosity," Walter said, "is the Army making this request of all mediums?"

"Yes, sir, we are. Even those who practice as part of their religion. The safety of our servicemen and the security of our military plans is of the highest priority."

"Naturally," Walter said.

"I hope you mean that."

"I'm not accustomed, Captain, to having my sincerity doubted."

"Doubting is part of my job. So is keeping an ear to the

ground and a nose to the wind. Fair warning, Mr. Schneider."

After Captain Fitzpatrick's visit, Ursula decided to cut back to one séance a month, with only her home circle in attendance. Walter and Emilie wanted Helen to quit altogether. Helen herself was of two minds about the situation. She didn't want to do anything that might put soldiers at risk, nor did she want to endanger her grandmother's freedom. But she knew she had a unique ability to comfort grieving people, and it seemed wrong to turn her back on them. She'd be turning her back on the spirits, too. Her grandmother told her they wouldn't hold it against her, that they were beyond such thoughts, and that, in any case, if they really wanted to communicate with the living, they'd find other avenues. But Helen still felt she'd be abandoning them. The spirits were teachers. They could benefit more people than just their own relatives. What good was a teacher without a class?

In the end, Helen reached a compromise with her parents. She'd do only one séance a week. Emilie and Ursula would carefully question sitters to see what they knew about the deaths of the men they were trying to contact. If Helen picked up any extra information, she would not announce it. The interlopers would be disappointed, and Helen regretted that, but it couldn't be helped.

She'd conducted one séance so far under the new arrangements, and she'd had to ignore one uninvited spirit, a pilot so new to the spirit world, odors of gasoline and smoke still clung to his uniform. She didn't completely ignore him. She listened patiently to his story and to his request that she comfort his sister, who was at the séance to contact a cousin lost at Pearl Harbor. But she didn't tell the sister or anyone else about him. She felt glutted with the force of him, as if she'd eaten his story and his wishes.

211

She didn't complain. The war was making demands on everyone. Some responsibilities and burdens were met openly, some privately. Helen wished Rosie were still around. With Rosie, she could show her feelings and not be squeezed to explain herself. And Rosie was bound to come up with some way to lighten Helen's mood, whether by dragging out their bicycles for a spin, or getting Helen to sing rounds with her, or making a contest of skipping rocks at the river. Helen tried to think like Rosie and then carry out the suggestions her friend might have made. It helped, but she still missed her.

Rosie was on her way to Algiers with the 149th Post Headquarters Company. She'd taken secretarial training, with a specialty in code transcription. The last letter Helen had gotten from her had been in December, from Daytona Beach, Florida, where she was finishing up her training. Helen had smiled to see that in a few months, the Army had succeeded where twelve years of schooling had failed. Rosie's letter was still smudgy, but this time it sported paragraphs and margins.

Dear Helen:

I can't stop saying how proud I am to be a WAAC. Not because there's anything so special about me, but because of the great gals around me. It looks like a bunch of us are finally going to get to really test our wings. Here's how it happened, and the story will tell you more about this outfit than any more crowing I could do.

Rumor was that Lieutenant General Eisenhower had asked for some WAACs for North Africa. Director Hobby called us all together and told us she wouldn't order anyone into a combat area. Since we're not part of the Regular Army, we have no military status. That means no protection if we're captured, no hospital benefits or disability allowance if we're hurt, and no death benefits. That's why she wouldn't order us. But, Helen, out of the 300 WAACs here, 298 stood up and volunteered. I'm sure I don't have to tell you I was one of them. Director Hobby got so emotional, she had to duck into a broom closet so she wouldn't cry in front of us. They never tell you a WAAC isn't supposed to cry. Not even any of the male instructors we had at basic said it, but you just know, or you know at least you should hide it. Anyway, half of us are going to Eisenhower. The other half will have to keep waiting for authorization from the European theater.

You've probably heard the bad things people say about WAACs. Some soldiers won't even let their sisters or wives be friends with a WAAC. Recruitment's down, which is a shame because we're just beginning to show how we can make a difference in this war. I know you wouldn't ever believe bad things about me because you're my friend. But don't believe them about any of us, okay? People just don't like someone trying to do new things, I guess. They don't like it that maybe they'll have to try new things, too. Director Hobby's still fighting to get us into the Army. Maybe if that happens, it'll help. Meanwhile, there's a job for us— 239 kinds of jobs, if you believe the recruiting posters— and we're going to do them all.

Fond regards, Rosie

Doing a job was one of the things people had against the WAACs. In towns near burgeoning Army bases, civilians feared they'd lose their new jobs to WAACs. Plus, the families of some soldiers, and some soldiers themselves, were none too anxious to have a WAAC free them up for combat duty.

But the worst of the "bad things" were accusations that WAACs were prostitutes and that half of them had already been sent home pregnant. A Washington columnist had written that there was a secret Army policy to supply all WAACs with prophylactics. The Army and the President and even Mrs. Roosevelt hotly denied this, and the columnist had to run a retraction, but suspicions about the morals of WAACs persisted among many people.

Helen suspected that Rosie's assessment was correct. People simply didn't like new ideas. Especially the soldiers far from home, living with danger and dirt and discomfort, like you read about in the columns by Ernie Pyle and John Steinbeck. Helen imagined those soldiers must want fiercely to believe that home was just as they'd left it, that people and routines were poised to readmit them with open arms, that places were being saved for them, at dinner tables and firesides, in offices and factories, in hearts.

Home was a front, too. The battle here, Helen thought, is to hold things steady, to stand by. It was a lot of what the WAACs were doing, actually, all over the country. It was what they'd do behind the lines overseas. It's what I've got to do, she thought.

CHAPTER 27
FEBRUARY 1943

"They're not very pretty," Billy said, staring at Helen's feet in a pair of brown oxfords.

"I know," she said mournfully. "But I need practical shoes that'll last."

"Take a turn outside," the salesgirl suggested. "You'll find they're very comfortable."

When Helen came back from walking up and down the sidewalk to be sure the oxfords didn't pinch, Billy was holding a black sling-backed pump trimmed with a flat grosgrain ribbon bow.

"How about this?" he said.

Helen turned the shoe over in her hands, then put it down.

"Very nice," she said, "but I can't use my shoe ration on high heels."

"You're allowed three pairs of shoes a year."

"I wouldn't get enough use out of them," she said, shaking her head.

"What if something special comes up? Then you might wish you had some fancy new shoes."

"Like what?"

"Like . . . like a party. Or a wedding."

"Who's getting married?"

"Nobody. It was just a for-instance."

Billy said nothing else as she paid for the shoes and gave the salesgirl her ration stamp. He remained quiet as they walked down to Millie's Corner Café, except for a few murmured assents to Helen's comments on the window displays they were passing. Seated in the café, he seemed nervous. He kept glancing around the room, turning back to Helen when she spoke, but not appreciably furthering the conversation.

"Looking for someone?" she finally asked.

"Huh?"

"Are you looking for someone?"

"Oh. No. I'm only . . . well, I'm having a hard time looking at you is all." He smiled at her. "Wow, that sure came out wrong, didn't it?"

Helen laughed. "Maybe I need those pretty shoes more than I thought."

"C'mon, Helen, you know I think you're a dish."

The waitress arrived with their hot chocolates and a grilled cheese sandwich they were going to share.

"I don't mind being reminded," Helen said when the waitress had left.

Helen blew on her hot chocolate and took a sip. Billy bit into one triangle of the sandwich and chewed slowly. He swallowed with apparent effort.

"I've enlisted," he blurted out. "Army Air Force. I leave for basic day after tomorrow."

"What?" Helen cried. "But you've got a deferment."

"I don't want it," Billy said fiercely. "I never wanted it. I kidded myself it was okay—the battlefield of the assembly line, like the radio's always saying—but it's not, Helen, it's really not. Lloyd's in it and most of the guys from my class, even some of our old teachers. And I'm still here at home like some kind of cripple. Or a coward." He put both his hands flat on the table. "Besides, the draft's started taking ordnance workers. I'd rather enlist and get some choice."

Helen put down the sandwich triangle she'd picked up just

before Billy began speaking. She felt sick to her stomach.

"Why didn't you tell me?"

"I *am* telling you."

"But why not sooner? The day after tomorrow. Oh, Billy." She felt tears coming, but she didn't want them, and she was sure he didn't want them even more. She pushed them back.

"It's better this way. Quick. Besides, it'll be months before I'm really gone. Over there, I mean."

Helen nodded, afraid she'd crumble if she tried to say anything. Sitting across from her, Billy looked so solid and familiar, she couldn't imagine that in one more day he'd be out of sight and out of reach of her hands for years. Though the war was beginning to shift, ever so laboriously, in favor of the Allies, anyone could see that a long road lay ahead, a long, rutted, agonizingly unpredictable road. Despite the songs and the movies, despite the cheery slogans and the boosterish posters, people had stopped expecting their men to come back soon. Everyone was digging in. Endurance was being tested at home as well as on the fields of combat.

Helen stood up and took her coat off the back of her chair. She wanted to flee the complacent noise and bustle of the busy café. How could everyone remain so ordinary on this extraordinary day? How could they continue to eat and babble and titter inanely as if nothing had happened? If she stayed one more minute in this indifferent place, she might begin tipping over tables.

"Let's get out of here," she said.

Billy put a dollar bill on the table. They left the café and turned immediately off Main Street onto Elm Avenue. Instinctively, they were heading for Brinker's Green. There'd be skaters on the pond, but Oratam Beach was likely to be deserted in the biting February air. Empty, open, harsh, it was the only suitable territory right now.

Beyond a fringe of gunmetal ice near shore, the river was blue-black, its surface glinting with tiny riffles when gusts of wind passed over it. Helen and Billy aimed for the farthest bench, where woods bordered the beach. But before they reached the sheltered spot, Billy grabbed Helen and they embraced, kissing each other ardently again and again. Some of the kisses actually hurt, but Helen didn't care. The roughness underlined their passion, in this frenzied moment and in all the sweet moments of their past. It was a protest against the void ahead.

They unbuttoned their coats, and Billy slipped his arms around Helen's waist as she nuzzled against his warm, hard chest. Helen felt as if they were the only living beings in the world.

"I'm sorry I didn't tell you before," Billy said. "I really thought it'd make it easier."

"It doesn't matter now."

"Well, it kind of does. To me."

Helen lifted her head and looked at him.

"Why?"

"It doesn't leave much time." He pulled away from her a little. "Gosh, Helen, I'm a deluxe dunderhead. I didn't think I'd feel so . . . I figured I'd wait, you know, until . . ."

"What are you talking about?"

"Helen, will you marry me? Right now?"

Helen was flabbergasted. She knew that lots of couples were making hasty marriages, and of course she'd thought before of marrying Billy. At times she'd even assumed it was predestined, though they'd never discussed it. She knew, too, that she was willing to wait for him, even with no guarantees of what would happen once he returned. Despite all that, she had, incredibly, never considered marriage as a full-blooded reality. She wouldn't hesitate to pledge to marry him, but to actually do it right away? Could she make that leap of faith?

"Billy, I—"

"Some folks would say it's not fair of me to pin you down when I don't know if I'm coming back or what banged-up shape I might end up in—"

She put her fingers to his lips. She didn't need reminding of the risks he was engaging, and she couldn't bear to hear them put forth so bluntly. She wished she knew some charm to protect him, or some trick for stopping the forward movement of time or for forcing it to make a grand jeté over the years of war into what had to be the sunny, sane days after. Lacking such powers, she was left only with the opportunity to link her fate to his. Maybe that would be charm enough.

"Yes, Billy. Yes, I'll marry you."

He clasped her to him as if he'd never let go.

The next day was Wednesday. They'd planned to take the bus to Elkton, Maryland, very early that morning. There was no waiting period after getting a marriage license there. They'd told their parents they were going to spend the day in New York and wouldn't be home until late in the evening. Everyone understood them wanting to have as much time together as possible. Thursday morning had been set aside for Billy's family. Thursday at noon he was leaving for boot camp.

Helen insisted they had to tell their news as soon as they returned from Elkton. Billy had agreed, but fearing one or the other of the two families would insist the couple stay the night with them, he'd already reserved a room at the Paper Mill Inn in Bogota. He was damned, he said, if he was going to spend his first night of married life within earshot of either his mother or Helen's father.

Helen got up at dawn. Snow was falling heavily, in big, wet flakes. By the looks of it, it had been snowing for hours. It would take extra time to walk to the bus station.

She slipped quietly out the kitchen door. She hadn't eaten breakfast. She didn't want to make noises that might rouse someone. Besides, she didn't feel like she deserved breakfast. She felt rather like a thief. But what was she stealing? Herself? What an absurd notion. Her family's trust? That was closer to it. But she wasn't stealing their trust so much as trading on it. They'd be hurt by her elopement, shocked maybe, and apprehensive for her, but they wouldn't disown her or even, probably, admonish her.

"It's the war," she'd say if she had to. Or they'd say it to one another. And go on. Just like everyone else. Still, she was sorry to be deceiving them, even for a short while. She wished she and Billy weren't starting out on such a footing. Her mother, especially, would be stung by her secrecy. But the duties of a daughter were not her only ones now. Now she was going to be a wife.

Billy was waiting for her in front of his house. From the snow accumulated on his shoulders and cap, he must have been waiting for a while.

"Good morning, Mrs. Mackey," he said playfully.

"Mrs. Mackey. That's your mother."

"Not for long."

"It still sounds strange."

He took her mittened hand in his and they started trudging through the soft snow, which was drifted nearly to their knees in places. Helen was glad she'd tucked her wool slacks into her galoshes. She was carrying a tote bag containing a beige rayon dress and the blue slip, an old pair of beige heels, and a bottle of leg make-up. She hadn't had silk stockings since the summer before Pearl Harbor, and her last pair of nylons had torn months ago.

"Before I went to sleep last night," Billy said, "I practiced saying *I'd like you to meet my wife, Helen*. Got so it sounded pretty good, I thought. But you're right about Mrs. Mackey. That's gonna take some getting used to."

By the time they reached the bus station, they'd each slipped and fallen once, yielding more laughter than pain, and they'd begun to feel they were off on a real adventure.

The station waiting room was crowded—several young women, an old man or two, and a good number of soldiers, some slumped in chairs asleep, a trio of them in a corner playing cards. Helen and Billy stomped the snow off their feet and went to the ticket window to purchase their fares.

"Better wait, son, to get your tickets," the clerk told Billy. "No buses running, and can't say for sure when they'll be cleared to go. May not run at all today. Especially going south. Weather's worse to the south."

"How about buses into New York?" Billy asked the man. To Helen, he said, "We could take a train to Maryland."

The man shook his head. "Might get over to the City later, but not now. Anyways, I hear the trains are stalled, too."

Sobered, Helen and Billy found seats facing the plateglass window. The sky was lighter than when they'd set out, but the snow showed no signs of letting up.

"What should we do?" Billy said.

"We'll have to wait."

They piled their hats, mittens, gloves, and scarves on an empty chair. They opened their coats, but left them on. Like most public places, the station was unheated because of the fuel shortage. To save on heating, schools were open only two hours a day, and restaurants were closed at night.

An hour later, the snowstorm had thickened. The few cars struggling down the street had their headlights on. Because the upper half of the headlamps had been painted black as a precaution against air raids, they shone only on those snow flurries close to the ground, but these were sharply illuminated, spinning thickly in mad whorls.

Billy ran his fingers through his hair and sighed. "Let's not spend the day here, okay? Us not getting to Elkton doesn't mean I won't still be leaving tomorrow."

It was a relief to get outside. The crowded waiting room had seemed to grow noisier and smaller as their chances of leaving town grew dimmer.

"Now what?" Billy said.

"I haven't had breakfast."

"Okay, there's a start. Let's head over to Millie's."

They had walked one block, faces lowered against the wind, when Billy stopped. "Gee, I should cancel our room at the inn. I think I can get my money back if I let them know before noon." He did an about-face. "There's a phone at the bus station."

"Wait," Helen said. "Why don't we walk to the inn after breakfast? It's a hike, I know, but we're bundled up good, and we can surely get there by noon. The snow really is lovely."

"Yeah, if you like disasters," Billy said. "But what else have we got to do, right? Okay, my lady, a hike through the lovely snow it is. On one condition."

"What's that?"

"That you marry me when I get leave after basic."

Helen smiled at him. "With pleasure."

When they got to the inn, they were wet and cold, but the long walk had been cheering, and they felt exhilarated. The desk clerk was busy with someone, so Helen and Billy decided to lounge a while in front of the fireplace in the sitting room off the lobby before conducting their business. The room was paneled in dark wood and furnished with large, overstuffed chairs. The fire was blazing. A big bowl of chrysanthemums on a piano in the corner added a touch of luxury. The brocade drapes on a wide bay window had been pulled open to showcase the snow-laden pines and yew shrubs on the sloping white lawn.

"Let's stay here forever," Helen joked, holding her hands out to the fire.

"You look beautiful," Billy said, regarding her appreciatively. "Like you're shining."

"I feel beautiful," she answered quietly.

They settled back in their chairs and watched the flames play over the thick logs. An inn guest came in and asked if they'd mind if she played the piano. A Chopin tune was soon coiling through the warm room.

"Helen," Billy said, leaning toward her and whispering beneath the music, "we can't stay forever, but we can spend the afternoon. We have a room."

His long-known, beloved face stood open to her, full of desire and trepidation. She saw that however she answered would be all right. The intention that had brought them out into the storm early that morning had been the big step, the real answer. All the rest of it was simply timing.

"I know we're supposed to make our promises in front of a preacher," Billy continued, "but even in a church full of people, it's the two of us talking right at each other that holds the meaning." He took her left hand in his and stared into her eyes. "I take you for my lawful wife, through thick and thin, war and peace—"

"I take you for my lawful husband," Helen interrupted, "through thick and thin, hard and easy . . . sunshine and snow."

They managed to smile at each other, then he squeezed her hand and went to check in.

Helen, her heart and gut fluttering, tried to concentrate on the dancing notes of the piano piece, but it was no use. She picked up Billy's cap and gloves and held them against her face.

She closed her eyes and did what she'd sworn to herself last night she would never do. She tried to sense whether Billy was going to his death. She was flooded with images—Billy leaning on the fence between their yards, Billy absorbed in trimming tiny pieces of balsa wood for a model plane, Billy swimming in the river, his muscular arms and shoulders rising rhythmically out of the water—but these were memories. She called to Iris. But for the first time ever, Iris didn't come. Helen put down the cap and gloves.

She was glad she couldn't discover anything about Billy, relieved that prophecy wouldn't be pouncing on her. She'd have to live like any other war bride, waiting, writing letters, praying. It made their relationship more honest somehow, and more their own. He'd be glad to know that their future was out of her ken, but he wouldn't like it that she'd tried to find out. But she wasn't going to tell him. Honesty was not a coin to be spent indiscriminately.

She wore the blue slip. And although he laughed at her for it, she kept on her socks because her feet were still cold. They took their time. They touched each other in all the delicious ways they already knew before they flourished into the new way. It hurt some. When Helen cried out, Billy stopped moving and raised up on his elbows to peer questioningly into her face. She lifted her pelvis to him, and he continued slowly, but soon, lost to his hunger, he increased his tempo. She rode the pain rather than stop him again. When he'd finished, he lay beside her kissing her neck and stroking between her legs until splendid pleasure drenched her soreness and she cried out once more, this time in happy triumph.

It was wonderful to have a bed. They fell asleep in each other's arms, woke up, made love again. Helen's climax that time came while Billy was still inside her, and she felt like singing, it was such a magnificent surprise. Billy went out to get them some food. Helen bathed and wrapped herself in a blanket and stood at the window studying the late-afternoon shadows on the fallen snow. It had finally stopped coming down. They ate tuna salad sandwiches and drank vanilla malteds sitting cross-legged in the center of the wide, tousled bed; made lazy, almost lackadaisical love once more; and dressed to go home. It was seven o'clock.

"So, first, we'll tell your folks we're engaged, then mine," Helen said, reviewing their plan, "because my mother will have lots of questions about wedding plans. She'll want a church ceremony, but with us not knowing just when your leave is, she'll have to settle for having it at home."

"You sure that's all right with you?"

"Yes, I told you. Besides, we've already had the wedding that counts."

She was sitting on the edge of the bed pulling on her galoshes. He bent over and kissed her.

"You're the top," he said.

Helen stretched out her legs and wiggled her feet in the ugly galoshes.

"You know what?" she said. "I'm taking another ration stamp and I'm gonna get those black heels. A bride's supposed to wear something new."

"A bride's supposed to *be* new," Billy ribbed.

"Is that a complaint, mister?"

"No, ma'am! I'm a lucky guy. I get to have two wedding nights."

CHAPTER 28
JUNE 1943

After thirteen weeks of basic training at Camp Boardwalk, Billy was coming home this afternoon, Sunday. He and Helen were marrying tomorrow, then spending Tuesday together before he had to board a train to somewhere for further training.

Helen had considered going to Atlantic City for the wedding—she liked the idea of being at the seaside, even if some of the beaches were oily with spills from torpedoed tankers, and the famous boardwalk had become a drill field—but since the Army had commandeered all the hotels as barracks, only private homes were left as accommodations, and Emilie feared it would be too difficult to find enough rooms for the two families.

Helen's wedding suit had been ready for a month. It was of pale green linen, with black piping to match the black heels. Emilie had made it with the War Production Board's style dictates in mind. The rules applied to manufactured clothing—a man's suit could no longer include a vest, nor could there be cuffs on the pants, elbow patches on the jacket, or wide lapels; production of zoot suits was stopped; women's bathing suits must be two pieces, and skirts must end one inch above the knees. Emilie decided to ignore the hemline rule and cut Helen's skirt to a more modest length, but she thought that however else possible, a soldier's bride ought to follow the guidelines for conserving cloth. The suit was neatly tailored, and though it lacked soft flounces and pleats, it showed off Helen's figure prettily.

An hour before Helen was to meet Billy at the bus station, Ursula called her to her room.

"Yes, Nanny?" Helen said, a bit breathless from having run up the stairs. She'd been running all morning while helping her mother clean. Running felt like the only possible way to locomote today.

"Come in, Helen. I have something for you. For tomorrow."

She held out a square of black velvet on the palm of her hand. Helen took it and carefully unfolded it. Inside, she found a fat, teardrop-shaped pearl on a short gold chain.

"Nanny, your pearl!"

Helen knew the story of the pearl, a gift from Ursula's husband, Oskar, on their tenth anniversary, the only such gift he, or anyone, had ever given her. Helen had only seen Ursula wear it on special occasions, but Emilie had told her that until Oskar's funeral, she'd worn it every day.

"Yours now. For your wedding. And to keep."

"Oh, Nanny." Helen hugged her grandmother, then rushed to the mirror over the bureau and held it up to her neck. "It's beautiful. Thank you. Thank you so much."

Ursula stood behind the girl and viewed the lustrous pearl against her smooth, young skin.

"It is the right place for it," she said. "My Oskar would think so, too."

"Helen," Emilie called from downstairs. "Billy's on the phone."

"Oh, dear," Helen said, "I hope he hasn't missed his bus. There's not another one until tomorrow morning. And Reverend Wittig wanted to meet with us tonight."

She handed the pearl to Ursula and rushed out of the room.

Billy's news was worse than a missed bus. Helen kept her hand on the receiver after she'd hung up, immobilized for the first time in days.

"What is it?" Emilie asked, coming in the front door with a large pail of garden roses. From outside came the slicing sounds of Walter's push mower.

"Billy's going to radio school in South Dakota."

"Yes?" Emilie said, puzzled.

"He wants to fly, you know," Helen elaborated, tears beginning to gather, "but it didn't look like they were going to let him be a pilot, so when he heard about the radio operator training, he signed up, and he has to leave right away."

"Today?"

"This may be his only chance to get in the air, he said."

"But his leave . . . The wedding . . ."

"He's changing trains in New York. There's an hour and a half between. I'm going to go see him there."

Emilie put down the pail of roses and came forward, reaching for her, but Helen wiped her eyes and made a slight side step, and with those small signals held her mother off. Commiseration now would unhinge her.

"I'll have to hurry to get into the City in time," she said, starting up the stairs.

Emilie began to follow her, then seemed to think better of it. She turned and went to the open front door.

"I'm going to tell your father," she said. "He can drive you in. If an OPA investigator stops you to ask why your car trip is necessary, I'm sure seeing off a soldier will pass muster."

Helen smiled gratefully at her mother and hurried to her room to change. Ursula came to the doorway and stood watching her dash back and forth between the closet and the dresser, pulling out clothes, considering them, tossing them onto the bed.

"You will be all right," Ursula said, her intonation neither wholly question nor wholly statement.

"I will have to be," Helen said shakily.

She put on a polka-dot sundress with wide straps and a square neckline and turned to let her grandmother pull up the zipper in back. When she turned around again, Ursula was holding out the folded velvet square.

"Still, this is for you," she said.

"No, Nanny," Helen said. "That should wait until my real wedding day."

"You give your heart. That is real enough for me."

Ursula unwrapped the necklace and laid it on the bed on top of the short-sleeved jacket that matched the sundress. Helen stroked the pearl with one finger.

"So, I let you get finished," her grandmother said.

Helen picked up her hairbrush from the night table.

"One hundred strokes," Ursula advised as she left. "To make it shine."

"Yes, Nanny, I know."

The heat of summer had come to roost early. During the week after Helen saw Billy off to South Dakota, the temperature and humidity climbed steadily day by day, finally stagnating at a muggy eighty-five degrees. The air in the house was close, but the dining room, well shaded by a large tree and kept shadowy by blackout curtains, held onto some of the previous night's coolness. Nevertheless, Ursula brought in two electric fans for Helen's weekly séance. She didn't want anyone fainting.

Emilie was no longer attending Helen's séances because she'd become a volunteer in the Hospital and Recreation Corps of the Red Cross. Four afternoons a week she donned a long-sleeved gray dress with white collar and cuffs and the Red Cross insignia on the bodice, and traveled to Halloran General Hospital in Staten Island. She waited until she got there to put on the gray veil and her white stockings and white shoes, to keep them fresh. At the hospital, she chatted with homesick patients, arranged flowers, played Checkers and Bingo, wrote letters for men too injured to do it themselves, and assisted the Red Cross recreation workers in arts and crafts with patients.

Helen and Ursula were Red Cross volunteers, too, but Ursula didn't have the stamina for hospital work, and Helen was still leery of getting close to soldiers, even ones who'd been wounded badly enough to be sent home. Instead, Ursula knitted sweaters, socks, and watch caps from olive drab and navy blue wool, and Helen, who was a novice knitter, made toe socks for walking casts and caps for bandaged heads. These didn't have to meet as exact military standards as the items Ursula made, which were part of a uniform. Helen worked at the Red Cross center twice a week. She rolled bandages, did the paperwork on blood donors, assembled packages for American and Allied prisoners-of-war, and sewed the "Gift of the American People through the American Red Cross" labels into sweaters headed for European refugees. But Helen never went to the center on a séance day, nor the day after. Her séance work was as demanding on her energies as an athlete's exertions.

Ursula set the oscillating fan so that its breeze would blow across Helen's place at the table. She'd just finished arranging the fans when the first clients arrived, a couple her own age whose grandson's plane had been shot down over France as it was returning to England from a bombing raid in Germany. Other clients arrived soon after this couple, bringing the group to twelve, including Helen and Ursula and Mrs. Durkin, who had puffed up the three front steps red-faced and sweating. Ursula assigned the overweight, heat-afflicted woman the seat beside Helen so that she, too, could partake of the sweep of the oscillating fan.

As was the routine since their visit from Captain Fitzpatrick, Ursula interviewed the clients to find out what facts they pos-

sessed about the deaths of their loved ones. She had to turn away one young woman who'd come hoping to ascertain her husband's whereabouts and condition. The woman had had no official notification that he was missing.

Mrs. Durkin served everyone lemonade while Ursula went upstairs to brief Helen so that she'd know which information she picked up was corroborative and which was new.

The clients watched closely as Ursula escorted Helen to the table. Though Helen avoided meeting anyone's gaze, she was aware of the hunger burning in their eyes. Their hopes were as strong as a lover's desire. In some of them, Helen knew, doubt lurked, too, and in a very few, scorn. They wanted to know what she heard and what she saw, but they also didn't want to know. Because what if it were not enough? What if they left the séance more bereft than when they arrived? What if she told them something that cancelled out burnished memories and comforting fantasies? Helen understood that that was how they'd see it—that she had spoiled things, that she had let them down, that she had robbed them.

"We begin with Bible words," Ursula told the group. "T Lord has anointed me to bring good tidings to the afflicte has sent me to bind up the brokenhearted."

"Amen," said the grandfather of the boy shot d France.

"Now we will not speak more," Ursula said. "W

Helen, whose head had been bowed during lifted her face and laid her hands on the tabl She began to breathe deeply, entering a se she felt dreamily detached from everyone them clearly and would have heard ther ing.

Sitting very still, Helen thought the table. She noted bewilderment

231

they, too, felt it, or were their expressions merely the jitters of first-timers? The vibration came again, lasting longer this time, undeniable. One woman gasped and pulled her hands away.

Despite the stuffy room, Helen felt enveloped in lovely coolness. Her stomach began to ache dully. A soreness asserted itself at the back of her throat, and an odd pressure.

Helen opened her mouth. A thin, white substance floated out between her lips. In the shaded room, it was difficult to tell what the substance was, or even if it really existed. It would be easy for skeptical sitters to deny later they'd seen anything at all. But Helen knew it was real because it was stinging her lips. The emanation lasted only seconds and was gone. The small discomforts were gone, too, and in her disinterested state, Helen considered the whole occurrence no more than a curiosity. She continued to sit silent and immobile.

Then she noticed that everyone's attention was trained on the center of the table. There, on a crocheted doily, a pale vapor hovered, almost indistinguishable against the white lace. Gradually, the vapor thickened until it resembled a piece of crumpled cheesecloth. The folds of material were shifting into a distinct shape.

"Lord, bless us!" exclaimed Mrs. Durkin.

The woman who had gasped when she'd felt the table vibrate reached out toward the luminous form.

"Do not touch!" Ursula said loudly.

But it was too late. The woman's fingers grasped the white be. At the moment of contact, the object vanished, and Helen s if someone had punched her hard in the stomach. She out sharply in pain and doubled over in her chair. Over sy, gulping breaths, she heard people firing questions.

t did it feel like?"

it solid?"

cold. Cold and clammy."

"Was it alive?"

"Did it move?"

"*Kommen Sie heraus!* Get out! Go!" Ursula shouted.

"But there's been no reading," a man protested.

"You do not get a guarantee," Ursula replied angrily. "Mrs. Durkin, give who wants their money back."

Helen felt her grandmother's hands on her arms helping her to straighten up.

"Helen. *Liebling*," she said.

Helen looked around. The room was empty of people. She saw Mrs. Durkin in the hallway using her bulk to good advantage to herd the clients out the front door.

"What happened?"

"First, *you* must tell *me*," Ursula said.

Mrs. Durkin returned, and Ursula sent her to the kitchen to make Helen a strong glass of iced tea.

"Bring her, too, a splash of sherry."

"My stomach hurts," Helen said when Mrs. Durkin had left again.

She untucked her blouse from her skirt to inspect her stomach. There was a large red mark on her skin that looked like a burn, though it didn't smart like one.

Ursula nodded. "It was the ectoplasm returning all at once."

"Ectoplasm?"

"What did you feel at the beginning? It was maybe not the same as other times?"

Helen thought a moment.

"Quieter than usual for a light trance," she answered. "And like I couldn't move if I wanted to. Except that I didn't want to. It was nice to be so quiet. Then I felt cool over my whole body—"

"The fan," Ursula put in.

"No, I'd been feeling the fan all along, and this was different.

The cool air was all over my skin, even under my clothing. Then I felt a cramp in my belly and my throat got sore, and next a stinging on my mouth, like when you drink orange juice with chapped lips."

"You saw something?"

"A sort of smoke? Then pow, there was this pain in my stomach—like a blow. What happened, Nanny? Was it something bad?"

"Nothing bad. Something special. Something rare."

Mrs. Durkin came in with a tray. On it were a tall glass of iced tea and three small glasses of sherry.

"I thought it was called for," Mrs. Durkin said in response to Ursula's raised eyebrows. "It's not every day, after all, that such a thing . . . It's not every day."

"Our good *frau* has waited a long time for this," Ursula said to Helen.

"What do you mean?"

"You don't know?" Mrs. Durkin said. "We had a materialization today. A spirit hand. Right on this very table. It was wonderful, wonderful. Who knows what would have followed if that silly woman hadn't interfered. Oh, Helen, I'm proud to know you. Proud." She picked up a sherry and drained it in one gulp.

"You are on a new step now, Helen," Ursula said. "I would not be so surprised at it if your wedding had happened. Such life changes can give a medium more power. But you have gone ahead without the help of becoming a married woman."

Helen took a hefty swallow of sherry.

"You must sip," Ursula scolded gently. "You took so much your cheeks are flushed."

"I can't wait to tell the rest of our circle," Mrs. Durkin said.

"Yes, they will have the proper respect. But we must be even more careful now who comes to Helen's séances," Ursula said. "She can be very badly hurt if someone grabs like that again."

The two women went on to discuss how best to screen sitters, what physical conditions of the room might promote more materializations, other ways to protect Helen. Helen herself did not participate. She got up and raised one of the shades so that she could look out the window. She stood there nursing her iced tea. A new step. But towards what?

CHAPTER 29
JULY 1943

After the materialization of the hand, everyone in Ursula's home circle began attending Helen's séances. This left less room for strangers, which Walter judged a good thing. Emilie sat in on three séances in order to witness Helen's new ability, but when nothing happened despite Ursula's careful re-creation of the darkened conditions of the first materialization, Emilie resumed her hospital schedule.

Ursula said that physical signs like the hand were very rare because so many conditions had to be just right. Obviously, Helen was able to attain the necessary degree of receptivity. That was why her automatic writings were so profuse. But physical manifestations depended as much on the thoughts and conditions of the sitters as on the medium.

"One person in a circle can make a block," Ursula told Helen. "And all sitters must have enough chemicals and energy for the spirits to pull out and pass through you."

"And there's nothing I have to actually try to *do?*" Helen asked.

"Only to concentrate and be meek." Ursula looked speculatively at her. "It is a help, too, if you *want* for it to happen."

This was, in fact, the problem. Helen wasn't at all sure she wanted another materialization.

Except for the stab in her stomach, which had been the result of interference and not an intrinsic part of the phenomenon, the production of the hand had caused her no strain and only minor discomfort. In fact, after that séance she'd felt a cascade of vitality, which was very different from the enervation she was accustomed to. It was as if she'd been infused with something, rather than having had something drained from her. So there were no physical costs to give her pause.

It was the requisite giving over of her will that troubled her. She began to wonder why she had the abilities she did if she was to be denied control; why, beyond easing grief, spirits bothered to contact the living at all; why she should offer herself as an avenue for them, an avenue unimpeded by any personal traits or wishes. Where was *she* in all this?

Helen decided that for the time being she'd continue entering séances prepared to generate physical phenomena. But she was going to pay more careful attention to every aspect of the experience—her sensations and emotions; the reactions of the sitters; the roles, if any, of Iris and her boys. If a broader purpose existed for her gift, she was going to find it. If one did not, she would find that out. And then, she hoped, she'd know what to do, how to take hold of the reins.

Ever since her time with Billy at the inn, the future had assumed a more definite shape for Helen. In that one afternoon, the future had become real. She could picture herself in it. She could feel herself moving towards it. Whether her psychic abilities would have a place there or not must not be left to chance. Billy would have a hard enough time accepting her continued mediumship if it were well thought through and demonstrably worthwhile. She couldn't ask him to be tolerant of something she hadn't made an effort to comprehend fully herself. The time for coasting and letting her parents and grandmother determine what was best had come to an end. She was an adult now. Her afternoon with Billy said so. Even the spirits said so.

For wasn't that one way to interpret the astonishing arrival of the hand?

Helen sat at the picnic table in her backyard with letter-writing materials spread around her. She'd just folded a V-mail to Rosie, congratulating her on becoming regular Army. The "Auxiliary" designation had been dropped on July 3, when Congress passed the Women's Army Corps bill into law. WAAC members were given the choice of returning to civilian life or joining the Army. The newsreels said seventy-five percent of the women had chosen to join up. Helen didn't need to hear from Rosie to know she was one of them.

From next door came the flapping sound of wet sheets being shaken out. Above the fence, Helen could see Mrs. Mackey's hands and forearms as she hung out the washing.

Helen took up her pen and began a letter to Billy by describing this ordinary sight, the rhythm of his mother appearing and disappearing from view as she bent to take clothes out of her basket, the brightness of the sun on the top edges of the tautly pinned white sheets. Helen wrote to Billy daily, so her notes often contained such small scenes.

She wrote to Rosie twice a week, and once a week or so to Rosie's brother Owen and to Lloyd, all by V-mail. Because it was put on film and then reproduced at its destination, V-mail was more compact than a normal letter and so could be sent by plane, reducing by a whole month the length of time it took to get a letter overseas. Helen had read in a magazine article that 1,700 V-mails would fit in one cigarette pack.

Helen was also writing regularly to three soldiers she didn't know, having gotten their names from a list in the newspaper of young men who received little or no mail. She sometimes found it easier to write to them than to her friends. To the soldiers she'd never met, Helen wrote about the food and the band music at the Independence Day picnic at Brinker's Green; about the girls' club, Little Orphan Annie's Junior Commandos, scouring the town's alleys for scrap metal; and about the sheen of the full moon on the river. She could tell her friends, too, about these things, and she did, but she couldn't write about the thoughts and events that most engaged her, namely the séances and her struggle to understand their larger meaning. For one thing, she worried that there might be details from her séances that shouldn't be put into a letter going overseas. V-mail was less likely to be captured than letters that went by ship, but the possibility still existed, and letter-writers were constantly urged not to include any information that might be useful to the enemy. For another thing, letters to soldiers were not supposed to make them anxious about friends and family at home. Wives were admonished not to mention money problems or leaky roofs or babies with colds. Helen figured her dilemma fit the category of problems better left unrecorded.

But the main reason Helen did not write about her quandary was that she didn't quite know how. She'd never gone into real depth with her friends about her abilities, except when she and Billy had argued about the stories dictated by her boys. A letter to someone on or near a battlefield wasn't the place to start. Billy was still safe on American soil, but he was preparing every day for combat, and she just couldn't clutter his mind with her ponderings, still so maddeningly vague.

Helen finished her note to Billy and sealed it in an envelope. She'd planned to write to Rosie's other brother, Jimmy, today, but she was hanging back from the task. It was so tough to imagine what news might cheer up a POW. Sometimes, she wondered if the Red Cross even managed to get those letters through. From all she'd heard of Japanese soldiers, she found it hard to believe they'd extend themselves to bring comfort to their prisoners. She decided she'd write to Lloyd first and work up to Jimmy's letter. Maybe she'd tell Lloyd, too, about his mother hanging the laundry.

Just as that idea was crossing her mind, she heard Mrs. Mackey's voice raised in a loud wail. She rushed to the fence and peered over it. Mrs. Mackey was sitting on the ground, her upper body sprawled across her laundry basket, her fingers gripping its rim. Bending over her and trying to get her to stand up was an elderly man in a messenger's uniform. Helen raced down her driveway, around the end of the fence, and into the Mackeys' yard. The man turned a doleful face towards her and held out a Western Union telegram.

Regret to inform you your son Staff Sergeant Lloyd F. Mackey was seriously wounded in action tenth July in Sicily. Mail address follows direct from hospital with details.

July tenth. Nearly three weeks ago. Helen shoved the telegram into the pocket of her skirt and gently grasped Mrs. Mackey's shoulders.

"Come on, now, let's go inside," she coaxed.

Mrs. Mackey lifted her face from the mound of wet laundry. She seemed baffled at finding Helen there, but slowly she got to her feet.

"You'll take care of her, Miss?" the messenger asked, obviously anxious to leave.

"Yes. But there's no phone in her house. Her husband works at the Curtiss-Wright plant. Gerald Mackey. If you could get in touch with him? Or their daughter Barbara? She's there, too."

The man nodded. "Yes, all right. Yes, Miss, I can do that."

Helen made Mrs. Mackey lay down on the sofa. She brought a sheet from the linen closet and lay it over her.

"Lloyd, Lloyd," the woman kept whispering. "My Lloyd."

"Try not to let your imagination run away with you, Mrs. Mackey," Helen said, speaking as much to herself as to the

240

stunned woman. "You'll know more when you get the hospital report."

Helen stayed at the house until Mr. Mackey and Barbara got home. When they hurried in the back door, she was in the kitchen with Linda cutting her a slice of watermelon. Helen had thought it more important to stay with the anxious nine-year-old than to sit with the oblivious Mrs. Mackey. The girl, who'd been down the block at a friend's house, was almost as alarmed by finding her mother stretched out on the sofa in the middle of the day as by hearing the news about her brother. Mr. Mackey went straight in to his wife, and Barbara sat down at the table with Linda.

Helen gave Barbara the telegram. She read and reread it. She even turned it over, as if she expected more or different news on the back.

"Do you think it's good or bad we haven't heard anything more yet?" she said. "I mean, if he was . . . worse . . . or if he . . . They'd be quicker to get you really bad news, wouldn't they?"

"I don't know."

Barbara slid her fingertips over the adjutant general's name at the bottom of the telegram.

"Thank God you were here, Helen."

"I'm glad I was."

"All done," Linda said, sliding off her chair. She headed for the back door.

"Here, wipe your chin," Barbara said, holding out a dish towel. "You've got watermelon juice."

"I'm only gonna go sit on the swing."

Barbara continued to hold out the towel, so Linda came and took it from her. She wiped her mouth and chin and fingers, then held her face forward for her sister to inspect. Barbara pulled the child close in a sudden, tight embrace. Linda endured the entrapment for a few seconds, then wriggled free and ran outside, letting the screen door slam behind her. Barbara rose.

Helen had an impulse to squeeze Barbara's hand or stroke her back, but there was a precarious composure about the young woman that made Helen hesitate. She recalled wanting to avoid her mother's touch right after she'd heard from Billy that he was on his way to South Dakota.

"I should show my father this," Barbara said, holding up the telegram.

Helen nodded and turned to go.

"We may want to come over later to call Billy if that's all right."

"Of course."

Helen walked slowly back home and returned to the picnic table. She didn't want to go inside to her grandmother yet. She sat there thinking about Lloyd, remembering little things about him—the way his voice cracked when he was talking excitedly; his fierce, sweaty speed on the varsity basketball team; his hammy performance of "Lydia the Tattooed Lady" at the Fall Follies senior year.

"Stop it," she scolded herself. "He's still alive."

To reassure herself of this, she smoothed out a V-mail form and printed "Dear Lloyd" in large bold letters. She'd have to leave the address blank for now, but she wanted to write to him today. She would tell him how still and hot it was on the day they'd learned of his being wounded, yet how the air became even thicker when the telegram arrived. She'd tell him about the sweet smell of the watermelon, how it snapped open under the touch of the knife, it was that ripe. She'd tell him they all missed him and were praying for him and were proud of him.

Helen's weekly séance was scheduled for that evening. It was the final one of the summer. She was going to take three weeks off in August to go with two girlfriends to pick blueberries near Tom's River in south Jersey under the auspices of the Women's Land Army. The girls would get paid, at an unskilled labor wage of thirty cents an hour, and out of that they'd have to buy food and lodging, but it was a patriotic thing to do, and, for Helen, it offered a break from the agog surveillance of the home circle. She hadn't liked the higher expectations of sitters since the materialization of the hand.

Helen thought later that perhaps her awareness that this would be the last séance for a while, plus the disconcerting news about Lloyd, still fresh in her mind, had rendered her more than usually receptive to the spirit world. Perhaps distraction was as powerful a state as concocted passivity. Perhaps the key was not to care what happened. But all these theories came to her later, when she tried to explain the remarkable events of the last séance in July, as she and her family would always call it.

Ursula and her home circle took up four seats, and Emilie filled another one. There were five newcomers: three strangers, plus Mr. and Mrs. Goldberg from up the block. The Goldbergs had a son in the Army, currently in California being trained in amphibious landings. They hadn't come about him, but about Mrs. Goldberg's sisters in Warsaw. After the Nazis took Poland, letters still managed to straggle through Switzerland, but she'd had no word in a long time. Mr. Goldberg made no bones about his disbelief in psychic powers. He was there only because his wife had been after him for months to come and because in recent weeks she'd been unable to sleep for worrying.

"She wanders the house like a ghost—you'll pardon the expression," he told Emilie and Ursula. "Just imagine—a man wakes up at three o'clock and finds himself in an empty bed. And where is his wife? Standing in the dark living room looking out at the trees, sitting in the dark kitchen turning around the sugar bowl in her hands."

Mrs. Goldberg stood beside him wearing a small, expression-less smile.

Emilie wanted to exclude them, but Ursula pointed out that the people they wanted to know about were not soldiers, so there could be no harm in seeing if Helen could discover something. Because the Goldbergs were long-time neighbors and because Mrs. Goldberg looked so haggard, Emilie agreed to let them stay.

Mrs. Goldberg had brought along the last letter she'd had from her sisters. Ursula let Helen hold it a few moments. The envelope was wrinkled and stained. The letter was written in Yiddish on soft, limp paper.

The séance began normally enough, though Helen thought her limbs might be feeling more leaden than usual. She slid into a deep quiet while the group sang *When the Lights Go on Again All Over the World,* their untrained voices wavering with emotion.

Helen became aware of a gray, twilit fog. She saw no figures, heard no sounds, not even, any longer, the singing. Either they had finished the song, or she was too deep in trance. A coolness washed over her skin. She felt a little crampy, as if her period might be starting, then that ebbed. Her throat and mouth and nostrils began to sting.

The center of the fog grew denser, until Iris became visible. The emerald green of her robe was muted to moss, and her flower was a dark, colorless silhouette against the drapery.

"I have brought no one, and I have brought all," Iris communicated.

"Pardon me?" Helen questioned silently, thinking she must have missed some part of this odd message.

"The living can not grasp the meaning. The living can only let it break their hearts."

Helen began to have a sense of many presences around Iris, but she still couldn't see anyone. She felt the presences multiplying. She thought that if she opened her eyes, she might find they'd invaded every corner of the room. Yet here, in Iris's territory, the fog hid them all. No one stepped forward with a message. No pictures appeared in Helen's mind. But slowly, a great heaviness entered her heart, a bottomless sorrow more profound than any she'd ever known. The feeling was coming from the fog, or from the spirits hidden there. They were drowning her in it. Helen felt pressed down, smothered.

"Iris!" she appealed. "I can't—"

Before Helen had finished her thought, the terrible sadness evaporated. The stinging around her mouth and nose stopped. The brief cramps came and went as before. The thick fog, now unpopulated, dissipated, and Iris with it. Helen came back to her surroundings as one wakes up from a long sleep, with gathering alertness.

But her surroundings had changed. Several people were on their feet and staring fearfully at her. Miss Simmons was repeatedly crossing herself. Mrs. Goldberg was leaning against her husband sobbing, and he looked close to tears as well.

"What does it mean?" a woman was saying. "What does it mean?"

"It's a hoax, that's what it is," another woman replied, though she sounded uncertain.

"That's all for today," Emilie said politely but firmly. She got up and opened the hall door. "If you'll exit this way, please. We'll notify you of future meetings. Thank you for coming."

Bewildered, the sitters filed out, some of them whispering urgently to one another.

"I can stay, Emilie, if you'd like," Mrs. Durkin said.

"Thank you, dear, no. What Helen needs now is privacy."

The large woman had no choice but to leave with the others.

Ursula remained at the table with Helen, mercifully saying nothing. While they waited for Emilie to return from the front door, Helen grasped the edges of her chair seat with both hands and pushed her toes against the floor. She wanted to be sure she was solidly out of trance and back in her own skin. For that's what the gripping sorrow had felt like—that she was out of herself and inside some horrible world from which there was no escape. Of course, that wasn't so. It had been a different experience than any she'd had before, but Iris had gotten her out of it. Iris would always help her escape. Nevertheless, she knew absolutely that she never wanted to repeat that kind of trance again.

"What happened?" she said quietly when Emilie had returned to the table.

"There was a materialization," her mother said.

"A hand?"

"More than a hand," Ursula said.

"A mist came out of your mouth and nose," Emilie said. "Then there were faces floating around your head. They were smaller than real faces, and they looked as if they were made out of white smoke or glowing clouds, but their features were distinguishable. No two looked exactly alike."

"Mrs. Goldberg saw her sisters," Ursula reported.

"She *thought* she saw her sisters," Emilie corrected.

"They came at the beginning, before the crowd," Ursula argued. "She got a good look."

"The crowd?" Helen said. "How many faces were there?"

Emilie and Ursula exchanged glances.

"Two, at first," Emilie said.

"The sisters," Ursula added.

Emilie frowned at her mother.

"Then more came, slipping out from behind one another. Some seemed to disintegrate, and as soon as they did, three or four more would fill that space. They got smaller and smaller, as if to fit better, though you could still tell they were faces. Men, women, children. It was impossible to count them."

"I have brought no one, and I have brought all," Helen said.

"What?" asked Emilie.

"Iris told me that. But I didn't understand." Helen rubbed her forehead. "I still don't."

"There came impressions to me," Ursula said tentatively. "From the faces." She paused. "Only impressions."

"Tell us, Nanny," Helen encouraged her.

"It came that they passed through together."

"So many at once?" Emilie said. "Was it from a bombing?"

Ursula shook her head. "It didn't feel so."

"Was there anything else?" Helen asked.

"That they made one family."

"Oh, there were far too many for that to be the case," Emilie protested. "Unless you were to go back several generations."

"*Nein*," Ursula said. "These dead were all new."

"Then how—?"

"There is even a bigger mystery, *meine Kinder*, and it is the feeling that came to me the strongest. That this impossible one family . . . that they all belonged to the Goldbergs."

CHAPTER 30
DECEMBER 1943

After the last séance in July, Helen never again allowed the dining room to be dimmed for a sitting. Keeping the room well-lit was proof positive against materializations, which required darkness like fish require water.

Nevertheless, the first several séances in the fall were jammed. So many people wanted to attend, the members of the home circle had to take turns. Despite Mrs. Goldberg's upset in July, she returned in September, bringing her rabbi with her, an old man with a voice as deep as a cello.

"So young," he said, taking Helen's hand when Mrs. Goldberg introduced him. He looked at her as if he wanted to know and understand her, as if he'd already decided he would like her.

"I don't know what Mrs. Goldberg told you, sir," Helen had said, "but I don't expect that any . . . that anything very unusual will happen today."

"My dear, young lady," the old man replied, "for me, just to be here is unusual enough." And he laughed softly.

As predicted, nothing spectacular occurred. Helen contacted the spirits of three soldiers. Two had died of wounds, one of dysentery in a POW camp. Each one established his identity to the satisfaction of his relatives. One mentioned his mother's walnut brownies, another the name of the family dog, the third his father's habit of falling asleep in his easy chair with his cigar still clenched in his teeth. Their messages sounded the same themes as always—there is no finality, the dead are content and progressing, the purpose of life is to help one another.

More and more, Helen was becoming convinced that it was these more general messages that were the true value of spirit communication. And how many times did people need to hear them? Belief was a decision. Belief without ongoing, tangible evidence was at the very core of being human. In October, she instituted a rule that no repeat clients would be permitted. She also began excluding clients who came wishing to know about the future, clients who sought spirit advice on specific matters, and skeptics who dared her, openly or not, to convert them.

The home circle and a number of Ursula's regular clients were disgruntled by the new standards. It left them all out. Miss Simmons had snorted something about Helen's having gotten on a mighty high horse. Ursula tried to get Helen to make exceptions, but the girl relented only in the case of the loyal Mrs. Durkin.

"I'm not a fortune-teller, I'm not salesman, and people can't turn me off and on like a water faucet," Helen told her grandmother. "You always said I had a gift. Don't you think I should spend it carefully?"

They were in the kitchen. Ursula was chopping cabbage. She put down her knife and looked at Helen. There was surprise in her expression and a pained tenderness.

"Du haben recht," she said, nodding. "Maybe when I was a girl like you, if I said the same, maybe now I could do more."

By early December, attendance at Helen's séances had diminished. That was fine with her. Better five or six serious, respectful sitters than a larger group peppered with petitioners, doubters, and thrill-seekers.

It was Emilie's idea that Helen visit Lloyd at Halloran. After five months in hospitals overseas, he was finally back in the

States, in the hospital on Staten Island. A discharge date was still to be set, but he was going to get a furlough home for Christmas. If he'd take it.

Lloyd had refused visits from his mother and older sister, and he'd only let his father come once. He put up with Emilie stopping by because it was part of her work with all the men on the ward and not geared strictly towards him. Emilie felt sorry for Mrs. Mackey, who was severely disappointed and frustrated, though she wouldn't say it outright, for fear people might take it as criticism of her son.

But Emilie was more concerned about Lloyd himself. She'd seen other young men sunk in gloom, pulled into themselves, frightened and angry and lonely. She'd watched some of them struggle out of these states, or at least successfully disguise them, while others left the hospital still lost. She wondered sometimes about those lost boys, about the confusion they'd raise in their families, about the unexpected paths their broken bodies had set them upon, about the stories you saw in their eyes that they wouldn't tell.

Lloyd had been wounded by a mortar shell. He'd had several operations to remove shrapnel from his body, but he was still riddled with fragments. The doctors said that some of the shrapnel would eventually work its way out of his muscles and emerge, bit by bit, through his skin, but that most of what was left was there to stay. There would be pain, especially in cold weather, gradually lessening over time, but probably never completely disappearing. Mrs. Mackey had told Emilie that she was sure her Lloyd, strong and stubborn and never a complainer, would be able to handle all that. It was the blindness that worried her. Lloyd had lost his right eye. And it was doubtful he'd have any sight in the left.

"Why do you think he'd welcome me, Mama, if he won't let his mother or Barbara in?" Helen had asked when Emilie suggested she go with her on her next day at Halloran.

"Well, maybe he won't exactly *welcome* you, but I think he might let you sit and talk to him. He seems to enjoy the notes you send when I read them to him."

"Did he say so?"

"No. But one day I came in and saw another volunteer was rereading them to him. You must have a knack for putting down things he likes hearing about."

Helen shrugged. "I just write ordinary stuff."

"He's supposed to come home at Christmas, you know, and I'm afraid he might choose to stay on the ward instead. It'd be a terrible blow to the Mackeys. But it'd be worse for him, I think, whether he knows it or not."

"All right. I'll give it a try. I'd like to see him, actually. And Billy would probably appreciate a firsthand report."

So it was that on a winter afternoon whose sky was threatening snow, Helen joined her mother on two rough ferry rides across the choppy Hudson River and New York Bay. Emilie went in alone to Lloyd to tell him Helen was there. After a few minutes, she came out into the hall and told Helen he'd agreed to her visit.

"I think we caught him so off guard he didn't know what to say but yes," Emilie confided with a satisfied smile. "His bed is the last in the row."

The narrow ward held eight beds, arranged along one wall. In the opposite wall, windows gave out on a courtyard where a large, rectangular garden lay dormant. In season, Helen's mother had informed her, the German U-boat prisoners held at Halloran tended vegetable patches there.

The ends of the beds were not far from the windowed wall, requiring Helen to walk down a space only somewhat wider than a sidewalk while the men propped in the beds watched her pass. A wan light was seeping through the windows, giving the room a dingy feel despite the crisp white sheets on the beds and the clean white bandages swathing various parts of the men. Helen felt she must nod and smile at each man, but her stomach lurched every time. None of them was horribly disfigured, and a couple of them responded with greetings as merry as any she might have met with from on-leave soldiers on a park bench—one fellow even managed a broad wink with the side of his face not covered by gauze—but they were all ruptured in some way, and it showed in their labored nonchalance as much as in their damaged bodies. It was this self-awareness that was so very hard to witness.

Helen would not let herself avoid looking at even a single man. She felt that if she did, she'd be adding to his hurt. At the same time, she felt that it was unfair to walk by them, that her youth and health and freedom of movement accentuated their premature dilapidation.

As Helen reached the end of the row, a male nurse was lifting a man out of the bed next to Lloyd's and settling him into a wheelchair. The man was missing both legs. Helen stepped aside and waited for them to go by on their way out of the ward, then she glanced over at Lloyd. He was lying on his side, with his back to her and the rest of the room. She walked around his bed and scooted a chair close to it so that she could talk in a low enough voice to give them some semblance of privacy. Lloyd's eyes were bandaged, and he was lying so still, Helen would have thought he was asleep except that she knew her mother had just spoken with him.

"Lloyd?" she said. "It's Helen."

He made no answer. He didn't move. Could he have dropped off to sleep that quickly? Helen wondered. Maybe some medicine was making him groggy.

"Lloyd? Are you awake?"

He rolled on to his back with a grunt.

"It's Helen," she repeated.

"I heard you the first time," he said.

"Oh. I couldn't tell because—"

"Because you can't see my eyes?"

"Well, not only that—"

"Welcome to the club. I can't see them, either."

Helen's mother had warned her that Lloyd's spirits were low, but she hadn't expected this terse bitterness.

"It looks like it might snow later on," she said, immediately cursing herself for using the word looks. But it was too late. She had to forge ahead. "The sky is that kind of heavy gray, you know?—like it's hanging down closer to the earth because it's too full to stay up where it belongs. The Hudson was gray, too, only darker, like . . . like the slate sidewalks on Larch Avenue . . . and just jumping with whitecaps. I stood out on the deck of the ferry—my mother thought I was nuts—to feel the wind. You could smell the snow in it."

"You can't smell snow."

"Yes, you can."

"All right, then, what's it smell like?"

Helen couldn't believe she'd been so mundane as to bring up the weather. And now he was arguing with her about it! But at least he was talking.

"Well, it's a damp smell," she began. "Something like when you dig down into the ground in the spring and the mud is still cold. Only it doesn't have that same dirt smell, not so obvious as that. It's a fresh smell somehow, like . . . well, like snow itself, I guess."

Lloyd's face was impassive. Helen figured they should move on from the topic of the weather, but she wasn't sure where to go. Since he'd refused to see his family, she thought she shouldn't mention them. And why would he be interested in any part of her day-to-day life? Maybe she could tell him about

Billy's latest letter, in which he'd described his first training flight. But maybe Billy had already written to him about that.

"You like to hear yourself talk, don't you?" Lloyd sneered.

Stung, Helen abruptly stood up.

"I'm happy to go, Lloyd, if that's what you want," she said angrily. "You just had to say so."

"You can smell snow coming," he replied in a tight voice. "Well, I can smell things, too. And you know what? Pity stinks."

"Oh, yeah? And who do you smell it on more, Lloyd Mackey, me or yourself?"

Helen instantly regretted her outburst. Lloyd was right. She did pity him. And she saw suddenly how corrosive that would be for someone as proud and fearless as he'd always been. Yet she was right, too. He was feeling deeply sorry for himself. Though justified, it was as dangerous as another wound. But she had no right to upbraid him.

She stood, irresolute, watching him. She could have left if she hadn't said that last thing. But she had said it, and she felt she owed him the opportunity of a retort. The exchange, though raw, had been too honest for apologies. To her amazement, he began to guffaw.

"That's the first square thing anyone's said to me in months," he said when he'd stopped laughing. "It felt like a sock in the puss, but maybe I needed one, huh?"

"Oh, Lloyd, I—"

"Hey, don't you get gooey on me now and say you're sorry or anything."

"No, I wasn't going to say I was sorry."

He laughed again, a short chuckling belch. "Atta girl."

She sat down. The chair made a little scraping noise against the floor. Lloyd turned his head toward the sound and folded his arms across his chest expectantly. His bare forearms were still browned, even after months away from the Tunisian sun.

There were a few small scars on them, but otherwise, looking at his arms in isolation, you'd have said they belonged to a man in the prime of his life, a man able to turn his muscles and his will to any task he chose. Helen wondered what to say next. She almost said welcome home, but it wasn't quite the right sentiment, and, anyway, he'd be sure to deem it gooey.

"My father and my grandmother said to say hello," she said. "They want to see you when you're home for Christmas."

"I don't know about that."

"Are you really thinking of not coming?"

"All the song and dance Ma's bound to go through," he said shaking his head. "I don't know if I can take it."

"You're gonna have to let her do it some time."

"Yeah, I guess." His brow furrowed. He gently touched the bandages over his eyes, as if checking that they were still in place.

"I should go," Helen said. "My mother wants me to meet the other Gray Ladies and help out a while in the recreation room."

"Sure," he said.

She stood up and walked around the end of the bed, then turned back to him.

"Nanny and I are home most days," she said. "You could come over to our house sometimes if you needed a change."

He leaned forward, as if he were ready to take her up on her offer right then.

"Okay," he said. "Okay, I'll take my furlough. You can tell my mother."

Helen smiled and nodded. Then remembering he couldn't see her, she said, "It's a deal."

"I guess it's about time I got out in the air again." He grinned. "To find out for myself what it smells like."

When Helen got home from Halloran, she was delighted to find a fat letter from Rosie waiting. She'd last heard from her friend in October, and that had been only a brief note to let Helen know that she'd transferred to the 6669th Headquarters Platoon, assigned to the Fifth Army under General Clark. She was still on the coast of Algeria, but in Mostaganem instead of Algiers. Helen wondered why Rosie had transferred, since her job had remained the same. She'd never voiced any complaints about her Algiers assignment except that the nightly bombings had made it hard to sleep.

Dear Helen:

Hope you're not too thick about my not writing, but I've been kept hopping the past month or two. In fact, I hopped all the way to Italy! Guess I better explain.

If there's one thing all soldiers are good at, it's rumors. Everyone's always trying to guess where their unit's moving next and when. Fellas even take bets on it, though that's not saying much since most soldiers bet as often as they eat. Oftener, sometimes. We gals in Headquarters hear a good share of these rumors, as guys think we might know something of what's true and what's not. (We do, but our lips are sealed.) Anyway, finally a rumor came my way that caught my interest, which was that the Fifth Army was going to experiment with females in the field by letting WACs staff temporary headquarters just behind the front lines. You know I had to get in on that!

So we came to Naples, which is a nice enough city for having a week's leave in, but still not the real goods. But now I'm in the field for sure. Our office is a tent with no lights, a few tables, a typewriter, barely enough paper. We plot troop locations, and requisition supplies and keep track of their delivery. When the troops move, we move, slogging through the rain and mud just like them, keeping six to thirteen miles behind the infantry. Between us and them is the artillery. You can hear the big guns up ahead day and night, both ours and the Germans'.

I have to tell you, Helen, that I have a sweetheart, and he's an artilleryman. His battery has four guns. Like us, they stay in one place for stretches of time, so they get to make drainage ditches around their pup tents and lay them with straw so they're dry inside. It's been raining here all the time, which makes the hills a beautiful green, but you do get tired of being wet. The Army keeps promising galoshes, but they never come. Anyway, the artillery is not in as dangerous positions as the infantry, which helps me not be so nervous if Arnie's safe.

Arnie Callendar is his name, from Des Moines. We met in Naples, when we both went to see the Pompeii ruins. He's a heck of a guy, Helen, no fooling, and he thinks I'm pretty choice, too. Just talking with him gives me a lift. It's like we know each other's way of thinking before we even say it. It's hard to explain, but he makes me feel more like myself. Even in ways we're different from each other, I still feel like I can count on Arnie to let me be just me, and that that's plenty good enough for him. I better stop now because I'm not making much good sense. It's hard to get words around it. But probably you know what I mean, because how you and Billy are together must be the same. The truck's here to take us to the showers, anyway. The guys mostly don't bother with showers, staying dirty for weeks on end, but I'm not that much of a soldier yet.

Love, Rosie

CHAPTER 31
JANUARY 1944

Lloyd was barely into the second week of his furlough, with another week looming beyond that, and Helen was feeling that maybe it hadn't been such a grand achievement to have talked him into coming home.

She'd visited the Mackeys on Christmas day with a Rita Hayworth paper doll set for Linda and a tin of homemade cookies, the product of weeks of saved sugar and butter. Lloyd said he wasn't hungry and had been, on the surface, courteous, but there was a peevishness about him, as if he regarded the cookies as part of some scheme hatched expressly to annoy or insult him, in league with his sisters singing *White Christmas* and his mother repeatedly asking him if he needed anything. He'd arrived only two days before, so Helen put his mood down to weariness or a reverse kind of homesickness. It must be tough, she thought, to be in such a familiar setting and yet feel out of place. For that was what he most seemed, out of place, like a garish souvenir in a simply appointed room.

Barbara told Helen he'd let Linda lead him through the house once—it was a game to her—but he'd refused assistance from anyone since. Which meant that he either sat for hours in one spot or felt his way awkwardly along the walls and among the furniture, swearing under his breath when he stumbled.

Helen went to the Mackeys' twice in the week after Christmas, intending to "spring" Lloyd, as they'd talked about in the hospital, but he declined both times and didn't bother to give a reason besides not feeling like it.

"I'm worried about him, Helen," Barbara confided one evening in Helen's kitchen, as they sat sharing a pot of tea. She'd come over specifically to discuss Lloyd. "He's not himself. I suppose it's foolish of me to think being away at war wouldn't change him, but, I don't know, I didn't expect this . . . this . . ."

"What?"

"Imposter comes to mind. Somebody who came home in my brother's clothes, looking like my brother, but without his dash and zest."

"Oh, I can't believe Lloyd would ever lose that."

"Well, then it's in hiding. And I'm beginning to wonder if it'll ever come out again."

"His injury must be a terrible thing for him to bear, Barbara. He's probably wondering what's going to become of him now."

"I know." She sat back in her chair and hugged herself.

"He hasn't told us any details about how it happened," she went on. "He tells funny stories about soldiers in his unit, he's got lots of colorful reports to give on Tunisia and the Arabs, and he'll answer my father's questions about battles in a general way, but I always feel like every story has another part to it that he's leaving out and that those are the important parts."

"What do you mean, important?"

"It's like he's in a prison, Helen. Those stories that he won't tell—they're the bars."

Helen refilled their teacups. She was thinking about the men on Lloyd's ward at Halloran and all the other men in hospitals at home and overseas. Were they all like Lloyd, trapped inside what had happened to them, going around in circles trying to find a way out, or maybe sitting and waiting for someone to point them to one? Whenever Helen worried about Billy, it was his dying she feared first, then a wound. She hated the idea of him torn and hurt, even if his wound were ultimately to have no lasting effects on his body. But she hadn't thought about how a wound might injure his mind or damage his outlook, how it might take a part of him away from her. She'd imagined herself, sometimes, nursing him if he came home wounded, and she believed she'd be up to anything, but if he ended up like Lloyd, a stranger of sorts, what would she do about that?

"Have you tried asking him specific things?" she said to Barbara.

"Yes, but it's no use. He clams up, or he gets angry. My mother made me promise not to do it anymore." She sighed. "I wish Billy were here. Maybe he'd be able to get through to him."

Helen knew that if Billy were home, he'd do everything he could think of to help his brother, and she thought that he'd expect her to do the same in his absence. But she couldn't even get Lloyd out of his house.

"That's not all," Barbara said hesitantly.

Helen waited.

"Lloyd would probably be furious if he knew I was telling you all this . . ." Barbara took a deep breath, as if bracing herself before plunging into a cold lake. "You know what? I don't care if he gets mad. It's like he came home with a huge, horrible rat sitting on his shoulder, and we're supposed to act like that's okay—more than that, like we don't even see it. Meanwhile, it's eating away at him. It's eating away at all of us."

"What else is going on, Barbara?" Helen gently urged her.

"He has nightmares. He wakes up yelling almost every night. Can you imagine Lloyd frightened like that? My parents went in to him the first time, but he threw a fit, said he wasn't a baby who needed his mother just because he'd had a bad dream. Now they don't go in. At breakfast, we all pretend we didn't hear anything. Even Linda has learned not to ask questions."

Nightmares. Here was something Helen could understand

without having to quiz Lloyd for details. The nightmares she'd suffered after Pearl Harbor had never recurred, but she could still vividly recall their terrifying images and the sucking reality of being detained within them. Additionally, the stories from her boys gave her some notion of what Lloyd might be seeing in his dreams. Maybe this was her avenue into his private fears.

"Do you think Lloyd would come for dinner?" Helen asked.

"I really can't say. He might worry about spilling food. He's actually quite accomplished at using utensils, but he might be nervous at a new table."

"What if my father went over and asked him?"

Barbara considered a moment.

"That might work. I don't see him being so rude as to say no to your father right to his face. But if he does come, what then?"

"I don't have any great plan," Helen said, not wanting to go into her history. "But maybe if he's able to relax a little, maybe then he'll start to let some cats out of his bag."

Walter decided that an invitation to after-dinner drinks would be more acceptable to Lloyd, and he was proved right. Not only did he get Lloyd to agree, he also succeeded in escorting him from one house to the other on the appointed evening without affronting the young man's pride. Helen reminded her father how Lloyd had insisted on hobbling around unaided after his bicycle accident years ago, so Walter was careful to let him decide how he'd manage. Lloyd used the stair railings to navigate his way down from the Mackeys' front porch and up onto the Schneiders' porch. In between, he held lightly to Walter's arm.

Helen watched their slow approach from the front window. It was a bitterly cold and windy evening, yet her father was strolling casually and chatting amiably, for all the world as if they were on a garden path in balmy mid-May. Helen was pleased to find when Lloyd entered the house that his mood appeared untroubled. In fact, he seemed quietly gratified at the accomplishment of his small journey.

The cold January air had forced Lloyd into a civilian overcoat, but underneath, he was in uniform, even though it was a lightweight, hot-climate issue. Barbara had told Helen he was refusing to wear his own clothes.

Helen took both men's coats and hats. Relieved of his outerwear, Lloyd stood almost at attention. Helen wondered if he were afraid of knocking something over.

"There's a good fire going in the living room," Walter said, raising a welcoming arm in that direction and taking a couple of steps. Then, confounded, he let his arm drop to his side.

Lloyd cocked his head slightly toward Walter's voice, but remained immobile. Before Helen had a chance to decide how gracefully to maneuver him, Emilie came from the living room with a pleased exclamation.

"Lloyd!" she said, "it's so wonderful to see you out of the hospital."

As she spoke, she put her hands affectionately on his arm, enabling him to casually take hold of her elbow. The motions were smooth and natural on both sides.

"My mother's impatient to see you," Emilie continued, moving towards the living room with Lloyd easily in tow. "When is that rascal Lloyd Mackey going to decide to pay us a visit? she keeps saying."

"Rascal?" He actually chuckled.

"Oh, you mustn't take offense. With her, that's a term of endearment. You *are* practically family now, remember."

Emilie led Lloyd to a fireside armchair next to Ursula's, ostensibly so the old woman wouldn't have any trouble hearing him. Helen marvelled at her mother's ingenuity. Lloyd might know he'd been managed, but Emilie had engineered it within such normal social forms, neither he nor anyone else found room for embarrassment. Helen realized that Emilie must have to deal with men's disabilities and shame every time she went to Halloran. For the first time, she saw her mother as someone outside the family might, as a resourceful, quick-witted person of action.

Walter gave the women sherry and poured brandy for himself and Lloyd, apologizing to him for the lack of whiskey. These days most alcohol went into making explosives. Conversation moved from home-front news, including national affairs like the coal miners' strike and catch-ups on which local men were stationed where, to theorizing about when a second European front might be opened in France, to descriptions by Emilie and Lloyd of the men on his ward. From this springboard, Lloyd introduced some of his experiences overseas. He avoided battle tales, except as framing references, such as, "I saw my first scorpion on the day before we met the panzers at the Kasserine Pass," and "There was a big air raid the night Bob Hope's troupe played for us." They all laughed at a long story about three GIs in Sicily bartering cigarettes and candy for wine and wonderfully ripe tomatoes, stuttering in pidgin Italian, flailing about with elaborate gestures, only to find that the peasant they were negotiating with had lived in Buffalo for eight years and spoke very passable English.

There was a lull after their laughter died out. It was a comfortable quiet. They sipped their drinks. Then Walter carefully asked Lloyd what invasion day in Sicily had been like. Helen thought that risky, despite the fact that Lloyd's wounds had come later in the campaign. But Lloyd didn't bark out an intimidating reply, as he might have done at home. He leaned his head against the high, padded back of his chair and seemed to reflect.

"Well, to start with," he said, "getting there was some show.

There were two thousand ships, half ours, half the Brits'—cruisers, destroyers, PT boats, sub chasers, troop transports, assault craft, barges carrying tanks—ships as far as you could see on all sides. And planes in formation overhead."

He paused, remembering the awesome sight.

"That first day was beautiful—the Mediterranean calm as a pond—but at night a big storm came up. Screaming wind, waves over the deck. The ship was up and down, rolling from side to side. We just about turned green, we were so seasick. If we'd got dumped on the beaches in that condition, a gang of first-graders could've whipped us."

"How long was the storm?" Ursula said.

"All night. All the next day. And that was the day we were supposed to land."

"What did you do?" Helen asked, caught up in the tale.

"We landed."

"But if you were all sick—"

"That night the storm quit cold. They took us in just before dawn. We were straight enough by then. We had to be."

Lloyd's tone of voice had shifted. Helen could tell he was done.

"Was it a tough fight?" Walter said.

Lloyd swallowed the last of his brandy.

"Been in tougher," he replied. Then he held out his empty glass. "Could I get a refill, sir?"

As Walter was obliging Lloyd, Emilie stood up.

"If you'll excuse me, Lloyd," she said, "I have to be up early tomorrow to go to the hospital."

"Tell the fellas hi for me."

"Of course."

"Time for me, too," Ursula said. She crossed to Lloyd and rested her hand on his shoulder. "Come back tomorrow at lunch, and I give you some sauerbraten. You'll be surprised how good it is from mutton. Better than the horse meat."

"As you can tell, Lloyd, the beef shortage has made for some adventurous cooking around here," Walter said.

Emilie signalled to her husband that he ought to exit, too. She knew Helen had hoped for some time alone with Lloyd. Walter lingered ten minutes after Emilie and Ursula had left, then excused himself with the claim he had some accounts to go over for a deadline the next day. Helen moved to her grandmother's chair to be closer to both Lloyd and the fire. For several minutes, they didn't speak. Helen was beginning to feel sleepy. Maybe she shouldn't try to draw Lloyd out any more tonight, she considered. Maybe enough had happened for the time being.

"So when are you and my big brother getting hitched, anyway?" Lloyd blurted.

Helen felt herself blushing. Silly goose, she thought.

"When he's done with his training at the end of February. He should get a couple weeks' furlough then, before he gets posted somewhere."

"He'll probably be attached to a bomber crew, you know."

"I know."

"But maybe cargo."

Helen really didn't want to speculate about Billy. Speculation could so quickly turn into apprehension.

"He shoulda stayed at the factory," Lloyd said, the simple opinion edged with exasperation.

"He didn't want to. He couldn't."

Lloyd leaned forward, elbows on his knees.

"Yeah, I know all about that," he said. "You wanna look brave. Hell, you wanna *be* brave. But it doesn't turn out like you think."

Helen missed not being able to peer into Lloyd's eyes. She'd never realized before how much can be learned about a person's feelings that way, how many words can be dispensed with by a look.

"Are you sorry you went?"

"Nah. It was the right thing. It's a war that's gotta be fought. But I'd still like to see Billy miss it."

"What was it like, Lloyd?"

He slowly shook his head.

"You wouldn't understand."

"I think I would."

"No, you wouldn't!" he snapped. "You weren't there."

Lloyd had been in North Africa for eight months, six of those months in combat with the Germans. Helen searched her memory for desert stories from her boys.

"It's hot, right?" she said. "There's constant noise from trucks and planes and guns. You're dirty all the time, and sometimes you don't get enough to eat or the food is bad. You walk and fight, walk and fight, day and night. You're scared sometimes, but what's worse is being exhausted. Exhausted and bored and sick of it. But it keeps going, and you do, too, somehow. You just walk and fight."

She said all this staring into the fire. It was down to red embers. She ought to put more wood on, but she didn't want to move. She looked at Lloyd. His face was oriented to her. She almost believed he could see through his bandages, he was so adamantly focussed on her.

"How do you know that?" he said, suspicion competing with awe in his voice.

"I've heard stories."

"From who—some crybaby at the USO?"

"I've . . . I've seen it, too."

"Seen it? You mean magazine pictures? Why, they can't begin—" He sat up straight in his chair. "Say, you're not talking about that spook stuff, are you? Billy told me about that, but I thought he must be exaggerating."

Helen winced at his characterization of her visions as "spook stuff," but she wasn't going to challenge him.

"Let's just say there are things I know that I don't tell everyone, either. Because I think they wouldn't understand."

"So, the walking and fighting and all—you really saw that? Like in a dream or something?"

"In trance. Which you could call a kind of dream, except I'm not asleep."

The room was getting cold. Helen got up and piled some kindling and two small split logs on the glowing embers. The kindling flared up. She stood watching it, to see if more would be needed to get the new wood to catch.

"It was on the road to Messina," Lloyd said to her back, each word so measured it seemed to stand as a statement all on its own. She turned around. He was running his fingertips gingerly across his bandaged eyes.

"That's where it happened," he continued at a quicker pace. "The Italians gave up quick on the beaches, but the Germans kept fighting. We were driving them over the hills to Messina."

Helen remembered from a newspaper map that Messina sat on the narrow strait between eastern Sicily and southern Italy.

"I was wounded before, you know. Near Algiers. A shell fragment in my wrist that went up my arm and came out here." He pointed to a spot just above his left elbow. "They doped me up with morphine at the battalion aid station, patched me up later at the collecting station. I didn't even make it to a real hospital."

"I didn't hear about that."

"I wrote Billy about it, thought he could tell the folks. But I burnt the letter."

"Why?"

"Because to tell about myself, I had to tell about my buddy who was hurt in that fight, too."

"So?"

"We were pinned down by enemy fire for hours. The litter-bearers couldn't get to us. I saw he was dying, but I kept telling him it was gonna be all right. After a while, he said to me *it's okay, I know,* so then I didn't tell him that anymore."

Lloyd rubbed the inside of his left wrist. Helen spied a shiny, ragged scar there.

"Then what happened?"

"Then . . . Then I fell asleep. Or passed out or something. When I woke up, he was dead. Flies all over the wound in his gut, flies in the corners of his eyes and inside his mouth. I couldn't even do that much for the poor bastard. Just stay awake and keep the flies off him."

Helen sat down on the floor in front of Lloyd's chair. She wanted to be near him, she wanted him to sense her nearness.

"Is that what you dream about?" she said softly.

"What?"

"Barbara told me you've been having nightmares."

"Barbara should keep her trap shut," he snarled.

Helen felt as if she were standing on one foot on a balance beam.

"I used to have nightmares," she said.

"About what?"

"About dying soldiers and sailors."

Lloyd twisted his mouth dismissively.

"If you haven't seen the real thing, it's not the same," he said.

"I'm sure you're right," Helen conceded.

She didn't want to make this into a contest. But she did want him to understand what she'd seen, especially what had been so hard about those dreams.

"Sometimes," she continued, "the men in my dreams reached out like they wanted me to save them. If they were already dead, they just lay there very, very still. But even they—the dead ones—even with them, I felt like they wanted something from me."

"They do," Lloyd said. "They all do."

She wished he'd elaborate, but something in his manner informed her he wouldn't. At least not tonight.

"You didn't finish telling me about how you were wounded this time," she said, tacitly agreeing to his closure of the topic of nightmares and what dying men might want.

"Yeah, and I'm not gonna finish, either. It was stupid even to start."

So, they were done all around, Helen thought. She got up and fiddled with the fire again, putting on a big log and banking chunks of burning wood around it. Then she returned to her place on the floor near Lloyd's chair.

"Helen?"

"Yes?"

"What do they look like?"

"Who?"

"My family. Do they look the same as when I left? Does the house?"

This must be the first time he's asked, Helen thought. Maybe the first time he's admitted so directly that his blindness will force him to rely on others for some things. It wasn't the story of his wounding, but it was just as good, perhaps better.

"Well, Linda's bigger, of course," she answered lightly. "Your mother got new curtains for the kitchen. Yellow, with red tulips along the hem. And Barbara cut her hair short. It was getting in her way at the plant."

Lloyd nodded intently, as if this were all vastly interesting.

"How about you?" he said.

"Me?"

"You didn't cut your hair or get bigger or anything, did you?"

She laughed. "No. But I do wear my hair up sometimes now. I never did when we were in school."

"Like Betty Grable?"

She laughed again. "Hardly."

"Is it up now?"

"Uh-huh."

"Can I see it?" He was reaching his hand out tentatively, and she realized he meant he wanted to touch her hair.

She took his hand and guided it to her head. Gently and slowly, he felt her hairdo, moving from the top of her head to the back of her neck. Then he put his hand on the arm of his chair and smiled.

"It's nice," he said.

She was a little flustered. No one had touched her so intimately since Billy. But she was grateful, too. For his careful, appreciative touching. And for his letting her feel, while they talked, that there was someone else who knew what it was like to have secrets that defined you yet also kept you apart from other people. She had set out tonight to help Lloyd, and he had ended up helping her. She hadn't known she needed help, and he didn't know he'd given it, but all that could be discussed some other time. She felt that she could tell Lloyd anything. He might tease or debate her, but he'd remain her friend. He'd never tell her not to be the way she was.

He stood up and announced it was time he was going. She got their coats. She felt awkward guiding him along the sidewalk, and neither of them spoke until they'd reached the bottom step of his porch, where he ventured a small joke.

"I'm okay now," he said, releasing her. "I coulda walked on my own, you know—if I didn't mind ending up in the river." She was glad he hadn't thanked her.

They exchanged good nights, and he felt for the stair railing. She watched him until he reached his front door. He must have

known she was still there, because just before he went into the
house, he turned and waved to her.

CHAPTER 32

The day after the night Lloyd touched Helen's hair, he returned to the Schneiders' for Ursula's sauerbraten, and he came again every day that week. Linda walked him over when she came home from school for lunch, so he always arrived shortly after noon.

Sometimes he ate lunch with Helen and Ursula, sometimes he simply kept them company with a cup of coffee. Then he and Helen would go for a walk. They'd been blessed with bright, dry weather. The air was cold, but tolerable. After their walk, there'd be mulled cider or cocoa, and Helen would read Lloyd the newspaper. And in all the small spaces that these pursuits afforded, they'd talk, idly for the most part, but with islands of serious exchange and connection. Or else they'd sit or walk in easy silence.

On the day before Lloyd was to go back to Halloran, the weather turned nasty. The air was damp and chilling, with occasional gusts of biting wind. Helen was reminded of the day Billy had told her he'd enlisted and they'd walked through Brinker's Green along the cheerless river. She marvelled that that had been nearly a year ago.

Helen knew this was the kind of weather that made Lloyd's hip and shoulder ache, but he didn't want to abandon their routine on this, his last day. They compromised on a short outing, just one circuit of the block. Before they were four houses away from home, Helen's face began to sting from the cold. She pulled her beret down over her forehead and her scarf up over her chin and nose. Lloyd wouldn't admit to any discomfort.

"All the same, you should be dressed better," she said. "Wool pants, a sweater."

Under his coat and muffler, Lloyd was in his lightweight uniform.

"Well, aren't you the little mother."

"Really, Lloyd, why *do* you wear your uniform?"

He didn't answer right away. Helen was getting used to this. She felt less and less that he was being secretive—though he still was about some things—and more that he was searching for the best way to express himself. She knew this because it had happened often enough for her to recognize the signs, and because she had experienced the same deliberation in her own mind when she had something, in her turn, to confide in him.

"One morning, after I was home a couple of days, I put on my old clothes," he said. "They felt heavy. And sad."

"How can clothes feel sad?"

"I guess I mean I felt sad in them."

"Why?"

"Because they're the same, and I'm not."

Helen resisted an impulse to assure him he certainly was the same. He wasn't, and his blindness was not the only difference, though it was the change everyone would react to and accommodate. She resisted her next impulse, too, which was to tell him that he was still the same in important ways, in his honesty and humor and toughness. She was too aware that she didn't know all the ways in which Lloyd was no longer the same person who'd left town so confidently two years ago. She would probably never know all the ways. But she was sure that, at the core, Lloyd remained the boy she'd known all her life. Adventurous, optimistic, wholehearted. That boy had simply stepped into another world where things didn't add up exactly as he'd expected them to, and now he'd stepped back, and things here weren't quite adding up either, even though this was where he ought to belong.

"And you don't feel sad in your uniform?" she said in the place of her impulsive sops.

"No, I don't feel sad. But it doesn't feel *right,* either. I'm still a soldier, technically, but yet I'm not." His next words were uttered harshly. "I wish they could just fix me up and send me back."

"Really?" Helen said, surprised.

"It can be hell, sure, but at least you know what's what and who's who, and you're part of something. You can actually have a kind of happiness if you just take the days one by one and don't think too much. Like a dog or something. Yeah, a dog's kind of happiness."

They continued on, hunched up against the cold, Helen alert for icy patches on the sidewalk. Lloyd's relaxed hand was on her elbow, and she walked a half step ahead of him, which allowed him to anticipate turns, stops, and curbs. They hadn't been as smooth on their first walk. It was like learning to dance with someone, Helen had thought, except that the roles of leader and follower were reversed. They were almost back to Helen's house when Lloyd spoke again.

"It's funny, when you're over there, all you think about is home. Guys are always talking about what they're gonna do when they get back. The jobs, the girls, the grub, lots of things. One guy in my outfit, all he could talk about was getting a little gas station and calling it Rogers and Sons, even though he's only got one kid who's not even a year old and who he hasn't ever seen. We all got so's we could've drawn a picture of that place, with the oil cans and the pumps and the tools that used to be his old man's, all in the right spots."

Lloyd was quiet a moment.

"But then you do get home," he continued, "and it's not like you dreamed about. And I don't just mean because of this." He pointed to his bandaged eyes. "If Rogers gets his gas station—and I hope he does—if he gets it, I'll bet you any amount of money it won't be like he imagined it. Even if he makes it look exactly right."

"Why not?"

"How could it be? How could anything? You think you're just taking a break to take care of some bad trouble that's got to be cleaned up, and that the time away won't count somehow, that your real life has just stopped for a while and is waiting there for you where you left off. But it's not true. Home's different, and you're different, and you can't figure which way to go."

Having reached Helen's house, they went inside and hung up their things. Helen left Lloyd in the living room while she went to make cocoa. When she brought in the mugs, she put Lloyd's down in the same spot on the end table next to his chair that she always put it.

"I haven't been to war," Helen said after they'd sat sipping their cocoa for a few minutes. "But when I first started getting premonitions and spirit messages, before I'd begun officially to do séances, I felt something like what you described. No matter how much I wanted to ignore it, I had changed, and I wasn't sure how I could still fit inside my ordinary life—school and friends and even Billy."

"But you figured it out."

"Pretty much. You will too, Lloyd."

He gave a slack smile.

"We're a pair, aren't we? You see things most people can't, and I don't see anything at all."

He set down his mug.

"How about the newspaper?" he said. "There was something about Anzio on the radio this morning."

Helen retrieved the afternoon *Record* from the hall. But when she'd sat down on the sofa, she laid the newspaper unopened beside her.

"Lloyd," she said nervously, "I'd like to read you something else."

"What?"

"Remember when I told you about the automatic writing?"

"The stories from the dead flyers and soldiers? Yeah, sure."

"I'd like to read you those. Or . . . or a couple of them."

Lloyd considered. It was on the tip of Helen's tongue to say "oh, never mind."

"What the heck?" he said. "Read 'em all."

Helen's heart was twitching as she went upstairs to her room to get the writings. Was she going too far? Would Lloyd think, as Billy had, that there was something unseemly, almost improper, about her communion with her boys? Would he turn away from her as he might from a freak? So far, Lloyd had accepted all she'd told him about her abilities and experiences with an open mind, even, she would say, with sympathy. She supposed his war ordeals had made him so receptive. She had met men after death, with the knowledge of battle still fresh in them and the wonder over their new state even fresher, but Lloyd had been with similar men just before they'd died, he'd seen their last bursts of animation and personality and, sometimes, the final brutal moments of their transition. Both Helen and Lloyd were burdened by what they knew. Both admitted they also cherished the knowledge. Helen found Lloyd's tales made hers easier to own. She thought it worked like that for him, too. But she'd never exposed him to as much as she was about to now.

Helen was so anxious about Lloyd's reactions, she read the dictated stories straight through, one after another, without looking up from the scrawled pages. Lloyd listened in silence, interrupting her only once near the beginning to ask her to read more slowly.

She finished with an airman who had related in awful detail the misery of being trapped in a burning plane on its way down. As the plane was breaking into pieces, he'd seen rays of light in the sky. At first, he thought they were German searchlights, but then he saw people walking on them. He and his crew climbed out of their plane onto one of these rays and found it was as firm as a wooden plank. The men were drawn through the air and deposited on the ground. Feeling drowsy, the airman went to sleep.

When I woke up, I was alone in a hilly place, like Scotland, where my grandparents are from and where I went once when I was a kid. Church bells were ringing from somewhere. It was sunny and warm, like a good day in June, which stumped me, 'cause when we took off from England, it was November and wet. And that was just hours ago, get it? Then I turned around, and there were all my buddies from the squadron, joking and talking, and right in the middle of them, my old Granpop. I was sure surprised to see him, and right away I took him to one side and start asking questions. All he'd say was that we'd been brought there because it was a good place to recover, and that questions could wait. "You've seen enough for now," Granpop said. "You're safe and well, warm and happy. What else could a man desire?" In a snap, all my curiosity was doused, like I'd been real thirsty and someone had given me a long drink of water and a full canteen besides, so I wouldn't ever have to worry about not having water when I needed it. Answers came later, some from Granpop, some from other folks, and more answers are ahead, too, but I'm in no rush. Some of us are still here resting, some of us have gone on, but no one is alone. We'll keep moving. It's what we're supposed to do. It's what you all are supposed to be doing, too.

"That's it," Helen said, laying the pages in her lap and looking at Lloyd.

He had slumped down in his chair, hands clasped behind his head, legs stretched out and crossed at the ankles. He let out a long whistle.

"Damn!" he said. "Pardon my French, but damn!"

"They're pretty amazing, aren't they?"

"I'll say!"

Lloyd resumed a more ordinary position in his chair.

"Then . . . you do believe them?" Helen asked with some trepidation.

"I have to. I know for a fact that what they say about getting shot or blown apart is right, so the rest of it must be, too. I can't buy *all* of it, but I don't think swallowing stuff like the light rays and the singing fountains and that kind of thing is really the point, do you? Probably different guys see different things depending on what kind of joe they are, what, maybe, would make it easiest for them. It's what's the *same* in what they say that's important to believe, don't you think?"

Helen felt like hugging Lloyd, she was so relieved at his response. Even her grandmother had not so thoroughly appreciated the messages from her boys.

"You know what else, Helen?" he continued more quietly. "I *want* to believe them. I want to hold on to the chance that all those guys I saw die—some of them screaming their heads off—that they all woke up some place sweet and peaceful, with people to look out for them, and that later, they helped look after the new guys that came. I'll never feel okay about them dying. None of them deserved it. Especially not the way they had to go. But to think they're okay somewhere—it does make it a little less hard."

"It was you talking about things being different now you're home that made me think of the stories," Helen said, patting the sheaf of writings. "These fellows are getting used to a new situation, too. They're the same, and yet they're not."

"Yeah, but they all met someone who told them it was gonna be all right in the end. Someone who was gonna stick around until it was. Someone they could bank on."

You can bank on me, Helen wanted to say, but she didn't dare. The very sentiment confused and unnerved her. What might its expression do to him? What did she really mean by it, anyway? What viable meaning existed for it?

"You don't think you're gonna be all right?" she said instead.

"Was I talking about me?"

"Weren't you?"

Lloyd grinned.

"Guilty as charged," he said. "But don't worry about me. I'm coming around. At least I know I'm luckier than your friends there." He pointed vaguely in the direction of the writings.

"More cocoa?" she said. "There's some left in the pot."

"Sure."

She went to the kitchen, warmed up the cocoa, refilled both mugs, and returned to the living room. She unfolded the newspaper.

"I found the Anzio report," she said, scanning the headlines. "It says the Fifth Army is there. That's Rosie's posting."

"Could I see the pages you wrote on for a minute?" Lloyd asked.

Helen gave him the automatic writings. He ran his hand over the top page, thumbed through the rest as if he were counting them, tapped their edges against his knees to make them into a neat stack.

"You still getting these stories?" he said.

"One every séance," she answered.

"I wonder if they'll stop when the war's over."

"They've slowed down already. I used to get three or four at a time."

"Slowed down, huh?" he said, interested. "Why do you think that is?"

Helen had already given this some thought, as part of her ongoing assessment of her abilities, their purpose and correct use.

"I think they come because they want to help us, to share some of what they're finding out. But they're on a path. I think they lose interest in us."

"That would explain why the same guys don't come back, but not why fewer of them are showing up."

"Maybe they think we've heard just about enough, and now it's up to us to use it as we can."

Lloyd nodded and sat quietly contemplative. Helen looked out the window at the gloomy day. It was a scene in gradations of black and white, like an etching—the dark tree trunks, the silvery weathered fence, the pearly sky, the gravel drive patched with milky gray frozen puddles. She felt dreamy, suspended, devoid of thoughts.

"You're gonna miss them, aren't you?" Lloyd said.

The same remark from someone else would have made Helen feel accused. But Lloyd's voice was soft and solicitous.

"Yes," she said simply. "I think I will."

CHAPTER 33
FEBRUARY 1944

Though Helen had promised Lloyd she'd visit him often at Halloran, she managed to get there only once, and that had been during his first week back. But she did give her mother notes to bring him.

Lloyd was forgiving. He knew that Billy would be home at the end of February and that Helen was busy, once again, with wedding preparations. It was surprising how many little chores stood waiting to be done. Just when Helen thought everything was ready, her mother would discover yet another task. Helen didn't bother Lloyd with the details, and during her one visit, he didn't ask for any. She supposed he'd have been bored by them. Even Billy had left it all to her to decide—the menu for the wedding lunch, the kind of cake, the musical selections. Helen didn't want to tell Lloyd about such things, anyway. She felt strangely embarrassed whenever she even contemplated mentioning the wedding to him, as if she were about to do something he disapproved.

"What's wrong with you?" she said to her reflection in the bathroom mirror one morning. "Lloyd's going to be your brother."

But Helen felt Lloyd would always be something other than a brother, something other than a friend, while being, at the same time, both those things, too. She knew they'd probably never repeat the leisurely camaraderie of his last week of furlough— the circumstances just wouldn't fall in place again. But the bond forged then would continue, an underground river beneath their separate lives, perhaps rising to the surface like isolated springs when time and chance permitted. She hoped so, anyway.

"Well, tomorrow's Lloyd's big day," Emilie said at dinner one evening. It was now a week to the wedding, and that event had been dominating most of the conversation at the table.

"What do you mean?" Helen said.

"Why, his surgery. He didn't tell you?"

"No."

"What's the surgery for?" Walter asked.

"A new doctor came on staff, and he thinks maybe he can restore some sight to the one eye. Lloyd was against it—it's quite a long shot, and he's already had so many operations. But the doctor kept at him. He's young and very devoted—you feel he'd like to totally restore every man in that hospital."

"So he got Lloyd to agree?" Helen said.

"He did," Emilie replied. "And you did."

"Me?"

"Lloyd asked me if I thought you'd want him to try the operation, and I said I was certain you would. It's going to mean he'll miss the wedding—he can't move around at all for a while—but I told him that you and Billy would understand."

Helen was filled with excitement and dread. No doctor had ever held out much hope for even partial return of Lloyd's sight. Of course he must grab at this opportunity. But what if it failed? Would he be grimmer than if it hadn't been dangled before him? If only she could talk to him before the surgery, to find out what he was thinking.

"Can he have visitors tomorrow?" she asked her mother.

"I doubt it. Why don't you plan on going day after tomorrow? Oh, but that's Saturday, and weren't you and Barbara going to take Linda shopping for a dress?"

"Oh, Mama, Lloyd's more important than that."

Emilie looked at Walter and at Ursula as if she were reminding them of something.

"Well, he is," Helen asserted, though no one had said anything. "Barbara can find Linda a dress perfectly well without my help."

"You've never liked Barbara's taste in clothes," Emilie said.

"I don't care."

"You don't care how your flower girl is going to look?"

Helen scowled at her mother.

"No, I don't."

Emilie looked again at Walter.

"Helen," he said, "you've been a great lift to Lloyd. We've all seen it. His family is very grateful, I'm sure. But young men . . . especially soldiers who've had a rough time of it . . . they can mistake kindness for . . ."

"What are you saying, Papa?"

"It appears to us that Lloyd may be a bit sweet on you."

Helen was mortified. Apparently, she and Lloyd had been a topic of conversation among her parents and grandmother. Was the Mackey household conjecturing, too? Had any of this absurd notion reached Billy?

"Lloyd sweet on me? That's ridiculous," she said.

But as soon as she'd said it, she realized it might not be ridiculous. With a sinking sensation, she recognized a vein of guilt vibrating beneath her annoyance. Her family's distressing observation was not so far off from her own puzzlement over Lloyd and the undeniable pull between them. She'd been disinclined to give that pull a name. She knew, intuitively, that Lloyd would never openly tackle it, either. But now the task had been taken away from them. Now, in self-defense, she'd need to find her own designation for feelings she'd been content to leave unnamed. Why couldn't people just let things alone? Especially things they obviously didn't understand, things that didn't fit neatly into labelled boxes on numbered shelves.

"You and Lloyd aren't children anymore," her mother was saying. "That changes things. It's why you don't really see men and women being friends."

"You're wrong, all of you," Helen replied hotly. "Lloyd is my friend and he's in trouble and I'm going to see him on Saturday no matter what anyone says or thinks or imagines. And I won't be ashamed of it, either!"

"No one is talking about shame here," Walter said in a steely voice.

"Such fussing!" Ursula interjected. "I think it is what the young people call the jitters. For you, Helen, and for all of us. Our girl grows up. It is a good thing—the only thing—but we don't always like it so much." She raised her hands in a gesture of futility. "We are a little, perhaps, afraid. But the world, it does not stop for that. Especially now. The war won't let anyone stop to think two times about anything."

"That's not so, Nanny," Helen countered. "The war makes you think about a lot of things that maybe you never would have before."

"About being ashamed, Helen . . ." Emilie said. "We don't doubt your character, or Lloyd's. But you have to consider appearances."

Helen looked at her mother, then at her father and grandmother. She didn't have the heart to keep arguing. Nanny was right about one thing. Soon the interplay among them all would be revised. Though she'd still be living with them, she'd be Billy's wife, a state that would confer a certain independence, a stronger right to be her own boss than getting older or graduating from high school or even becoming a successful medium had given her. These, then, were the final days of her being their child, or, at least, of that being her chief position in life. She didn't want to mar the time with strife.

"Nanny's right," she said, dropping her embattled tone. "I've got the jitters. It makes me touchy, I guess."

"Just bear in mind, Helen, what your father said," Emilie told her. "That's all we ask."

Helen nodded and got up to start clearing the table. Bear it in mind, she thought sourly. How would she ever get it out of her mind? Nevertheless, she would go to visit Lloyd on Saturday. For now, she wouldn't think past that.

On Saturday morning, Helen was at home alone. Her father was off rehearsing songs for the wedding with two men from the *Sängerbund,* and her mother and grandmother had taken a roasted chicken to a sick friend in Carlstadt. She was writing a letter to Billy, telling him she was going to see Lloyd that afternoon, expressing her hopes that the operation had worked, though they wouldn't know anything for a while. Mentioning Lloyd to Billy did not feel awkward or phony, and Helen took this as proof that her feelings for Lloyd were not imprudent and wouldn't have to be disowned.

The doorbell rang. Helen was expecting a neighbor's boy to stop by for the stack of newspapers sitting just inside the front door. The Oritani was admitting kids free to a special matinee if they brought in bundles of newspapers. But when she opened the door, Barbara was standing there. She was coatless and hatless in the frigid wind, and she was crying.

"Barbara, what is it? Did something go wrong for Lloyd?"

"I came right over. My mother said I should wait 'til I calmed down, but I just couldn't."

"What's happened?"

"Oh, Helen." Barbara put her face in her hands and began crying harder.

"Come into the kitchen," Helen said, taking her by the elbow.

Barbara sat at the kitchen table while Helen put on water for tea. Then Helen sat down opposite her and waited while Barbara wiped her eyes with a handkerchief and struggled to gain control of herself.

"It's Billy," she said, staring down at the table.

"Billy?"

Helen couldn't fathom what she might mean. Billy was in North Dakota. Billy was going to be home in less than a week. What could he possibly have done to upset his sister so?

Barbara looked at Helen and let out a long, shuddering sigh.

"There was an accident," she said, unfolding a crumpled telegram that she must have had wadded up in her hand all this time.

"An accident?"

Alarm was flooding in. If Billy had been in an accident, she'd go to him. Right away. He mustn't be left to languish in a hospital so far away, with no one to sit by him and cheer him along. She stood up.

"I've got to pack. I've got to find out which train—"

Barbara reached up and put a staying hand on Helen's arm.

"Helen," she said, "he's dead."

Helen's sight went black. Behind her, the kettle began to whistle, its shrill piping rising quickly to a scream. Trembling and nauseated, she staggered against the edge of the table. Barbara jumped up to steady her, then lowered her to a chair. The kettle kept screaming. Helen looked at it and started to rise.

"I'll get it," Barbara said, crossing to the stove and turning off the gas.

"The telegram doesn't say much," she explained when she'd returned to the table. "His plane crashed during a training exercise. They . . . they're sending him home in a few days."

"Oh, God, oh, God," Helen said.

Her heart was galloping. Her insides had liquefied. Her body felt clumsy and hot. Everything in the room was flat and unreal.

She felt mocked by the stove and the dish cabinets and the clean counters, all audaciously unaltered, stolidly awaiting use, no difference to them by whom. Billy was gone. How could that be? Billy was gone. It was torture sitting still while within her a maelstrom whirled, dragging her down into a bludgeoning darkness. She got up and paced the room in quick steps, round and round, wringing her hands, pressing her fists to her temples, swallowing down terror.

Barbara interrupted her wild circuit and put her arms around her. Immediately, Helen began to sob.

"No, no, no, no," she moaned. "Not him, not him."

Barbara was crying again, too. Helen held on to her tightly. The bony press of Barbara's shoulder against her face and the firm circle of her thin arms were the only things keeping Helen from the full dominion of the heaving inside her.

She didn't know her father had entered the room until Barbara twisted around to hand him the telegram. She heard his voice, but not what he said. She felt herself transferred from Barbara's arms to his. She smelled the pipe tobacco in a pouch in his jacket pocket. She felt more comforted by his big, familiar embrace than she had by Barbara's. She leaned into him like a weary child. He couldn't help her—no one could—but she felt safer with him there. She didn't feel as much that she was falling, falling, with no bottom in sight.

The crying was coming more quietly now, like an idling motor. She didn't care if it ever stopped. She wasn't falling anymore. That was enough. As much enough as anything could be.

CHAPTER 34
MARCH 1944

The day of the funeral was a blur to Helen. Her mother shepherded her through the viewing at the funeral home, the church service, the cemetery rituals, the reception at the Mackeys. Helen was sorry that the Mackeys chose to have Billy buried in his uniform. He'd been a soldier such a small portion of his life. But maybe it's what he would have wanted. She didn't say anything. She wasn't his widow, however much she might feel like one.

Helen did request that the Mackeys put some of Billy's cherished model planes next to the casket in the funeral home and display others around the living room during the reception. Mrs. Mackey hadn't wanted to do it. A plane had taken her son's life. But when Mr. Mackey brought back a message from Lloyd that he thought it was a good idea, she gave in. Lloyd, still recuperating from surgery, couldn't attend the funeral.

The first few days after the funeral were less blurred, but they had the same boundary-less quality. It was morning, then it was afternoon, then it was evening. Meals happened, though Helen ate sparingly, lacking appetite or feeling full after only a few bites. She performed small household tasks. She slept a lot. She sat on the front porch and watched the mailman come and go, the milkman, the bread man. Children passed on their way to and from school.

Helen was keeping her bedroom curtains closed. The window looked out on the Mackeys' backyard, where scarcely a square foot stood without memories. Among many other things, it was there Billy had kissed her for the first time.

The newspaper was a minefield. War news was impossible to read, and seemingly benign sections like the funnies or sports or the society page could also waylay her. *Lil Abner, Blondie,* and *Popeye* presented her with the comic trials of coupledom. Sports stories reminded her of Billy's days on the high school track team. The society page described engagements and weddings and births, and showed pictures of groups of smiling women at teas. Even the obituaries made her feel strangely left out. Old people had died of illnesses. Soldiers died in battle.

Inexorably, days passed. Then, amazingly, it was three weeks since the news of Billy's death. Helen emerged from her daze and entered a dull, ceaseless ache scattered with sharp jolts of pain from out of the blue. Bing Crosby came on the radio singing *"I'll Be Seeing You"*, and Helen burst into uncontrollable tears. Someone on the bus loudly gloated about the overtime pay at a munitions plant, and Helen had to get off before her stop to keep from shouting the woman down. A young man of Billy's height and hair color and wearing the uniform of the Army Air Force crossed in front of her on the street, and she followed him two blocks, almost convinced that it was Billy, that some terrible mistake had been made and the boy they'd sent home in a box hadn't been him after all.

The fact of Billy's death was like a new house Helen was learning to inhabit. In it, every ordinary action felt altered, every unconsidered routine foreign, every expectation challenged. She'd been evicted from herself. Billy had taken part of her with him, and that part would never belong to her again.

Ursula and Emilie were careful with Helen, letting her dwell within her bereavement as deeply as she wished. They never brought up Billy, but if Helen did, they listened sympathetically to whatever anecdote she had to spin, sometimes adding their own small embellishments to her reminiscences.

Walter was of the opinion that the best thing for Helen to do was to swallow her sorrow and put on a brave face. He never said so, but Helen guessed his position. If she got weepy at the dinner table, he'd quickly introduce a trivial topic of conversation. When he found her on the sofa rereading Billy's letters, he set about cleaning his pipes, whistling softly through the task, keeping her company and wordlessly implying she ought not linger over the letters. One evening, he asked her if she'd cultivate the Victory garden this season, since Emilie was so busy with her Gray Lady work. Helen assented, and despite the listlessness of her response, he immediately plopped the latest Burpee seed catalog on her lap, and the very next Saturday, he turned the earth for the garden, making the plot larger than last year's.

Helen didn't find more comfort in one way of being treated than the other. There were times when her mother's tenderness and her grandmother's patience were balms, allowing her to retreat into an inattentive state free of serious responsibility. At other times, the same coddling chafed her. Likewise, her father's attempts to gently bully her into resuming some kind of normal life felt, in various instances, bracing and encouraging or cruelly dismissive and unfair.

One thing everyone kept talking about was time. How time healed broken hearts and all wounds, how in time it'd get easier, how she wouldn't feel like this forever, unmoored and raw. She wanted to believe them. She did believe them, in some recess of her benumbed mind that was managing to evade being smothered by grief, but it was difficult to get to that recess, and once there, it was difficult to stay for long.

Every night after dinner, Walter spread out maps on the dining-room table. It had been more than three years since the United

States joined the conflict, yet Walter still kept daily track of military events in all the theaters of war, drawing battle lines, recording dates and the names of generals and of towns and forests and rivers. Since Billy's death, Helen had avoided going into the dining room during her father's record-keeping sessions. She used to look in on him three or four times a week and let him update her. He always pointed out where people they knew were posted, though you could never be sure of anyone's exact location. Letters from overseas came with headings such as "somewhere in Italy" or "somewhere in the Pacific."

Finally, one evening, Helen decided she wanted to see how it would feel to look at her father's clean maps and listen to his battle summaries.

"Helen!" he said, surprised, looking up when she entered the dining room. He had spread a map of the Pacific on the table and was anchoring the corners with beer steins from the sideboard.

"What have you got tonight?" she said, walking over to the table.

He stared at her a moment, then turned and pointed to an expanse of ocean dotted with two curving parallel lines of islands.

"The Marshall Islands," he said. "They're all very small, but together they cover four hundred thousand square miles of ocean, and they're key to our push towards Japan." He tapped at one spot. "The Marines and the Infantry took this island, Kwajalein, a few weeks ago, and now they're moving out from there to take the rest."

Helen sat down at the table.

"Were many men killed?" she said.

"No," Walter replied. "The Marines learned some hard lessons on Tarawa back in November, and it saved lives in the Marshalls."

Helen remembered hearing about Tarawa. In three days, more men were lost there than during the six-month battle for Guadalcanal.

"They bombarded Kwajalein much harder than they had Tarawa," Walter went on, "both from the air and with naval gunfire, *before* landing any troops. They said the island looked like it had been lifted up into the sky and dropped."

What must it be like, Helen thought, to be under such bombardment. In this case, it was Japanese forces getting hit, and any fellow-feeling she had was mitigated by the recently released reports of the Bataan Death March, which had occurred two years ago. Rosie's brother Jimmy had been captured in Bataan. If bombing an island so hard it looked like it had been dropped from the sky would move the end of the war one day closer or keep one American boy out of a prison camp or out of a hospital or morgue, she would stomach it. Still, it made her shiver. Horrible, she thought. It must have been horrible.

Walter picked up a green pencil and circled three currently embattled atolls. In red pencil, he noted the Marine and Infantry divisions involved. He had other colored pencils for other designations, such as guesses at fleet locations, sites of sinkings, sites of amphibious landings. He was subscribing to two New York newspapers now, in addition to *The Record,* to glean as much information as he could. He knew that the more specific the information was, the more out-of-date it was. The details of future troop movements and even of current engagements were necessarily sparse. But his maps helped him place all the activity in some comprehensible order. It was his way of being a part of the war.

He'd wanted to volunteer as a plane spotter for the Civilian Air Warning System, but Mr. Collins was in charge of River Bend's unit, and he resented all things German, including his neighbors. Walter had taken classes in survival techniques during air raids and in first aid, but hardly anyone expected air raids anymore. River Bend's blackout sirens hadn't sounded in two years.

"You know, Papa," Helen said, "you ought to have a map of the United States, too."

"What for?"

"For things that happen here."

Walter closed his pencil box and studied her a moment.

"You mean like Billy's accident?" he said softly.

Helen nodded. She wouldn't cry. She wouldn't.

"And maybe, too," she said, speaking quickly to hold on to her composure, "where the war plants are, or where the Army does different kinds of training. You could mark Crystal City and the other internment camps, and the relocation centers for the Japanese from the West coast, and the POW camps."

"It's an idea," Walter said, though Helen felt he was simply humoring her.

"The war is here, too, Papa, don't you think? Even though we're not getting bombed, and we don't have to eat tulip bulbs to stay alive like they're doing in Holland, or have horses pull our cars, like in France."

Walter slid out the chair next to Helen's and sat down.

"The most important way the war is here or anywhere, Helen, can't be shown on a map," he said. "It's in people's hearts and in their faces. It's in the way so many lives will never be the same again."

"Then why do you keep the maps?"

Walter laid his hands flat on the map on the table and surveyed his notations.

"It's so big, this war. The men and the machinery, but also the ideas. You have to hold on to the bigness to see that winning is worth all the individual tragedies. Now that the other side is losing ground, when I make my marks on the maps, I actually get to watch the darkness being pushed back."

Helen nodded. She knew Billy's death was part of something bigger, something necessary. He'd have been the first one to say so. But it was too soon and he was too particular and special a person for her to derive any solace from the thought that he had died in a noble cause, that he had willingly put himself in harm's way for an ideal. Her head could call him a hero, but her heart could only count him stolen.

Walter looked intently at his daughter.

"If I could have spared you this, Helen," he said, "I would have done anything, anything at all."

"I know, Papa."

He stood up then and busily unrolled his map of Europe, laying it on top of the map of the Pacific, lifting and replacing the steins at the corners. He took up the front page of the *New York Times* and looked back and forth between the map and an article about the campaign in Italy. He grunted. There'd be no pushing back of darkness on this map today. The Allies were still bottled up below the Gustav Line, where the Germans at Monte Cassino and the mountainous terrain and cold winter rains had been fiercely opposing them since mid-January. Even after Cassino had been bombed so heavily that the Germans were reportedly burying their dead with bulldozers, they were still holding on.

Helen got up and left the room. It wasn't important, really, she thought, if her father didn't get around to adding a map of the United States to his inventory. The map that counted here was time. The conquest of hours, not miles or hills or beaches. Hours of waiting. Hours of making do and getting by and readjusting. Like everyone kept telling her. Give it time, they all said. As if "it" were a pet she had to feed. As if she had a choice.

CHAPTER 35
APRIL 1944

Lloyd's operation had failed. Tomorrow, he was being transferred to Valley Forge General Hospital near Phoenixville, Pennsylvania. Barbara had told Helen he'd be there three months, learning to use the recently developed long cane and working on improving his tactile perception and manual dexterity and his ability to retain and follow verbal directions. Then he'd go to a new center in Avon, Connecticut. They were doing things there no one had ever tried with the blind before, teaching them to move about independently by using their hearing and other cues to judge distances and the location of obstacles. President Roosevelt had pushed for the program, insisting he would send no soldier home who hadn't first received training to help him meet the problems of blindness.

Helen stood in the hall outside Lloyd's ward. She'd come to Halloran without having given much thought to what might transpire, knowing only that she had to see Lloyd before he left. That had gotten her onto the train and then the ferries. But now, just steps away from him, she faltered. What would she say? He'd sent no messages summoning her. They'd exchanged sympathy notes, personalized but formal. Yet in the past few excruciating weeks, when she could think only of her loss or of nothing at all, she'd been quietly aware that he was here waiting for her and thinking about her, despite his own grief over Billy, despite his feeling, as he must be, lost and alone. This awareness was a small piece of flotsam on a wild sea, but it had kept her from sinking more than once. She couldn't let him leave thinking that she'd forgotten him.

Lloyd was seated in a chair beside his bed. As Helen approached, she saw he had a small loom on his lap. His hands were unerringly weaving a strand of yellow yarn over and under a red warp. The rapid play of his fingers was so sure, she realized he must have done this many times before.

She stopped a short distance away to watch him. There was something about the sight of him, so self-contained and intent, that relieved her. He didn't look like someone who was weak or helpless or discouraged. Except for his dark glasses and the incongruous loom, he could have been any strong, handsome young man sitting expectantly in any room, maybe in a café waiting for friends to arrive for a jolly dinner, or maybe in some girl's living room waiting for her to come downstairs and go out dancing. Lloyd loved to dance. Helen got the impression— though perhaps it was only a desperate wish—that no matter what, Lloyd was unquenchable. And if he could be, with all he'd been through and all he had yet to face, there had to be a chance, too, for her.

"Hello?" Lloyd said in her direction. He'd sensed her presence. He kept at his weaving.

"Hello, Lloyd."

His hands stopped. She saw him swallow.

"Helen," he said. It wasn't a question. He knew her voice. She found that pleased her tremendously.

She moved closer and perched on the edge of the wide windowsill opposite his chair. The top half of the window was open a crack. Cool air drifted in and touched the back of her neck. She recalled her first visit to this room and how she'd talked about the weather. How very long ago that seemed, yet it'd been only three months.

"What's it doing outside?" Lloyd said, as if he were also thinking of that first visit and their argument about the smell of approaching snow.

"Oh," she said, "a bit breezy. Cool for April, but not cold."

He nodded.

"I'm getting out of here tomorrow," he said.

"Yes, I know."

"Come to wish me luck?"

There'd been the tiniest bite in his tone. His chin was lifted slightly, the line of his mouth straight and serious, prim she would have said of anyone but Lloyd.

"No," she said.

He smiled, but not fully.

"I mean," she amended, "of course I do wish you luck. But, really, I think I just wanted to see you again."

"You think?"

"I wanted to," she said definitely.

"Good. Because I've wanted you to come."

They both shifted in their seats, as if some great hurdle had been crossed, or as if one were rising up ahead.

"I guess you know all my news," Lloyd said, pointing to his eyes.

"Barbara told me. Sounds like you've got a lot of work in front of you."

"Yeah, well, better than staying parked here or on some street corner with a tin cup."

"Oh, Lloyd, don't say that, not even as a joke."

"It's what people think, though, isn't it? That a blind man can't do anything. I'm just saying it before they do."

He picked up the loom in his right hand and tossed it onto his bed. It was an angry gesture, but Helen noticed he'd reached out with his left hand first to gauge the distance and temper the force of his throw.

"I wouldn't say that about a blind man," she told him. "I

wouldn't think it, either. Especially not about you, Lloyd."

"Hey, I'm no hero," he said. "I'm going to Valley Forge and to Avon 'cause that's where Uncle Sam's sending me."

"Don't you want to go?"

Lloyd frowned in concentration.

"The thing of it is, Helen," he said earnestly, "I want it to work. I want it so bad, it kinda scares me."

"Scares you?"

"When the operation didn't take, it was like somebody shut a door and locked me out. For the first time, I really believed that I was gonna stay blind the rest of my life. But the crazy thing is, as soon as I knew there was no hope, I started feeling hopeful— not about seeing again, but about getting along as I am, about learning whatever they can show me. Because now I *need* it." He wrung his hands. "But what if I can't do it? What if I'm no good at it?"

"Are there special requirements?"

"You have to have good hearing. I suppose you have to practice a lot."

Helen reached over and put her hand on Lloyd's wrist.

"The Army must think you can do it or they wouldn't send you," she said. "I believe in you, too, Lloyd, for what that's worth."

He lowered his head, as if he were regarding her hand resting on him, then he lifted his unseeing gaze, seeming to follow the line of her arm up to her face.

"It's worth a helluva lot," he said.

Helen removed her hand and slid farther back on the wide sill. Lloyd rubbed his hands on his knees.

"How have you been?" he said softly.

He meant Billy, of course. She'd known it would have to come up. But the answer was so big, she didn't know how to begin. Other people had asked her the same thing, in the exact same words, and she always managed to say that she was all right, or that it was hard but she was getting by, or that she didn't want to talk about it right then. Such responses, while not false, were woefully incomplete.

Coming from Lloyd, the query felt new and vast and very personal. She wanted to show him everything that was inside her, but she was afraid she might not be able herself to bear hearing all of it laid out together. She took a deep breath and sighed. Lloyd was waiting, but she didn't feel his waiting as pressure. He was just there, like a burning candle.

"What did you do yesterday?" he finally said. It was a starting place.

"I took a long walk."

"Uh-huh."

"It was too muddy near the river, so I just walked through the streets, up around the high school and over by town hall. I didn't really think about where I was going."

She had thought about Billy. She didn't need reminders, but they were everywhere nonetheless—the high school steps, Benson's Hardware, the hobby shop where Billy bought supplies for his model planes, the bridge over the railroad tracks where Lloyd had dared her, when she was ten, to walk on top of the railing. To Billy's horrified amazement, she'd done it, but he'd become so nervous watching her that he'd wrapped his arms around her waist and lifted her down when she was only halfway across. Yesterday, near that bridge there'd been a poster urging people to buy war bonds. It featured a drawing of a young soldier's unsmiling face. "I died today. What did *you* do?" it said.

"Does it help to walk?" Lloyd asked.

"Now it does. In the beginning, I was so exhausted I could barely move around my house. I try to walk really fast. It helps me breathe."

"Otherwise you feel like you're suffocating?"

She studied his face. Did he feel that way, too?

"Exactly," she said.

"The last time I saw Billy . . ." Lloyd began, letting the name hang suspended between them a few seconds, ". . . was the day I left for Camp Kilmer to be staged through for England. He played the big brother to the hilt that day, telling me to watch my back, keep my nose clean, be sure to write to Ma. He didn't try to do that very often."

"He told me once that nobody could ever tell you what to do."

Lloyd grinned.

"The Army knocked that out of me," he said.

"Not all of it, I suspect."

Lloyd's expression became serious.

"I like to be my own man," he said, "but now I know what it's like to have somebody depend on you for their life and to have to depend on other guys the same way. I'm still stubborn, I guess, but I don't believe anymore that I can do it all on my own, or that it'd be the best way even if I could. I want you to know that, Helen."

"Okay."

"I was a lousy brother," Lloyd said in an anguished voice. "I shoulda pitched in more when Pop was gone."

"That doesn't make you a lousy brother."

"It doesn't make me a good one."

Helen thought about Billy and Lloyd, what she'd seen of their interactions over the years; she thought about Rosie's brothers, and about Teresa and Terence. It seemed to her that the brothers of girls behaved differently towards their siblings than did the brothers of boys. The brothers of girls could be disdainful, bossy, fiercely protective. Two brothers, however, could create what was almost a third entity, to which each donated a piece of his living, beating self. They might fight or have different interests, they might be envious and competitive, but they were bound together in an unbreakable way. That third entity continued to exist, if shrunken at times, ever at the ready to defend and nourish them.

"Billy loved you," she said to Lloyd. "That's all that matters now." And she began, quietly, to weep.

Lloyd cleared his throat. He felt on his bedside table for a cup of water and took a couple of gulps through a bent glass straw.

"Are you crying?" he said.

"A little."

Helen dug a handkerchief out of her purse and blew her nose. It had been a relatively mild spate of grief, more relieving than engulfing.

"I didn't mean to upset you," Lloyd said. "I haven't had anyone much to talk to about it."

"It's all right."

"No, it's not. I should be helping you, not making you cry."

"You *are* helping me."

Helen put away her handkerchief and stared at Lloyd. Suddenly, she wanted to feel his arms around her. They'd probably both start crying in earnest then, but it would be fine. It would be right. Then, in the next moment, she felt that their embracing wouldn't be right, that it would be chancy, even perilous. The peril wouldn't come from Lloyd, nor from her, but from somewhere outside them, somewhere that they were part of despite its being outside them. It was not just brothers who could spawn a third entity.

"Whenever I'm with you, I feel good," she dared to say. "I relax. Even now. I know I can cry or not cry, I can talk about Billy or not talk about him, and either way, it'll be all right. That's how you help me. It's something nobody else does."

Lloyd seemed to mull this over for a moment. Abruptly, he stood up.

"You wanna take a walk?" he said.

"Where?"

"Down the halls, outside, anywhere. I just feel like moving."

Helen put on her jacket and tied a scarf over her head. She crooked her arm, and Lloyd took her elbow. In the hall, she fetched him an olive green sweater out of a closet.

There was not much to look at in the central yard—the surrounding walls and tall windows of the hospital, the turned earth of the bare garden plots, the cracked concrete of the rectangular walkway, a few men wrapped in blankets and sitting in wheelchairs. Helen and Lloyd slowly walked the perimeter. The yard was sheltered from the wind, and most of it was bathed in afternoon sunlight. Helen loosened her scarf and let it drape around her neck.

"I thought he was safe," she said after they'd gone halfway around the yard in silence. She felt a catch in her throat on the word "safe," but she wrestled it down.

"He was a soldier, Helen."

"But he wasn't in the war yet."

Lloyd stopped walking and turned to face her.

"My unit went ashore at Gela in Sicily," he said. "Do you remember reading anything about what happened there? We heard General Eisenhower asked the war correspondents not to report it because of morale at home."

"Gela? I'm not sure."

"While we were fighting on the beach, they flew in reinforcement troops. Only, the transport planes happened to come in right on the tail of a heavy German bombing attack. Our gunners got confused. They thought the German bombers were back. They shot down our own men. Our own guys, Helen. Twenty-three planes went down. More than four hundred GIs were killed."

"I remember it now—but the report didn't come from anyone in the field. There was a leak from the War Department, and there weren't many details."

"The point is, Helen, that war's messy. You listen to news broadcasts, you look at neatly drawn maps in the papers, you hear the President or the generals talk, and it seems like everything's all worked out and under control, like some kind of gigantic football game. But it's not under control, really. It can't be. There are rules, sort of, but everyone knows they can be crossed if you have to. There's people giving orders and other people following them, but they're all winging it a lot of the time. And there are accidents . . ."

He shoved his hands in his pockets.

"When you sign on for war," he continued, "you sign on for whatever comes down the pike, and you find out quick that anything can and that if you live long enough, you'll see plenty, and not a lot of it will make sense—not in the way things used to make sense."

"That's how I've been feeling about Billy—one of the things I've been feeling. That his death didn't make sense."

"It made as much sense as any of them."

They started walking again. Gray Ladies came to take the men in the wheelchairs inside. One of them reminded Lloyd that dinner would be arriving on the wards soon. He said he wanted to make one more circuit before returning to his room.

With the men in the wheelchairs gone, Helen could pretend they weren't in a hospital yard but in some undergroomed city park. She didn't want to think about the soldiers shot out of the Sicilian skies by their compatriots. She didn't want to think about the maimed men in the buildings around them. She didn't want to think about war and its jumbled mix of sense and nonsense, of hard necessity and profligate waste. Would Billy's death have been any easier to take if he'd died in battle? He was gone. That cold fact overrode its own trappings.

"We're back at the entrance," Helen informed Lloyd when they'd done their last tour of the yard.

"Is there a bench we could sit on a minute?"

There was, and she led him to it.

"Do you think, Helen, that you're gonna hear from Billy? Do you think he's gonna come to you?"

She hadn't expected this. It was something she'd wondered herself. She'd even talked to Nanny about it. But she hadn't thought anyone would broach the subject with her.

"My grandmother says he won't," she said.

"Why not?"

"She's never known it to happen. Besides, I'm not holding séances now."

"Do you think *she* could do it? Call him for you?"

Helen had considered this, too, but Nanny had refused.

"She doesn't think her ability's strong enough," she answered.

The old woman had meant not only that she might be unable to bring Billy through, but also that she wouldn't know how to supervise the energy between a new spirit who'd passed violently and a grieving, powerful medium.

"Nanny said we have the proof of all the others that Billy is all right. She said that's enough."

"Is it enough for you?"

Helen picked at a loose thread on her jacket. Lloyd was making her think, making her shape her thoughts into explanations. She balked at the effort, but she was grateful to him for forcing it.

"No, it's not," she said. "But seeing him wouldn't be enough, either. It wouldn't be the same as really seeing him again. And it wouldn't last."

Lloyd turned, angling his body towards Helen. When his

knee bumped hers, he pulled back a few inches.

"He didn't really believe all that stuff, did he?" he said. "About what you can see."

"He had his doubts."

"Would that stop him from contacting you?"

"I really don't know, Lloyd. He'd have to want to, certainly. He'd have to think it would help me."

"Would he come, do you think . . . would he come to help *me?*"

Helen was startled. Lloyd sounded as needy as any mourner at one of her séances. Was he asking her to bring Billy to him? Now that the wish was issuing from someone other than herself, the notion of fulfilling it suffused her with anxiety. Perhaps Nanny was right that mediums were not meant to call up their own dead.

"Is there something specific you want to hear from him? Or something you want to tell him?"

Lloyd slowly shook his head and stood up.

"Forget it," he said. "It was just a cockamamie idea."

Helen, too, stood up. Lloyd took hold of her elbow in preparation for entering the building.

"You know what else my grandmother says?" she told him gently. "She says that the dead hang around a while watching how the people they left behind are doing. So, if there's something you want Billy to know, you can talk to him like he's right in front of you. Because he probably is."

CHAPTER 36
MAY 1944

Rosie was home on a month's furlough. The day after her arrival in town, she was on Helen's doorstep, looking fit and trim and serious. Helen immediately threw her arms around her, and they both burst into relieved laughter.

"Come in," Helen said, pulling her by the hand. "I didn't think you'd stop over for a day or two. My folks are all out. They'll hate it that they missed you."

"I couldn't wait to see you," Rosie said. "There's plenty of time for everyone else later."

They went through into the kitchen. Helen filled two tall glasses with iced tea made with spearmint from the Victory garden and cut two pieces of Ursula's *Linzertorte*. They took their glasses and plates into the backyard and dragged two Adirondack chairs under the big maple in whose shade they'd spent so many summer afternoons. Rosie peered around the yard.

"It all looks the same," she said. "And yet it's not like I remember it."

"What do you mean?"

"It's smaller, for one thing. But that's not all." She scanned the yard again. "I feel it at home, too. It's not a *bad* feeling, just a little confusing. When I was overseas, I'd picture this yard sometimes, and my mother's kitchen, and Oratam Beach, and a couple of other spots. To remind myself of what our guys were fighting to save and why I was living in a wet, muddy tent or letting myself get eaten alive by desert flies. But it turns out the real places don't fit the pictures I thought up."

"Lloyd Mackey said he thought home could never be like what you dreamed about. He said when you're away at war, you build up a dream of home, and you've got the dream, and then when you're back, you've got nothing, and it's like you're moving slower than everyone else and you're not sure how to join in."

Rosie nodded thoughtfully.

"How is Lloyd?" she said.

"He's all healed, but he won't ever see again. He's in a rehab hospital in Pennsylvania."

"Gee, that's tough."

"Oh, he'll be all right. He'll be better than all right. He's got so much heart, Rosie. And guts. When you're with him, you feel like . . ."

Helen interrupted herself with a swallow of iced tea.

"Well, you know, same old Lloyd," she continued brightly. "Nothing could ever keep him down for long."

Helen thought she saw a question in Rosie's eyes, but her friend turned her gaze to a couple of robins on the grass. She crumbled up a bit of torte crust and threw it to them.

"Helen," she said quietly when she'd turned back, "I'm so sorry about Billy."

"Yes, I know. I got your letter. It was wonderful, the things you wrote."

"I can't even think how I'd feel if anything happened to Arnie, and we've only known each other seven months, while the two of you . . ." Rosie shook her head. "Gosh, Helen, you were in love with Billy even before there *was* a two of you—your whole life practically."

"A kid's crush," Helen said, shrugging.

"But not later."

"No, not later."

Rosie set her empty plate on the ground and her empty glass on top of it. One robin hopped a little closer, cocking its head to inspect the plate for crumbs.

"Do you miss him a lot?"

Only Rosie would dare to ask so blunt a question, though it wasn't really daring, but simply an expression of her guileless nature and her deep affection for Helen. Rosie's bluntness made Helen feel daring, too, which was not particularly natural to her. It was as if Rosie had leant forward and cajoled Helen, as she'd done so often when they were children and she was proposing some mild trespass or chancy exploit. "C'mon," she'd say, "you can do it. It'll be okay. Cross my heart and hope to die."

"I miss him," Helen said. "But maybe not as much as I should."

"Who says?" Rosie spouted. "That mooning mother of his? Say, Mary Steltman hasn't been needling you again, has she?"

"No, no," Helen said, smiling.

"What then?"

"Oh, Rosie, I'm afraid to say it out loud. I've hardly even said it inside my own head."

"C'mon, it'll be all right," Rosie said, reaching out to squeeze Helen's arm.

Helen took a deep breath.

"Sometimes I think it was just the nearness of the wedding making me nervous. You know, like you hear all brides get? That my nervousness mixed me up."

"If me and Arnie ever get to where we set the date, the only thing could make me nervous is whether he'd show up on time! But you've got to be a little plainer, Helen. What happened?"

"Lloyd happened."

Rosie raised her eyebrows and sat back in her chair.

"Plainer," she instructed.

"Well, I visited him in the hospital, over in Staten Island, and then he came home on furlough at Christmas, and he got in the habit of stopping by. We'd take walks, I'd read him the newspaper, we'd talk."

"Did he make a pass at you? 'Cause these soldiers, sometimes they can be—"

"No, nothing like that. But one day, my parents and my grandmother kind of warned me about him, that they thought he was falling for me. I was mad about them saying that, but then I started to think that maybe *I* could be falling for *him*. At least a little. And I got scared. 'Cause how could I fall for somebody when I was about to get married? Especially, how could I fall for my fiancé's brother?"

"Well, how could you? Honestly. Tell me what's so swell about Lloyd that you'd think for one minute about throwing over the love of your life."

Helen slid forward on her chair.

"I *didn't* think of throwing Billy over," she protested. "But I did think maybe . . . I did start to wonder, Rosie . . . if he really was the love of my life."

"Look, Helen, like you said yourself, it was probably just bride's nervousness."

"I didn't say probably."

"What was it then?"

"Being with Lloyd is so . . . so *easy*. And Lloyd's not an easy person."

"And being with Billy was hard? C'mon, Helen, you were ready to marry the guy. You can't tell me there was nothing there."

"Of course there was something there. There was a lot. He was . . . well, I guess he was my definition of what being in love is. I couldn't imagine him not being part of my life. I still forget, sometimes, that he's gone."

She looked over at the fence along the driveway. The old wooden box she used to stand on was still there, a clump of dandelions growing pressed up to one side of it. Rosie was right. She had loved Billy practically her whole life, with a naïve ardor that would not tolerate doubts. When misgivings or misunderstandings did crop up, a kiss, a touch, the fulcrum of private history eviscerated them so handily she barely knew it was happening. She looked again at Rosie.

"It was something you wrote me about Arnie that gave me my first twinge of not being sure."

"Arnie?"

"Not about him, exactly, but about how you felt with him. That you felt more like yourself. You thought I'd know what you meant because of Billy. But I didn't."

Helen fiddled the fingers of her right hand on the broad wooden arm of her chair.

"Later, I thought of your letter again," she continued, resting her hands in her lap, where she stared down at them. "Because later, I thought I did know what you meant. But not because of Billy."

"Because of Lloyd?"

Helen nodded.

"Oh, brother," Rosie said, shaking her head. Quickly she added, "Gosh, I guess that's not the best thing to say."

Helen couldn't repress a wry smile.

"What's Lloyd got to say about all this?"

"Nothing," Helen replied, appalled. "We've never talked about it. Never even come close."

"And what about now?"

It was the very question that had been dogging Helen since the last time she'd seen Lloyd, when she'd had that shameful desire to feel his arms around her. She kept pushing the question down, refusing to give it any berth. She felt guilty that it even arose. Now, agitated, she stood up and walked away from the chairs and along the fence a short distance. Rosie didn't interfere. Helen returned to her seat.

"There's more," she said.

"Okay."

"Billy hasn't . . . come to me yet," she said hesitantly. "Not even in a dream."

"Is he supposed to?"

"I keep wondering if he's not coming because he knows that I was worrying about us. Oh, Rosie, what if he knew it before he died? What if somebody said something to him?"

"I don't get how these things work, Helen, but just because you haven't seen Billy in a dream or anything doesn't have to mean he knew you were trying to decide between him and his brother."

"I wasn't! It wasn't ever a choice between him and Lloyd—I could never, ever think like that. I was still gonna marry him. I *wanted* to marry him."

Rosie reached over to hold Helen's hands.

"Well, there's your answer, then. You didn't do anything wrong, Helen."

"But I *feel* wrong, Rosie. Even now, when I think about us getting married, there's this scared lump in my stomach."

"Maybe that's why Billy isn't coming."

Bewildered, Helen made no response.

"Maybe he doesn't want you to be scared."

"Seeing Billy wouldn't scare me. It's my own feelings that scare me."

"Could be it looks the same to him. Could be he thinks you don't want to see him. Do ghosts think?"

The back door of the house opened, and Emilie poked her head out.

"Rosie!" she called, crossing the yard. "I didn't know you were coming over. Here, let me give you a good hug. You're not too much of a soldier for that, are you?"

"No, ma'am," Rosie said, getting up.

Over Emilie's shoulder, Rosie shot an appraising glance at Helen. Helen made a gesture that said it was all right that their talk had ended so abruptly. Rosie had given her something to ponder.

Helen had resisted going into trance to seek Billy. She'd wanted him to do the seeking. Even as part of her dreaded what he might say. But maybe it was a mistake to avoid trances and séances. She still preferred that Billy come without her sending Iris to find him, but she could let him know the door was open, couldn't she? Shouldn't she?

Yes, she decided, only half listening as her mother and Rosie chatted, she'd hold a séance, or a series of séances, a fuller giving over to trance than she'd ever made before. She'd discard the careful rules and schedules she'd set up in the fall, after the materialization of all those faces had so unnerved her. She'd let anyone attend, allow any questions, give Iris free reign, welcome any spirit. She wouldn't pull back no matter what she saw or heard.

CHAPTER 37

Iris brought every departed soul that every sitter requested, and more—people's grandparents and distant relatives, children no one in the circle knew, and, always, at the end of each séance, one of Helen's boys. But so far, after ten days during which Helen had sat five times, no Billy. Not that Helen had asked for him. As planned, she was simply putting herself at the disposal of the spirit world and waiting.

The round of trances was influencing the intensity of Helen's dreams. In them, she climbed long ladders whose tops she couldn't see; she swam in still, green waters that had no shoreline; she watched, transfixed, as swarms of tornadoes headed her way; and always, she awoke before her exertions exhausted her, before calamity struck. Once, in one of the quieter dreams, she stood at a fruit stand piled with bright tomatoes and lemons, cucumbers and figs, utterly convinced that Billy was standing right behind her, only inches away, and equally convinced that if she turned around, he'd disappear. She felt him concentrating on her. His attention was as powerful as a touch. She smelled lemons for two minutes after waking up. She smelled him.

"Today has only Mrs. Durkin and Miss Simmons," Ursula told Helen as they walked to Mrs. Durkin's house on the eleventh day of Helen's campaign. Ursula had suggested a different room might produce different results.

The four women were experienced at séances, and each had

her own wishes for this one. Mrs. Durkin was hoping for another materialization, she didn't care of what or whom. Miss Simmons was worried about her fiancé, Mr. Howard, who was in the Aleutian Islands, which had been recaptured from the Japanese last summer. Ursula wanted Billy to contact Helen. She was beginning to be concerned about the strain the girl was subjecting herself to.

Helen, too, wanted Billy to come, but that was no longer the only thing driving her. The close succession of trances had left her in a constant state of heightened awareness, as if she were a simmering pot. What, exactly, was simmering in her she couldn't say, but she felt during each trance that something was coagulating, gathering strength and momentum, and that it would soon be revealed. She understood that it was a force or message or spirit unrelated to Billy. She was opening herself to it as much as to him.

She entered trance calmly and automatically, but she soon sensed that today something was different. The usual detachment from her surroundings had set in, the usual feeling of being in a featureless antechamber, but Iris was not there to greet her, which was not usual.

As she paid closer attention, she discovered some familiarity about the state. It was reminiscent of the day in front of McCutcheon's when she'd had the vision of Pearl Harbor, except that she felt none of the fear and confusion she had that day. It was similar, too, to the certainty she'd encountered when she'd looked at the *Life* photo of the children in the trench shelter. Then she knew. There'd be no spirits today. She was going to receive a premonition.

Helen found herself looking down at a beach at night, as if she were hanging above it in a hot air balloon. It was absolutely quiet except for the barely discernible *whoosh* of the waves. She could see a broad area of shingle at the water's edge and an open swath of sand stretching to the base of high, steep cliffs. A deep, V-shaped ditch had been dug into one section of beach, and concrete walls had been erected elsewhere. Only by filling the ditch and downing the walls could anyone pass easily from the water to the cliffs, though Helen did spy a few funnel-like avenues of access.

Large concrete structures sat on top of the cliffs. Helen recognized them from newsreels as gun emplacements. Planted on slopes below them were machine gun nests, angled so that, together with the artillery in the concrete emplacements, they could cover every inch of the beach with firepower.

All at once, the air filled with the deafening roar of big guns from the water. In flashes, Helen picked out an armada of battleships and destroyers bombarding the cliffs and the concrete walls on the beach.

Then, for a split second, Helen was encased in an inky darkness thick with noise. Added to the naval gunfire were blasts from the big guns on the cliffs, the loud chatter of machine guns and the answer of rifle shots, the shriek of whistles, the rumble of explosions. And tangles of screams, so many screams—men shouting to one another, men crying out in agony. Helen put her hands to her ears, but she couldn't block the sounds. Her chest was vibrating with them.

Suddenly, dawn-like light obliterated the darkness. But the light hadn't arrived softly, like a normal dawn. It had leapt instantaneously into being, as if by the flick of a switch.

The exposed scene was seething with horrors. The beach teemed with soldiers. Soldiers running and crawling, soldiers falling, soldiers spinning and flying, hit by bullets or mortar shells, thrown and torn by land mines, cut in half by machine gun crossfire, writhing wounded with no one to evacuate them, men scrambling on their bellies over the dead bodies of their comrades. Some men staggered to their feet after being hit, only to be hit again and fall again. Even then, some of them got up and pressed on. There were flamethrowers and smoke, sand bursting up in sprays from bullets and hand grenades and mines, beach grasses on fire. The soldiers were heading for the cliffs via the funnel openings Helen had noticed earlier, but it was a deadly route, peppered with land mines, tangled with barbed wire, and strafed by machine gun fire.

Helen saw landing craft disgorging yet more soldiers, some of whom sank out of sight, never to reach the beleaguered beach. The water between the landing crafts and the beach was red with blood, and churned by gunfire, shell fragments, drowning men, and the detonation of underwater mines.

The artillery noise and the shouts and screams were even louder than they'd been during the short spell of blaring darkness. Bombers and fighter planes howled overhead. It was a huge, hellish pageant of gore and clamor. Helen's heart felt like it might explode, and her stomach was in knots, yet she could not look away.

Slowly, words insinuated their way into her cringing mind. *Festung Europa.* Fortress Europe. It was what Hitler arrogantly called France and the other German-held lands. Another word was tapping at the edge of her mental grasp, an English word. An American, not a European place. Omaha. Could that be right? Yes, it was clear now. Omaha. But what did land-locked, placid Nebraska have to do with such a field of slaughter?

As soon as she was sure of the name, Helen felt herself begin to slip out of trance. The sickening vision and the din evaporated. Everyday sounds met her ears—a car horn outside, the creak of Mrs. Durkin's chair as she shifted in her seat. Helen's neck was tight with tension. She opened her eyes. The friendly faces of the three women at the table filled her with relief. At the same time, she wished they weren't there. How could she tell them what she'd seen? What description would be adequate?

Her hands were trembling and would not stop.

"Helen?" her grandmother said. "There was no one today?"

Helen looked at each woman in turn.

"I saw a terrible battle," she said. Her voice felt throaty and unused.

"Where?" Miss Simmons asked.

"I don't know. Maybe nowhere . . ."

"Nowhere?"

"It felt like . . . like it hadn't happened yet."

"A presentiment," said Mrs. Durkin, impressed.

Helen sat on her hands to calm them. She turned to her grandmother.

"I think I should tell someone, Nanny."

"You are telling us."

"No, someone official. Like Captain Fitzpatrick."

Mrs. Durkin and Miss Simmons looked at Ursula for explanation. Ursula sat up straighter, letting them know by the set of her shoulders that they wouldn't be getting one.

"It's her duty," Mrs. Durkin said, in an attempt to remain included.

"It might save lives," Miss Simmons offered.

"First, Helen must think some more," Ursula declared.

"Yes," Helen agreed. "There were some things about it that were puzzling."

She was trying to placate her grandmother. She shouldn't have brought up Captain Fitzpatrick in front of the others. Also, putting herself under her grandmother's direction prevented Mrs. Durkin and Miss Simmons asking more questions.

But she knew she didn't need to think anymore before taking her information to Captain Fitzpatrick or someone like him. Nor would she ask her family's permission. It didn't matter that the vision had been indefinite as to time and place. It didn't matter that she didn't understand why she'd heard the

incongruous name of an American city. Those were things for
the captain to figure out. Mrs. Durkin and Miss Simmons were
right. She had a duty, and if she did it, lives might be saved.
Plus, if she told someone, as she hadn't done with the Pearl
Harbor vision, she might be spared nightmares later on. She
never wanted to see that beach again.

Helen set out early for New York. She didn't have an appoint-
ment with Captain Fitzpatrick, and she wanted to have the
whole day in case she had to wait to see him. Additionally, she
couldn't count on how long it would take her to get there.
Because of gas and tire rationing, more people were using public
transportation. Military personnel had first call on tickets, and
there were always military personnel on the move. Train cars
and buses were sometimes packed shoulder to shoulder. And
troop trains had priority on the rails, requiring civilian trains to
pull off onto sidings and let them pass, which could take an
hour or more.

The train to the city was crowded but on time, and Helen
had to wait only half an hour to see the captain.

"You're in luck," his WAC secretary told her. "Some days, he
doesn't come to the office at all."

Captain Fitzpatrick stood up when Helen entered his
cramped office. He indicated a chair in front of his desk, and
when she'd sat down, he resumed his own seat. He rested his
folded hands on his blotter. Papers were stacked at the desk's
corners like miniature sentry towers.

"You told my secretary, Miss Schneider, that you had some
vital information for me," the captain prompted. "Is it something
about mediums? Some bunko artist? We had to throw a
hypnotist off Camp Shanks just the other day."

"I'm not a hypnotist," Helen said, bristling.

Hypnotism was a current craze. There were hypnotists on the

radio, and hypnotists giving public demonstrations in nightclubs, in lecture halls, even at schools. Lindbergh's admiration of the Nazis before the war was blamed by some people on his having been hypnotized when Goering pinned a medal on him. But now Lindbergh was teaching American pilots and flying combat missions in the South Pacific.

The captain sat back in his chair and waved his hand vaguely. Clearly, hypnotism and mediumship were all the same to him.

"I had a vision, Captain," Helen said. "I saw a large, very violent battle on a beach."

"Half this war is being fought on beaches," the captain said. "It's no wonder you had such a dream."

"Not a dream, a—"

"Let's not quibble over terminology, Miss Schneider."

"It was a European beach, I believe," Helen continued, businesslike. "And there were an awful number of men getting killed. I thought you ought to know about it, that maybe something could be done, because, you see, this battle hasn't happened yet."

Captain Fitzpatrick narrowed his eyes.

"Miss Schneider," he said heavily, "men do get killed in battle. I'm regularly at staging areas all over New York and New Jersey, and I see men leave every day who will most certainly face death. I'm sorry you had such a frightening dream, but I really don't have the time to—"

"Omaha," Helen said.

The captain started.

"What did you say?"

Helen knew he had heard her clearly.

"I don't know what it means," she said, "but it has something to do with the battle I saw."

"Wait here." The captain got up and left the room.

He was gone twenty minutes. Helen was just about to ask the

WAC in the outer office about him when he returned. He had two young corporals with him, both wearing bifocals, which explained their stateside posting. They were also wearing MP armbands and shouldering rifles.

"You will have to go with these men, Miss Schneider," he said.

"Go where?"

"For tonight, you can bivouac at Ellis Island."

Astonished, Helen stood up.

"I don't understand," she said.

"I'm not at liberty to explain further. Tomorrow someone from the Counterintelligence Corps in Baltimore will talk with you. Until then, you are not to repeat anything that was said here today."

"If you let me go home, I promise I'll come back tomorrow."

"These men will escort you to Ellis now."

The captain went around his desk and sat down. He took the top few papers off one of the stacks and picked up a pen. The corporals stepped closer to Helen, one on either side of her. At the threshold, Helen stopped and turned.

"My parents . . ." she said.

"We'll notify them," the captain replied without looking up. "Someone's already on their way there."

CHAPTER 38
JUNE 1944

The next day, Helen sat nervously on a hard chair in a small room while Captain Fitzpatrick and another man, Major Levy, looked through some papers on a bare table set under an open window. She was wearing the same clothes as yesterday, and she felt unkempt, despite having washed up in a basin as best as she could that morning. Her stale appearance, especially in contrast to the two crisp military men, increased her nervousness. She wished she'd been issued the standard khaki shirt she'd seen all the internees wearing. At least it would be fresh. She hoped the fact that she hadn't been given one was a sign they didn't expect her to be staying.

She shifted her position, trying to relieve a stiffness in her back. For most of last night's long hours, she'd lain tensely awake on a narrow iron bed and listened to the other women in the dormitory—their snores, their turnings, their coughs. Once some dreamer cried out a few unintelligible words. The dormitory was off a balcony above the huge registry room where the internees spent their days reading, playing cards and chess, knitting, carving eidelweiss from deer horn or doing other crafts, and writing letters. Whenever during the night someone walked across the empty, cavernous room, his steps echoed up to its arched, tiled ceiling and from there into the dorm. Near dawn, Helen had dropped off for two hours, but she was far from rested. The insides of her eyelids felt grainy.

She was beginning, too, to regret her empty stomach. A

Border Patrol Agent had escorted her to the dining hall for breakfast, but she'd taken only a cup of black coffee. He'd directed her where to sit, well out of conversation range of anyone who might decide to be friendly, and he'd stood close by while she drank her coffee.

Helen was the only person in the large hall accompanied by a guard. Several people gave her sidelong glances as they passed, and one little boy stopped and stared frankly at her, moving on only after a woman, presumably his mother, had hissed *sich bee-ilen* at him. In spite of everything, Helen smiled at that. How many times in her childhood had Nanny hurried her along with the very same command? Helen ignored the remainder of the curious looks by examining a WPA mural about the role of immigrants in industrial America. From her seat, she could see coal miners, a pigtailed Chinese man working on the railroad, and a young family consisting of a man shouldering a large bag and a woman wearing a kerchief and carrying a baby in a sling.

At last, the two officers turned towards Helen. Captain Fitzpatrick folded his arms across his chest and leaned back against the edge of the table, observing Helen with the kind of expectant interest people give to dozing zoo animals. Major Levy, hands clasped behind his back, smiled at Helen. He had a beautiful smile, but seeing it didn't make Helen feel any safer.

"Miss Schneider," the major said, "you brought some information to Captain Fitzpatrick yesterday that holds some interest for us."

Helen wondered who "us" was. The Army, she supposed. But Ellis Island was run by the Immigration and Naturalization Service. Why hadn't they taken her to an Army facility? Why had they taken her anywhere at all?

"What we need to know now," the smiling major continued, "is who gave you that information. Also, when and where he gave it to you, and how."

"How?"

"Was it a face-to-face meeting? A phone call? Perhaps an encrypted letter . . ."

Helen looked past Major Levy to Captain Fitzpatrick. Hadn't he told him?

"It was a vision," Helen said, returning her gaze to her inquisitor.

His smile slipped a little. It occurred to Helen that it was more like a tic or a scar than a real smile. There was something involuntary about it. At the same time, it was vaguely predacious, like bait.

"Come, come, Miss Schneider, you don't expect us to believe that, do you?"

"It's the truth."

The smile, or whatever it really was, vanished. The major, with the air of having to do something he wished he didn't, went to the table and opened a drawer. He drew out a sheaf of oversized papers. As soon as he'd turned around again, Helen saw what they were. Her father's maps. She couldn't imagine how they'd gotten to this room, but their presence frightened her.

"I see you're familiar with these," Major Levy said. "Why don't you tell us about them?"

"They're maps," Helen said, embarrassed at sounding stupid, but unable to come up with anything better. "About the war."

The major nodded encouragingly.

"Lots of people keep maps," Helen added, rallying a bit.

Major Levy selected one map and handed the others to Captain Fitzpatrick, who set them on the table.

"Very few people," Levy said, "keep maps like this." He held it up. "In fact, I'd venture to say that no one whose allegiance is in the right place would have any occasion to create such a map."

It was a map of the United States. It was incomplete, but Walter had entered a good number of symbols and names, especially along the Eastern seaboard, and he'd worked out a careful key, pasted into one corner. Red squares for military training camps, blue squares for embarkation points, green squares for defense plants, green circles for airfields, blue circles for detention camps, red circles for relocation centers. Helen saw a blue circle in the Hudson off lower Manhattan and realized it must be Ellis Island.

"That map was my idea," she blurted.

"Was it now?" A bit of smile slunk back. "And who told you to make it?"

"No one."

"Who were you going to give it to once it was done?"

"No one."

"One of your father's German friends?"

"No."

"One of your grandmother's connections, then."

"No, no. The maps aren't *for* anyone. It's just a hobby. You're making it sound like—"

"Like a conspiracy?" Levy carefully rolled up the map.

"Your mother volunteers in a veterans' hospital, doesn't she?" he said. "I imagine a sympathetic, motherly woman could pick up some useful tidbits of information from homesick soldiers without them even realizing what they're saying. Quite the family operation you've got going, *Fräulein* Schneider. *Nicht?*"

"Why are you saying all this?" Helen burst out. "My family has never done anything wrong."

"Very commendable."

The major handed the rolled-up United States map to Captain Fitzpatrick without turning around. He kept his eyes fixed on Helen.

"Would you have any objection, Miss Schneider, to signing

an unqualified Pledge of Allegiance to the United States of America?"

Helen wondered if this were some kind of trick. She no longer trusted anything this man might say. He could turn ordinary statements into attacks. But she felt it would be a serious mistake to refuse to sign a pledge of allegiance.

"No, of course not," she answered. "No objections at all."

"That's fine," Levy said. "We'll get the captain here to take care of that later."

He walked thoughtfully up and down the room a few times and looked once at his watch.

"While we're on the subject of your family, we have a few more questions. Purely routine."

He lifted his arm, and following his cue, Captain Fitzpatrick picked up a pen and a clipboard from the table.

"Do you have any relatives serving in the Armed Forces of the United States?" he began.

"I have . . . that is, I had . . ." Helen stammered, unwilling to bring the tender fact of her and Billy into this harsh room. She touched her thumb to the back of the ring Billy had given her. A delicate band of diamond and emerald chips, it had once been his great-grandmother's. Helen had moved it to her right hand on the day of his funeral. "My fiancé was in the Army Air Force."

"That would be William Mackey?"

"Yes, but how did you—?"

"You kept his letters."

"Well, of course I did, but—"

"They were among the materials the FBI confiscated from your residence yesterday."

A flash of nausea assailed Helen.

"Those letters are *mine*," she said fiercely. "I want them back."

The captain was unmoved. "Everything not pertinent to our

inquiry will be returned to you in good time," he said.

"Do you have them here?" she demanded.

Fitzpatrick scowled at her. "I strongly suggest, Miss Schneider, that you calm down and let us get on with the interview."

Helen glared at him. He returned her stare with one of his own, icy and implacable and clearly meant to intimidate her. It was working. Fear and awful helplessness were rolling back in. Retreat was her only option. But she was determined to retreat with dignity. She nodded assent to the captain, but she didn't lower her challenging gaze. In the periphery of her vision, she saw Major Levy bend to the table and write something down.

"Do you have any relatives serving in the German Army?" Captain Fitzpatrick resumed in a wooden tone.

"I don't know for sure," she said, trying to keep meekness out of her voice. "We might. I don't exchange letters with anyone, if that's what you want to know."

"Have you at any time been a resident or visitor in Germany?"

"No."

"Do you speak German?"

"No."

"Did you ever hear anyone in your family speak German?"

"My grandmother."

"Did you ever hear her, or anyone else in your family, or any friends of your family, praise Hitler?"

"Never," Helen said, quickly deciding not to mention Uncle Franz's brother Erich. He wasn't a close relation. He'd never even been to the Schneider home. Anyway, she honestly didn't know whether Erich had ever praised Hitler.

"Has your grandmother adhered to the regulations for enemy aliens regarding curfews and restricted zones, and the prohibitions against plane travel and the ownership of photographic equipment?"

Helen nodded.

"Please answer aloud," Major Levy instructed her.

"Yes, she's obeyed the rules," Helen said.

"Will you, for the duration of the war," the captain asked, "avoid any typically German clubs, associations, and organizations?"

"I guess so."

The captain glanced up from his clipboard, where he'd been reading out the questions and recording her replies.

"You guess so?"

"Well, I'm not sure what that might include."

"We can supply a list," Major Levy put in, brushing away the digression.

"Your father, I believe, is a member of the *Nord-Amerikanischer Sängerbund,* a national federation," Captain Fitzpatrick said.

"A federation of men's singing societies!" Helen said. She almost could have laughed at the absurdity of them thinking the *Sängerbund* might be in any way threatening. *Sängerbund* members were like any other Americans. They bought Victory bonds, they had sons and grandsons in the military and wives and daughters in the Red Cross.

"And your grandmother pays dues to a local organization, the *Krankenkrasse,*" Fitzpatrick pressed on, unfazed by Helen's disdain.

"The *Krankenkrasse* is a sick and death benefits society," Helen said, feeling worn out. "I'd guess every old-time German in Bergen County is probably in it."

Fitzpatrick returned his attention to his clipboard.

"Are you willing," he said, "to give information to the proper authorities regarding any subversive activity you might note, or which you might be informed about directly or indirectly?"

Helen hesitated. As with the loyalty pledge, this appeared on the surface an easy thing to agree to, but shadowy distinctions seemed to be hiding below the easy surface, like the slimy, jagged branches of sunken logs that sometimes snagged boats and fishing lines on Hunter River.

"Do you have a list for that?" she asked, genuinely hopeful.

Major Levy's face darkened.

"This isn't a game, Miss Schneider," he said. "There are already enough questionable activities and ties associated with your family for us to deem the lot of you potentially dangerous to the public peace and safety of the United States, and intern you all for the duration."

"That's crazy! This all started because I came to Captain Fitzpatrick with some information I thought he ought to have."

"A correction, Miss Schneider," said Captain Fitzpatrick. "This all started because you demonstrated that you knew things that you shouldn't have known."

"Things I shouldn't have known?"

"How and where certain soldiers died. When a certain ship sank."

"But I told you—"

"Yes, we know: the spirits."

Now it was Captain Fitzpatrick's turn to go to the drawer in the table and pull something out. This time it was a thick sheaf of papers tied with a black ribbon. The automatic writings from Helen's boys. The instant she saw them, she put out her hand for them. Major Levy stepped forward. Fitzpatrick gave the papers to him.

"Tell us about these," he said in a suspiciously gentle voice.

Helen lowered her hand.

"Haven't you read them?" she said.

"Yes, we have. The captain thinks they're stories you pieced together out of newspaper accounts and flights of fancy, to use in your séances with gullible parents and wives of servicemen."

"What do *you* think?" Helen knew Levy outranked Fitz-patrick. She thought he also might have a more open mind, if only because he seemed honestly curious.

"I think that whether you made them up or not, they *sound* true."

Helen clasped her hands tightly together in her lap.

"They *are* true," she said.

"And you received this information how, exactly?"

"From the spirits," Captain Fitzpatrick interrupted.

"That's right," Helen said, ignoring his mocking tone. "Those boys came to me, unasked. I wrote down everything they said, and I didn't put in one word that wasn't theirs."

"Why would they do that?" Levy said. "Come to you and tell these incredible stories?"

"I didn't ask them why."

"Do you usually write down your . . . spirit communications?"

"Not usually. They wanted me to."

"Again, Miss Schneider, one has to wonder why." He turned to put the papers down on the table, then turned back to face her. "Quite apart, of course, from wondering if any such appearances really did—or ever could—occur."

So, curious or not, the major had limitations on how far he'd go.

"All right, Captain," he said, "I think we're through for the time being."

The captain began stacking the papers and maps.

"What's going to happen to me?" Helen asked, getting up. It felt good to be on her feet rather than craning her neck up to look into the faces of the standing men.

"Your family will be here shortly to visit you," said the major. "They've been advised to bring you a few personal items. Later this afternoon, you'll be sent to Camp Seagoville by train."

"Seagoville? Where's that?"

"In Texas."

"Texas!"

"It can't be helped. Seagoville's the only long-term facility for single women."

"But how long will I be there?"

"That depends. We'd like to have some more discussions with you."

"Why can't I stay here?"

Major Levy caught the eye of Captain Fitzpatrick, who had finished gathering the papers and was standing near the door.

"She's almost as inquisitive as we are, isn't she, Fitz?"

"Miss Schneider," the captain explained, "Ellis Island is a transit facility. The people here are awaiting deportation or repatriation."

"But don't I get a hearing?"

"You can put in to the Justice Department for a hearing at Seagoville if you like," Major Levy said. "But you don't get to ask questions of a Hearing Board."

Captain Fitzpatrick opened the door and went out into the hall, where he waited for his cohort.

"There are no locks here, Miss Schneider," Major Levy said. "You're free to go to the main hall or the library, or to walk in the compound outside."

Free, Helen thought miserably. That's a joke. It struck her that an island made a perfect prison. Levy gave her a curt farewell nod.

"Major," she said, staying him. "I still don't know what it is you suspect me of."

"Why, Miss Schneider," he said, his strange and coldly beautiful smile materializing again, "we suspect you of exactly what you claim for yourself: that you have access to knowledge beyond the grasp of most people. And in this war, we can't afford to ignore any possible advantage, however farfetched, now can we?"

Helen was too flabbergasted to respond. The major exited the room. Helen heard the receding clicks of the men's shoes against the hallway's cement floor, and then, through the open window, the screech of a sea gull.

CHAPTER 39

Helen was on the train to Seagoville for three days, in the custody of a Border Patrol agent. She let Helen roam the train freely, but whenever they neared a station, Helen had to return immediately to her assigned seat, with the agent beside her. They'd been handcuffed together from the time they stepped off the ferry from Ellis Island to the moment the train pulled out of Grand Central Station, and the woman said she wouldn't hesitate to use the handcuffs again if Helen wasn't in her place every time the train arrived at a stop.

Miss Pierce wasn't a cruel person, as far as Helen could tell, only a very conscientious one. Not that she got to know her very well. They dined separately. They didn't converse beyond small talk about the passing countryside. Miss Pierce reminded Helen of her high school gym teacher. She had the same no-nonsense air, the same earnest attachment to the rules of the game. But when they were walking down the crowded Manhattan sidewalks and through bustling Grand Central, she'd hidden the fact of the handcuffs by linking elbows with Helen and laying a sweater over their manacled wrists so that they looked like two chums connected by affection, not law, thus sparing Helen deep embarrassment. She hadn't had to do that, and Helen was grateful to her for it.

Seagoville looked more like a college campus than a prison, though before the war it had been a federal reformatory for women. Six two-story, colonial-style red brick buildings connected by paved walkways framed a grassy quadrangle. These buildings were where most of the camp's 700 internees lived. There were also sixty pre-fab wooden "victory huts" assigned to married couples, with and without children. Other brick buildings housed a library, a beauty shop and a barber shop, a hospital, the power plant and maintenance shop, and storehouses for food and household items. But the collegiate grounds were fenced, with a white line marking a "kill zone" ten feet in from the fence, and armed guards patrolled the perimeter on horseback.

The first thing Helen was asked when she arrived was what language she spoke. She was surprised to learn that the majority of Seagoville's internees had been brought there from Central and South America, and many of them spoke only German and Spanish or Japanese and Spanish. The Italians were long gone, Italy having surrendered in the autumn of 1943. It was the German army fighting the Allies on Italian soil. But on June 4th, while Helen was still on the train, the Allies had at last entered Rome.

An English-speaking Panamanian woman was appointed to show Helen around. Marta was a voluntary internee. Her husband, a German national, was interned at Camp Stringtown in Oklahoma.

"He's coming soon," Marta told Helen as they walked across the lawn. "Then I shall move to the colony."

"The colony?"

Marta pointed to the group of "victory huts" and their mess hall.

"You have a husband in another camp?" she asked.

"No."

"You won't have to be waiting, then," she said. "The waiting is hard. Also the not knowing what is our future. That you will have."

Helen's negative reply seemed to have doused any remaining curiosity Marta had. She didn't venture more questions.

They entered one of the brick residences. Marta took Helen through the dining room, which was furnished with tables set for four, and into the kitchen.

"We make our own crews for the dining room and for cooking," Marta explained. "They bring the food and we prepare it. We can make requests."

"Oh?"

"Of course. You can't expect us to eat the same as the Japanese," Marta said.

As they proceeded along the hall of the dormitory upstairs, Helen glanced into several rooms whose doors stood open. They were all identically equipped with one or two twin beds, a dresser, a desk, and a washstand. She spotted some individual touches—a few books stacked on the floor beside a bed; a flower in a vase; a large, framed photo of Adolf Hitler on a wall. When they arrived at her room, Helen was relieved to find she'd been given a single. She set down the satchel her mother had brought to Ellis Island.

Marta lingered in the doorway, counting silently on her fingers. Helen supposed she was checking that she'd covered everything she was supposed to.

"We have tennis and ballet, sewing machines, and more things," Marta said. "You can go to the recreation building to ask. You remember which one?"

Helen didn't remember, but she nodded anyway, hoping Marta would leave. Now that she was in her room—she was tempted to call it a cell, but that would only make her feel worse—she yearned to be alone.

"The Quakers come sometimes with music and lectures." Marta spoke staring at the ceiling, concentrating on her recitation. "There's jobs, too, but they can't force you to work. Ten cents an hour. We get three-fifty a month clothing allowance. All in scrip. So we can't save up to bribe nobody."

Marta lowered her eyes from the ceiling.

"Herr Stangl is the Speaker for the Germans to Dr. Stannard," she continued. "But if you want to complain about anything, see Herr Wiedemann in our building. He is who we elected to the Council. He was a Bund official. Very strong man."

Helen nodded again. She'd briefly met Dr. Stannard, the camp commander, that morning. The woman had struck Helen as patient and respectful, which was close enough to kindness in a place like this.

Finally, Marta left, promising to return the next day with Helen's slot on one of the meal crews. Helen immediately closed the door and sat down on the bed.

She took Lloyd's letter from her skirt pocket. She'd had to let someone in Dr. Stannard's office read it, but it had been returned to her uncensored. She'd already read it during the train journey, so censorship now would have been pointless, but she was glad nevertheless that none of it had been blacked out. It would have been painful to see it defaced. In the past few days, the letter had come to stand for all the sustaining connections in Helen's life—Lloyd, because he'd written it, and her family, because they'd had the consideration to bring the letter to her on Ellis Island, and even Rosie, because it was through the conversation with Rosie about Billy that Helen had decided to hold the series of séances that had led her to Major Fitzpatrick's office and ultimately landed her here.

She unfolded the letter. What a strange twist, she thought. In his letter, Lloyd had struck the pose of an explorer writing of a new world to someone secure at home. Yet here she was in a setting as novel and challenging, in its own way, as the one he was describing.

335

Lloyd was learning how to maneuver through the buildings and grounds of the hospital and through the streets, buses, and taverns of Phoenixville, probing and pushing against the limits of his blindness and against self-doubt. Helen, too, had involuntarily entered a kind of darkness, but in her darkness there were neither guideposts nor guides, Marta and Herr Weidemann notwithstanding. Lloyd had helpers and teachers. She had interrogators. The Army was trying to expand Lloyd's freedom. The same Army had fettered her.

Helen smoothed the letter flat on the desk. Most of it was typed, Lloyd having dictated it to a Gray Lady, but the final paragraph was in pencil. The handwriting had the unsteady, careful quality of a child's script, displaying an obvious effort at control. He explained, in the dictated section, that to write by hand he had to place a piece of corrugated cardboard under the letter paper and use the ridges of the cardboard to keep his lines straight. As he wrote, he followed the tip of the pencil with his left index finger, and when he finished a word, he moved his finger to the other side of the pencil point to create even spaces between words. It sounded like a laborious process.

Lloyd conceded he'd need to learn to write and read Braille. At first, he'd decided against it. He had enough else to master, he reasoned, and would simply rely on getting through that aspect of life by listening to talking books and getting people to take his dictation. But then he'd met a young amputee who was learning to read Braille with the stump of his wrist and another veteran who was using the tip of his tongue, so Lloyd figured he could and would do it, too.

The typed segment of the letter was full of stories like that. How you could tell if a lamp needed to be turned off by feeling if the light bulb was hot. How following a rubber mat in the mess hall with the edge of your foot led you to where you picked up utensils and food and where you dumped your garbage. He went on at length about his new plastic eye and how much better it was than old-fashioned glass eyes—lighter in weight, unbreakable, able to move from side to side, more natural-looking and better fitting. Helen couldn't help but feel queasy at Lloyd's pleased declaration that he could smooth away any irritations with a nail file.

She skipped to the hand-written postscript, which was phrased like a telegram, probably because of the concentration required to shape every word.

Am going to Avon early. Bunch of new guys coming here need beds. Grapevine says Avon tough as nails. Hope I'm ready. Still working on how to hold a cane. But can light a cigarette. Will show off when I see you again. Miss showing off. Too many champs here. Kidding. Regards, L.

Helen wondered if Lloyd had left Valley Forge yet. She didn't know his new address, but if she wrote to Old Farms Convalescent Hospital in Avon, Connecticut, her letter would likely make it to him. But what should she say? She could tell Lloyd where she was, but not why. Would he think that the simple fact of her detention meant she must be guilty of something? Hadn't she herself once thought as much of Erich?

What she wanted to tell Lloyd was how she was feeling—confused, fearful, lonely. She had downplayed these feelings in front of her family. They were already worried enough. Her father had sworn to take every legal recourse to get her released. There'd been several successful court cases where German-Americans had protested orders from the Army that they move out of their homes and jobs in restricted military zones. Helen's wasn't an exclusion case, but Walter held up these examples as evidence that her plight wasn't hopeless. Helen had acted more reassured than she was.

She would go tomorrow, she resolved, to Dr. Stannard's office and inquire when she could expect to be questioned again. Major Levy had said she would be. The sooner that happened, the sooner she'd know what was going on. Then she'd write to Lloyd.

Helen had spent many hours on the train going over her interview on Ellis Island. She'd become convinced that though her battle vision had activated Captain Fitzpatrick, it was not the real focus of his and Major Levy's interest. The questions about her loyalty seemed, in hindsight, beside the point. She kept turning over the major's parting words. He wanted something from her. But what? Surely not merely another promise to restrict her séances.

A sliver of optimism perforated Helen's gloom. When someone wants something from you, she thought, it gives you leverage, however moderate. You have capital to spend or trade. You are not defenseless. She opened her satchel and started unpacking her clothing and toiletries into the dresser.

The following morning, Helen was on her way to the commander's office when she heard a raucous honking of car horns. Through the chain link, she spied eight automobiles speeding along, horns blaring in a jumbled medley, headlights flashing on and off. Three men in a convertible were standing up in the backseat waving small American flags and shouting. The drivers kept making U-turns so that they could pass the front gate again and again, then they finally tore off down the road, still leaning on their horns. Helen saw nothing but fields and pastures on all sides. The cars must have come from Dallas, where she'd disembarked from the train, or perhaps from some small farm town nearby.

Other internees had stopped to stare at the noisy motorcade. Their quizzical expressions made Helen think this was not a regular occurrence. Some faces showed alarm as well as bewilderment. Helen recalled reading about a murderously angry mob wielding hatchets and shotguns that had marched on a Santa Fe relocation camp for West Coast Japanese in 1942, when American troops were suffering terrible losses in the Philippines. The camp commander had turned the vigilantes away by convincing them that violence against the internees could backfire into the Japanese military mistreating or killing American prisoners of war. Yet the occupants of the honking cars at Seagoville's gate had seemed more exuberant than inflamed.

Dr. Stannard's office was crowded with staff gathered in a semicircle in front of a radio at the far side of the room. The clerk who'd registered Helen yesterday looked over at her when she entered, but the woman didn't come to ask what she wanted. No one paid Helen any mind at all. She went to stand at the edge of the group to find out what was captivating them.

"It's the cross-channel invasion," a man whispered to Helen. She guessed he was a guard because of his Sam Browne pistol belt. "Started last night." He pointed unnecessarily to the radio.

A stream of reports was being issued. Eyewitness accounts from reporters who'd dropped into France with paratroopers or landed on the beaches with the first or second wave of infantry. Bulletins from Berlin and London. Local reactions from all over the United States.

Seagoville was not the only place where motorists were sounding their horns and flashing their lights. Across the country, church bells were pealing, air raid sirens blaring, factories and trains blowing their whistles. But despite the excitement, the reporters said, the overall mood was solemn. Churches were filled with praying, weeping people. There were prayer services in offices. Stores were closed, sidewalks deserted. On Army bases, men stood in silent crowds around loudspeakers piping in the news. Tonight, the Statue of Liberty, dark since

Pearl Harbor, would be lit for fifteen minutes, and at ten o'clock, the President would come on the radio and lead the nation in a prayer for their fighting men.

"The liberation of Europe has begun," an announcer quoted a White House statement, adding his own enthused comment, "Brother, we're on the road to Berlin!"

While more home-front stories were being broadcast, the guard leaned closer to Helen and filled her in on what she'd missed.

"They hit five beaches in Normandy," he said. "The Brits and the Canadians are at Gold, Juno, and Sword, and our boys are at Utah and Omaha. Sounds like they got it the worst on Omaha, by a country mile."

Helen's heart jumped.

"Fooled the Jerrys," the man continued. "They thought we were coming in at Calais, so they were better dug in there. They said Rommel was off at a birthday party in Berlin! Bad as it was on Omaha, it coulda been worse if they knew we were coming in there."

"Omaha?" Helen said. "That's a beach?"

"Well, it's not what the Frenchies call it, I'll wager, but, yeah, it's a beach. More like a combination grave pit and junkyard now, from what they say." Again, he indicated the radio. Omaha had just been mentioned.

Helen listened, frozen. It was late afternoon in Normandy. The troops on Omaha Beach had reached the cliff tops, and tanks were beginning to move inland, so the terrible shore fighting was over, but the reporter was recapping the morning landings. He was describing her vision—the falling and fallen bodies, the floundering landing vessels, the men pinned down on the sand by machine gun fire, the choppy, bloody sea, the whole cacophonous storm. Now, the reporter said, the beach was quieter—an occasional mine explosion, some sniper fire. Ships as far as the eye could see waited off-shore to unload supplies and more men. The next phase of Operation Overlord would be the taking of Normandy's Cotentin peninsula, followed by a break-out from there toward Paris.

Yes, the beach was quieter, the reporter repeated soberly, and weary soldiers were moving doggedly on to the tasks of cleanup and build-up, but the wreckage of battle, both human and machine, lay about on every side. Burning trucks and jeeps, overturned boats, twisted wrecks that used to be mine detectors and portable radios, dead tanks, smashed bulldozers, rolls of telephone wire, bloodied shoes, writing paper, first aid kits, thousands of cartons of cigarettes, oranges, toothbrushes, family snapshots, life belts. And bodies—bodies arranged in rows and covered with blankets, other bodies as yet not collected. During the battle, the reporter noted, there'd been so many bodies everywhere, you could barely take a step. He named the divisions that had landed on Omaha. One of them was Lloyd's. If he hadn't been sent home from Sicily, he would have been there today on that horrific beach.

Helen turned and left the office. She wanted to sit out in the hot Texas sun a while and try to calm her mind, then find a chapel. There must be one somewhere on the grounds.

What had made her think she could prevent anything as vast and convulsive as Omaha? She'd strode into Captain Fitzpatrick's office with such self-confidence. She'd felt so important. How like a silly, vain schoolgirl.

Why had she been given the vision? Or any of the messages she received? It was an old refrain, but one she'd lost sight of. Maybe here, locked away and alone, the answer would come at last.

CHAPTER 40

Marta had warned Helen about "barbed wire sickness," the excruciating boredom and sinking worry that afflicted those who didn't stay busy, so Helen quickly devised a routine. Each morning, before the day's heat had gathered force, she walked the grounds. After breakfast, she helped out in the children's classrooms, teaching conversational English. She spent the rest of her day in the weaving room, where she was working on a small rug. Some days, she had to put in time in her building's kitchen. Marta asked her to join a group of women who were planning to put on a play, but Helen declined. She was trying to make the best of a bad situation, but she wasn't ready to conceive of it as being a long-lived one.

The evenings were emptier. There'd been an open-air song-fest once, where the standard *Leiderkranz*, or wreath of songs, was punctuated by *Deep in the Heart of Texas* and *Home on the Range*, both belted out with gusto. Another night, Helen went to a Hopalong Cassidy movie in the auditorium.

The movie show was the only time she saw Japanese internees up close. She studied them surreptitiously, curious about their appearance and their uniformly mild-mannered demeanor. These people had not been interned as part of the wholesale removal of Japanese and Japanese-Americans from the West Coast. If they had been, they'd be in a relocation camp instead of at Seagoville. Everyone here had been interned as individuals, for specific reasons. Helen caught herself wondering what their "crimes" had been, but as soon as she'd thought it, she felt ashamed. What had *her* crime been? Surely, she was not the only person interned on flimsy, circumstantial, or secret evidence. Marta informed her that the Japanese at Seagoville who were not from South America were language teachers from California, or were, like Marta herself, voluntary internees wishing to stay with their spouses.

Except for the songfest and the movie, Helen stayed in her room evenings reading newspapers. For days after June 6th, almost every story was about the invasion of France. Advertisements had been dropped to make room for reports from Caen, St. Lo, and Cherbourg. Radio stations, too, had cancelled commercials. The radio in the rec room was on continuously, even though at times Helen was the only one there. She knew this was in stark contrast to homes across the country where people were sticking close to their radios and hanging on every detail of the dramatic, first-hand accounts of the fighting. She'd read that factory workers were so news-hungry, bulletins were being broadcast over loudspeakers on the factory floors.

Helen would have sought out the news in any case, but she had the added spur of a directive from Iris. Or her interpretation of a directive from Iris.

In her room on the night of June 6, still shaken up from having had her premonition about Omaha beach so exhaustively confirmed, Helen had called on Iris. Because she was nervous about entering trance in such an alien environment, she placed her chair against the door. If someone tried to come in, she'd be jarred, and simultaneously, her weight would impede the opening of the door, allowing her a moment to collect herself.

Despite her nervousness, Helen slipped easily into a light trance. The characteristic sense of well-being was restorative. Iris soon shimmered into view, surrounded by a pink mist.

"Iris," Helen addressed her mentally, not daring to speak

343

aloud. "I don't know why I'm here—here in this place, and here in your company. I need guidance."

"Here is the same as anywhere," Iris answered.

"For the moment, yes," Helen countered. "But I have to function in two worlds, not just in yours."

"Mine is also yours."

"Yes, yes."

Helen fought down irritation. It would only disrupt her trance and cause Iris to be even more vague. She concentrated on cultivating the paradoxical state of being alert enough to interact meaningfully with Iris, and detached enough to let in whatever she might offer, especially the unexpected or mysterious. Attempts at interpretation should come later. This frame of mind was much easier to achieve when Helen was doing a reading for someone else, or when Iris had an agenda, like when she brought the newly dead soldiers. It was different now that Helen herself was seeking a message.

Iris waited patiently, as always, while Helen reinforced her trance state. Though, Helen had thought in the past, could Iris ever be said to be truly waiting? There was no air of expectancy in her, no sense that her time was being ill-spent, no sense of time passing at all. Iris didn't wait, really, Helen had finally decided. Nor did she have patience. Or not have it. She simply existed. She didn't struggle to understand things, nor to elucidate them. Maybe she already understood everything, or maybe she didn't deem full understanding to be necessary or even particularly interesting. It was an enviable state.

"You desire to understand," Iris communicated, as Helen was trying to think of how to say just that. "It is natural. No act bears fruit without this desire."

"There must be a reason you come to me," Helen said, "and a reason my boys come, and all the spirits who appear when I call on behalf of other people."

"We come out of love."

"But *why?*"

"For that question."

Helen felt a fluttering of despair. Talking with Iris was like trying to grasp flowing water. Except that Iris wanted to help her. She was sure of that. Though wanting was perhaps too muscular a notion.

Helen envisioned a stream of cold, clear water, eddying around rocks, sliding through a quiet forest. She elaborated the image until she could smell dampness, hear the stream gurgle, pick out individual pebbles in the streambed and water striders near its green banks. She stared at the stream, as mesmerized and content as she might have been beside a real stream in the woods by Hunter's River on a summer afternoon at home.

Her fledgling despair lifted. It wasn't her responsibility to steer the stream. She had no control over what the stream might carry to her or past her. Iris had control. Or something or someone beyond Iris. It was a liberating realization.

"We can guide anyone," Iris said, "but some are easier to reach. Some stand by the door. You are one."

"What is your guidance?"

"Prepare to live evermore. You make your own rewards, your own regrets, in your earthly world and in ours. Live in joy here and now, and prepare to live in joy."

Helen recalled the mundane questions people put to their departed loved ones during séances. Requests for advice on practical problems, pleas for release from sorrow or guilt, applications for glimpses into the future. They all seemed so small compared to what Iris was offering. Yet most of the time, the spirits had obliged.

Helen had started discouraging these kinds of inquiries last October because she'd begun to feel such use of her powers, and of the spirits' tolerance, was actually a misuse, or, at best, a mistaken use. But she'd never broached her theory to Iris, and Iris had never made any overt notice that Helen was approaching her mediumship differently. In the series of séances last month, Helen had lifted all restrictions in an attempt to pave the way for Billy to appear. Iris hadn't shown notice of that shift, either.

"If there's this higher purpose," Helen pressed now, "why do spirits bother to answer earthly problems and petitions?"

"They answer so people will believe," Iris said, "so people will pay attention. Those answers are not the real answer."

"Why do they send me visions I didn't ask for?"

"There is a sea of nows," Iris continued. "The boundaries do not always hold."

"But what am I to *do?*"

"Choose. Give what will help. Everything has its time."

To Helen's dismay, Iris began to fade.

"I still don't understand," she called to her.

But Iris was already part of the mist, distinguishable merely as a thicker area of cloudiness. Only her flower was still identifiable, hovering unsupported in the air.

"You will know," Iris said from out of the mist. Her voice was unusually melodious and sweet.

Despite Iris's confident words, when Helen came out of trance, she felt frustrated. Then, Iris's tone, lingering in her mind, began to soothe her, in the same way she'd been soothed as a fretful child by her father singing her a lullaby or her mother stroking her head.

It occurred to Helen that though she wasn't in control of the elusive stream of the spirit world, nor of the boundary-cracking visions, she *was* in charge of what information from these sources she shared with others. And just as she'd learned to enter and leave trance at will, she would learn how to "schedule" opportunities for receiving visions. After all, hadn't she succeeded years ago in "turning off" seeing auras all the time? She stood up and stretched her arms above her head. She felt better.

The next evening, Helen began her intensive newspaper reading. She tried to pry out the common, human experiences behind the facts of battle statistics and geography. She read about families and schools and churches, and how the war was touching them. She read editorials and analyses, and letters from local boys overseas. If, as Iris had instructed, she was to choose what was helpful, she had to know what was needed. Not what people thought they needed, not what they would say at first blush if you asked them, but what they might say in an unguarded moment after a tiring day, when they were sitting with a friend who fell quiet at the right time, or when they took a gamble on a compassionate stranger's shoulder.

Major Levy arrived in Seagoville ten days after Helen. A clerk from Dr. Stannard's office found Helen weeding in the flower garden and escorted her to a meeting room in the administration building. The major was seated at a long table when Helen entered. He stood up and said good morning. She nodded to acknowledge his greeting, but she didn't say anything in return. He seemed not to mind.

"I trust you've been comfortable, Miss Schneider?" he said when they'd sat down on opposite sides of the table. "This camp has an excellent record."

"Being kept in the dark is not comfortable, Major," Helen replied.

She wasn't afraid of him, as she'd been on Ellis Island. What could he threaten her with now? She wanted to get out of Seagoville and go home, but if she had to stay, she would manage. The war against Germany couldn't last much longer. The experts were saying it'd be over by Christmas. In any case,

Major Levy was not likely to be swayed by displays of humility
or timidity, nor by appeals. She didn't know what, in fact, would
sway him, but she believed that the stronger she was, the better
chance she had. And she did feel strong. So why not show it?

"Kept in the dark?" Levy said roguishly. "I assume you don't
mean literally."

"No, not literally."

"Well, Miss Schneider, perhaps by the end of this meeting,
you won't have that complaint any longer. It's all up to you."

Helen doubted this was true. The major bent to open a
briefcase on the floor at his side. He took out an olive green
folder and set it on the table between them. It was stamped
"Top Secret." Helen looked from the folder to the major. He
seemed to be waiting for her to speak. But why bother to ask
about the folder? He was obviously going to tell her about it
whether she asked or not.

"What did you think of the news of D-Day, Miss Schneider?"
Levy finally said.

"I thought what everyone thought—that it was horrible and
yet good news."

"Nothing more?"

Helen hesitated. This must be what people mean, she
thought, when they speak of playing cat and mouse.

"I thought that I'd been right."

The major nodded.

"I thought that, too," he said quietly.

He laid his hands flat on top of the green folder. His fingers
were hairy, and he was wearing a wedding ring.

"I'd like to ask you some questions about how you . . . *see*
such things."

"All right."

"They aren't dreams, correct?"

"No, I'm awake. I'm usually in the middle of some ordinary

activity, and a vision just arrives. Though when I saw that beach, I was in trance."

"In trance?"

"It was during a séance."

"A séance." The major sat back in his chair and shook his head. "Where dead people in white sheets float around the room and levitate furniture."

"It's not like that."

"Whatever you say," Levy conceded, sounding fatigued. "Séances are not my concern. What I want to know is whether you can bring on visions like the D-Day battle at will."

"I've never tried."

"Do you think you could?"

"I don't know."

Major Levy stood up and walked the length of the room twice. He seemed to be weighing the advisability of some course of action.

"Miss Schneider," he said returning to the table but not sitting down. "I've been granted some discretionary leeway, and I'm going to take a chance on you. I'm going to be candid—up to a point—and I'm relying on you to hear me out without prejudice, and then to see and fulfill your duty to your country."

Helen was taken aback. She hadn't known what to expect from this interview. She'd girded herself for insinuations, insults, threats, brow-beating, even some form of bribery. She hadn't counted on a plain request. She'd never imagined being taken into the major's confidence. Was this simply another, more sophisticated tactic in the cat-and-mouse game?

"Everything I'm about to tell you," the major went on, "is not to go beyond this room."

"But you said I'm a danger to the peace and safety of the United States," she said.

The major looked at her with a mixture of amusement, annoyance, and admiration in his eyes.

"I said *potentially* dangerous," he replied.

"Yet here I am."

"At the time of our last meeting, detaining you was a necessary precaution. In wartime, Miss Schneider, niceties must sometimes be dispensed with. I trust you won't hold it against us."

"Niceties? Like liberty?"

"Don't be naïve," the major said, irritation winning out over decorum. "We were on the eve of the biggest, most important invasion of the war, for God's sake, and there you were, a girl with a multitude of German connections, spewing forth all kinds of details about beach landings and casualties and code names—"

"But you didn't believe me!"

The major exhaled audibly and sat down again.

"We couldn't take the risk that someone else might believe you," he said. Then he tapped the folder with his index finger. "There was this, too. If your vision turned out to be even partially accurate, we wanted you available to discuss this."

"Do you always lock up people you want to talk to?"

The major stared wearily into Helen's eyes. Let's not do this anymore, he seemed to be saying.

"Very soon," the major said, "you will be free to go. Now can we dispense with this topic?"

"I guess so."

"All right, then."

He got up again and went to the door. A woman appeared in the hall, and Major Levy asked her to bring them coffee. When he came back into the room, he went to the window and stood staring out, his back to Helen. The view was hardly absorbing—just two buildings for staff housing outside the gate—but he remained steadily turned towards it. Five minutes later, there was a rap on the door. Major Levy opened it, and the woman he'd spoken to entered with a tray on which sat two mugs, two napkins, a pot of coffee, a small pitcher of milk, and a plate of jelly doughnuts. After the woman left, Helen and the major each poured themselves some coffee. Helen took a doughnut and put it on her napkin. The major let the doughnuts be.

"The Army has begun an experimental program," Levy said without preamble, "to explore the possible military uses of certain apparent mental abilities. The Russians have reported some success with a similar program."

"Mental abilities?"

"Your visions," the major answered, lifting his eyebrows just a tad.

"You don't think this program is worthwhile, do you?" Helen hazarded.

Levy shrugged. "Wiser heads than mine have decided this is worth a look-see." He smiled conspiratorially. It was the first time his smile had held any genuineness. "Heads higher up, at any rate."

"What kind of program is it?"

"We ask people like you to try to get information for us on target areas—through the air or the spirits or however it is you do it—plus, we look for soldiers who have traits that lead us to believe they could be trained to do this sort of thing, and we test them, too. Remote viewing, we call it."

"What do you mean by target areas?"

"We ask you to concentrate on specific locales and to describe what you see—buildings, weather, anything. Some of the viewers make drawings. Some of them claim to hear sounds or even smell things from the target area. Me, I'd take aerial reconnaissance over this stuff any day, but we can't always get our planes in everywhere."

"So it's a kind of spying."

351

"You could say. We haven't used it in the field yet. We're still giving the viewers coordinates of places we know, so we can check their accuracy. But the Russians claim they've got men zeroing in on enemy targets already and that they're right on track."

Helen took a bite of her doughnut and a swallow of coffee. She purposely stared at the wall to forestall the conversation's continuing. What would Iris think of this surprising development? Was this a proper use of Helen's capacity for visions? Choose, Iris had said. She probably wouldn't ever say more. But that was all right. Because, Helen suddenly thought, this is mine. My ability, my decision.

"What happens to this information?" she said, turning back to the major.

"Once we get to feel okay relying on its accuracy, then it'd figure into military planning—troop movements, air strikes, timing. Not everyone in the program is convinced yet it isn't all a bunch of malarkey, or at best, lucky guesses and coincidence. That's not much to build a plan on. Not enough to stake lives on."

"What about what the Russians say?"

"Could be they're exaggerating."

"What about my Omaha Beach vision?"

"Could be you're the real McCoy."

He stood up. He set his briefcase on the table and put the "Top Secret" folder into it.

"I'll be in the area a few days," he said. "You think about it. Dr. Stannard knows how to reach me."

He walked to the door. Helen stood up, too.

"Can I ask you one more thing, Major?"

"Shoot."

"Did you ever really intend to lock up my family?"

"I intended you to feel the full might of the U.S. Army," he said soberly.

Helen tried hard not to show how much this remark unbalanced her.

"I wasn't kidding when I told you there were enough grounds," he continued. "In hindsight, maybe I *should* have taken you all in. Your father's been kicking up a lot of dust. Got a lawyer to file a writ of habeas corpus. We had to send Captain Fitzpatrick to tell him to back off, that your release was imminent."

"Is it?"

"We won't know which paperwork to process until you've decided about the remote viewing."

"But you're going to release me either way?"

The major looked disappointed.

"Either way," he said. "Still, you must remember, Miss Schneider," he added, perking up, "the Army is a machine whose wheels grind slowly at times. 'Imminent' doesn't give you a date to mark on your calendar, now does it?"

CHAPTER 41

Major Levy had left a one-page description of the remote viewing project, and the day after her meeting with him, Helen went to the administration building to look it over. She had to sit in the warden's office to read it, with the warden present. Helen reviewed it several times before handing it back to Dr. Stannard.

The major had outlined only the testing and training phase of the project. Presumably, the details of exactly how the Army planned to use remote viewers were too classified for the warden of an internment camp to see, let alone a civilian who hadn't yet signed on to the project.

The brief document reiterated that Helen would be asked to concentrate on certain geographic coordinates and to verbally describe or make sketches of any mental impressions she received. She'd also be asked to work with a beacon, a person in another room who would be staring at a National Geographic photograph. Again, she'd record any impressions of the place in the photo. If her rate of accuracy on these tasks was adequate, she'd move on to the training phase, which entailed the same activities, except that a monitor would help her refine her impressions as she was receiving them, by asking her questions and by guiding her to center on particular aspects of a target.

After Helen left Dr. Stannard's office, she wandered over to the baseball field and stopped to watch some boys playing. They were running and shouting like boys anywhere, their enthusiasm unhampered by either their confinement in a camp or the unforgiving Texas sun. But beyond noticing that, Helen wasn't really paying attention to the game. Her mind was still on the remote viewing project.

Describing the physical features of a place could be construed as benign or trifling, especially during training exercises, but, of course, if the program ever truly entered the arena of war, there would be consequences, and those consequences would be lethal. This made Helen very uneasy.

She told herself her qualms had to be overcome for a greater good. She reminded herself that decent people everywhere were having to do so. Lloyd had killed. Billy would have. Rosie was a helpmate to killing. What were scrap collecting and bond buying, really, but ways to fund killing? The posters encouraging such activities made no bones about it. To save American lives, they said in no uncertain words and pictures, German and Japanese lives must be taken. Many posters showed vicious-looking Nazi and Japanese soldiers brutally murdering women and children, or gloating over the bloodied bodies of handsome American infantrymen, sailors, and airmen. But giving the Army information that would be used to guide specific attacks was more direct, more soldier-like, than buying bonds or even working in a defense plant, and Helen was not sure she wanted to be a soldier. Major Levy had implied it was her duty to join the project. Why was duty so commonly presented as straightforward and simple, when it was often, in reality, a complicated affair?

Putting aside the spiky question of duty, Helen recognized that participating in the project could have personal benefits. For one thing, she'd earn a definite release date. But more important, the training might give her skills for controlling her visions. She might discover how to live a full, ordinary life and keep within it a limited but authentic space for her extra-ordinary sensibilities. She wished she'd been able to assure Billy she had such control. Then she could've belonged to him *and* to herself. Or could she have? Maybe even well-managed psychic abilities would have been too much for him to countenance. What would she have done then? But, oh, why ask herself that now?

Helen moved off from the ball field and headed for the weaving room. Weaving always emptied her mind. That's what she needed now, a bit of empty-headedness.

On her way to the recreation building, she passed two women strolling arm-in-arm. They were speaking German. Helen caught the words *Feld* and *Frankreich,* and she knew they were discussing Normandy.

The success of D-Day had evoked tepid reactions among many of the internees at Seagoville, but Helen knew from her newspaper-reading that it had been a shot in the arm to the rest of the nation. Since then, however, the national mood of excited optimism had become muted. Fighting on the peninsula was dragging on. The push inland was going to take longer than expected.

The roads and fields of Normandy were lined with high earthen banks topped by hedges. Hedgerows were excellent hiding places for the Nazis' dreaded 88-millimeter guns. Able to knock out tanks, aircraft, and buildings, versatile enough to mount on a tank or set up in a ravine or a village, the 88 was extremely powerful and accurate, even against fast-moving targets. It was by far the best and most feared gun of the war. When used against infantry, it fired fused shells that created bursts of piercing flak. Flak was a chilling new word in the language, taken from the German *Flugzengabwehrkanone.* Lloyd said a number of the vets at Valley Forge had been blinded by steel splinters from an 88.

Helen looked at the backs of the women walking on. Were they pleased that the campaign in Normandy was proving to be hard? Helen was living in the midst of these people, but she didn't know any of them well. It was easy to pick out the dedicated Nazi sympathizers. They were explicit about their allegiance, singing party songs and marching to mark anything "important," like Hitler's birthday or the departure of one of their own from the camp. In Helen's short time at Seagoville, more than a hundred of them had chosen to be repatriated to Germany and had left to meet a ship in New York. Marta had told her that active Nazi agitators were soon transferred to stricter camps. Escapees and repeated brawlers, for example, were sent to Camp Kenedy.

But what about the others? A swastika flag stood opposite the American flag on the stage in the auditorium, yet how many internees actually believed in Hitler and his doctrines, and how many were just trying to get through their internment with the least amount of trouble?

It occurred to Helen that if she found it difficult to ascertain where other people's feelings lay, then her own attitudes might present an equally mysterious face. She wouldn't have it. She had a German name and unknown German cousins who might right now be fighting and dying on the other side of those Normandy hedgerows, but she was an American, and this was a time that required the firm taking of sides. She felt squeamish about becoming a link in the death-dealing chain of war, but she didn't doubt for a moment the dire necessity of that war.

Maybe most of the Bundists at Seagoville weren't really dangerous. Walter had called them self-important blowhards. Maybe if they hadn't been locked up, they'd have done nothing more than follow the course of the war in the papers in the same way people followed their favorite football teams. When Germany lost, they'd probably quietly fade away. But Helen felt sure that if Germany won in Europe and later invaded the United States, these same passive Bundists would greet them on the streets with flags and confetti and aid them however they could. She didn't want anyone to think for a moment she might be part of such a group, or even indifferent to them. She would become a remote viewer, she decided. She would do her part.

July 1944

The combined bureaucracies of the Army and the INS delayed Helen's departure from Seagoville for several weeks. Knowing she would be leaving made being in the camp harder than it had been when her release was uncertain. She felt even more apart from the other internees. The camp was a warren of subgroups. The Germans were divided among German nationals, U.S. citizens, and South Americans, and then, across those lines, among dedicated Nazis, moderate Nazis, and neutrals. No one of Helen's acquaintance knew if or how the Japanese were aligned among themselves. In all this, Helen felt herself a population of one. She might find other like-minded souls if she stayed, but she wasn't staying, so she didn't try.

On July 21st, the camp was abuzz with the news that the day before, a group of Nazi officers and others had attempted to assassinate Hitler by placing a bomb underneath a table at a meeting. The Führer survived with only minor injuries. A wave of arrests and executions quickly followed. Some of the conspirators took their own lives rather than be captured.

"It is like the Führer says," Marta had declared to Helen. "This only shows it is his destiny to lead and prosper."

Marta was conveniently ignoring recent positive news out of Normandy. Despite the hedgerows and the daunting 88s, the Allies had finally broken out of Normandy. They were racing across France, meeting little resistance on their way to Paris.

Helen was buoyed by the news, but it didn't alter her resolve to train as a remote viewer. The GIs might be doing a bang-up job in Europe, but there was still the war in the Pacific, with its massive naval battles and its ground fights inching along, island by bloody island.

A few days before she left Seagoville, Helen received a letter from Lloyd full of stories about Old Farms Hospital. He'd gone fishing and horseback riding. He was taking courses in business and insurance and Braille. He wished he could show her the beautiful rolling hills of Avon and the magnificent red sandstone buildings that the sighted staff had told him about.

"The place used to be a fancy school, and its architecture is famous," he wrote, "but I bet you could tell me better than the Army dopes here how it all really looks—tell me in a way that I could see it, too."

Helen didn't know if or when she might manage a trip to Connecticut to visit Lloyd, but the mere possibility made her believe, in a way she hadn't before, that she actually was going to be free again.

CHAPTER 42
AUGUST 1944

When Helen saw Major Levy again, it was in Captain Fitzpatrick's small New York office on an afternoon in late August so sweltering the whole city was as stuporous as an old dog. Major Levy had wanted Helen to go to Fort Meade in Maryland for testing and training, but she'd had enough of being away from home, so he'd arranged for a monitor to work with her in Manhattan and keep him informed of her progress.

A fan at the open window was doing little good. It was simply pushing the heavy air around. Traffic noises rose from the streets and conspired to make the room feel even closer. Helen pitied Major Levy, who was wearing a tightly knotted tie and a long-sleeved khaki shirt. At least he'd doffed his stiff jacket and hung it on the back of the desk chair. Helen wore a sleeveless seersucker dress with a scoop neck, and she'd fixed her hair in a Victory roll. She was grateful for the exposure of her neck and arms to the currents of air stirred up by the fan.

"The captain's down at Camp Boardwalk in Atlantic City today," Major Levy told Helen soon after she'd arrived. "Not a bad assignment in weather like this, eh?"

Helen managed to respond with a weak smile, but at the mention of Billy's basic training camp, a trap door had opened in her belly. It was like that now—she stayed on an even keel emotionally most of the time, but she could be sideswiped by a word, a picture, an unexpected object. The stimulus could be utterly mundane. In fact, the mundane prompts evoked the strongest reactions because she was unprepared for them. The other morning when a toy bombsight, complete with a map of Germany and a little bag of marbles for bombs, fell out of a box of Kellogg's Pep cereal, she'd started to cry.

Would she ever grow a tough enough skin that such stray reminders couldn't wound her? She was tired of the little ambushes; tired, too, of the constant kernel of missing at her core that gave the ambushes their force, and yet a part of her was afraid to let the ache of missing go. It was as if she were holding Billy's hand in some dark place, and if she opened her fingers and released him, she'd never find him again.

She believed what her boys had told her. She believed that Billy was content, at peace. She also believed he was going to move on, change in some way she couldn't understand. But she wasn't ready yet to think of him so gone, so finished with her.

The major had an open folder in front of him on the desk. He was leafing through the papers in it.

"Things seem to be going all right in your sessions," he said, looking up.

"Yes, I think so. My monitor is satisfied."

"Indeed." He picked up a paper with a graph on it. "Apparently, you usually make more hits than can be accounted for by random chance."

Sometimes, after Helen's monitor had given her the longitude and latitude of the remote target, she received only general impressions—that a man-made structure was present and that it was tall or squat, clustered with other structures or off by itself, or that some sort of transportation corridor existed. Other times, she perceived details of buildings, both exterior and interior, and she could distinguish a road from a river, pavement from dirt.

"My accuracy increases if I go into a light trance first," she told the major.

"As opposed to . . . ?"

"As opposed to just sitting with my eyes closed and waiting for pictures to come."

"There's a difference?"

"Trance is like looking out an undressed window instead of looking through a lace curtain. Same view, but more clear."

"I see." Major Levy smiled his crafted smile. "If I may be so bold as to use that phrase."

"Of course." Helen was irked. Would he never let up trying to disconcert her? Weren't they supposed to be collaborators now?

"The beacon exercise seems to give you trouble," he said.

Helen got only hazy images with this system. Even trying various people as beacons hadn't improved her performance.

"It's too made up," she said. "I can't get going."

"I didn't realize your ability was so discriminating."

"Well, it seems it is." Helen watched Major Levy put away his smile as someone else might fold and pocket a handkerchief. "And I rather like it that it is."

"You like it?"

"I'm not a machine, Major."

Levy closed the folder.

"No, you're not. None of you viewers are. We haven't gotten a single piece of actionable intelligence from any of you."

Exasperated, Helen pointed to the folder under his hand.

"Does it say in there that twice I saw things that were happening at a remote site and that both times I was correct?"

"Simple events, as I remember. Someone washing a car, wasn't it? But you couldn't tell the make or model. And someone raising a flag. The American flag, you said, but that was a safe guess, whether or not you were aware you were guessing."

"I focussed on that site several times. I knew it in detail."

"You knew it, or you have a clever imagination? With the

inadvertent help of contaminating hints from the monitor, perhaps."

"I won't say imagination doesn't step in sometimes," Helen
objected, "but I've gotten so I can tell the difference between
my imagination or other 'contaminating' information and true
signals from a site."

"Can you now?"

"Signals have their own feel. A kind of pop. An invigorating
pop."

"A pop." Levy sounded more than skeptical. He sounded
downright derisive.

"Have you ever attended a viewing session?" Helen asked.

"No," he replied, in a tone that implied such duties were better suited to men of lesser rank and greater gullibility.

"And I don't suppose you've ever attended a séance, either."

The major cocked a disdainful look at her. "What do you
think?"

"I think, Major, that you ought to see for yourself, at least
once, what it is that you so off-handedly dismiss as preposter-
ous and delusional."

"I don't believe, Miss Schneider, that I ever used such words."

"You didn't need to."

The major sighed and leaned forward, resting his forearms
on the desk. Helen noticed a gleam of perspiration at his
hairline.

"I don't mean to offend you, I really don't," he said. "I can
accept that you believe in what you claim, but as for its being
actual truth, that, I'm afraid, I can only judge as highly unlikely."

His tact was as annoying to Helen as his disbelief.

"Would you object to attending a séance?" she said.

"Please, Miss Schneider, we are off the point of our meeting."

"What about a private reading? Just you and me. No monitors or beacons. No witnesses."

"And you're convinced that would change my mind?" He seemed amused.

"No, but I'm willing to take the chance. Are you?"

She could see he felt tempted.

"We could do it right now, today," she added, spurred by his hesitation, excited by her own daring.

He regarded her thoughtfully. She knew enough not to say more, to let him chew on the challenge.

"Very well, Miss Schneider," he said cautiously. "Perhaps I should, after all, know a bit more about . . . all this . . ." He waved his hand over the report folder. "For the sake of the fullest evaluation of the project."

The major put on his uniform jacket and left Helen alone in the hot office while he went to secure a room for their séance. She stood up, plucking at her slip where it clung to the backs of her legs, and squeezed around the desk to gaze out the window. The Hudson River was visible some blocks away. She watched the passage of tugs, barges, and shad fishing boats. A ferry was docked on the Jersey side near the houseboats at Edgewater.

Helen began to worry about what she'd rashly set into motion. She'd never before tried so directly to impress someone. Did she care so much that Major Levy doubted the value of the remote viewing project? All along she'd reckoned that its usefulness to the Army would turn out to be limited at best. In fact, at times, she'd hoped that it would prove a failure. She'd gone faithfully to her sessions and honestly tried her best to follow instructions, and she'd mostly put aside consideration of whether remote viewing was an activity she ought to be doing, but every once in a while she still had twinges of conscience.

No, it wasn't the project she felt compelled to defend. It was herself. Though she was a little ashamed to admit it, she wanted to bring the major and his mercurial smirk up short. It was a matter of pride. Pride goeth before a fall, she remembered from a Sunday school lesson. But what if one was already down? Couldn't pride also be the first rung of a ladder leading up? Rightful pride, that is. Like hers.

The ferry was plying its way across the river. Helen scanned the deck railings. She could see patches of color that must be the clothing of passengers, the dark monotones suggesting men and the brighter ones women. It was the kind of surmising observation her monitor sometimes urged on her. Before practicing remote viewing, Helen had never attempted to plumb a vision or address ambiguities within it. Now, she was not only doing that, she was getting better at it. The reading for the major would go fine, she told herself. She was strong enough to *make* it go fine. But she still felt keyed up.

Levy returned, rescuing Helen from further second thoughts. He escorted her to an empty meeting room on another floor. It wasn't much larger than Captain Fitzpatrick's office, but it was far less cluttered, containing only an oblong table with six chairs around it.

Helen asked him to switch off the overhead light and lower the blackout shades. Enough light leaked in around the edges of the shades to render the room murky rather than dark, as if they were standing at the place in a cave where the rays of the sun still barely reach, just at the lip of total blackness.

"Now what?" Levy said.

Helen divined that the major, too, was nervous about their impromptu undertaking, and that realization restored her equilibrium. She was in charge here, a switch from their past interactions. She was the expert, he the novice. His skepticism couldn't shield him from that. He had agreed, however implicitly, to follow her. The proverb about being able to lead a horse to water but not being able to make him drink came to

Helen's mind. Very well then, she thought, the water I show him must be irresistible.

"First we sit down," she said.

Levy pulled out a chair for her at the head of the table. He took the place to her right.

"Does it really have to be so dark?" he asked.

"It helps," she said. "It would also help if I could hold something that belongs to you, something that is only yours."

The major was baffled for a moment, then he worked his wedding band off and gave it to her. She placed it in the palm of her hand and closed her fingers around it. The thick gold circlet was still warm from his body.

She closed her eyes.

"May we be put in touch today with good and helpful spirits," she intoned.

"Uh, must I close my eyes, too?" Levy said.

Helen shook her head no.

"You need to be quiet now, Major," she said. "You may get a chance to ask questions later. I'll let you know when."

She began her deep breathing. She passed quickly through the state where her body felt as if it were swelling and her mind raced with rapidly tumbling thoughts, into the phase where all activity was suspended and she felt as if she were a reed swaying in the wind. As her grandmother had taught her, at this point Helen took one quick, short breath, propelling herself into the phase where she was open to the spirit world.

This was the time to ask what she wanted to see or know. Often, at this moment, Iris appeared. Helen usually confined herself to summoning the specific spirits her sitters wanted to contact. At more general séances, she simply remained open to whatever messages might come. But Helen had learned—not from her grandmother, but from her own experiences—that now was also the time when she could insert her own requests.

She'd never exercised this possibility, but she'd known for a while it existed, and she knew, as well, that if she were to exercise it, she would have to do so fearlessly.

A brightness radiated behind Helen's closed eyelids, and Iris came into view against a white background. As always, the guide's face was hidden within her deep hood, but today Helen thought she could make out two glittering spots. Iris's eyes?

"I want you to bring a spirit for this man," she said silently to Iris. "An unmistakable spirit entity. And I want to hear and see everything, and to remember all I see and hear."

"Tell yourself to see and hear, and you will see and hear," Iris replied. "Tell yourself to remember, and you will remember. As strong as is your desire, that strong will all the consequences be."

Helen nodded.

The whiteness behind Iris dispersed like clouds thinning. A figure seemingly made out of fog was forming beside the guide. Though Helen's eyes were still closed, she saw a stream of bluish gray vapor moving along the floor of the room towards the vague figure. She beheld, in fact, the whole room—the drawn shades, the empty chairs, the incredulous face of Major Levy. He was staring, awestruck, not at Iris and the coalescing vapors—Helen understood that he *couldn't* see them—but at her.

She felt a stinging around her lips and nostrils, and realized that the vapors forming the spirit presence were emanating from her. They were sliding down her chest and lap, onto the floor, and across to the spirit, who was beginning to take the form of a bent old man. At the sight of the vapors flowing out of her, she felt the prick of panic, but with an effort of will and the aid of Iris, who at that moment floated nearer, she quelled it. As soon as Helen's fear was gone, Iris moved back and slipped behind the old man. As he gathered substance, she faded, first her colors draining away, then her shape.

Levy continued to stare at Helen, his body tensed towards her like a cat about to spring. He was gripping the edge of the table, as if to hold himself back. He was a man of action, after all, and he must be considering what he ought to do about the placid young woman exuding mysterious vapors within easy reach of his hand. He seemed to decide she was all right for the time being, because at last he let his gaze slowly follow the trail of the vapors. When he let out a strangled cry and got up from his chair so abruptly it fell over, Helen knew he could see the materialized spirit.

The old man wasn't as clearly delineated as Iris had been, and his clothing, skin, and hair were the same bluish-gray as the vapors, his long beard and his large, liquid eyes somewhat darker. The fringed shawl around his shoulders was almost white. His gnarled hands were clasped loosely together at his waist. He was looking affectionately at Major Levy.

Helen received the name Efraim. She knew from signed documents she'd seen that Major Levy's first name was Sid, but the old man was clearly communicating Efraim, and he was directing it towards the major. Ursula had taught Helen to report exactly what she saw and heard without trying to make corrections.

"Efraim," she said.

"What did you say?" Levy demanded.

"Efraim, don't you know me? Don't you know your *zaida?*" Helen said, voicing the words that were swimming into her mind from the spirit.

Levy looked back and forth between Helen and the spirit, as if he didn't know which to answer. He finally chose to speak to Helen, in a harsh whisper seemingly designed to exclude the old man.

"What are you doing?" he hissed. "Whatever trick you used

to learn my Hebrew name, that . . . that *thing* . . . over there *isn't* my grandfather."

"Efraim, Efraim, still with the hard head," Helen said, exactly in the style of an indulgent grandparent. "You remember when you fell out that tree? Oy, how the women fussed! I told to them, better his head than the backbone or the ankles, because in the head our Efraim is strong like a rock, like a young oak. And wasn't I right? A bump and a scrape you had and not a minute in the sick bed. But what's good for falling out trees is not so good for making up the mind. On this, also, I am right."

"Stop it!" Levy shouted. "Lots of boys fall out of trees. Stop it!"

The beginning of this outburst was aimed at Helen. She was gratified to see, however, that before he'd finished, Major Levy had turned and was addressing the old man.

A quietude came into Helen's mind. Was the major's grand-father preparing to depart, or was he simply waiting for his grandson to calm down? Breathing hard, Levy stood watching the old man intently, although the spirit wasn't moving. His face wore the same benevolent smile as when it'd first come into focus. Helen centered her attention on the major's breathing. When it had slowed, she ventured to speak.

"Do you have any questions, Major, for your . . . for our visitor?" she asked softly.

"How . . . ? It's not possible," he said, "not possible."

"Efraim," Helen said, again picking up a stream of thought from the spirit, "a man can be strong without being hard. A man can carry the weight he must and not let it bend him so low he forgets to look up at the sky. Don't forget the sky, my boy."

"He gave me . . . ," Levy said, his voice low. "I mean, my *grandfather* gave me a telescope when I was twelve. It was old, in a cracked case—"

369

"—lined with velvet," Helen interjected, "and the velvet was worn threadbare in spots, and he said—"

"—he said, *It's old and stiff like me, Efraim, older even than me, but it can still see the stars.*"

Major Levy stepped hesitantly towards the spirit.

"Is it really you?" he said with emotion.

"And who else should I be?" Helen responded drolly on behalf of the old man.

Unexpectedly, the major lunged at the spirit. His hands appeared to take hold of the old man's shoulders, but the instant he made contact, the spirit evaporated. At the same moment, Helen felt a severe blow to her chest, as if she'd been struck with a baseball bat. The violent pain spurred her to cry out, but the breath had been knocked from her, and she couldn't make a sound. When the spirit disappeared beneath his hands, Levy wheeled around and in three strides was upon Helen, digging his fingers into her upper arms. A sensation like an electric shock shot through her. Then all was black and blank and hushed.

CHAPTER 43

Helen thought she must be dreaming. She was shuffling down a long corridor, someone's arm around her waist. With great effort, she turned her head to see who was beside her. It was Major Levy. His brow was covered with perspiration. He ought to wipe away the sweat before it runs into his eyes, she thought foggily, but to tell him that was too intricate a feat, and besides, if he were to take his arm away, she'd probably fall to the floor. Not that lying on the floor didn't have its appeal. Why was he making her walk? Where were they going?

She shook her head to wake herself. The action made her dizzy, but she came to enough to recognize that the hallway and the major were not a dream. The smiling, slightly scolding face of an old man came vaguely to mind, like the beginning consonant of a forgotten name. Then Helen recalled everything, most distinctly the brutish thump on her chest and the electric jolt through her limbs. She moaned.

"What is it?" Levy said anxiously. "Do you want the smelling salts?" He fumbled in his pocket.

Helen shook her head no. She had a hazy recollection of the sharp, burning odor of ammonia, and a woman in uniform waving something back and forth in front of her face. When had that happened? Where?

"I've arranged for a car," Levy was saying. "I'll drive you home myself. You're going to be fine. Do you understand me? You're going to be fine."

"Okay," Helen said, in order to make him stop talking. His words were like pellets of hail against her aching head.

"It's just a little farther to the elevator," he said. "You're going to be fine."

"Shhh," Helen managed, beginning to shuffle forward again.

The major obliged. Even when they'd reached the street and he had to maneuver her into the backseat of a shiny, black sedan, he did so in silence. Still silent, he got behind the wheel and pulled out into traffic.

Helen felt as if she were covered head to toe with a thick blanket. She heard street sounds, the hum of the car's wheels, the change in the hum as they were crossing the bridge, and once, the major coughing, but she was too weighed down by the enveloping blanket to stir or speak or open her eyes or care.

Then she was walking again, this time up to her own house. She felt more alert than she had in the endless hallway or the car. The major again had his arm around her, but she was leaning on him less, and she wasn't shuffling. When they reached the porch, she pushed him away, trying to gather her wits. Levy waited a moment before ringing the bell.

Emilie answered the door.

"Helen?" she said, looking back and forth between her daughter and the strange Army officer. "What is it?"

She reached up with both hands and pushed Helen's hair back behind her ears. It seemed a strange thing for her mother to do, but then Helen realized that somewhere along the line her hair had come down out of its roll and was hanging around her face tangled and awry. She began to lift her hand to her hair to neaten it, but Emilie took her by the wrist and led her inside. Levy followed, closing the door behind him.

"Mrs. Schneider?" he said. "I'm Major Levy. I oversee the project your daughter is working on. She had a fainting spell. We had a nurse check her over, and she's fine, absolutely fine, but we didn't want her to travel home on her own."

"Fainting spell? Why didn't someone call us?"

"Mama," Helen said softly. "I'm all right. I fainted, that's all."

She sat down heavily on a bench in the hallway. It was a struggle to keep her eyes open. She wondered how normal she was managing to appear. Not very, she suspected.

"She doesn't look absolutely fine to me," Emilie snapped at Levy. "What exactly did this nurse check?"

"Well, her pulse, her temperature—"

"What is all this?" Ursula said, coming into the hall.

"Oh, Nanny, Helen fainted in New York. This man brought her home," Emilie replied.

Ursula felt Helen's forehead and the back of her neck, then glared at the major.

"You were there when this happened?" she asked sharply.

"Yes, ma'am."

"What is it she was doing?"

"Doing?"

"What was she doing to make her faint?"

"Nothing, Nanny," Helen put in. "It was the heat."

"I'm sorry, ma'am," Levy said, "but I can't discuss Miss Schneider's work in any detail. I thought that had been explained to you when she began to—"

Ursula waved her hand at him.

"Yes, yes," she said testily. "We were explained to. But there was nothing about maybe a young girl might faint in this work."

"Major Levy," Emilie said, "we are fully aware that it's Helen's mediumship the Army is interested in in some way. We were content to leave it at that. But when she comes home in this condition, I think we deserve to know what's been going on."

"It's a hot day, ma'am. The office was poorly ventilated. I

blame myself for not offering her water, but aside from that, there's nothing more to say about it."

"I'm taking Helen up to bed," Emilie said, helping Helen to her feet. "Nanny, if you'll see the major out?"

As Helen climbed the stairs beside her mother, she heard the front door open, and in the major's voice, she heard again the words "going to be fine."

Helen opened her eyes. She was in bed in her own room. A rectangle of sunshine lit the lower half of her white cotton coverlet.

"*Guten Morgen.*"

Helen looked across the room to find her grandmother seated in the old rocker near the open window. Outside, a mockingbird began its repertoire of trills.

"Morning?" Helen said, pulling herself up into a seated position. "How long—?"

"Your mother sat up the whole night to watch you. I sent her now to rest herself."

Ursula came to stand beside the bed.

"Almost asleep on your feet you were when that Mr. Levy brought you yesterday."

There was a glass of water on Helen's bedside table. She took a long drink.

"I think, *Liebling,* that you must tell me more what happened."

Helen wanted to tell. She wanted her grandmother's help in understanding what had happened. But the little girl in her was afraid of the old woman's censure. She slid down in bed again.

"I can't, Nanny."

"Because of this secret work?" Ursula was scornful. "You don't have to tell that. Only why you fainted."

Ursula sat down on the edge of the bed. "If that is what you did."

"Mama and Papa will be angry."

"They are too worried to be angry. And because they are worried, it is enough to tell it only to me."

Ursula put her hand on the coverlet over Helen's knee. It was a reassuring, encouraging touch, wise, if such a word could be used, so unlike Levy's electrifying grasp, unlike, too, Emilie's perplexed tenderness as she'd helped Helen into bed.

"It was not your ordinary work, was it?" Ursula said.

"No."

"You had another vision? Like the beach?"

"Not exactly."

Helen sat up, crossing her legs like a tailor. "There was a materialization."

"Who?" Ursula asked, surprise flashing across her face.

"Major Levy's grandfather."

"This is what you are doing? Calling up grandfathers? How is that supposed to help the war?"

"It's not. It's like you said—I wasn't doing my usual work. I was . . . I went into trance for Major Levy. It was all my idea. I wanted to prove . . . I wanted him to stop treating me like . . . oh, I can't explain it. I shouldn't have done it, but I did."

"Hmm," Ursula muttered, managing to sound, at the same time, both contemplative and disapproving.

"A medium does not collapse like you were collapsed unless someone has interfered," she said.

Eyes downcast, Helen began twisting the edge of the coverlet between her fingers.

"Everything was going all right," she said, "until Major Levy tried to take hold of the spirit." She looked at her grandmother. "And then . . . he grabbed at me, too. And then I passed out."

"He tried. He grabbed," Ursula reiterated. "But did he touch?"

Helen nodded, ashamed at her recklessness, obvious now in the telling.

"Then it is no wonder."

Ursula said this so quietly she could have been talking to herself. She stood up from the bed.

"Please, Nanny, don't be cross. I've learned my lesson. I won't do anything like that again. Honestly, I won't."

"No, you won't," Ursula said sternly. "It will be the miracle if you are ever able to call a spirit again."

"What do you mean?"

"Your major seized a materialized spirit, and he put hands on you while you were in the deepest kind of trance. For your gift to survive one shock would be a matter for thanksgiving. But two?" She shook her head slowly back and forth, as if she were receiving bad news.

"How can I find out?" Helen said.

"With time," Ursula replied. "Only with time."

Abruptly, the room felt terribly small. It was hot, and too cheerfully cluttered with remnants of childhood. Helen needed to get out, to take a long walk beside the river, or to pedal her bicycle through the peach orchards west of town. She couldn't begin, yet, to consider in any depth the damage to her powers her grandmother was positing. The notion loomed too large, like a figure in a nightmare. Yet if she stayed cooped up in her room, how would she stop herself thinking about it? She flung back her covers and swung her legs over the side of the bed. Ursula shooed her back.

"But I'm fine, and I'm hungry," Helen protested, even as she was obediently lifting her legs back into bed.

"Your body, too, could be hurt or sickened from this," Ursula said, straightening the sheet and coverlet. "You maybe still will show some harm. Better let's wait in bed one day."

The advice was sensible, and was, in any case, not really advice, but an order, however mildly put. Helen's own folly had landed her in this predicament. She didn't bother to argue.

Ursula fixed Helen a breakfast of sweet, milky tea and dry toast and brought it to her on a tray. Helen was disgruntled by the meagerness of the meal, but, again, she didn't bother to argue. It was her grandmother's standard sickbed fare. And unfortunately—Helen would so have liked to prove the old lady wrong—within an hour of the breakfast, Helen began running a fever. After a quick rise, her temperature leveled off at an intransigent 101 degrees. Neither aspirin nor cool cloths made a dent in it. There were no other symptoms. No aches, no nausea. Her grandmother was willing to let her try eating more, but the fever sapped her appetite. She had to force herself to drink the tall tumblers of watered-down juice her mother brought her every half hour.

The day's humid heat, too, had stalled. Helen's neck and underarms and the backs of her knees were slimy with sweat. The oppressive heat and the furnace of Helen's body became one undifferentiated experience. She moved in and out of brief, deep naps, not fully awakening between, but only opening her eyes for five or ten minutes and gazing fixedly at whatever her face happened to be oriented towards. Sometimes, just before closing her eyes again, she'd pat her damp forehead with the edge of the sheet or turn over onto her back or her other side. When Emilie brought the glasses of juice, she'd gently shake Helen's shoulder, and the girl would pull herself up only enough to be able to drink, then drop down again onto her stale pillow and into another bout of somnolence.

She didn't dream during her naps, though once, as she swam up out of sleep, an impression of the color purple trailed her like a stream of ink in clear water, and she wondered if Iris had been trying to get through to her. After that, each time she felt herself dropping off again, she made a conscious wish to meet Iris in a dream or to receive a sign from her, but neither happened.

As dusk shrouded her room and cooler air leaked across the windowsill, Helen's fever began seeping away. By nightfall, her temperature was normal. She got up and took a tepid bath scented with lavender salts. Her mother changed the sheets. Her grandmother let her venture down to the kitchen for some cold chicken and a pear salad and ginger ale. Her father came into the kitchen just as she was finishing.

"Feeling better?" he said.

"Yes, much better."

"Major Levy called to see how you were."

"Did he?"

"He wanted to know if you'd be in for your next scheduled session, or if he ought to tell the people you work with that you'd be absent."

"Yes, I'll go in," Helen said. She took a gulp of soda.

"Sip!" Ursula instructed from across the room, where she was putting away dishes.

Emilie came into the kitchen carrying the sheets she'd stripped from Helen's bed. She deposited them in the back room, where the washer was, then returned and sat down at the table with her daughter.

"Bed's all ready with clean linen," she said smiling. "Don't sit up too long."

"Sit up?" Walter said. "She's already planning to go back to work!"

"What?" Emilie said.

"I'm not due there for two more days," Helen told her parents. "I'm sure I'll be in the pink by then."

"Hmph," Ursula grunted loudly. Helen gave her a quick glance, but the old woman was reaching to a top shelf with her back turned.

"Nanny thinks that you've been overdoing it," Walter said to Helen. "Whatever exactly it is that you do. That that's why you fainted and fell ill. Your mother and I agree with her."

"So we don't think it would be a good idea for you—" Emilie began.

"It was the terrible heat is what *I* think," Helen said carefully, watching her grandmother's back for any signals she was about to contradict her. "The same thing might have happened to me here, or on a stuffy bus, or somewhere else."

Ursula, having completed her task, came to stand behind Emilie's chair.

"I did do . . . I was trying something new when I fainted," Helen continued hesitantly, "and it was a bit difficult, so maybe that *plus* the heat . . . But you all don't have to worry. I won't be doing that kind of thing again."

"Are you certain of that?" Walter said. "Because, frankly, Helen, it may be Katie-bar-the-door, but I'd prefer you call in today and resign. Heat or no, any job whose demands are enough to make you ill is not a job I want you to have."

"But, Papa, I *need* to go back. I need to see if I . . . that is, I should at least—"

"Perhaps, Walter," Ursula put in, "Helen wants just to make her ending there the right way. It's how you raised her, to be responsible and fair."

"Yes, that's it," Helen said. "I can't just all of a sudden walk out on them. And if it turns out I'm able to work like before and feel fine doing it, then I'd rather not walk out at all. I'd like to stay on."

Emilie looked anxiously at her husband.

"I don't like it," she said to him, and turning to Helen, she repeated, "I don't like it one bit."

Helen was aware that her mother wouldn't have appealed to her father unless she'd perceived he was leaning Helen's way. Helen couldn't read his inclinations, but she knew her mother could.

"I promise, Papa, that if I feel at all weak or sick, I'll quit immediately," she said.

"Walter?" Emilie attempted.

He cleared his throat loudly.

"Helen knows better than we do, Emilie, what the work entails and how she's feeling."

"You didn't see her when she came in yesterday," Emilie said, getting up in agitation.

"I saw her last night when she was so dead asleep I couldn't rouse her to say hello. Is there something else I should know?"

The question was coated with annoyance. To Helen's father, the matter had been settled, if not to his total satisfaction, then at least to a point that begged off further debate.

"No, of course not," her mother quickly answered him.

"I saw Helen when she is just home yesterday," Ursula said soothingly to Emilie, "and I didn't like, either, but tonight I see she is herself, and she has made the good promise to her father, so I tell myself it must be all right."

"Very well," Emilie said reluctantly. "I can't argue you all down. It's true the symptoms were consistent with simple heat exhaustion."

She turned to Helen. "But I still don't feel easy with you going back there."

"Nor do I," Walter said. "I'm trusting you to be smart about this, Helen. And one last thing . . ."

"Yes, Papa?"

"Don't let yourself get carried away with any foolish notions that the war can't be won without you."

"Yes, Papa."

Walter and Emilie left the room, Walter pausing at the doorway to let Emilie pass through first. Helen doubted there'd be any more discussions between them on the decision, at least not tonight.

"So," Ursula said, "you think to make that work into a test, no?"

"I can't simply wait for time to tell."

Helen carried her plate and glass and silverware to the sink. Ursula followed and reached past her to turn on the tap.

"I'll wash," she said. "You go back to bed."

"Thank you, Nanny."

"It's nothing."

"No, I mean thank you for helping me with Mama and Papa, and for not saying anything about . . . anything."

The old woman shrugged.

"It is yours," she said. "It is for you to decide, and for you to live."

CHAPTER 44
SEPTEMBER 1944

Helen didn't get back to the remote viewing project as soon as she'd hoped. She'd conceded to her mother's wish that she wait until the heat wave broke. An unenterprising weather system, it had stagnated over the region for nearly two weeks.

The day she finally went into the city was beautiful, the sky peacock blue with racks of immaculately white cumulus clouds as bulbous and buoyant as a child's drawing. Infected by the beauty and the lenient air, New Yorkers, stylish and purposeful, strode briskly along the crowded sidewalks. Everything and everyone looked bright, freshly made, optimistic. But Helen was too nervous to be cheered by the day's fineness or invigorated by the busy flow around her. As she approached the building where the Army had its three floors of offices, she looked up, trying to pick out the window of the room she usually worked in. What was going to happen there today?

During the sluggish waiting period, Helen had had no dreams, at least none she remembered. She hadn't dared to call Iris or go into trance. Once, outside a theatre where *Arsenic and Old Lace* was opening, she'd tried to see the auras of people waiting in line, but nothing had appeared. The remote viewing exercises would be a better trial, she'd told herself. They were orderly, supervised, scientific. Yet now, literally on the threshold, she hung back.

She'd gotten used to living suspended, like someone waiting for a very late train that might never come or whose whistle might be heard around the bend in the next minute. She was neither here nor there, nor even on the way somewhere, and she was content to be because she'd trusted it was a temporary state.

Helen had taken to gardening very early every morning, as soon as light showed in the sky. It was the only cool time of day. Most of the neighborhood was still asleep, so it was quiet except for the dawn chorus of birds and, briefly, the clink of the milkman's bottles in his metal basket and the crunch of the paperboy's bicycle on the gravel driveway. It amazed her that her mind didn't wander in such stillness and solitude, but it didn't. She found herself utterly absorbed in where on a stem to make the best pruning cut, or whether she'd thoroughly routed the weed roots she was digging up.

For two hours, sometimes three, she gave herself over totally to the garden, like a pig in a mud wallow, and each night she was able to fall quickly to sleep, without useless mulling over what might have befallen her psychic abilities and how long it might last. But now, the intermission was over.

Yesterday, American troops had crossed the German border for the first time. Thinking of them, Helen entered the building.

Her monitor, Lieutenant Boddington, was pleased to see her. But was that wariness she saw in his expression, too? Wasn't he observing her more closely than usual? And they hadn't even begun to work yet. He asked how she was feeling, which he'd never done before, and there was a pitcher of water and a drinking glass on the table. That, too, had never happened before. Stop it, Helen chided herself. It was highly unlikely that Major Levy had disclosed the full story of their remarkable afternoon, but her having fainted was probably common knowledge in the office. The lieutenant's apprehension and the precautionary water were only natural. He'd always been a bit of a mother hen.

After Lieutenant Boddington had made sure Helen was comfortable and ready, he gave her a set of sealed envelopes. In each envelope was the name of a city. Helen was to open an envelope at random, read the city's name, and describe its current weather conditions. The lieutenant then called someone in that city to check her accuracy. Out of five cities, Helen correctly described the weather in only one of them, was partially correct in another, and substantially off in the other three.

"Not your best showing," said Lieutenant Boddington, "but perhaps you're a bit rusty, eh? I shouldn't have started with a new test. Besides, even weathermen get the weather wrong sometimes. Notorious for it."

Lieutenant Boddington believed deeply in the remote viewing project and wanted to see the Army adopt it as a permanent program. He was perpetually concerned that Helen not lose confidence in herself. He tended to minimize her misses and make much ado over her hits. Major Levy was right to worry that monitors might inadvertently give viewers leading information.

The nervousness that Helen had felt on the street ratcheted up. It was not so much that her score had been poor. It was that the experience had felt so different from other times. The "pop" she'd told Levy about was absent. She'd had some vague notions, but she couldn't honestly attest that they weren't simply guesses dressed up as perceptions.

"Maybe it's like beacon work," she said hopefully to the lieutenant as he was writing on his notepad. "Maybe this just isn't my cup of tea."

Lieutenant Boddington smiled at her.

"Exactly what I was thinking," he said. "Let's move on to something with more meat, shall we? Something familiar. The old tried and true, as my mother used to say."

He produced a stack of index cards. Helen took one and

turned it over. Printed neatly on it was a series of four numbers, indicating a target place. The numbers had been randomly selected and assigned to the target. They weren't geographic coordinates, as had been used when Helen first started remote viewing.

Helen stared at the numbers a minute, turning off her intellect and her everyday reliance on the conscious mind. She closed her eyes and waited for signals from the target. A rippling surface came to her. A lake? She cast out that idea. A rippling surface, period. Too early to name it. Besides, the image felt like it was coming from her imagination, not from the remote site. It didn't have that distinct mental flavor that true signals did. She tried to elaborate on the elusive surface, to see its edges, its color. Nothing. She strained to hear sounds from the site. Nothing.

She wasn't completely discouraged yet. It wasn't uncommon to spend an hour on one target, gradually obtaining information, making sketches, giving Lieutenant Boddington verbal descriptions. Always, in a successful session, there came the thrilling moment Helen called "dropping in." It was as if she'd been taken somewhere blindfolded and then had the blindfold removed. She was, then, in two places at once—at the table with the lieutenant and alone at the remote target. Often, after Helen felt securely "in" a place, Boddington would direct her where to look.

As minutes passed and nothing more than the unidentifiable ripples appeared, Helen began to feel impatient.

"Anything?" the lieutenant said softly from the other side of the table.

"A rippling surface. A lake maybe?"

"There's no lake at the target," the lieutenant said. "Nor nearby. No bodies of water at all. Try drawing it."

She opened her eyes. He slid a pencil and sketchpad across

to her. She drew rows of wavy lines. They could have been interpreted as water, cake frosting, ridges of windblown sand or snow, an animal's curly pelt.

Helen knew Lieutenant Boddington was disappointed, but she didn't care, as she would have in the past. Today, she only cared about how he could serve her quest to evaluate the state of her abilities.

"Let's do another one," she said.

It was what they did—move on to a new target—when she couldn't make a connection, but it was Lieutenant Boddington who decided when. He looked a little taken aback by her suggestion, but he didn't object. He respected her talents too much.

Helen took another card and stared at another four-digit number. Again, she closed her eyes and waited. Nothing. Not even an ambiguous image.

"How're we doing?" Boddington asked after ten minutes.

Helen shook her head and opened her eyes. The sight of the lieutenant's crestfallen face nearly tipped her over into tears.

"I'll tell you what," he said sunnily. "Let's try front-loading."

Helen hadn't needed to be front-loaded since her second session. All he'd give her was the name of the remote place. She'd still have to rely on her psychic abilities to describe it, especially if Boddington asked her to zero in on a particular neighborhood or building. But it was a crutch nevertheless, a beginner's tool.

"Ever been to Detroit?" the lieutenant asked.

"No."

"All right, then, let's do Detroit. My hometown, by the by."

Helen closed her eyes yet again. She called up everything she knew about Detroit in order to cleanse her mind of it. She banished what she'd read about the huge plane factory at Willow Run now putting out one B-24 bomber an hour, and about the murderous race riots in the city last summer. She saw smokestacks and skyscrapers and dismissed them as suppositions of how Detroit might appear. She saw federal troops and policemen, smashed store windows, and hate-wrenched faces. These, too, she dismissed as leftovers from newsreels. Her mental canvas finally blank, she waited to drop in.

Time lengthened like a stretching cat. Helen perceived nothing.

"Now, Miss Schneider," Lieutenant Boddington said gently. "I'm going to ask you to focus on one section of Detroit. It's called Paradise Valley."

Helen nodded. The image of a green cleft between rounded mountains came to her, but she knew it was just her association with the word valley. Detroit couldn't contain a place as rural as that. She thought, for the briefest moment, that on the far right side there was a razor's edge of glowing purple, but as soon as she turned her attention to it, it was gone, and she couldn't swear it had ever been there at all. That was the last straw.

"I can't do this," she said, standing up suddenly.

"Please, Miss Schneider, don't be upset. It's your first day back after an illness. You can't expect to—"

"I can expect better than I've gotten today. I *do* expect it. And so do you. You know you do."

"I gave you Paradise Valley because the look of it is so distinctive, so unlike, I'm sure, anywhere you've ever been yourself. Maybe it was a mistake. Too harsh for a young lady. Paradise Valley is a slum. Sixty thousand Negroes in sixty blocks, sewage running in the streets—"

"It's not the place, Lieutenant. It's *me*. It's gone. What I had is gone."

The lieutenant stood up, too. He reached over and laid his hand on the table in front of Helen, patting it soothingly, as if it were her hand he was touching.

"Oh, I don't believe that for one moment," he said. "A gift like yours doesn't just disappear. You're tired, or I chose inappropriate materials today, or—"

"Maybe it can't disappear, but it can be driven out, extermi-
nated."

He pulled back his hand and straightened up.

"Well," he said, befuddled, "I wouldn't know about anything
like that."

He started gathering his papers and cards and envelopes.
Helen didn't know what else to say, whether to leave. Usually
they exited the room together, and he walked her to the elevator. Should she tell him she wouldn't be coming back? She
didn't want him to try to talk her into staying with the project.

"Is Major Levy here?" she asked.

"Yes, he is," Boddington replied, "But you're not scheduled
to see him until his next visit. We'll have more for him to review
by then."

"I'd like to see him today."

Boddington regarded her curiously.

"Very well," he said. "I'll go see if he's available."

Helen was alone in the room for fifteen minutes before Levy
showed up. In that time, she stood at the window staring at
pedestrians and traffic far below, sat down and got up, walked
around the table twice, sat down again, folded her arms on the
table, and rested her head on them.

It was gone. Her mysterious, unearned, sometimes onerous,
sometimes exciting gift was gone. Boddington could tut-tut all
he liked, Nanny could advise waiting longer, but Helen knew.
She just knew. It had felt good to say so out loud and
unvarnished to the startled lieutenant. It was like admitting a
guilty secret. She felt disencumbered and heady, and at the
same time off-balance and anxious. She didn't try to parse her
emotions. That would have been like trying to dissect the wind.

When she heard the door open behind her, she lifted her

388

head and turned in her seat.

"Miss Schneider?" Major Levy said in an apprehensive voice. "You're not feeling well?"

"I was just resting."

"All right, then," he replied awkwardly.

He shut the door and walked to the table. Helen expected him to take Boddington's place across from her, but instead he sat down in the chair next to hers and leaned slightly towards her with an inquisitive look in his eyes.

"I wanted to let you know," she said in an official tone, "that I'm leaving the project. I won't be back."

Levy raised his eyebrows and straightened up in his chair.

"That's your prerogative, of course," he said.

As leery as Helen had felt about the intimacy of Levy's attitude when he'd first sat down, now she regretted its evaporation. She hadn't known how it would feel to see the major again, but the formality they'd both adopted was definitely dissatisfying.

"I should caution you," Levy continued after a pause, "that strictly speaking, your . . . performance . . . the other day was part and parcel of your work for the Army, and thus classified information, not to be shared with anyone outside the project."

"My performance?"

"I didn't mean—"

"So, Major, as it was part and parcel of my work, I assume there'll be a full account shared *within* the project. To whom should I report for de-briefing? The Army is bound to want someone other than you to interview me."

A wish was lodged beneath Helen's sharp words, a wish that she and the major could move together onto more open, more honest ground. But at the moment, she had no interest in shaking off her justifiable pique. She couldn't help but feel gratified that Major Levy looked truly miserable.

"I seem always to be putting my foot in my mouth with you, Miss Schneider," he said dejectedly.

"When you're not trying to put it on my neck."

Levy threw up his hands.

"I had that coming, and more," he admitted.

"Don't worry," Helen said curtly, "I only told my grand-mother, and she won't tell anyone else."

Levy tapped his fingers irresolutely on the tabletop.

"The truth is, Miss Schneider," he finally said, "that you flat out scare me a little, and even a little fear can make a man say and do stupid things."

Helen sighed. She'd wanted the formality dispensed with, and now she'd have to rise to the occasion.

"That séance was scary for me, too," she confided. "The fainting part."

"But you *have* fully recovered, haven't you?" Levy said with genuine warmth. "You really are all right?"

Suddenly, as when Boddington had looked so disappointed, Helen felt close to tears.

"Physically, yes," she answered shakily, "but . . . I seem to have lost my abilities."

Levy made a disbelieving grimace.

"Lieutenant Boddington told me you had some problems today, but *lost* them? How?"

Helen waited to speak until she could trust her voice to be steady.

"Because you grabbed the spirit and you touched me while I was in trance."

"What?" Levy jerked his head back as if he'd been struck. "My God, if I'd known, I wouldn't have—"

"It's only technically your fault. I shouldn't have been trying to show off."

"But can't you get your abilities back?"

"I don't know how."

Levy looked towards the window. The view was of a shorter office building across the street and a stunning band of blue sky. A pair of pigeons flew by, their heads iridescent in the sunshine. Levy returned his gaze to Helen.

"And I've been worried about the hell there'd be to pay if my superiors ever find out," he said, shaking his head ruefully.

Acknowledging his imprecise apology with a nod, Helen stood up and retrieved her hat from the end of the table. She took it to a small wall mirror and began pinning it on. Major Levy came to stand some feet behind her. His reflection spoke to hers.

"I'm glad it happened," he said quietly.

Helen's hat was in place, but she continued to face the mirror.

"Why?"

"I can't answer that completely yet," he said. "Something that I *know* is impossible nevertheless occurred. I don't expect ever to understand it. But I won't be able to insist anymore that there's only one way the world works, only one 'right' way to describe it."

"My spirit guide . . ." Helen began, then paused to see if Levy would scoff. When he remained attentive, she went on. "My spirit guide says that we're not supposed to understand everything, because understanding doesn't have an end or a top, it just keeps going."

"I'll have to chew on that one a while," Levy said with a sincerely self-deprecating smile.

Helen turned around and took a long look at the major. She wanted to remember his face, especially his face at this moment. He withstood her scrutiny patiently. Maybe he was harvesting her face, too. It was unlikely they'd ever meet again. Finally, a hint of official demeanor returned to his expression. It was time to go. Helen tucked her clutch purse under her arm.

"The Army appreciates your service, Miss Schneider," Levy said, extending his hand to shake hers. He held on a moment. "For myself," he added, "thanking you doesn't seem exactly the right thing for what you did the other day, but . . . Let's just say I'll never forget it. And I hope it turns out you're wrong about losing your gift."

Helen moved towards the door. Levy stepped ahead of her to open it. Before passing out of the room, she paused close by him.

"All my life people have called what I can do—what happens through me—a gift," she said. "But maybe, Major, it was only a loan."

CHAPTER 45

When Helen came back from New York, her mother and grandmother were in the living room listening to *The Cisco Kid*. Emilie switched off the radio and urged Helen to take off her shoes and lie down on the sofa. She propped pillows under Helen's head and feet and gave her a tablespoon of cod liver oil, as if she were a sickly child. Helen didn't resist.

"You need to take things more slowly," Emilie said, recapping the cod liver oil bottle. "Next time, go in for half as long."

"I've quit," Helen said dully.

"What?"

"I'm not going back."

"Oh, darling," Emilie exclaimed, "I'm so glad. Your father will be, too."

"The job, it is finished?" Ursula asked.

"For me it is."

"Well, I'm going right to the butcher's for a roast for dinner," Emilie announced, plumping the pillow at Helen's head. "It'll fortify you."

She bustled happily out of the room. Helen closed her eyes.

"Helen," Ursula said quietly a few minutes later, "you aren't sleeping?"

"No," Helen replied, opening her eyes, but holding her gaze to the ceiling.

"What did you find out?"

"I found out that you were right," Helen said in an adamant

whisper. "My abilities are gone."

"The work today didn't go well?"

"The work didn't go at all."

"And you think it would be the same another day? That it would be the same, too, at the home circle, or in solitary trance?"

"I know it would." Helen irritably kicked the pillows out from under her feet and onto the floor. She sat up.

"I could probably still go into trance," she continued, "but I wouldn't receive anything. Or anyone."

"Not even Iris?"

Helen shook her head.

"I think she tried to come through a couple of times, but it was no use. I guess now she'll be moving on. No sense knocking her head against a brick wall."

"She is your guide," Ursula said. "She will stay. You maybe won't see her again, but she will stay."

"If I can't see her, what good is that?"

"Whenever you know, deep inside, what to do, where to go, there will Iris be."

"Like some kind of puppeteer?" Helen snarled.

"Did she ever feel so?"

Helen would have liked to be able to make another negative comment, but she felt too drained and deflated.

"You are not a puppet, Helen. If Iris brings a desire, it is your own desire she shows you, your right place. And you are free to ignore."

Ursula bent over from her chair to pick up the pillows Helen had kicked off. She tossed them back onto the sofa.

"You remember you asked once about my guide," she said, "and I told you he didn't come so much?"

"Yes."

"That was a little *Flunkerei,* a fib. He hasn't come at all since

I was only a bit more than your age. And I can blame only myself."

"Why?"

"I hold the hands, but I read the faces. I am a good guesser. Sometimes, too, there is a small trick here or there, for the little excitement. To have the people come back."

"And that's why your guide stopped coming?"

"*Ja*, I think so. Yet I feel him sometimes, like he is right here." Ursula pointed to a spot six inches above her left shoulder. "And when, once in a while, true spirits come to sittings, I believe it's Gerard who brings them. Iris, maybe, will do the same."

"But why should I ask her to, Nanny? So people can get their puny questions answered? So they can stop feeling afraid and guilty and lonely?"

"These are not puny things, Helen." Ursula hesitated a moment, clasping and unclasping her hands in her lap. "And there is yourself, too."

"Myself?"

"You were on the way to being a great medium, someone people will seek out and reward. This you can still have."

"What do you mean?"

"You say the gift is gone. But you remember what it was like. You do not have to wish Iris will help. You already know what to say, how to act."

Helen had never used gimmicks to court clients. She'd never felt the need to make excuses or reparations when a séance "failed." She could be almost haughty to clients who complained of too meager results. But now her grandmother was showing her an alternate path, crass but definitely inviting. She could still be special. She could still feel powerful. But it was such self-importance that had lost her her gift.

"Nanny," she said at last, "I can't . . . cheat . . . like that. I know you've said that telling people what they want to hear can help them, and I've seen it, but I just couldn't. It wouldn't bring back Iris or my boys or any of it, and it would be like . . . like spitting on them, like . . . like spitting on myself, and on you."

Ursula let out a long breath redolent with melancholy, and yet, she was smiling.

"You are right, *Liebling*. But more people than me will ask you to keep having séances. It's good to wonder here, quiet in your own house, what to answer."

"You mean you didn't really want me to—"

"I would like it, your company and help. But not in this way, to be *eine Fälschung*. You make the choice as I had hoped. To lead you to this is my gift to you, and my gift to spirit. To make up for all the tricks I have done, and all the *Flunkereien* ahead."

Ursula stood up purposefully. The topic was unmistakably closed.

"Your mother will be home soon," she said. "I'm going to scrub some potatoes and set the oven for our roast."

"Nanny?"

"*Ja?*"

"I feel so lost. Like I've forgotten my own name and there's no one around to tell it to me."

"Emilie had a boy in her hospital like that," Ursula said. "His head was hurt, and he couldn't remember his name or his town or if he has a sweetheart . . ."

"What happened to him?"

"Some pieces, they leaked back in. For the rest, he must figure them out—he ate chocolate ice cream to see if he was a person who likes chocolate ice cream."

"Did that really work?"

"Pretty good, your mother said. Because the same person was still there underneath. That person knew he likes chocolate, and maybe that person is who has the idea to make the test with the ice cream. What you had, Helen, maybe it is not gone forever."

"You can't be sure of that, Nanny."

"Just so," Ursula said with a small shrug of her shoulders. "But it is what I think all the same."

Helen slouched down into the sofa, tucking a pillow behind her back.

"I wonder, Nanny," she said quietly, "if they're disappointed in me."

"Who?"

"My boys."

"*Ach,* child, spirits have no interest in such feelings."

"I know, but I worry anyway that I let them down, that their stories were wasted on me."

Ursula considered her granddaughter.

"Did their stories change you, Helen? Did they teach you?"

"Yes Yes, they did."

"And you shared these stories, no? With the home circle, with clients at séances. So, maybe some of those people, they are changed, too. Maybe they learn to live a little bit in a different way, a bigger, more hopeful way. And maybe each changed person meets along his way another person and makes a change there, also. Quietly, with no fuss or hooray. Do you think this is possible?"

"I guess so."

"Then where can be the waste or disappointment? The spirits, they do not have expectations. They only give, and leave us to take it or not."

Helen nodded. Her heartsickness softened to wistfulness.

"It's so strange, Nanny, to think I'll never see Iris again, never hear any more stories."

"Then don't think so," Ursula declared. "Don't wait for them, but don't wash your hands, neither. Always there is change. Spirit teaches that."

Helen reached for her shoes and slipped them on.

"Want some help with the potatoes?" It was a halfhearted offer.

"*Nein.* I will do by myself."

CHAPTER 46
OCTOBER 1944

Rosie hadn't been posted back to Italy after her leave in May, but had been sent, grumbling, to an office in Washington, D.C. After the Allies landed in Normandy in June, overall strength in Italy had been gradually decreased, even though fighting was still going on in the northern Appenines, Americans on mules pushing Germans on mules towards the Po Valley, a crawling campaign of hard-hammered inches according to Rosie's Arnie. Rosie's letters to Helen from Washington were as full of news about him as about herself. Now, Rosie was coming to River Bend on a three-day pass. Helen sat in the bus station waiting for her.

Helen scanned the waiting room. A year ago, there would have been more soldiers. More young women, too, many with babies, on their way to the bases where their husbands were posted. All that had slowed down. There weren't as many people moving to get to jobs, either. Some defense plants had even taken steps to convert to nonmilitary production. Just today, Helen had seen a poster that showed a crying child and the caption, "Mother, when will you stay home again?" It'd been many months since she'd seen any posters encouraging women to work or praising women workers for doing a man-sized job.

Despite these subtle changes, the national optimism of the summer was waning. American casualties had so exceeded estimates that the Army, for the first time, was putting boys younger than nineteen into combat units and drafting men over twenty-six. Some people were still hoping for peace in Europe by Christmas, but the Germans were showing no signs of surrender. In fact, they'd recently launched new rockets against England, the V-2s, which traveled so high and so fast, there was no way to warn of their approach and no defense against them. And Hitler was boasting that Germany was at work on even more formidable wonder weapons. American newspapers rumored that these weapons might employ atomic bombs and be capable of crossing the Atlantic.

Just a few days ago, at Leyte Gulf in the Philippines, the largest naval battle in history had been fought, with the American navy victorious. Among the battleships had been several raised from the mud of Pearl Harbor. The Japanese navy was virtually destroyed, and the Japanese had so few planes left even before the battle that some of their aircraft carriers had entered the fray without a single plane aboard, acting only as decoys. But Leyte Gulf had seen the birth of a shocking new tactic, suicide pilots who flew planes loaded with explosives straight into the decks of ships. The pilots were called *kamikaze,* which meant "divine wind," the radio said.

It seemed the Japanese, like the Germans, were not likely to concede defeat easily. The more sober commentators were positing that the war was likely to stretch until 1946. The Allies' superior might would win, but doggedness on the other side would drag it painfully out.

Helen wondered where Billy would have been sent, what battleground she would have received letters from, which dangerous skies he would have risen into. She hadn't followed the course of his unit's deployment. Lloyd might know. He kept close track of war news, but in their weekly exchange of letters, the details of war were a rare topic.

When the bus from Washington pulled up, Helen went out to the curb. Rosie was the third passenger off. She was in uniform, her hair pulled neatly into a tight bun below her cap, a duffel bag slung over one shoulder. When she saw Helen, she dropped the bag on the sidewalk and gave her a hearty hug.

"I'm starving!" she declared.

"How about Millie's?"

"Sister, that's music to my ears."

It was a bit of a hike from the bus station to the café, but Rosie was tired of sitting, and the day was lovely, cool yet sunny, with some of the trees along West Main beginning to turn color. In truth, they wouldn't have noticed if the walk had been twice as long, they were so glad to be together.

"Remember I told you I got small arms training right before my leave in May?" Rosie said after they'd caught up on family news.

"How could I forget? You were so excited."

"Well, they took it back."

"Took it back?"

"They're not training any more WACs to use pistols, and the War Department's not letting the ones who *were* trained carry them."

"But you don't need a gun now."

"Even if I was near the front lines, they wouldn't let me carry one. We're not even allowed to wear the badges that show we got the training."

"Why?"

"That's a question you don't ask in the Army."

Rosie shifted her bag from one shoulder to the other.

"My guess is everybody's still spooked about girls being soldiers," she went on. "You know, like the smart alecks who say WAVES stands for Women Are Very Essential Sometimes. But a pilot on a strafing run doesn't turn the other way when he sees a skirt, and a bomb doesn't see anything at all. And just 'cause you're working in a cartography tent or a mail hut, or you're some officer's driver doesn't mean you're safe."

"You're right to be angry," Helen said.

Rosie shook her head slowly.

"I shouldn't kick," she said, softening her tone. "I had my turn in a combat zone, like I wanted. The girls in the Navy and the Army Air Force and the Coast Guard and Marines have all been stuck stateside or in quiet spots like Hawaii and Alaska and the Caribbean. Anyway, me getting what I want isn't important."

There was the trace of a frown on Rosie's brow, despite her moderating words.

"It's only not important for now," Helen suggested.

Rosie flashed her friend a grin.

"I know," she said.

When they reached Millie's, they chose a table near the wide front window, as they used to do in high school. Rosie ordered a hot turkey sandwich with mashed potatoes and gravy and a chocolate malt, Helen an egg salad sandwich and a Coke.

"How about you?" Rosie asked. "How's your secret war work going?"

Helen picked up her napkin and smoothed it on her lap.

"Uh-oh," said Rosie. "Too hush-hush? I was just asking in a general way—like if it's interesting."

"Actually, I've quit."

"Quit! What happened? And don't give me that look—I *know* something happened, because you're no quitter."

"I'm not supposed to talk about it."

Rosie shook out her napkin with a snap. She gave the impression that if there'd been a blameworthy neck handy, she would have used the napkin to strangle it. Helen smiled at this display of unquestioning loyalty.

"Okay, so it's a loose lips thing," Rosie said, "but you can tell me how *you're* doing. Are you sorry? Glad to be out of it? Did you just get fed up? The Army can do that to you. Don't I know it!"

"Oh, Rosie, I'm feeling lots of things, so many things I don't know where one ends and another starts, or what goes with what."

"Well, look, your head's on your shoulders, and you know how to use it. You'll figure it out."

The waitress came with their food and drinks, causing them to suspend conversation. After she'd left, they remained quiet a few moments, shifting utensils, using the salt and pepper, beginning to eat.

"It's more a matter of my heart figuring it out than my head," Helen finally said, annoyed at the catch in her voice.

Rosie put down her knife and fork and looked straight into Helen's eyes.

"You're an ace in that department, too," she replied warmly. Then she took a long swallow of her malt. "Also which: who says everything always has to be figured out all the time? Is there some new law I don't know about? Because if there is, a lot of us are gonna be in a lot of trouble."

Helen laughed. How good it felt to be with Rosie. Her mind was like a new pair of scissors, clean and candid. Rosie was right. Life didn't have to be, *couldn't* be, tidy. Some mystery, even about oneself, was part of the package. Hadn't Helen said much the same thing to Major Levy?

"What's the latest on Arnie?" Helen asked.

"Still in Italy. Mostly, he writes about what he wants to do when he finally gets home—little things, like wear a silk shirt or eat a good steak. And he tells me about his buddies that I know." Rosie paused. "He hardly ever mentions the fighting, but I've seen for myself what they're up against."

"That must make it harder for you."

Rosie shrugged unconvincingly.

"Arnie wouldn't want me to stew. Anyway, I swear the guy was born under a lucky star. Two years in combat, and all's he's gotten is athlete's foot, and a broken wrist from jumping out of a moving jeep."

"Any other plans for home besides shirts and steaks?"

Rosie's freckled cheeks pinked up. She concentrated on poking her fork gingerly into a ball of bread stuffing as if it were an unknown object. Helen had never seen her blush before.

"Well?"

Rosie put down her fork and looked up from her plate.

"Well . . . we do have an understanding, Arnie and me."

"Which is . . . ?"

"Which is . . . that when the war's over and he comes home . . ."

Rosie leaned forward over the table. Lowering her voice, she spoke rapidly, as if she feared someone might try to stop her.

"I keep thinking, Helen, that if I tell anyone, I'll jinx it—or, worse, jinx him—but I'm busting with it, and I guess I can tell you. I'm waiting for him, Helen. I'm waiting for him, and when he gets back, we're gonna get married and have a nice little place somewhere, and babies even—I can hardly believe it's me saying I want babies, but he does, so I do, too—and we're gonna forget the explosions and the mud and the fires and all of it. Arnie's not gonna have to be afraid to go to sleep, or to wake up, because he'll be safe. We'll be safe."

Rosie sat back, and Helen saw that her eyes were filling up with tears. Just then the waitress arrived to ask if they wanted dessert. Helen ordered two pieces of lemon meringue pie and two coffees.

"It won't get jinxed," she said when the waitress had left. "It'll happen just like you said."

Rosie looked hopefully at her. "Is that one of your . . . you know . . . one of your future-telling things?"

Helen shook her head. "I don't do that anymore."

"Oh. Then you were just being nice."

"Yes and no. I don't . . . see things . . . anymore, or get messages. But I feel in my gut that Arnie's luck is going to hold."

Rosie nodded. "Yeah, I feel it, too, most days. Even on the days when the worrying won't let go, I never really believe I could lose him."

"There, you see? We can't both be wrong."

The pie and coffee arrived. Helen added cream to her coffee, stirred in a cube of sugar. Rosie watched her thoughtfully.

"Did you ever think Billy wouldn't make it?"

"No," Helen said, smiling wanly. "But I was able to put off thinking about that because he wasn't in harm's way yet."

"Do you mind my asking?"

"Not at all. People usually avoid mentioning him to me—I guess they think they're being considerate—but it only plays up his absence. If that makes any sense."

"Sure."

"It's nice to hear his name every once in a while. It can make me sad, but it's nice anyway."

The girls paid their check and left the café. They walked at a more leisurely pace than they had earlier.

"Helen," Rosie said cautiously, "did you ever get to . . . did you ever see Billy, like you wanted?"

"No, I never did."

"Does that bother you like it used to?"

Helen shook her head. "He doesn't have to come buck me up."

"So you're not fussing anymore that his not coming means he's mad at you or jealous or something?"

"I doubt any of that matters where he is. Besides, he knows what he meant to me. What he means."

"How do you figure that?"

"It's something I used to feel in trance sometimes. I'd get a sort of flash—not specifically about Billy, but about everything—that everything and all of us are connected. *More* than connected. Nonstop. That it's all one piece—you, me, what we see around us—and that there's no past, no future. Not really. Everything that happens was already happening before we noticed it and keeps on happening even when it looks like it's over and gone. Even individual lives."

"Whew," Rosie said, whistling. "You've lost me."

"Sorry," Helen said. "It's something I've been thinking about a lot lately, but this is the first time I've tried to talk about it."

"It seems to me that things happen and people do things, period. People can make plans, and we remember things and read history books, so how can you say there's no future or past?"

"That's the common sense viewpoint. It fits into mine, except that it's a very small part of it. It only seems like it's big and complete because we use it so much to get through day-to-day living. But it doesn't explain everything. It doesn't explain what I've seen and heard in my trances."

"Didn't you say you weren't doing trances anymore?"

Helen, who had been invigorated by this conversation, felt her mood punctured.

"That's right."

They'd reached the River Bend Savings and Loan, at the corner where they'd parted ways so many times over the years. Helen hadn't the mental energy to continue the discussion about what was real and what was not, but she wasn't ready for Rosie to leave, either. Rosie must have felt the same, because instead of saying good-bye, she sat down on the low brick wall in front of the bank. Helen sat down beside her.

"And what about Lloyd?" Rosie said.

"What about him?" Helen replied, caught off-guard.

"Well, I could say how's he doing—and I do want to know that—but what I mean more is, what about him and you, and what about him bringing up Billy—is he one of those people that won't talk about him—and what about you and Billy and Lloyd?"

"Whoa there," Helen said, putting up her hand like a crossing guard.

Rosie laughed. "Too much too fast, huh? Maybe my dad's right that being in the Army has made me brassy."

"I don't know where to start."

"So there *is* something to tell. More than a report on how he's getting along in his program?"

"Lloyd and I *don't* have an understanding, if that's what you're getting at," Helen said.

"But you keep in touch?"

"Yes. And we do talk about Billy sometimes—that is, neither of us is afraid to mention him or memories of him."

"Do the memories ever get in the way?"

"Get in the way of what?"

"If you have to ask, I guess not," Rosie said, sounding nettled.

"I'm not trying to put you off, Rosie. I do . . . feel something . . . for Lloyd. But he doesn't know it. So there's really nothing for memories to get in the way of."

"Feeling something isn't 'nothing.' "

"I suppose."

"It *isn't.*"

"Well, to answer your question, then—no, my memories don't get in the way of my feelings for Lloyd." There was that annoying catch in her throat again. "But it's crazy, Rosie, because I still love Billy, too."

Rosie took her by the shoulders, as if Helen were a drunk or an hysteric she was trying to steer back toward reason.

407

"You know what, Helen? Someone else might say 'crazy' is the most important word in all that, but I say the most important word is 'too.' "

Rosie let go of Helen's shoulders. A car paused at the corner before making a left turn. Helen looked away from her friend to follow the car's progress down the street. Rosie stooped to pick up her bag.

"One other thing before I go, Miss," she said lightly.

Helen hauled a matching lightness into her voice. "What's that, Corporal?"

"Lloyd Mackey?" Rosie had dropped her bantering tone. "He knows, all right. I'd bet my last dollar on it."

CHAPTER 47
DECEMBER 1944

The black sky was clean of clouds. The snow-laden hills and trees surrounding the frozen lake glowed in the light of a full moon. Holding Lloyd's elbow, Helen was ice skating with him, cold air brushing her face. She didn't mind a chilled nose and cheeks. Her exertions were keeping the rest of her warm. After the long train ride to Connecticut, it felt wonderful to be outdoors with her body pumping and her blood singing. There were other pairs of skaters on the lake, and many single men standing around a roaring bonfire on shore. The skating party was the first of the season at Old Farms, and few soldiers wanted to miss it, whether they had a girl to bring or not.

Everyone was skating in the same direction, following the shoreline some distance, then curving out to form a wide oval route. The large bonfire, tended by two sighted staff members, cast a flickering ocher radiance over one section of ice. When skaters passed through that area, individual features were discernible; otherwise, they were silhouettes in a Currier and Ives print.

"Which way to the center of the lake?" Lloyd asked Helen after they'd gone several times around the oval. "They say it's solid clear across."

Helen steered Lloyd out of the stream of skaters and faced him away from the shoreline. They stopped, and she let go of his arm. After standing very still for a moment, he crouched like a sprinter and shouted, "Let's go!"

409

He set off at a brisk pace away from the party. He'd taken only two or three strides before Helen followed. As soon as she was beside him again, he began skating even faster.

Going in a straight line allowed for a greater build-up of speed than going around an oval. Helen was skating at the limit of her strength to keep up with Lloyd, but there was a sense of partnership in their headlong flight. She never felt that she was chasing him, or that he was on the verge of breaking away from her.

It was quieter away from the bonfire and the other people. Soon, the only sounds were the rhythmic scrape of their skates and their hard breathing.

Helen was watching, as best she could, for treacherous lumps in their path. This was no groomed rink, and a rough patch could appear anywhere. It was difficult to see very far ahead, even with the bright moon. Her heart was pounding as much from trepidation as from the labor of her legs. She cast a quick glance at Lloyd. His knit cap had blown off, and his dark hair whipped back from his forehead. His artificial eye glinted. His mouth was open in a wide grin. A grinning man skating full tilt into total darkness! She wished he'd slow down, but she didn't want to ask it. It seemed important to let him go until the urge to stop came to him spontaneously.

Finally, Lloyd started coasting. He stretched his arms wide, as if to embrace the night. They were still moving fast.

"Oo-ee!" he shouted.

His glee was infectious. Helen laughed.

When their momentum had slowed considerably, Lloyd spun to a stop. He sat down abruptly on the ice.

"That wasn't a fall, by the way," he said, panting.

"What would it matter if it was?" Helen replied.

She sat down, too, carefully tucking her long coat under her so that the cold wouldn't seep through her wool pants to her skin.

"Some people," Lloyd said, "take one gander at a guy with a cane and dark glasses and think they know everything about him. When the bunch of us came here, we changed trains in Philadelphia, and I'll tell you, conversations in the station waiting room stopped dead when we got close. Picked up again in whispers at our backs. One lady's whisper wasn't soft enough, though, and I heard her tell somebody that she'd rather her son didn't come home at all than to have him come home 'like that.' "

Helen put her hand on Lloyd's coat sleeve and shook his arm gently.

"I'm not 'some people,' " she said.

"I know. I've gotta get better at remembering I don't have to prove myself to everybody all the time."

Helen studied Lloyd's profile in the moonlight. Sitting there, a lock of his windblown hair falling over his brow in the same endearing way his brother's used to, Lloyd appeared completely whole and normal. It was only when he started to move that you noticed a difference. Even then, it was subtle. At Old Farms, they trained the men to avoid the stereotypical bent posture and shambling gait of the blind. Most of the soldiers Helen had seen on campus didn't even use canes.

Looking at the defiant lift of Lloyd's chin, Helen wondered how difficult it was going to be for him and other disabled veterans to fit back into their former lives and how difficult it was going to be on the rest of the population to let them fit in— where, on both sides, misunderstandings and unexamined assumptions and just plain inexperience would place extra obstacles. There were also hundreds of thousands of men and women who'd been permanently disabled by accidents in ammunition factories and defense plants.

"Anyway," Lloyd added, "they've taught us how to fall like paratroopers. And how to bump into things without jarring our bodies."

They sat in silence a few minutes. From the other side of the lake came the plaintive call of an owl.

"Owl," Lloyd said.

"Yes, I heard it."

"Do you hear Johnny singing?"

"Singing?"

"From over there." Lloyd pointed towards the distant bonfire.

"I can see people moving around, but I can't hear any of them."

"The bonuses of blindness, Miss Schneider," Lloyd said in a professorial tone. He held up a gloved hand and began counting on his fingers. "Sharper hearing. More refined senses of touch, smell, taste. And for the lucky few—yours truly included—facial vision. You can't hear because you're too distracted by all you see."

"And you can hear well enough to know who's singing?"

"I flimflammed there. Johnny always sings when we have a social event with girls," Lloyd said, smiling. "He thinks he's Frank Sinatra."

"What's facial vision?"

"It's when you're able to tell something's in front of you and how near it is. Sighted people probably have it, they just don't need to use it. Some guys don't ever get very good at it, but I'm lucky—I seem to have a natural capacity. I just *know* when there's a wall there, or a table or whatever. It's like I feel a shadow pass over me when I get close to something. The docs think it might be a change in air pressure against your face."

"Is that how you all are able to walk around here without canes?"

Lloyd gave a short laugh and shook his head.

"Facial vision's the least of it, though I'm glad I have it," he said. "Mostly, we pay attention. Deep, deep attention. Remember that scale model of the grounds I showed you this afternoon? Every new guy spends hours and hours feeling that model to memorize the layout. Then he takes walks with a guide, and after a while, the two things click, and he knows where paths and steps are, where to turn. We listen to how voices and footsteps change depending on the size of the room and on where we are and where other people are, so we don't have collisions."

"What about outside of Old Farms?"

"That's where cane work comes in. We have bus steps here for practice, and once a week the New Haven Railroad brings in a train half an hour early so we can learn how to move around the train and the station. And for new places that you're gonna be staying in a while, there's brailling."

"Brailling?"

"Feeling with your hands. When I first got to Valley Forge and here, too, I brailled the whole ward again and again until I knew how to get to the bathrooms and the water fountains and my locker without groping. You cold?"

"Beginning to be."

Lloyd got to his feet and brushed off the seat of his pants. Helen got up, too.

"Let's skate back more slowly," he said.

"That sounds good to me."

Helen oriented Lloyd and they set off. Lloyd didn't offer her his arm, and she wasn't about to take it on her own. She supposed he was listening to her skates to stay so neatly beside her.

"It's a beautiful night, isn't it?" he said, after they'd gone some distance.

"Yes, it really is."

"I can taste it in the air."

"There's a full moon," she elaborated.

"A full moon. Clouds?"

"None."

"Stars?"

"Some. The moon's washed out all but the brightest."

"How's the snow look?"

"White."

"What kind of white?"

Helen stared at the hills and the woods. Lloyd was right. There were different whites.

"On the far hills," she said, "the snow's a bluish-white, like skimmed milk, and almost gray in the shadows. Closer in, it's a thicker kind of white, and where there are open spaces between the trees, the snow sparkles like sugar."

"Yeah," he said. "I can see it. And ain't it grand?"

Helen slept in the next morning. The Red Cross bus that took her and the other girls from the skating party to Hartford hadn't left Old Farms until close to midnight, and by the time she'd settled into her room at the boardinghouse where she was staying, it was almost two o'clock. Lloyd had things to do in the morning, anyway, starting with breakfast at seven, the compulsory daily gripe session at eight-thirty, and then classes. He had a pass for the afternoon and evening, and they'd arranged to meet for a late lunch at a diner. He'd gone there several times with friends and was ready to find his way on his own.

Helen arrived early at the diner, which was crowded and busy. She took a booth with a view of the front door. When Lloyd came in, he'd probably pause there, and she'd be able to spot him and go to him. She ordered a cup of coffee and opened the morning edition of *The Hartford Times*.

Two days ago, under cover of a low fog, German panzers and troops had punched through the sparsely manned American lines in the Ardennes Forest in southern Belgium. American troops, astonished and outnumbered, were fighting fiercely. Nevertheless, many of them had been forced to retreat, and some had had to surrender. Hundreds of American prisoners, hands on their heads, had been summarily shot by SS troops. Eisenhower was speeding Patton to the area with reinforcements. More than a million men were going to be fighting one another. Soldiers who, last summer, had dreamed of a stateside Christmas with their families were now facing the reality that Christmas Day and New Year's Day, and maybe beyond, would be spent in cramped, frigid foxholes or advancing from tree to tree in bitter cold, through deep snow, under fire from tanks, machine guns, and 88s.

Helen recalled the variations of whiteness in the snowy woods last night and the prettiness of Old Farms' red sandstone buildings set in smooth lawns of fallen snow. How horrible to think that in the thick woods and rocky gorges of the Ardennes Forest, snow was only making miserable, endangered men more so. Lloyd's old division was there.

Helen folded the newspaper shut. She'd just read that the soldiers in the Ardennes were stuffing newspapers under their clothes for insulation. In an attempt to take her mind off the bad news, she looked out the plateglass window and watched the passing cars and pedestrians. She wondered from which direction Lloyd would be coming.

"Excuse me, Miss," a male voice said.

Helen turned to find a young man in civilian clothes standing beside her booth. He had an overcoat draped over one arm, and Helen spotted an eagle pin in the lapel of his suit jacket, indicating he'd been honorably discharged.

"The place is full, and the waitress suggested maybe you might share your booth . . ."

"I'm sorry, but I'm waiting for someone. He should be here

any minute."

The young man smiled. It was a pleasant, easy-going smile, Helen thought.

"Of course you'd be waiting for someone," he replied. "And he's one lucky son of a gun—if you don't mind me saying."

Before Helen could answer, Lloyd came up behind the man as if out of nowhere and gave him a shove. The man stumbled forward against the table. Coffee splashed out of Helen's cup.

"Hey! What the . . . ?" The man spun angrily around.

"*I* mind, buster," Lloyd said loudly.

Helen jumped up to intervene, but as soon as the man saw Lloyd's cane, he dropped his aggressive posture.

"Sure, sure, soldier," he said. "No harm done, and none meant. Ask the lady. She'll tell you."

Helen put her hand on Lloyd's arm, but he shook her off and took a step in the direction of the man's voice, his cane sweeping out in front of him like a menacing tentacle. A burly older man in a stained white apron hurried out of the kitchen and headed for the trio.

"If you boys got a beef with each other, you'd better take it outside," the cook called to them. As he came closer, he, too, noticed the cane.

"Say, you must be from over at that school in Avon," he said to Lloyd.

"That's right, mister. What of it?"

Lloyd shifted his attention to the cook, but in his agitation he turned his head too far and ended up facing the waitress, who was standing nervously beside the cook. She slunk back a little.

"Now take it easy, son. I just mean I want you veterans to always feel welcome in my place and not be bothered by nobody while you're here."

"Hold on!" the stranger protested. "I'm a veteran, too."

"You can sit at the counter, hot shot," the cook growled.

416

"Forget it, I'm taking my business elsewhere."

The young man jammed his hat on his head and pointed a finger at Lloyd.

"You had a tough break, buddy," he said, no sympathy in his tight voice, "but you and I both know there's plenty who had it just as tough, or even tougher. And you're in for one helluva hard landing if you forget that."

Lloyd's scorching scowl dissolved. The young man strode out of the diner, and Helen nudged Lloyd into the booth. The cook and the waitress went back to work, the other patrons quietly resumed their meals.

"I guess you're gonna give me a thorough raking now," Lloyd said glumly.

"What possessed you to push that fellow? Whatever did you imagine he was up to?"

"I don't want anyone annoying you."

"I'm perfectly capable of handling a mildly flirtatious young man on my own, thank you," Helen said indignantly. "And without making a public scene over it."

"But you shouldn't *have* to handle fatheads like that on your own."

"Come on, Lloyd, it's not as if you found him accosting me in a dark alley somewhere."

"And what if he did, huh? I couldn't do a thing about it. Not a goddamn thing. 'Cause I *live* in a dark alley and I'm never getting out."

Lloyd's hands, propped on the edge of the table, had curled into fists.

"I haven't heard you talk like that in a long time," Helen said softly. Her irritation had slipped away like sand down a slope. "Not since you were at Halloran."

Lloyd opened his fists with a quick motion, as if he were flinging something away.

"I was scared at Halloran, and plenty mad, too."

"And now?"

Lloyd peered at her with his dead eyes. Helen knew he'd been trained not to let his facial muscles go slack because if he did, it looked to people like he wasn't listening to them, but in this moment, his steady attention was not mere technique. It was as if, somehow, he were really seeing her. She felt, incredibly, like he was touching her.

"With everything they've been teaching us, I figure I'm gonna be able to take care of myself, and that feels good," he answered. "I'll get a pension from the Veteran's Administration, so I'll be okay that way, and I expect to work, too—and not in some sheltered workshop, either. But now all of it, the training and the money and even feeling good . . . well, I don't know now if it really is going to be enough."

"Enough for what?"

Helen felt the force of his concentration on her across the table. She had to will herself not to look away.

"Enough for you."

Helen was inundated with emotions. She was surprised, flattered, frightened, joyous, guilty, and flustered, all at once. She had an impulse to find something light and deflective to say, but she heeded, instead, a deeper, stronger instinct not to defuse the moment. Whatever followed between her and Lloyd, right away and on into the future, this moment would be its origin, and she wanted it to be immaculate. So she didn't say anything.

"Well, at least you haven't run away," Lloyd said with a wry smile.

"No."

"Do you want to? Run away, I mean."

Helen took a deep breath. She was sure Lloyd heard it. What would he make of it? If she were in his place, she'd probably think it was not a good sign. But maybe he was smarter about people's sighs than she was, because he had to be.

"No, Lloyd, I don't want to run away," she said, "but—"

"But—now there's a lousy word. Listen, Helen, I know it might be too soon after Billy for you to think about anybody, let alone me, and I know I'm no basket of roses, but I just figured I'd go for broke. Because we—not just me and you, but all of us that've survived this war—we gotta get on with it, you know? We've got to take risks and build stuff and help each other out and . . . and fall in love."

The waitress arrived then. She'd left them alone quite a while, maybe, Helen thought, to be sure Lloyd had calmed down. Before the waitress could ask and without consulting Helen, Lloyd ordered burgers and Cokes for them both and a black coffee for himself. He obviously wanted the interruption to be as brief as possible.

"Do you remember, Helen, when you read me those stories? From your automatic writing?"

"Of course."

"And when we talked about how it seems like the dead want something from the living? The war dead, anyway."

"Yes."

"Well, I think that's what they want. What I just said. They want us to dive into life, to make something of ourselves, to make being alive count for something. Leastways, that's what we ought to do, whether they really 'want' it or not, because they're not here to do it for themselves. Otherwise, what does it matter that we made it through?"

Helen had never felt so close to Lloyd before, nor to anyone else ever. It was an unanalyzed, emotional reaction, and it was a physical experience, too, as if tangible fragments of free-floating matter in her heart and gut were gliding unerringly into hollows she'd grown so used to she'd stopped noticing their ache.

"I think you're right, Lloyd," she said.

"And it's you I want to do all that with. Will you give it a chance, Helen? To see if I'm right about that, too?"

Helen swallowed hard. She wondered if he heard it.

"I do want to, Lloyd. I want to give it a chance."

"Sounds like there's a 'but' in there somewhere."

The waitress brought their sodas and Lloyd's coffee. Helen thanked her, but Lloyd ignored her.

"I'm no basket of roses, either," Helen went on. "I've changed since we were last together, back before you went to Valley Forge. I didn't write to you about it because it was too complicated. In a nutshell, I've lost my abilities, Lloyd, and I'm not exactly sure yet what kind of person that leaves me being."

"A lunk muddling through like the rest of us!" Lloyd exclaimed.

Helen couldn't help smiling.

Lloyd carefully found his cup and picked it up. He took a sip of coffee, then set the cup perfectly on the saucer.

"See that?" he said. "That's muscle memory. People who can see do things like that all the time without having to think about it or even look at what they're doing. For me, every motion is a mental chore, but with practice, I can get where some things— the muscle memory things—come automatically. Maybe, Helen, your case is like that. You lost your gift, but there might be something like muscle memory inside you that you can wake up."

"I don't know, Lloyd. I do feel like a lunk."

"That's good."

"Good?"

"You gotta go through a time of fumbling around. Those fumblings are the muscles trying to remember. That's why they don't move things out of our way at Old Farms or help us too much."

"Does it always work?"

"I'm not gonna lie to you. Some guys never get it."

Helen put her straw in her soda and took a long drink.

"It wouldn't be the same," she said. "If it could happen at all."

"Of course it wouldn't be the same, but it'd be *something*. For me, it's a kind of freedom, a bunch of small freedoms, actually, not having to wrestle with every single movement in my day. For you, I don't know . . . maybe for you, it'd be like an off-the-cuff sureness sometimes about things, a kind of knowing what's what without having to puzzle it through."

Lloyd reached across the table, his hand open, palm up. It was a bold gesture—nothing had been agreed, really—but his fingers were trembling a little, and that added great tenderness to his audacity. Helen felt a stirring in her core, a yearning that, somehow, was its own answer. Her brand of muscle memory? She laid her hand in his, and he gripped it gently.

"Lloyd, I—"

"A chance, Helen. For both of us. That's all I'm asking."

In reply, she squeezed his fingers. He inclined his head and softly kissed her hand.

"Vanilla," he said, grinning. "And moss. You smell like vanilla and moss."

CHAPTER 48
APRIL 1945

Franklin Delano Roosevelt was going home. In a steady rain, his funeral train was moving slowly north from Washington, D.C. to Hyde Park, New York, where he'd be buried in the garden of the house where he was born.

When the train carried his body from Georgia, where he'd died, to the White House, where his coffin lay in the same room Abraham Lincoln's had, hundreds of thousands of weeping, praying, singing, and silent people had lined the tracks at stations and crossings along the entire route. The same thing was happening on this final leg of the solemn journey.

Helen was on a bridge over the Harlem River in the sad, wet dawn. The president's train would pass on the tracks below. Many others were waiting, too, people of all ages and races and backgrounds. The rain stopped, but the air remained moist. The crowd milled, and people conversed a bit, but they kept their voices low, as they might in church. It had been like that on the streets of River Bend, and all across the country, yesterday afternoon, at the time of the funeral in Washington. Buses and cars stopped where they were. Stores that weren't already closed locked their doors for a time. People cried openly, men and women both.

Twelve children were bunched together near the middle of the bridge. Each one was holding a red rose. Some of them fidgeted, twirling their roses or hopping from foot to foot, some leaned over the railing to watch for the train's lights, but they were, overall, quieter than you'd expect a group of children to be.

"We've come to say good-bye to the president," one girl had told Helen when they'd trooped by a little while ago.

A few yards away, Helen's father was standing between her mother and her grandmother. On Helen's right, close beside her, stood Lloyd. He put his arm around her waist and pulled her even closer.

"He's coming," he said. "I hear the engine."

A few minutes later, everyone else heard it, too. People pressed up against the bridge railing and leaned towards the sound like sunflowers turning to the sun. The headlight of the locomotive came into view, then the locomotive itself, with its plume of white steam. The children stopped fidgeting. The soft conversations ceased. A few people knelt and bent their heads in prayer. Walter reached one arm around Emilie's shoulders and the other arm around Ursula's. Helen took Lloyd's free hand and entwined her fingers with his. A man near them lifted a small boy up so he could see.

It was a long train. It had carried the president in life, too, with all his retinue, so there were club cars and a diner, a line of sleepers for the press and staff and the Marine guards, a baggage car, a vehicle-carrying car, a communications car, and the president's private car. After the noisy locomotive had passed beneath the bridge, the children with the roses began singing *God Bless America.* Train wheels clacked, couplings squealed, but the children's high-pitched voices prevailed. Some adults joined in, the song spreading along the bridge like a creeping grass fire. Helen tried to sing, but after only one line, she couldn't continue.

Finally came the last car, the president's private car. Its seats had been removed to make room for a pine bier. The circular windows were open. FDR's long, flag-draped coffin was clearly

visible, resting on the bier and flanked by uniformed servicemen at attention, one from each branch of service.

"The casket's passing now," Helen told Lloyd. "It's got a flag
over it, and an honor guard."

"Is Fala there?"

"I don't see him."

"He loved that dog."

Helen recalled all of the times she'd seen photos of FDR
with his Scottish terrier. The president always seemed to be
smiling in those pictures. But now that she thought of it, he had
smiled quite a lot for a man with his heavy responsibilities. He
was large. That was all there was to it. He was a large man in
every way, including joy and mirth. She smiled to herself, thinking that he'd probably make a large spirit, too.

People had begun leaving the bridge, though a few continued
to watch the train as it moved away from them, heading north.
Helen remembered the trains from early in the war, lively with
jovial young men jostling one another at the windows to reach
into the baskets of fruits and doughnuts being offered by pretty
girls alongside the tracks. She remembered, too, the trains that
had passed through River Bend in later years, shades drawn
down over closed windows, trains full of wounded men and cof-
fins.

"You two ready to go?" Walter asked, approaching Helen and
Lloyd. His voice was husky.

"I'd like to stay until I can't hear the train anymore," Lloyd
replied.

"We'll meet you at the car," Helen said to her father.

Walter waited for Emilie and Ursula, who'd been walking
arm in arm a bit behind him. Then the three of them continued
on.

"The president used to say 'my friends' all the time in his
radio talks and speeches," Lloyd reminisced as he and Helen

began walking off the bridge several minutes later. "And he really felt like one. I feel like I've lost a friend."

"And a protector," Helen added.

"Right. That, too."

"It's hard to believe he's gone. He'd been looking so tired since Yalta, but somehow I never thought of him dying. It's shocking."

" 'Cause it was so sudden, I guess. And 'cause we need him so much."

Helen was glad, for FDR's sake, that the death had been sudden. It would have been hard for a man like that to linger. And she was glad he'd been in a place he loved, a warm place, where spring was already well established. April in Georgia. There'd be peach trees in bloom, and dogwoods.

"It doesn't seem right that he won't get to see the end of the war," Lloyd said.

"He will if he still wants to."

"Well, he knew it was coming soon, anyway."

Patton and Montgomery were ready to cross the Rhine, meeting only sporadic opposition from German troops, many of whom were green boys hastily armed. The Russians were in Vienna and nearing Berlin. German cities had been devastated by intense American bombing. On the day Truman was sworn in, two more large concentration camps, Buchenwald and Belsen, had been liberated. Negotiations were underway for the surrender of the Germans in Italy. In the Pacific, the invasion of Okinawa was continuing. Clearly, Allied victory was inevitable, though the ferocious resistance of entrenched Japanese soldiers and *kamikaze* pilots would make it costly.

So many dead, Helen thought. Over 13,000 from New Jersey alone. People she had known. Her first love. She held more tightly to Lloyd's elbow. This was life now, this man's solid arm, this daybreak bridge, her own body and darting mind. This is what life had always been, a seamless ball of exaltation and sorrow and many pedestrian moments. She wanted to savor it all, to remember to stand still at some point inside each living hour, pleasant or heartbreaking, bland or crucial. She believed it was the only way. Because, really, there was no standing still. Every moment was a departure. She wanted to notice the fall of scarlet leaves and the apple-green budding of new ones, the scent of swelling yeast, the fullness of laughter, the taste of icicles, the hundreds of tiny ways people cared every day, whether it was a man washing his car on a sleepy Sunday afternoon or a girl pushing her brother on a swing, the smile of a stranger or the wordless, confident touch of a friend.

The dead were at her back and in her heart, but they were leaving her to her own devices, successful or mistaken, as they did everyone. They'd come to her, Helen believed, simply to say that life was important and life was not all. She'd passed on the message as best she could. She'd continue to pass it on by how she lived, how she treated other people. She was keeping her inner ear open to whatever subtle variations on the message might emerge, but she wasn't expecting again anything as dramatic as Iris or other spirit visitors, nor vivid premonitions. That door was closed. It was enough, now, to know it existed.

"Do you want to go home right away?" Lloyd asked.

"What do you have in mind?"

"I'd like to walk a while. Maybe find a place for breakfast later. I don't feature sitting just yet."

"Me, either. But we have to stop by the car and tell my folks."

"Sure."

Helen, only inches in front of Lloyd, stepped off the curb. He followed without hesitation, almost simultaneously. They crossed the street into the brightening morning.

ABOUT THE AUTHOR

Noëlle Sickels grew up in northern New Jersey, the setting of *The Medium*. She is the author of two other historical novels: *Walking West*, the story of an 1852 wagon train journey from Indiana to California, and *The Shopkeeper's Wife*, a tale of murder in 1856 Philadelphia. She's also had contemporary short stories and poems published in numerous anthologies and magazines. Ms. Sickels is a retired teacher living in Los Angeles and Ojai, California. She isn't psychic, but she did see a ghost once.